The Pastor's Kids

By Connie Kronlokken

The author believes that all quotations in this book have been used under the "commentary and criticism" fair use of copyrighted materials.

Published by

Lightly Held Books

DEDICATION

In memory of our wonderful parents,
John and Florence

The Pastor's Kids

"Turn out the light, Ellie," demanded Line, her thin chest quivering with energy as she cupped her hands around her eyes against the glass. "We can't see." Her younger sister and brother's faces were also pressed against the cold glass of the living room window. Ellie, who at eleven was the eldest, read a magazine under the lamp. Alone, in a white frame parsonage in a snow-covered town on the flood plain of the Red River, the kids peered into the darkness, looking for headlights in the distance.

The house faced the railroad track along which the little town was built. In the daytime Line could see the great grain elevators holding Bryson's wheat crop until it was shipped by rail to Minneapolis. Line looked out past the dim streetlight on the corner, past the railroad tracks, toward the flat snowy fields which glowed dully under a clear, moonless sky. Headlights, moving toward town on the road that came from the highway, could be picked out a mile away.

"My hopes!" piped up Paul. He was almost four, tow-headed, and so tired he was leaning on his sister. "My hopes!"

"That's not a car," said Marty scornfully. "It's not moving." A year younger than the eight-year-old Line, she had the same Norwegian cat face, but darker hair.

"It's okay, Paul," said Line, lifting Paul up from behind with two strong hands and holding his little knees on the window sill. "Look. There's the road," she pointed. "That's where they'll come from." The radiator steamed beneath them.

Lights cutting the darkness were few. Line watched silently. But then, twin lights appeared and moved at a reasonable speed in a straight line towards the little town.

"My hopes! My hopes!" shouted Paul and Marty together.

1

Ellie, pale and blonde with a droop in her long back, turned off the lamp and now came slowly to the window, putting her head under the curtain.

Line bit her tongue. She didn't know why Ellie irritated her so much. Line suspected Ellie, who was weak and had a morbid streak, was thinking of the Wheeler boy, only 19, whose car sat on the tracks while a night train plowed into it. Dad went out the next day to help pick up the arms and legs, wheels and car doors strewn along the track. But Line mustn't speak of it. It would scare the younger kids.

The four watched wordlessly, as the car crossed the railroad tracks and was hidden from view by the tall grain elevators. Now the lights disappeared and might be heading up the street toward them. Would it be Mother and Dad returning home from a day of shopping?

Line waited. Moisture seeped between the glass and the storm window and lay in the corners in triangles of glittering frost. Paul blew hot small breaths at the window to see if it would melt. The road was outlined by snow plowed into banks under the street light at the corner, but no car came up their street. They were marooned, as if on an island, the little town asleep around them.

"Paul, you've gotten so heavy," said Line, lifting him down. She looked around. Boiling water in the iron radiator made it too hot to touch. "Marty, can you bring a chair?"

Marty obediently began dragging a chair in from the adjoining dining room. She was too small to carry it.

"My hopes," stated Ellie flatly from the window.

Marty rushed over, leaving the chair in the middle of the room. Two pairs of headlights were now crawling along the road toward them, one higher than the other.

"It's a truck," said Paul, excitedly. "A truck and a car."

"My hopes! My hopes!" chorused Line and Marty. If only it would be Mother and Dad and the house no longer forlorn and empty. It wasn't that Line was afraid, but they were losing control of their courtesy, of their sweetness. For once, they all wanted exactly the same thing. They wanted Mother to come home and be the rock in the middle of the house, upon which they could dash their small passionate waves, sending up emotional spray without incident. They were tired of themselves and of time.

The town itself was empty without Dad, the young and beloved Lutheran pastor. Like everyone else, Dad wore khakis and was as at home on Bryson's main street as he was in church. He liked being called Pastor Carl, not Reverend Mikkelson. The stores, which faced the railroad track further down the main street were empty. The farmers who came in on Saturdays had gone home, though the tavern lights might still be burning. The school and its big yard outlined with leafless cottonwoods, to which the kids walked mornings and evenings, was definitely empty.

The white church across the alley from the parsonage was empty. It was made of two churches when the Swedes and Norwegians finally agreed they could worship together, as the services were now in English. The old brown church, two blocks away, was put on rollers, moved down the street and attached to Immanuel as a parish hall.

* * *

It had been a very long Saturday. Line woke up when she felt Paul climbing over her to get under the covers between her and Marty. His cold feet dug into her back.

"Ellie's up," said Paul. "And Mother and Dad are gone."

Line smiled to think of Paul climbing out of his crib, looking for the others. "They went to Grand Forks," she said. The men gathered at the Post Office the day before had agreed that no snowstorm was expected. It would be clear and cold, a reasonable day for Dad and Mother to go shopping in the larger town, buying things not available in Bryson. On winter mornings at the Post Office there was a lot of fat to chew. It might take Dad half an hour to get the mail.

On the other side of Paul, Marty's big blue eyes blinked open, dark, wavy hair falling over her forehead, but she didn't move. Line stretched her whole body like a cat. She felt warm under the covers. The light at the windows was grey with a bit of pink in it, the radiators hissed and she could hear the wind blowing.

"No school today," said Line, for Paul's benefit. "We can play with you."

"We could play school," said Marty, hopefully. "Paul would like it."

"Oh no," said Line. "Not me." She pushed back the covers and jumped up.

All three went down the wooden stairs in their pajamas, passing Ellie who had claimed the dining room table. They found cereal boxes in the kitchen cupboards, rice krispies and Quaker puffed wheat, which they ate with cold milk. The breakfast nook where they all fit closely on built-in benches still felt shiny and new.

The door to the outdoor entry was painted with thick blue and rose swirls of Norwegian rosemaling. Eating her puffed wheat, Line remembered their neighbor June's brown hands painting it. She loved June, but June had moved to Idaho, to grow potatoes with her new husband.

Ellie's books and homework papers were spread around her as she sat at the dining room table in the snow-bright glare of the big windows. A large woodpecker attacked a piece of suet firmly nailed to the bird feeder, noisy, his small red crest showing up against the bluish shadows of the snow.

"Mother said you should play outdoors," Ellie said to the backs of Line, Marty and Paul as they scampered past her on their way back upstairs. "It's going to be a nice day."

Line turned around and stuck out her tongue at Ellie, while Marty and Paul rushed past giggling.

Ellie, scandalized, used their long names, as Mother would have. "Caroline, Margaret, Paul!" she said, as forcefully as she could.

But the three of them didn't stop to listen. They ran up the stairs and fell on Line and Marty's bed, suppressing their laughter. Dad called Line Sparky. Her gang, Marty and Paul, were usually right behind her.

"Play bear! Play bear!" shouted Paul.

Line opened a door to the long, low closet under the eaves, in which she could barely stand. On the floor was a bearskin rug with the bear's head attached, his red mouth open and his teeth showing. She put the skin around her shoulders and, aiming the teeth and the glass eyes downward, rushed out of the closet at the bed, growling and crawling on top of the shrieking Paul.

"You smell like mothballs," said Marty.

Soon all three of them were sitting on the floor of the closet, making houses for the miniature dolls and corrals for the small rubber animals they collected. Low closets like this opened under the eaves of each of the bedrooms. The other closets were full of boxes of letters and papers, cardboard missionary barrels stuffed with old clothes, rags and blankets, wooden apple boxes of books and most especially Mother's trunk, with its tantalizing mementos of the life she had lived before marrying Dad.

Line and Marty marked off the territories of their houses and ranches on the closet floor. The bear rug was a wild, dark woods between them. Paul was content to look on, offering to run his small John Deere tractor through their fields. Line's favorite doll was a seven-inch Indian maiden with dark skin and braids on either side of her face. Though she professed not to like dolls, Line was willing to play at ranching. Marty happily played dolls all day, naming them after characters in books and telling their stories to anyone who would listen.

A delicious, sweet, buttery smell drifted upstairs and penetrated the closet.

"Oatmeal muffins," said Line. Ellie must be baking muffins, their favorite lunch.

"I'm hungry," said Paul, getting up and heading for the stairs.

Line sat back on her heels, remembering that she had put out her tongue at Ellie. Her stomach growled with hunger. Oh well, she thought, I'll just be extra grateful. There was no question of apologizing.

Line followed Marty downstairs. They were still in their pajamas, and milk and crumbs were hardening in the breakfast bowls, which were still on the table.

"The muffins will be done in fifteen minutes," said Ellie sweetly. She stood in the new kitchen in her limp Saturday sweatshirt and brown corduroy pants, licking a spoon.

"Thank you for making them," said Line, aiming a big smile directly at her. She could see there would be a truce, at least until Mother got home. "We'll go put on our clothes." She raced upstairs, followed by Marty and Paul.

* * *

Marty was the first one down. She put the cereal bowls in the sink, carefully laying out four Melmac plates and glasses, with knives for each of them. She poured the cream off the top of a new milk bottle, and put the milk on the table. Marty felt bad about being mean to Ellie, but she was so in tune with Line she could hardly help it.

To Marty, Ellie was a tragic figure. Ellie was eleven, four years older, and it was as if she lived in a different world. When Dad and Mother married during the war, Mother worked in an orphanage near Red Lake, waiting for Dad to finish his training at the seminary. Ellie was born a year later and she had to share Mother with many other children. Marty, Line and Paul, all of whom were born after Dad took his first call as a pastor, grew up as a family.

Marty knew Mother loved Ellie and tried to make it up to her. There were photographs of her, the baby Elizabeth proudly held up to a camera. She had been dressed up for Dad, who drove out from St. Paul on Sundays. But Marty noticed that Ellie was sad and expected little.

When Ellie lifted the muffin papers out of the tins and put them on a rack on the table, Sparky and the gang were sitting in their places watching. They looked at each other and habit prompted them to fold their hands together for a moment before grabbing a muffin. "Come Lord Jesus, be our guest, and let these gifts to us be blessed. Amen."

"Amen," said Paul loudly.

Marty spread butter on her muffin, sweet with buttermilk and brown sugar. It melted into the golden texture and Marty blissfully popped the pieces in her mouth.

After a moment of chewing, Paul fussed, "I want the same color plate as Line." The hard plastic Melmac plates came in two colors, brown and chartreuse, to go with the new kitchen.

Marty smiled to herself. She knew what Paul wanted, but she had not given it to him on purpose. No one ever noticed her, dark and small and sandwiched between the bright Line and Paul, the only son.

"Here," said Ellie, exchanging her plate for Paul's. "Are you happy now?"

How silly it was that Paul wanted a particular color of plate, Marty thought. And how quickly they forgot that Jesus was a guest at the table.

"So, is one of you going to help me with dishes?" Ellie asked defensively.

Marty and Line looked at each other reluctantly, but Marty felt guilty. "I'll help Ellie if you take Paul up for his nap," Marty said to Line. Neither of them wanted to do the dishes, but no one had cleaned up all morning and they hadn't yet sunk so low they could leave the house in a mess for Mother.

"I'm a big boy, and I don't need a nap," said Paul, predictably.

"Never mind," said Line. "We'll just go read a little." He might go to sleep, or he might not. "If you don't take a nap, you won't be awake when Mother and Dad come home tonight," she wheedled.

Ellie put the uneaten muffins in a washed plastic bag. Marty helped her clear up the dishes, rinsing as Ellie washed them in the double kitchen sink, humming a song Marty didn't know. The china animal planters Dad had bought each time Mother had a new baby, stood in the cut out shelves over the sink. Marty's was a white china hippopotamus with a drooping sprig of green in it. No one ever watered them.

The house felt very empty. Marty sat down at the dark, upright piano in the room Dad used as a study, sifting through the red books of simple tunes and finger exercises. But she realized that Paul might be sleeping, so she turned on the light table in the corner opposite Dad's built-in desk. It was a light bulb in a wooden cabinet with a piece of opaque glass on top. Dad and Mother used it to trace designs on carefully-typed stencils, making mimeographs for church programs.

Marty began to make copies of Betsy McCall, a paper doll which appeared each month with new dresses in the *McCall's* magazine. She took a clean white piece of paper and put it on top of Betsy and drew what the light showed her with a pencil. There was plenty of paper. Old church bulletins, old school tablets and packages of clean white sheets. Although frugal about food and electricity and gas, Dad didn't say anything about how much paper the kids used to write stories, make puppet shows and draw animals, elves and paper dolls.

Soon Line and Paul appeared. "Did you sleep?" Marty asked.

"No," said Line. "He didn't. I'm going to make Paul some horses."

Marty moved over, giving Line room to copy her best paper horse. It was standing, not walking or galloping. Paul crowded next to them, watching. When Line finished tracing it, she gave it to Paul to fill in with colored pencils.

"You always make horses," said Marty.

"I wish I had one," said Line. "But I don't, so there you are." She had lots of cut out horses, photographs from magazines, traced copies from books. Morgans were brown or black with a black mane and tail. Pintos were white with black or brown spots. An Appaloosa was spotted, especially its rump. "You always make clothes," said Line. "I would think you had enough!"

Marty was coloring dresses with little paper tabs on them, cutting them out and folding the tabs over her favorite paper doll. She had a Whitman's candy sampler box full of clothes and dolls. "The glass is too hot," said Marty. She reached over and turned off the switch so the glass could cool down.

Paul was too little to use scissors, so Line cut out the horses he colored, and Marty helped him name them, writing the names carefully on their backs.

The long day drew on. When the light began to fade at the windows, Marty looked up at the clock. "It's almost 5:00 o'clock. Time for 'Sergeant Preston'!"

The gang scrambled to get close to the old brown upright wooden radio in the living room. Line turned the dials and found the station. The musical theme rolled out into the room and an announcer described the Yukon, a wild place in Canada where Sergeant Preston and his dog King brought the law to people during the gold rush. Blizzards and rough weather made it difficult. The kids sat on the floor and pressed their ears to the speaker to make out the story from the deep, occasionally static-ridden voices. Even Ellie looked up from her magazine.

Sergeant Preston talked to his dog as if he were a person. "King knows the trail," he said in a deep voice. "On, King!" Marty imagined herself in the wild north, mushing dogs, fighting storms and wild animals, and setting things to rights. In the end Sergeant Preston said, "Well, King, this case is closed."

Marty set the table for supper, which was boiled baloney tied at the end with string, cooked macaroni on the side. Ellie cut the baloney into pieces with a sharp knife. There was milk, of course, as much milk as they wanted. Paul smashed down his macaroni and dug roads through it with his fork.

After supper they couldn't think what to do with themselves. A subdued Ellie did the dishes by herself. No one wanted to take their Saturday night bath or memorize their Bible verse. Line pulled out the Parcheesi board and made Paul and Marty play with her, though Paul was becoming whiney. Time spun more and more slowly as the day wound down.

Finally it was so late that Mother and Dad must come. Marty couldn't do anything but wait. She had a hollow pit in her stomach. She pressed her nose on the frigid glass under the living room curtain. "Come on," she said. "Let's say 'my hopes' whenever we see a car that might be theirs."

"Okay," said Line. "It can't be long now." She turned out all the lamps in the house, except for the one over Ellie, who was reading about whether someone's marriage could be saved in *The Ladies' Home Journal.*

Marty couldn't see anything moving in the little town, sleeping under its blanket of snow. The people were tucked up in their houses. Next door were an older couple who had deeded their farm to their son and moved into town. The kids could have asked them for help if they needed it, but they didn't want help. Beside Marty, Line and Paul pressed their faces against the cold window and cupped their hands around their eyes, looking out into the dark flat distance.

* * *

Paul didn't see where the truck went, but lights flashed across the ceiling as the car turned the corner. Paul followed Marty and Line as they rushed through the dark house toward the kitchen. Crash! Paul yelped as he toppled into the door jamb, having tripped on the chair Marty had left. He felt a sharp pain on his head and couldn't do anything but sit on the floor and howl.

Ellie came, turning on lights. She got a piece of ice from the refrigerator and, wrapping it in a dish towel, held it to the bluish bump which was appearing on Paul's forehead.

"There, there," Ellie said, calmly. "No harm done. It's not bleeding." She lifted Paul up and carried him into the kitchen.

Paul whimpered and in came Mother and Dad, carrying brown paper bags and packages, stamping the snow from their galoshes and taking them off in the entry. Paul blinked in the brightly-lit kitchen. Mother and Dad were like angels with light around their heads. He could smell the cold they brought in.

Marty jumped up on Dad and tried to put her arms around his neck. Though not very tall, Dad was muscular and wiry, with the warmest eyes behind his rimless glasses. He smiled broadly as he lifted Marty up in a bear hug. "How's my girl?" he said. Putting her down, he went back outdoors.

Line took packages from Mother's arms and helped her take off her woolen coat. "We're so glad you're home safe!"

"I am too!" said Mother. She shivered. Relief sparkled in her brown eyes, as she shook out her dark curls and opened her arms, taking Paul from Ellie and kissing his forehead. "Oh, Paul," she said.

Paul started to cry. He was so tired and his head hurt.

"You'll be okay, Paul," said Mother gently. "My darlings, I missed you all. How did you manage?"

Paul felt better. He put his head in the soft wool of the cardigan on Mother's shoulder, and sniffled. Here he was, where he was meant to be.

"We were fine," said Line. Her face shone, mirroring Mother's smiling face.

"We played camps, and we made paper dolls, and we had oatmeal muffins for lunch," said Marty.

Mother looked at Ellie, quizzically. "You were fine?"

"Line stuck her tongue out at me," said Ellie flatly.

An exasperated look crossed Mother's face. "Honestly, Ellie. You're three years older than she is. You're much more grown up, don't you think?"

"Yes, I guess so. We didn't fight, or anything," said Ellie grudgingly.

"Good," sighed Mother. "Thank you girls, for taking care of yourselves. I'm glad nothing worse happened. You are my good girls," she said.

Ellie looked confused. She just stood there, watching. But Paul saw Line smirking at Marty.

"I guess you can get along without baths tonight. But we'll be a sleepy crew in church tomorrow!" continued Mother.

Dad came in with the last of the packages, boyish and animated. He beamed with pride at his little family. Handing the packages to Ellie, he pulled off his coat, gloves and felt hat. He took Paul and lifted him up.

"You know whose birthday it's going to be tomorrow, don't you?" Dad said.

"Birthday?" No one had mentioned it to Paul, but he knew what a birthday was. "Is it mine? My birthday?"

"Yup," said Dad. "Four years ago you were inside your mother's tummy, and the next day you were born, and now, here you are!"

Paul was too sleepy to take this in. He put his head on Dad's shoulder.

"Let's go see about the furnace," said Dad. He carried Paul down the steps to the basement and put him on a bench against the stone foundation.

The iron door to the furnace creaked as Dad opened it with a worn potholder. The coals at the bottom of the opening glowed, hot, red and gold. Dad loaded two shovels full of black lumps from the coal bin into the mouth of the furnace. Little flames licked up from the coal as it lay on the cinders. What's coal? wondered Paul, yawning. Why did it burn? Dad closed the door. Sleepily, Paul connected the glowing mouth of the furnace and the hot water in the radiators, too hot to touch.

Paul was mostly asleep as Dad carried him upstairs and put him in bed.

* * *

In the kitchen, Line asked, "Can we see what's in the packages?" She had her hands in Dad's fur-lined gloves. They felt so soft, she wondered if they were made from a rabbit.

"I'm sure they'll keep until morning," said Mother. "You kids should be in bed!"

"Please," Marty wheedled. "Just one?"

But Mother was excited too. "Just this one," she said, finding a thin flat package from a stationary store.

In it were booklets full of printed Valentines to cut out, and envelopes to paste together and put them in. Line turned the pages, running her fingers over the brilliant reds and pinks and spelling out the phrases. Jokes, rhymes and sweet words to give to friends at school.

Line looked up at Mother with wide eyes. "They're beautiful!" Mother smiled, her cheeks pink. Line saw that she was happy after a day out in the world. The color of Mother's scalloped corduroy dress was Burnt Sienna, according to the names printed on the crayons in the crayola box.

Marty kept fishing in the package. Out slipped a new red piano lesson book, and three Hallmark cards printed with paper dolls, delicately colored girls on stiff paper, with several colored outfits for each. She handed Ellie the piano book.

Line opened the cards and looked at the paper dolls. One was blonde with a blue ribbon in her hair, one had jet black hair and blue eyes, and the other auburn hair in reddish gold pigtails. Beside her, Marty's head bent over the dolls, her eyes soft with longing.

Line thought the paper dolls very well-drawn. They had pale tinted skin, and the one with red hair had freckles. She wanted the red-haired one, and she would keep trading until she got it. Their clothes were perfect, lace dresses, hats, beautifully colored coats with nipped in waists, an ermine muff. They were much better than limp, floppy magazine paper dolls.

"There's one for each of you," said Mother, putting her arm around Ellie's thin shoulders. "Marty can choose first, because she's the littlest. But leave them here now and go to bed. You can play with them after church tomorrow."

Mother followed the girls, to make sure they brushed their teeth and said their prayers. At the top of the stairs she said, "Don't let the sun go down on your anger, girls. Give each other a big hug before you go to bed."

Line put her arms around Ellie, and looked up. Ellie was half a head taller. Deep down, she did love Ellie. Line thought she herself would have made a better oldest sister, but it couldn't be helped. She was glad Mother was home to keep the peace.

Ellie brushed Line's cheek with her mouth. "Good night, Line," she said softly.

"Good night," chanted Line, yawning. "Sleep tight. Don't let the bed bugs bite."

2

That summer Paul fell sick. Dad came home from a church convention with a light flu, and Marty had some fever too. Mother put an army cot in the study, and first Marty and then Paul slept there feverishly, in June, during the long, warm days.

Paul couldn't wait to get better and get outdoors. There was a new sidewalk, a long ribbon of unbroken concrete running beside the parsonage for an entire block. Paul longed to ride his tricycle on it, up to the church and all the way back.

Dad had found turtle eggs in the spring buried in a gravel road. Four tiny turtles hatched from the eggs. They lived in an aquarium with a puddle of water in it. They couldn't climb out of the high glass walls, though Paul could take them out to play. They were the most precious things in the world, with their tiny green patterned shells. Paul loved feeling their little feet walking on his skin. He fed them fish food and bugs.

Marty was fine and Paul was up after a day or so, but Mother said he should not touch the turtles until he was quite well. His knee wasn't bending the way he wanted it to and he let Line pull him in the wagon, surprising her. She mentioned it to Mother. "See, he's dragging his leg when he walks."

Mother was horrified and called Dad to look. They watched Paul walking. Mother felt his forehead. Her hand felt very cool to Paul's hot head. Dad made a telephone call. That afternoon Mother made a bed for Paul in the back of the car, and she and Dad drove him to a hospital in Fargo, as fast as they dared.

Within hours, the doctor drove a needle into Paul's back, Dad holding him down on the cold table. It hurt so much he yelled into Dad's kindly, sad face above him. Afterwards, Dad held him tightly, shushing him. "It's going to be okay," said Dad. "You'll have to stay here in the hospital, but we'll come back tomorrow."

Mother's eyes were damp, but she was trying to put on a brave face. "Don't forget to say your prayers tonight," she said softly, before they left. "I won't be here to remind you, but we'll be with you in our hearts."

Paul was put into a white crib in a white room with nurses coming and going, wearing masks. He was alone. The next day he was moved into a room with three other boys. They had what he had, a new word, polio.

He wasn't allowed out of bed. A nurse brought him a bedpan in the morning and told him to use it. She dressed him in clean pajamas that smelled funny. He didn't feel bad, just hot and his legs ached. Paul knew he was sick, but he wasn't a baby. All of a sudden he was being treated like a baby.

And Mother and Dad didn't come. Paul waited and waited, sinking back and forth into hot, feverish sleep. The other kids didn't talk much. One of them snuffled in the corner. Grownups, doctors, and women in black and white came and went.

In the late afternoon, a woman in black robes, with a stiff white collar and her hair hidden under a veil, lifted Paul out of the crib. Her soft brown eyes shone out from her pale face framed in white. "Your parents are outside. I'll hold you up so you can see them," she said.

Paul felt the stiff white starch against his chest as she held him. Everything in him yearned for Mother's softness.

"Don't cry, you'll make them feel bad," the woman with the big eyes said.

At once Paul started wailing as if it were the end of the world. His parents, outside! And here he was being held by a woman in a black dress with a stiff white frame around her face. It was like he was in a fairy tale.

"I want to go home!" he sobbed.

"Shhhhh," hushed the nun. "Let's wait until you feel better. Don't cry. There's a big boy." She wiped his eyes gently with a handkerchief, smiling at him.

Paul tried to stop. He was shocked to be touched by other hands than those of his family. And he wasn't a baby. The woman held him in her lap, her big brown eyes close to his face, her expression solemn but not soft. She looked like the pictures Paul had seen of Mary, the mother of Jesus, except that Mary wore blue.

Paul gathered up his small courage. If he didn't stop crying, he was sure the woman wouldn't let him see Mother and Dad. With a big effort, he shushed himself and his tears froze.

The nun picked him up and held him up to the window, and there, two floors down, under a tree on the grassy lawn were Mother, Dad, Ellie, Line and Marty. They were waving, waving hats and scarves. Mother and Line were crying, Paul could tell.

"Wave," said the nun, and Paul waved.

"I want to go home," he said.

"You can't go home right now," said the nun. "You're sick. You'll get better soon, and then you can go home."

But that didn't turn out to be true either.

The days went by very slowly. Breakfast, lunch, supper. Paul didn't feel like eating. The sun stayed late into the evening and the sheets were wet with sweat. Paul longed to be home in his bed in Ellie's room. He longed for his family to come. They did come, but not every day. Paul waited, listening. When supper arrived on a day they didn't come, he whimpered to himself, knowing another long night stood between him and seeing their faces.

In the evening, a nun came into the room and said prayers with the boys, clicking a long necklace of black beads. At the end of the string of beads was a cross with Christ crucified on it. The nun made the sign of the cross over Paul and each of the other boys at night. Randy, the boy in the bed next to him, seemed to understand.

"Ain't you a catholic?" he asked Paul. His shock of dark hair and dark face stood out against the white sheets.

"No," said Paul. "I don't think so." He had never heard of nuns. At night he lay awake, watching the headlights of cars move across the ceiling and listening to the rustling leaves in the big tree outside the window. When clear silver moonlight fell in on the beds, Paul imagined a thick web, like a spider's, built across the sky between the earth and moon, especially for sick kids. On the moon, they could play.

In the afternoons, the Mikkelsons stood in a line outside under the tree. Paul stared at them intently, trying to remember everything. The girls wore summer clothes, seersucker shorts and blouses. Marty and Line had short hair, dragged to the side of their heads with barrettes. Line held up his John Deere tractor.

Ellie looked grownup in a skirt and blouse, her blonde hair in tight curls at the ends. While he watched, she lifted up the pair of shoes Mother and Dad bought for him when the summer started. New brown shoes, with shoelaces he wasn't quite able to tie. The shoes were waiting for him.

Dad wore a suit and tie, his arm around Mother. Oh, how hard it was not to reach for Mother, to have glass between them. She wore a dress Paul had never seen, a white dress with black flowers on it, and a hat. It looked as if his parents were going visiting.

The nuns wouldn't hold him up for very long. They brought in the cards and notes that his family sent and read them to Paul. He put them under his pillow. He couldn't read them, but he knew who wrote each one, because he knew their drawings and their handwriting.

They didn't bring his toys. Why? Paul wondered.

Randy explained, "We're catching. Polio is catching. Anything they bring in here has to be burnt." That made sense, thought Paul.

Paul pulled out the letters which would have to be burnt. There was a card with a cowboy swinging a lariat on the front. Line's letter was on white paper, with a small pinto horse in color in one corner by her name. There was a letter from Ellie in cursive and a printed one from Marty, in big letters on lined school paper. Paul had memorized what they said, "We miss you, Paul. Get well soon. Your place at the table is empty. We are praying for you every night."

"Randy," he said. "Can we get well?"

"Oh, yeah. I think so. Depends on your legs. Might need a wheelchair."

"A wheelchair!"

"Believe me," said Randy. "We're the lucky ones. We're not in the iron lung."

It was all too much. Paul didn't know what to think. He tried to stretch his legs. They felt fine, he thought, though they ached a little. It was hard to straighten out his left one. He badly wanted to get out of bed. It seemed he had been in the hospital forever. But he wasn't so hot all the time now, and he was sleeping more at night.

One morning the nurse dressed Randy in a cowboy shirt and pulled jeans on over his stiff legs as Paul watched. "Are you going home?" asked Paul.

"Yup," said Randy. He looked taller than Paul as he sat on the bed. Several years older. "My brother's gonna take care of me."

"At the store?" Randy's family had a hardware store in town.

"Yup," said Randy. "Don't take any wooden nickels." He grinned as the nurse lifted him into a wheelchair and rolled it out the door.

Finally, a few days later, it was Paul's turn. Before the sun was even up, a nurse wheeled a wooden wheelchair with a high back into the room. She dressed Paul in new clothes. "Your father and mother are here," she said.

"I'm going home?" asked Paul.

"They'll tell you," she said.

When the nurse wheeled him into an elevator and down to the front waiting room, there were Mother and Dad. Mother's eyes were shining, but Paul was shy. It was so long since he had talked much.

Dad picked him up and carried him out to the car. The sun wasn't up yet, the sky pale blue and alive. It was so wonderful to be under the open sky at last.

"I can't wait to get home," sighed Paul, relaxing in the warmth of Dad's arms.

"We're not going home," said Mother. "We're going to drive to a clinic, where they will take care of you and get your legs well." She was beaming all her love straight at him. Paul could feel it. "You've been such a brave boy. We love you so much."

"We're going to Rochester, Minnesota," said Dad. "It's 400 miles away, so we'll be driving all day." Again there was a bed in the backseat of the car for Paul.

Paul felt unsure of everything. But, he was much less sick than he was on the way to the hospital. Couldn't he just go back to his happy life at home? "Where are my sisters? Can they come?"

"They're going to stay with your cousins for a while," said Dad. "They miss you, but they can't come to the clinic."

"I can walk," said Paul. "They just won't let me."

"Maybe," said Mother. "We'll have to let the doctor decide about that."

How odd this new world was, in which other people knew more than his parents.

At the clinic Paul was given a bed in a long white room with high ceilings and tall windows where there were beds for 30 boys. Most of them were older than he was, but there were a few cribs for smaller kids too. The bed was high off the ground. Paul tried to slip off the bed and stand on his legs when no one was looking, but his left one crumpled and he fell on the floor. He lay there, thinking about this, until one of the other boys yelled at a nurse that Paul had fallen out of bed.

Some of the older boys had wheelchairs parked at the ends of their beds and Paul watched them swing themselves out of bed with their arms and hands and into their chairs. Like monkeys, Paul thought. It looked like a possible future. He resolved to become a monkey.

Daytime was for therapy. In the morning, in a treatment room, Paul was wrapped in a hot, wet sheet from head to toe, where he lay like a dead mummy unable to move, finally falling back asleep. After the hot wrap, he did physical therapy with a man named Ed who stretched his legs. It hurt some, but Paul was beginning to understand, from what he saw around him, that getting well was partly going to depend on him. And that it might hurt.

"How's that?" Ed would ask gruffly, gently pushing his bent leg as far toward his head as it would go. Ed was almost bald with a fringe of dark hair around his ears and he had big hands. They felt warm and strong on Paul's thin legs.

"Okay," said Paul, trying not to wince.

Ed held it, longer than Paul wanted him to. Paul's hands tightened on the bars on the table. "Good," Ed said. "Better than yesterday. Don't worry. You're a good man. You're going to be okay." He was a medic in the war, on a ship stationed off Iwo Jima. All the boys liked him and at lights out they told stories about Ed and the other doctors and nurses, some of them perhaps true.

After lunch, Mother came and sat with him. She was staying in a nearby town with her mother and sister. Every day she took the bus to the clinic, and her sister, who was a teacher, drove up later in her car and picked her up when Paul went to supper.

Mother wanted Paul to have time alone with her, so she helped him into a chair and wheeled it outside under a tree and read to him. Paul was terribly happy to be outdoors, away from the white room and the metal beds and the noise. She read Bible stories, and she brought a big book called *Treasury of Children's Literature*. In it were fairy tales from Hans Christian Anderson and the Grimm Brothers. Stories about Robin Hood and pirates. Paul closed his eyes and listened, feeling the fresh air on his skin and going far into the story.

Some days Paul sat in a hot whirlpool bath in the afternoon and Mother sat by him and read to him. There was a row of bath chairs each sunk into a tank, and all the kids in the other baths wanted to hear Mother read. The sound of the whirlpools was loud, though, and it was hard to hear her. Her voice was low and smooth, not like a teacher's voice, and she couldn't raise it very loud.

After a month or so, Paul could get out of bed. His left leg was skinny and too weak to stand on. His hips were stiff, but he could get his legs over the side of the bed and then grab for his wheelchair. The trouble was, it didn't have any brakes, so it skittered away when he tried to grab it. It was an old wooden one, quite low. If he could get a hold of it, he could stump with his strong leg, and then swing himself into the seat. His arms were getting stronger, because they pushed the wheels as he propelled himself around. If he missed the wheelchair, one of the other boys would corral it, and back it up to his bed with his own wheelchair, so it couldn't go anywhere and Paul could get into it.

Several of the boys had metal wheelchairs, with brakes. Much better in Paul's eyes. The metal chairs were smaller and easier to control. These boys could do anything. At night they would sneak into their chairs and out into the corridor and have races! Paul didn't dare get out of bed at night. His chair would slip and slide and he would have been lying on the floor in the dark, so he just listened. The boys who raced were four and five years older than he was anyway. When they came back to bed, they bragged about who won. The one Paul liked best, Lloyd, didn't brag. He was quiet, but he often won. When he did, someone else told the story.

One day black clouds hung in the sky and it looked as if there would be a rainstorm. Paul rolled his wheelchair out onto the enclosed sunporch after lunch, where he could look down the walk to see if Mother was coming. He could watch her turn in at the gate, walk up the wide sidewalk and come up the steps to the front door. The sunporch was dark and the air felt heavy, warm and wet.

Paul felt sad because he was afraid Mother wouldn't come, but he was excited by the lightning crackling across the sky. If you counted how many seconds between the lightning and the roll of thunder which followed it, you knew how many miles away the storm was. At least Dad said so.

The lightning and the thunder were coming very close together. All of a sudden, as Paul watched, the rain came coursing down in sheets. It poured through the trees, flattened the spirea branches and splashed hard on the sidewalk. The rushing water sounded all around him. Paul felt ecstatic. He wished he was a frog sitting out in the storm, croaking.

Then two people came dashing up the sidewalk under one umbrella. They didn't have coats on, just summer clothes, and one of them looked a little like Mother! The two people dashed in the door and Mother shook out her umbrella, while Dad raced to Paul and caught him up in a big damp bear hug. Tears streamed down Paul's face and he didn't even care. Mother's too, and none of them cared.

The heavy rain stopped at about the time they all quieted down. The damp, wet pressure of the air was lighter too. Dad pushed Paul in triumph in his chair around the clinic, with Paul telling him where to go and introducing him to everyone he knew. Mother followed, beaming, in their wake.

Late in the afternoon, they came back to the sunporch and settled around a table. Dad had stopped in Renville, where the girls were staying with his family. He brought letters from them. Mother spread out the letters on the table, pointing to each word as she read.

"Dear Paul, We miss you. We went to an ice cream social. I hope you are getting enough ice cream this summer. I feel bad having fun when you are sick in the hospital. Dad says we are coming to see you before we go back to school. Yay! We can't wait to see you! Love, Line."

Paul didn't really like the sound of that. "How long do I have to stay here?" he asked.

"You're going to get better, Paul," said Dad. "You're much better already. You'll be home soon." Dad's face looked tired, but his eyes were steady and warm, the way he looked after he preached two sermons on Sunday.

Line could write cursive, but Marty couldn't yet. Her stiff penciled letters crawled across the page, each line sloping up a little more. Paul could see his name at the top.

"Dear Paul, Dad says the turtles are still alive. Dad has been feeding them. Grandma and all the cousins send you a hug. The cousins have comic books and a player piano. See you soon. Love, Marty." Comic books! Mother and Dad would never spend money on comic books, but the boys in the clinic had some. They were full of little pictures that made up a story. Paul could never resist picking one up to look at the pictures if it were lying around.

"What's a player piano?" Paul asked.

Mother rolled her eyes. "You put rolls of punched out music in a special piano, and the piano plays by itself. Those girls are lowering themselves!" she humpfed. Dad seemed to think this was funny, or maybe he was just happy to be there, his smile wide.

Ellie printed her letter, as if Paul were going to read it. "She didn't know what to write," said Dad. "I told them to just write what they were doing."

"Dear Paul, I am staying with Grandma and helping in the garden. The strawberries are over, but they have radishes, squash, onions, carrots, beans and beets. I know you would like to be out in the dirt with us. Grandpa bought some peaches and Grandma canned them for the winter. I helped, so I get to take some home for us. We will save them for when we see you. Love, Ellie."

Mother sighed. "Such good letters," she said. None of them wanted to be this far apart, but it couldn't be helped. The letters, and Dad having just seen Line, Marty and Ellie, made it feel like they were all there, circled around Paul.

"Dad," said Paul. "Could I get one of those metal wheelchairs, with the brakes? They work so much better, and I could get around really well."

Dad's eyes twinkled as he took Paul out of his chair and put him in his lap. "I'm not going to help you get a better wheelchair, Paul. I'm going to help you get some crutches."

Mother smiled. "You are here to get strong enough to walk again, Paul," she said.

"A better wheelchair would just cripple you," said Dad, "Make you not want to leave it. Let's see how much you can walk right now." He put his strong arms around Paul's middle and held him while Paul tried to get his legs to walk. His right leg was better than the other, but his left one was skinny and caved in. He couldn't hop like a bunny. A person needed two legs to walk.

When they left at supper time, the clouds were fluffy and white and the sun was shining on the freshly washed trees and plants, water standing in bright puddles in low places along the sidewalk. They would come again tomorrow, but then Dad would drive the long way back to North Dakota. The church needed him and he needed to make money for all of them.

That evening, Paul pondered all that he had learned. Some of the boys used crutches, but they did seem to prefer to zoom around in their wheelchairs. They were like hot rods. Wheels were the best. Paul had never been around so many boys. It was exciting. But he wanted to walk again. He wanted to be free.

Paul was glad the turtles were still alive. He longed to feel their dry little feet on his skin and touch their stiff green patchwork shells.

The next day, when Dad and Mother came, Dad watched Ed doing physical therapy with Paul. Paul kept his mouth firmly shut until it was too painful, as all the boys did. The staff called them little soldiers and told them that polio couldn't keep them down if they worked hard. Mother wiped her eyes. She hadn't had the stomach to come to physical therapy before. Paul was her baby, not a soldier. But Dad watched approvingly and thanked Ed for working with Paul.

At Dad's questioning, Ed found a small pair of crutches for him. "Yeah, I thought he was about ready for these too," Ed said. "It's okay if he compensates with his arms for now. He's going to be strong in many ways." Paul swung the crutches out in front of him and dragged his feet after, leading with his right. He was clumsy, but the smile on his face made up for it. Mother smiled too, her eyes moist.

"He's a good man," said Ed.

"You're right about that!" said Dad cheerfully, as if Paul and he were one person. "Nothing's going to keep this kid down." When Paul walked over to him, Dad lifted him high and the crutches clattered to the ground.

At the end of the summer, Dad brought Line, Marty and Ellie to visit. Paul showed them all how well he could walk on his crutches, but then he let Line push him in the wheelchair when they went outdoors.

Line was sharp and a little bitter. "This place looks more fun than Renville," she whispered to Paul. She loved the excitement and noise. The kids at the clinic might be disabled, but were no less active for all that. There was an atmosphere of struggle and camaraderie that even visitors could feel. Marty followed along, watching and listening, but Ellie seemed removed, off in her own world.

When they left to go back to school, Mother went with them. Paul stayed at the clinic, having physical therapy and hot baths every day. At night he got out of bed and sneaked out into the hall on his crutches with the big boys.

In September, the clinic brought in teachers in the afternoons. Paul was too little for school in North Dakota, where there was no kindergarten, but he went to class at the clinic and began to learn the alphabet, and what the letters sounded like. He had a box of letters from home by his bed now, and he pulled them out to see if he could read them.

On the weekends, Aunt Rose came to see Paul. She was a big, high-spirited woman, Mother's sister, who was used to kids as she was a school teacher. Paul asked her if she thought the letters from home would have to be burnt, but she said she didn't think so.

Aunt Rose brought books and sketchpads and an Uncle Wiggly game. She too seemed delighted by the big collection of raucous boys in Paul's ward. She talked to them as if they were grownups, and they liked her too.

But Paul was tired of being so close to everyone. The cries of the staff sounded loud throughout the day as they corralled the noisy kids. Whenever he could, Paul stole out under the great trees so he could think and look at the sky. Evenings, he sat in the quietest corner he could find, a place in the dining room where one of the older girls kept up an almost continuous chess game, testing herself against anyone who would play. He was too little to play, but Betty smiled at him when he sat near. He had almost given up expecting to go home.

On Halloween, Paul was fitted with a brace on his weaker, thinner leg. This leg was strong enough to stand on now, and the brace kept his knee from caving in. Paul knew it was Halloween because the boys carved a pumpkin into a jack-o-lantern and put a candle in it. They plotted to put sheets on their heads and go over to the girls' ward and scare them. Two of the braver ones tore tiny slits in their sheets so they could put them on their heads and still see. No one would know who the culprits were.

One of the boys put the jack-o-lantern in a wheelchair and pushed it in front of him. The ghosts made eerie-sounding cries, "Woooo-ooooo-oooo." Paul went with them and heard the girls screaming. The boys clattered back to their room, leaving the jack-o-lantern in the wheelchair outside the door.

Dad came to the clinic the next week. He went to every one of Paul's therapy sessions to learn how to work Paul's legs. He learned how to put on the brace, and how to oil it and take care of it. He was going to take Paul home.

Paul could hardly believe it. After all the long months of being sick, he was going to go home. Dad put a pillow in the seat in the old black Ford where Mother usually sat, but Paul could hardly see over the dashboard. Wrapped in a warm blanket, he peered out across the land as they drove. It hadn't snowed yet and the fields were bare, with a stubble of greygold cornstalks in them. The trees were leafless, black lace against the grey sky. Paul had missed that whole summer and most of fall, but he would be home for Thanksgiving, and they weren't even bringing his crutches.

3

Line's school year got off to a bad start. One morning she looked over and saw Clyde staring out the window instead of copying out the answers to the social studies questions. It was a brilliant day, the sun crusting the new snow with its warmth. Outside on the window ledge, a row of green glass coke bottles was stuck in the snow.

The same ten kids were in Line's class as the year before, but they were in a new room with the fourth grade class, and a new teacher. Line didn't like Mrs. Soderberg, who seemed to pick on the same kids all the time.

As Line watched, Mrs. Soderberg, rapped Clyde's knuckles with a ruler to get his attention. Clyde, who wore a Hopalong Cassidy shirt, his hair parted on the side and slicked down, hardly even flinched.

"You can do your social studies questions after school, Clyde," said Mrs. Soderberg, a tiny woman with tightly-permed, graying hair.

Line was outraged. Without even raising her hand, she said, "But, Mrs. Soderberg, Clyde gets up early to milk the cows and has to walk a mile to the bus."

"No back talk, Line," said Mrs. Soderberg.

"But how will he get home?" cried Line. She knew Clyde's dad would be mad if he had to come and get him.

Mrs. Soderberg turned around and stood next to Line's desk. "Not one more word, young lady," she said. Her pearls clicked against the buttons of her cardigan as she summoned up all her importance. "You can stay after school as well."

The whole room, including the fourth grade class, was quiet. Line looked down at her desk and felt her heart pounding and a blush spreading over her face. She knew that in school, Mrs. Soderberg ruled the class. If she didn't behave she would be sent to the principal's office, the principal would call Dad and she would get a bad mark in conduct. She was probably already getting a bad mark in conduct, but she did not want anyone to call Dad.

The school was an old, perfectly symmetrical building which sat in the center of a block at the edge of town. A line of cottonwood trees planted when the school was built marked the edge of the schoolyard. They were tall now, their leafless branches spreading wide under light snow. On the first floor of the school, four large classrooms held two classes each. Upstairs, in one large room which was also used for assemblies, was the high school. The lunch room was in the basement, next to the furnace room.

Line was in third grade, leaving Marty behind in second grade with the wonderful Miss Onstead, who never reprimanded Clyde. Miss Onstead had a different way of involving her students, helping them learn together. But Line would be in Mrs. Soderberg's class for the next two years. She would have to get used to her old-fashioned methods.

Clyde said the same thing after school. It turned out that Clyde's mother was at Ladies' Aid at church. So, after an hour of writing quietly under Mrs. Soderberg's watchful eye, Line and Clyde put on their galoshes, hats, mittens and coats, and left school, walking together toward the church. The sun was low in the sky and their shadows were long, angling in front of them.

"It's okay," said Clyde. "I don't care if she raps me." The sidewalks were mostly shoveled, as it was a few days since the first snowstorm. Clyde picked up a stick and dragged it through the sunlit drifts. The stick dug a line, making a blue shadow. In his other hand was a shiny tin lunch pail, very bright in the sun.

"But Miss Onstead never did that," said Line, sliding in her boots on the icy sidewalk, as if she were skating.

"School was easy then. All that music and art. I don't need that," Clyde sniffed. "Pop says I need to learn arithmetic and reading. He don't care about the rest of it." Line knew that Clyde's dad didn't come to church, while his mother was one of its most important members. Clyde's mother came to talk to Dad by herself, but Line didn't know what they talked about.

"If you stick up for me," said Clyde, smiling, "they'll say you're my sweetheart." He began to draw his name in the snow with the stick, then added a plus sign and put "Line."

Line laughed. "I don't care." She took the stick and wrote on the fresh snow on the other side. "Line + Clyde". There it was, for all the world to see, just across the street from the church.

Line felt herself growing warm under her coat. She started running down the long new sidewalk which was shoveled all the way to her house.

"See you tomorrow," she shouted back at Clyde.

Mother and Dad were still at church and no one seemed to notice that Line was late from school and excited. Ellie was in the kitchen making cinnamon toast, because it would be a while until supper. Marty and Paul sat together on the sofa, their heads bent over the Sears Roebuck Christmas catalog which was splayed between them on their knees.

It was wonderful to see Paul sitting on the couch as if nothing had happened. The months that Paul had been gone had felt very long to Line. Once the novelty of staying at the cousins for the summer wore off, Line felt she was marking time, like it wasn't her own life. And when school started, Paul was still missing. Finally, things were beginning to feel okay again.

When Paul first got home, he was shy, quiet, very close to Dad. Three times a day he went into Dad's study and Dad laid a mat on the floor and stretched Paul's muscles. Paul didn't want the girls to come in, because it hurt, and he didn't want them to see. Sometimes they heard him squawking. After physical therapy, Dad got down on the mat and wrestled with Paul. Line knew because she spied on them. That part looked like fun.

Line helped Paul buckle on his brace in the mornings. It fitted tightly to his leg and flexed at the leather knee caps, ending up in a pair of shoes. He didn't wear it at night, but he couldn't sneak around without it during the day. Most people didn't even notice it under his pants, but Mother and Dad did.

In December, the mornings were bitter cold, but the house was warm. Lying in bed, Line heard Dad get up early and go down to the basement to shovel coal into the furnace. She hugged herself under the covers. Christmas was coming! Nothing could prevent it. All of the preparations for it were beginning.

Line waked up Marty and then got Paul, whose bed was in Ellie's room. They went downstairs in their pajamas, Paul gimping along behind holding onto the banisters. They wanted to see what was behind that day's door on the Advent calendar.

The calendar was a gingerbread castle, with snow on its roofs, mullioned windows, and a big gate with deer outside. It came all the way from Denmark. Each day they opened one door and when they had opened them all, it would be Christmas.

Line and Marty let Paul find the next door and open it, because he had been away from home so long. Behind the door marked "4" was a tiny fairy. Line turned on the light behind the calendar. In the darkness of the early morning, light shone through the thin paper where doors had been opened. It was like a castle in a fairy tale, with its windows full of bright elves, toys and fairies.

On Sunday night, Mother said they would have a candle-lit supper. Line put out the candles as Marty set six places in the dining room. In the middle of the table, Line put the painted wooden Advent tree, an evergreen made of two pieces of wood slotted together so it would stand up. At its four corners were red holders with candles in them.

Paul begged to light the table candles, but Line said he was too little. She scratched the match across the matchbox and the small hot flame appeared. She carefully touched it to the wicks of the candles. Once they were lit, Paul didn't move, watching the wax drip down the candles and pool at the base.

Mother made a big plate of toasted cheese sandwiches, and let Line put a marshmallow in each cup of cocoa. After the meal Dad began devotions in a soft, gravelly voice. He was tired, as he had preached and sung two services already that day. But his face had an uplifted look, Line thought, as if he had been communing with the angels.

"Grace be unto you, and peace, from God our Father, and from the Lord Jesus Christ," he said, in the words of the apostle Paul to the Corinthians. Around the table, the faces glowed in the candlelight as Dad looked at them. "The season of Advent is our anticipation of God's great gift to us, the birth of Christ our Saviour." He moved the little Advent tree with its red candles close to the edge of the table. "Come Paul, stand next to me." He lit a match and handed it to Paul. "You have to hold the flame down," said Dad. Paul touched the match to one of the wicks, holding his breath.

"In him was life; and the life was the light of man. And the light shineth in darkness; and the darkness comprehended it not. John 1:4," said Dad. "Let us all prepare our hearts for the coming of the Christ Child. We'll go around the room and each say a prayer."

Mother began by thanking the Lord that they were all together, and for Paul's recovery and the good health of all of them. Ellie prayed that they all stayed safe, that there wouldn't be any blizzards, the car wouldn't get stuck and they would stay warm that winter. Marty was thankful for the birds, the beautiful world and the food they had to eat, and Paul said his little piece: "God bless us every one."

When it came to Line, she couldn't think of anything more to say. Pictures passed through her mind, of the church, the school, their house in the snow. Horses, the sled they got for Christmas last year. She was thinking of asking Dad if he would take them out on it. There were no hills to use the sled on, but sometimes Dad tied it to the back of the car and dragged them through the snowy streets. It was dangerous, but fun!

The minutes dragged by in silence. Everyone's heads were bent over their folded hands. Line opened her eyes and peeked. She knew they were waiting, but she couldn't think of anything to say.

"Line," said Dad, a little sternly.

Line rubbed her nose with her folded hands, but nothing she thought of seemed to be right in a prayer.

At last, Mother's contralto broke the silence, "Oh, come. Oh, come, Emmanuel," she sang softly. "And ransom captive Is-ra-el, that mourns in lonely exile here." The unfamiliar words rolled around in Line's head to the haunting melody.

Dad's beautiful tenor joined in, and so did Ellie. "Until the Son of God appear. Rejoice! Rejoice! Emmanuel shall come to you, oh Is-ra-el."

Mother stood up and pushed her chair away from the table, clearing cocoa mugs and plates into the kitchen. Everyone left the table, but Line just sat there feeling bad. Dad looked at her, tired and a little hurt. He took Paul into the study to work on his leg. Ellie and Marty evaporated up the stairs, leaving Line to help Mother. She stood rinsing the dishes and putting them into the rack, wiping the glasses and the silverware.

"I just can't wait!" Line said. "I keep thinking of all the toys and fun we are going to have."

"You could thank the Lord for that," said Mother.

"Nooooo," said Line. "That's not the Christmas spirit, is it?" She was thinking of all the times Dad told them that there might have been a St. Nicholas, but Santa Claus wasn't real, didn't come down the chimney, and that the songs about reindeer were just made up for fun. The presents they gave each other were in honor of the gift God gave to the world, his Son, the Christ child.

"It's part of Christmas. Gift giving is about love," said Mother. "Rejoice. Rejoice!" she sang. She smiled at Line.

Line climbed up on the stool to put glasses away, wondering why it was so easy to talk to Mother, but not to listen to Dad's voice reprimanding her.

"Now, what do you think," said Mother, conspiratorially. "I'd like to take all the miniature dolls and dress them up as shepherds and wise men, and Mary and Joseph, and the angels of course, and make a manger scene."

Line looked down at her. They already had one manager scene, made of beautiful colored figures on stiff cardboard. But it would be fun to put rags on some of the dolls for shepherds and dress others in fancy scraps for wise men and angels. "Dad has those stamp boxes, they could be the gold, frankincense and myrrh," Line said. It was like playing at ranches. "We have those plaster sheep. And there could be horses, couldn't there?"

"Of course," said Mother. "Everyone wanted to worship the Christ child."

"My Indian doll would have to be Mary," said Line. "Because she's the only one that can sit."

It turned out to be a project that occupied them for many days. Robes were easy to cut out of cloth scraps, velveteen tied with gold ribbon for the wise men and burlap tied with rope for the shepherds. The Indian doll, which was getting slightly bald on one side, was dressed with a blue headdress as Mary. Dad nailed together a wooden stable, and Paul glued on tiny willow sticks for thatch. The crib for the baby Jesus was made of willow sticks tied together with twine. One of Ellie's blonde dolls, which came wearing a Dutch dress and hat, was dressed in blue and hung in the sky for the angel who sang to the shepherds.

The finished manger scene was displayed on a tall bookcase, with folds of cloth for the hills and blue paper stuck with gummed gold stars for the sky. Dad rigged a tiny light behind the biggest star in the sky that led the wise men to Bethlehem and pricked the paper so light shone through. In a darkened room, it looked like a starry night. The kids were terribly proud of it.

Only two turtles were left by this time. One died and one wandered off, probably under the refrigerator. Line found it very funny to see Paul standing on a chair in front of the manager scene with a green turtle bigger than the Christ child crawling across the hills. "Turtles don't like deserts," she said. "I don't think there was any water for miles."

"My turtles do," said Paul. "Maybe they saw the star, just like the wise men did, and came to worship."

Ellie got to be the star of the best Christmas celebration. On St. Lucia's day, December 13, according to Scandinavian tradition, the oldest daughter put a crown of candles in her hair and carried breakfast up to members of her family, singing carols.

Line was despondent. "I'll never get to be the oldest," she told Marty as they climbed into bed the night before.

"Me neither," said Marty.

"Dad calls me Sparky," said Line. "I should get to bring light into the darkness."

"Do you think she's going to put candles in her hair?" asked Marty. "Her hair might get singed right off!"

"I would," said Line. "I'd put candles in my hair." She remembered St. Lucia's day last year, but didn't know whether Ellie used real candles or not.

"Never mind," said Marty. "Let's play Snow White and Rose Red." They took tiny dolls to be the characters and pushed the covers down to the bottom of the bed. They humped the covers into folds, making caves for Snow White and Rose Red to live in. The bear, who would become a handsome prince when they were kind to him, lived in another cave. But somehow, planning how they would play always took much more time than actually playing, and it wasn't long before they pulled the covers up and fell asleep.

In the morning, they heard carols. Ellie was playing them on the record player, turned up loud enough so the songs came drifting upstairs. Eventually they heard her coming up the stairs with a tray full of coffee cups and orange juice glasses. She put it on a dresser in the hall and ran downstairs again.

Line and Marty stood in their bedroom door as Ellie came up the stairs very slowly. She had put a white kerchief over her blonde hair, and pressed it down with a wooden ring with holders for four tall candles. Three of them were lit, but one had gone out. She wore a white robe made from a sheet with a red shawl for a sash. This time she was carrying a tray of frosted buns and another plate with silver things on it, trying not to trip. She was singing along with the record in her thin, reedy voice, "O Holy Night, the stars were brightly shining ..." She did look like a queen.

Line ached with envy. "One of your candles is out," she hissed.

Ellie frowned. There was nothing to do about it now. "Go get Paul," she said to Line.

Line went to wake him. They all trooped in to Mother and Dad's bedroom and sat on the floor. Ellie took off the wooden crown of candles and put it carefully on the dresser. Dad and Mother poked their heads out of their cocoons in bed and Ellie passed them coffee cups, moving carefully in the dark. The candles were the only light in the room. Ellie had made the coffee herself.

"Pretty good," said Dad, tasting it.

The kids drank orange juice and ate the rolls Mother made with raisins and cinnamon and brown sugar. The silver things turned out to be wrapped Hershey's kisses! They could never remember having chocolates at breakfast.

"I think I died and went to heaven," said Marty, softly.

"Not yet!" said Mother, encouragingly. "Things might get better. You never know."

They all laughed except Line, who was trying to keep her mouth shut to avoid saying something envious and mean. She did manage to do it, but she could feel a hard little lump of anger in herself. Nothing was fair. Why did Paul get polio, and no one else? She was mad at Ellie because she went on with her own life when Paul was so sick, and because Ellie would always be older. She was mad that she had Mrs. Soderberg for a teacher, who picked on some kids and not others. And she felt, that though Dad was Christ's representative to people on earth, it was up to her to remind him that he wasn't perfect. Nobody was perfect.

Line's bad temper dissipated as she laid her school clothes on the radiator to warm up, corduroy pants under a green printed cotton dress with a white collar. The clothes Mother sewed for her were usually fall colors, golds and greens and browns because of her red-gold hair. Marty minded that they wore homemade clothes, dresses handed down from Ellie and dresses out of mission barrels, but Line didn't care.

No one in school seemed to know about St. Lucia's day, even though many of them were Scandinavian. It was just an ordinary day, and Clyde wasn't even there. He was probably at home helping his dad. Line realized that it was Mother who knew about these delightful Christmas customs and taught them all to celebrate. It was Mother's ideas that made the house festive with music and light.

After school, Mother said that if Line went to the grocery store and got eggs and some bread, she would make scrambled eggs with bacon for supper.

"Can I come?" piped up Paul. "Can I come?" He had been in the house all day. A light snow was falling in the grey light that was rapidly becoming darkness.

"Of course!" said Line, ready for adventure. "Let's go!" They went out in their coats to the cold entry. Fishing through the sea of black galoshes on the floor, they found their own, buckling them over their shoes. Only Ellie got new ones. Her old ones kept being passed down as their feet grew.

The snow made the sky and earth hardly distinct from each other. Paul and Line were two short figures going down the walk, using the street lamps to see.

Line caught snowflakes on her mittens, but it wasn't very cold out and they melted as soon as she caught them. Her mittens just got wet.

Paul put his tongue out. "The snow tastes dirty," said Paul. "I like it."

"Me too," said Line. She tasted the snow she was mounding up in her mittens.

"Where do hobos go when it's winter?" asked Paul. They walked down the sidewalk along the main road, past houses, with the railroad tracks on the far side of the street.

Line knew where hobos had a campfire near the tracks and had seen men walking from the railroad tracks after a train had passed through. Sometimes they came to the back door to ask Mother for food. They were always respectful, in their caps and extra layers of dirty clothes. They seemed happy when Mother gave them cans of beans and meat. Some of them were quite young, Line thought. But Mother was saddened by them and acted as if she didn't want them to come in the house.

"California or Florida," said Line. "Somewhere warm." She pulled a leafless stick out of a shrub and put it over her shoulder. Though she was willing to play with dolls and fairy tale characters, she much preferred being a hobo. It was one of the many reasons she had missed Paul so much that summer.

"I saw a movie about a tramp," said Paul. "At the clinic one Saturday."

"Oh?" said Line. They hardly ever saw movies, except sometimes in assembly. "What was he like?"

"His clothes were too big. His trousers dragged around his feet. He wore suspenders to pull them up, and a little round hat, and a mustache."

"I wonder if a tramp is the same as a hobo," said Line.

"He didn't ride the railroad. I just know that the boys around me called him a tramp. And he carried his things in a handkerchief at the end of a stick."

"Maybe for tramping," said Line. "Maybe a hobo rides the train and a tramp walks."

"Yeah!" said Paul. "That makes sense."

"I think I would rather be a hobo," said Line. "It would be fun to go to California on a train."

They passed the gas station, a wide space where cars came at you from almost any direction. Line grabbed Paul's mittened hand and craned her neck to look up at the red and white flying horse fixed to a pole high above their heads. A yellow light shone inside the horse to light it up. She also liked the men who worked at the station. When she walked by with Paul, or even with Marty, the men often teased them, calling out, "Hello, boys!"

Beside her, Paul dragged along, looking into the gathering darkness. Line could see he was struggling. "Is your brace bothering you?" she asked. The metal was wrapped in cotton wadding, and the kneecap was leather, but the metal did run up his leg and it never warmed up. Line knew it just got icy cold, and took a long time to warm up when they went inside.

"Yeah, a little," said Paul.

They passed the bank, the post office and the dark tavern that smelt sour and old, even in the winter. It was four o'clock and the bank was shut, but a colored glowing neon sign saying "Miller" shown in the window of the tavern.

"I think I'd rather be a tramp," Paul said finally. "I'd rather see things. You can see more things when you walk."

At the grocery store, Mr. Ellingson welcomed them, standing at his long counter in a red woolen sweater. He was a church councilmen, a good friend to Dad. He was talking to a farmer Line didn't know. The farmer wore overalls with his flannel underwear sticking out and a big parka. He was chewing tobacco. His stubbly grey beard and the smell of tobacco and tractor grease were so strong, he felt pleasantly foreign to Line. Maybe he was Clyde's dad.

Line and Paul went to the back of the store to get the eggs. They were too warm in their bundled coats and hats, but they were going right back outdoors.

"Wa'll, you know, I'll bet he'll be back by springtime," the farmer was saying slowly to Mr. Ellingson. "The mills of God grind slowly, but they grind exceeding small." Line froze, listening.

"You're probably right," replied Mr. Ellingson.

Bringing the eggs and a loaf of white bread in a plastic wrapper up to the counter, Line waited while Mr. Ellingson wrote them down, with their prices, on a little yellow tablet with a carbon paper underneath. He put one copy in the cash drawer to put on their bill, and one into a paper sack with the eggs and bread which he gave to Line.

"You kids ready for Christmas?" Mr. Ellingson asked.

"Yes," said Line and Paul together. They were told so often that children should be seen and not heard that they didn't try to talk to grownups.

"How about a piece of candy to keep you warm on your way home," he said. "It won't spoil your supper, will it?" To the farmer he said, "They're the pastor's kids."

"No," said Line. "And thank you." She and Paul each picked a wrapped candy from the bins near the counter. They pulled off the paper and put the candy in their mouths.

"Thank you," mumbled Paul sidling out the door behind Line, released from the alien world of grownups.

Her mouth full of Tootsie Roll, Line savored the phrase she heard the farmer say as they walked home. "The mills of God grind slowly, but they grind exceeding small." What did it mean? She carried the sack of groceries carefully because it had eggs in it. Paul seemed absorbed too. Line held his mittened hand, feeling his uneven steps as they walked. The snow still fell lightly, softening the edges of things and laying lightly on the bare branches of bushes and trees.

In the windows of the houses they could see colored Christmas tree lights. When they got to the corner where they could see their own house and the church across the road, they stood for a minute, looking at the windows. The back porch light was on, and there were lights in the kitchen and dining room, and upstairs in Marty and Line's bedroom. The living room was dark, except that Line could just barely see the tiny lamp above the manger scene on the bookcase that made the Christmas star.

They crossed the road and hurried toward the back porch. In the entry they stripped off their coats and snowy galoshes, their faces glowing from the cold. Line went into the living room and looked at the beautiful manger scene, at the angel, the shepherds in their tunics and the wise men in velveteen robes. One of the shepherds wore the same green calico tunic as the dress Line wore to school that day. A small bronze stamp box held the wise men's gold. The myrrh was a tiny glass perfume bottle produced by Mother. Mary looked demure and tender, her arms stretched out toward the tiny pink plastic baby in the manger, the Christ child, with Joseph standing protectively nearby.

It's not up to me, thought Line. The mills of God grind slowly, but we are all in His hands. She stretched out her finger toward the baby, the Christ child, and stroked his little white swaddling clothes. The angry, hard place in her softened and the mantle of responsibility for the world slipped off. "Oh come, oh come, Ema-nu-el," she sang softly to herself. "And ransom captive Is-ra-el."

4

Marty pushed her chip boat with a long stick, feeling the sun on her chapped red hands. A small batch of sparrows lit in a tree all at once and then rose together to fly to another. The tree branches were bare, but the smell of life was in the air, buds rising along the twigs. If you could smell at all, winter was almost over. There might still be another snowstorm, but the lengthening days proved that winter's back was broken. Spring was on the way.

Marty loved being outdoors. It was Saturday and Mother had turned Line, Paul and Marty out to play while she washed clothes and Ellie cleaned the house. They could play anywhere on the block, as long as they didn't cross any roads.

In March, the world was full of puddles, watery slush and chunks of ice in sunken places and ditches next to the road. The kids found wood chips for boats, which they guided with sticks around the ice floes. Marty tried to stay out of the deep parts, so the water wouldn't surge into her galoshes. If she did get thoroughly wet, it didn't matter anyway because the temperature was no longer freezing.

The ditches alongside the road flowed into culverts, big cement pipes under the sidewalk. Line stood on one side of a culvert and Paul and Marty on the other, calling to each other that their boat arrived.

When the morning freight train roared down the tracks across from the parsonage, the kids stopped and watched. In the house, they hardly noticed, though the chugging of the engine and the rhythmic clacking of iron wheels on steel was sometimes so loud it shivered the plates and the cups off the hooks in the green cupboard. But the train rarely stopped in Bryson, and the long, musical whoooo whooooo, which alerted the depot master, never surprised them.

They waved to the engineer who leaned his head out the window, looking back in a blue and white striped denim hat and a red handkerchief around his neck. They were too late. He didn't see them. The train with its two engines roared on past, going north. Paul counted the cars, the flat cars, box cars, hopper cars and cattle cars, and Marty read the names on their sides, Rock Island Line, Georgia Pacific, the Soo Line, Burlington Northern, Illinois Central.

Down the street, at the trim white train depot, the outgoing mailbag was suspended on an iron arm. As the train whistled by, slowing a little, one of the men on the caboose, the last open red car, put out a grabbing hook and retrieved the thick canvas mailbag as the train passed. Another threw out a similar bag full of Bryson's mail.

Marty couldn't see things in the distance very well, but Paul and Line could. Standing in the slushy ditch, they all waved. The caboose men, who wore uniforms with stiff black caps, waved back. The musical sounds faded, as the train clattered off into the distance.

"I see the mailbag! I see it," shouted Paul. Johnny, who worked for the depot, went out and retrieved the mailbag to bring it to the post office.

"Let's race from this point to the other side of the culvert," said Line, turning back to the chip boats, and laying down a stone which would be the starting point.

"But how do we start?" asked Paul. "Someone's boat has to start first." The ditch water was a thin trickle in places. Not enough room for all of their boats in a row.

"Eenie, meenie, meinie moe," said Line. "Ok, Paul, you start. Marty, get your boat in line."

But Marty was lost in thought. Looking across to the depot made her think of Eileen, the depot master's daughter. She was Marty's arch-rival for the friendship of the only other town girl in her class, Anne. Eileen had prettier clothes than Marty, including buckle shoes, and she wore white stockings under her dress in the winter. Marty had only corduroy pants like the other girls. Marty was a better student, but in her eyes, pretty clothes and buckle shoes counted for more than a good report card.

Just that week, when Marty asked her to play marbles, Anne said she couldn't because she had promised to sit with Eileen at lunch. Marty ate hot goulash on a tray in the lunchroom, hurrying before the noisy high school kids came down. Then she joined the boys playing marbles on the basement floor in front of the furnace. They rolled marbles against the wall and tried to hit each other's with special shooters, claiming the ones they hit. Loren had an iron ball bearing shooter and a terrific aim, and he took her favorite red cat's eye before she knew what happened. But, when he saw how sad this made her, he traded it back for a white glass marble that Marty didn't love as much.

Standing in the puddle, Marty reflected that Eileen couldn't play on the floor of the basement at school because her white stockings would get dirty. Marty was sure Anne would rather play marbles than pretend to be grown up and talk to Eileen. It was more fun to play with the boys, or to get wet out in the ditch than have pretty clothes, she decided, reluctantly. She wanted to have everything. She pushed her boat toward Line and Paul, who were shouting at her to race with them.

That year there was no late snowstorm in April. Rains came and the earth softened, new grass replaced the old, and by May the sun was strong, even hot in the middle of the day. Eileen came to school with white cards for each girl in the class. Marty was postmistress that day, so she put them in the small wooden cubes with the first and second graders names on them, their own post office.

When Marty opened hers, she found a printed party invitation, with the date and place handwritten in. She was excited by her first printed invitation, and couldn't wait to see the inside of the train depot, where Eileen lived. At home birthdays were only celebrated with the family.

On Saturday Marty walked to the depot by herself, but hesitated outside the door until Geraldine's mother dropped her off. Geraldine lived in the country and didn't come to Marty's church. She wore a dress with a big white collar, red cherries appliquéd on it to match the dress. Marty wore last year's store-bought Christmas dress, a blue print with a longish waistline and a tiny row of lace around the collar. But she despaired of her shoes. Her only pair of saddle shoes were polished to cover up the scuffed part, but they looked old, the laces dirty and the leather worn. Dad couldn't afford to buy them more than one pair of shoes.

Together, the girls were brave enough to open the door. The depot was a big room with painted wooden benches, and a glass window on one side with a hole in it, so people could talk to the depot master. Along one side, windows looked out on a platform next to the railway track. Marty and Geraldine stood still and looked around, until they saw Eileen, standing in a doorway on the far side of the room. She wore a blue velveteen dress with a white collar and shiny patent leather buckle shoes with white socks. Her blonde hair was curled and tied with a big white bow.

"Come in, come in," she called. "We live over here. May I take your things?"

The girls didn't have any things, except the packages they carried. Marty handed Eileen a birthday present wrapped in tissue paper left over from Christmas, taped together, with a card she made herself. Geraldine's present was wrapped in paper printed with pictures of balloons and dogs, with a white card and a ribbon bow. Marty could see that the present and its wrapping were very important. Eileen put them on a table, in what looked like an ordinary, living room.

Lace doilies covered the backs and arms of the sofa and a big chair, as they did at Grandmother Mikkelson's house. The bookcase, with only a few *Reader's Digest* books on it, held tiny porcelain figures and plates. A vase of roses stood under a lamp on an end table and lace curtains hung at the windows. At one end of the room was a dining table set with flowered china plates.

Eileen's mother entered. Young, and rather plump, she looked stylish to Marty in an apron and high heeled shoes.

Eileen introduced them, practicing as they did in school. "Mother, this is Marty and this is Geraldine." Mrs. Sundby took their hands and smiled lazily, as if she had heard a lot about them. She went back to the kitchen.

Just then Anne and Melody arrived. "I didn't invite any boys," said Eileen. "So we are all here."

Anne's family was poor and her father worked at the gas station. Marty had played in her ramshackle frame house with its big kerosene stove in the front room. Heat traveled upstairs through a pipe, and Marty knew it was cold in the bedrooms, two rooms with old iron bedsteads crammed against the sloping eaves, in the winter. But Anne wore her Sunday School dress, a print dress with a ruffle in front, and carried a present. Melody was taller than the other girls with a big crop of freckles and red, frizzy hair. She linked her lanky arms behind her navy corduroy jumper, because she had no present.

Eileen showed them into her bedroom, where they could put their sweaters if they wanted to. An old-fashioned doll with a china head lay on the pink chenille bedspread. "It was my Grandmother's," said Eileen, "and she passed it on to me." The bureau was covered with an embroidered cloth, and displayed a tiny jewelry box, and a comb, brush and mirror set in matching pink plastic.

Marty looked out the window to see what Eileen saw when she woke up. The bedroom looked toward the grocery store and the tavern, not toward the railroad track, but there was a tree. She imagined that the trains must sound in Eileen's sleep the way they did in Marty's. In the closet were Eileen's dresses on hangers and below them a row of pairs of shoes. Everything was neat and it all belonged to Eileen.

Eileen invited them to play a game of pin the tail on the donkey, blindfolding each of them with a handkerchief, spinning them around and letting them try to find the place on a printed wall poster where the tail should go. After that they dropped clothespins from a chair into a milk bottle. Marty thought the games were tame. She imagined that she and Line could have made up much more exciting things to do in that big depot waiting room. But she was anxious to find out how you were supposed to behave at parties, and she tried to do as the others did.

All the girls looked to Eileen. They were in the same class at school, so they knew each other, but none of them seemed to know what you talked about at parties. The party was rather subdued, like a party in a picture in a magazine.

Finally Eileen's mother invited them to the table. There was a plate of egg salad sandwiches on white bread with the crusts cut off, a dish of carrot sticks and glasses of kool-aid. The girls passed the plates and ate stiffly and carefully.

Mrs. Sundby sat at one end of the table. "Now Anne," she said, "do you have plans for your vacation?" There was one more week of school, and after that, the long months of summer.

Anne looked down, "No Ma'am."

Marty jumped in, trying to help her friend. "I just want to play outdoors every day," she said.

"We have a garden," said Geraldine. "I help my Mom in the garden. We cook and bring food out to the men in the fields. I love summer, but it's hard work!"

"A big garden?" asked Mrs. Sundby, showing polite interest. "What do you grow?"

"Everything. Strawberries, carrots, beans, peas, radishes, squash. I help my Mom canning."

But Eileen couldn't be quiet any longer. "We're going to Chicago to stay with my aunt, for two months! I can't wait!"

The girls all turned to her. Chicago was a big city, unimaginable.

"What's Chicago like?" asked Marty, curious. She remembered Eileen had been there last summer.

"They have really nice stores. Dress stores and department stores, and shoe stores. You can try things on. Lots of tall buildings and restaurants. We're taking the train!" Marty imagined four or five towns like Grand Forks put beside each other.

"Well, of course we're taking the train," said Mrs. Sundby, laughing pleasantly. "Your father works for the railroad."

Melody said, "I'm going to my Grandma's house in Minnesota."

But Eileen wasn't finished. "Last summer we went to concerts in the park, and everyone was beautiful, and they had little dogs." Whenever a city was mentioned, Eileen acted as though she knew more than anyone.

Marty was only vaguely jealous. She wanted to be outdoors all day, every day in the warm weather with no school. The dew on the grass made your bare feet wet in the summer, and the mourning doves cooed in the dovecot above the barn across the street. Dad said there were also homing pigeons there. You could attach a message to their legs, and they would carry it to someone. Chicago seemed very far away.

"Eileen," said Mrs. Sundby, "You can tell the girls about Chicago when you see them at school in the fall." She went into the kitchen and returned with a white frosted cake with candied letters saying "Happy Birthday Eileen" on it, and eight tiny pink candles stuck in candy holders. Before cutting the cake, she placed the pile of presents in front of Eileen.

"Ok, girls," said Mrs. Sundby. "Let's sing." She began the birthday song up a little too high for Marty, but they sang loudly and happily, and afterwards, she said, "Make a wish, my sweet girl."

Eileen screwed her eyes tight and wished. Then she tried to blow out all the candles with one breath. She missed two and blew them out with a second breath. She sighed.

"What did you wish?" asked Melody.

"It's a secret," said Eileen. "I can't tell." She smiled and inclined her head so her hair bow stood erect. Marty thought she must be happy to have them all at her command for once.

Eileen opened the presents, a tiny silver locket, a package of printed paper dolls (from Marty), a small plastic purse, and from her mother, a pale blue cardigan with little pearl buttons. As each present emerged from its paper Eileen squealed delightedly, as if it was the most wonderful thing in the world. Marty made note of the squealing, but knew she couldn't have done it herself.

The cake wasn't very good. The frosting tasted like sugary, greasy paste, not like her own mother's delicious butter cream. But Marty ate every bite, plus the hard candied "H" from the word "Happy."

Now that the party was over the girls became more relaxed. Melody was going home with Geraldine's mother, who waited for them in town after shopping. Anne and Marty could walk home, but in different directions. Marty wasn't sure she could make it home without going to the bathroom, so she asked Mrs. Sundby.

"Could I use the bathroom, please?" She always liked to see what houses were like. She loved houses and collected her favorite house plans from the *Good Housekeeping* magazine or the *Better Homes and Gardens*.

Mrs. Sundby led her into a room off the depot waiting room, where behind a calico curtain was a ledge with holes for two people to sit. Beneath the holes were huge, metal slop buckets. In the corner was a china washbasin with soap and a pitcher of water to wash your hands. A little stool allowed children to climb up and go to the bathroom, but Marty was so shocked, she didn't think she could do it. She decided she could wait until she got home.

"It's okay," Marty said as politely as she could. "I guess I don't have to go."

The girls all left together, saying their goodbyes and thank yous, and how pleased they were to be invited to the party.

Marty walked home as fast as she could, thinking that never again would she envy Eileen. The stark fact behind her little velvet dresses and patent leather shoes was that the depot didn't have indoor plumbing! No wonder she couldn't wait to go to Chicago. Maybe her aunt had a real toilet. Marty couldn't wait to tell Line.

At home, Marty tried to decide what was different about the Mikkelson's house. On the dining room table was a vase of tall pussywillows Dad cut for Mother because she loved them. Pussywillows were the soft, velvety seeds pods of the willow trees. The table was a wooden door, its plywood veneer varnished smooth as silk, with wrought iron legs. Beside it was an oak sideboard painted green. The green shelves above it had a curved jigsawed frontpiece painted with Norwegian rosemaling. Mother's china cups, which Marty had often dusted, filled the shelves.

The curtains were in dark cotton fabrics to match the browns, greens and golds of the worn upholstery on the sofas and chairs in the living room. A piece of glass, set in wrought iron by their neighbor, made a very modern coffee table. On the wall were pictures of Christ in brown tones. One was just his head, with flowing curls, and the other showed him knocking at a wooden door, dressed in a robe, with his head inclined, to show that he was knocking on their hearts, waiting for them to open.

Marty decided that lace made a place old-fashioned, while the parsonage had a modern feel. Mother read the magazines, just as Marty did, and she was full of ideas. Though there was little money, there was enough to paint and make old furniture look up-to-date. Even Line and Marty's bed was modern. Dad sawed the top of the ironwork off an old-fashioned bedstead, and fitted a plywood cover over it. Mother painted the wood blue, and trimmed it with Norwegian rosemaling.

Marty felt the soft pussywillow catkins. Unlike the felt roses at Eileen's, they wouldn't last long. Outside the hollyhocks were beginning to grow tall under the window. The bird feeder had been taken down with the storm windows, and the windows let in the breeze through the screens. Spring and summer were lovely, following the dark, breathlessly cold winters, which were beautiful in their own right. There was no need to envy Eileen, who went to bed every night alone with all of her own things.

And they were going on vacation too! All of a sudden Dad and Mother were packing and planning. It was early June, and they could have the Bible camp on Red Lake in Minnesota all to themselves for a week before it opened for campers. The kids packed their clothes in boxes which went into the trunk of the old black Ford. They sat in the back seat with their pillows and Mother stuffed blankets and quilts into available corners around them. It was still cold, so they wore their spring coats.

The trip was short. The Minnesota state line was near their house and they were soon in the mythical Land of 10,000 Lakes, where they had all been born before the family moved to North Dakota. Marty spent the whole trip looking out the window as the surroundings changed from wheat fields to woods. If she kept her eyes on a certain point in the middle, the land in the distance seemed to flow behind them, while they rushed into the land in the front. It was like a circle.

In the late afternoon Line, with her sharp eyes, called, "Look!"

As the car rushed past, a mother deer, a doe, and her fawn stood at the edge of the road against the dark evergreens. A deer was a magical animal, as they saw few of them in North Dakota.

"I'll bet they're fat and happy now that winter is over," said Dad. Deer could eat bushes under the snow, but they really wanted grass and weeds, especially new soft grass.

The Bible camp was a group of frame buildings at the southern edge of a huge lake, with a chapel, a kitchen and dining hall, and barracks for sleeping. A sandy path went down through the grass to the lake, where a dock pushed out with reeds on one side and a patch of sand on the other. It was too cold to swim, because the lake ice only left in late May. But they could go out in one of the aluminum boats that were beached, upturned at the edge of the lake.

Marty, Paul and Line followed Dad to the end of the dock. Line and Paul lay down on their stomachs, looking into the dark water. Dark clouds lowered and the wind was strong, blowing white-capped waves toward them across the long fetch of the lake. Marty could not see any land on the far side. It was like an ocean, she thought. Dad shaded his eyes and smiled over at her against the grey, cloudy sky. The wind whipped at the calico kerchief tied around her dark hair.

"Red sky in the morning, sailors take warning; red sky at night, sailor's delight," he said. "Guess we are in for some rain."

"I can't see anything down there," said Line. If there were fish, or minnows, they might have gone fishing, but they hadn't brought fishing gear anyway. Paul stood up as a white cap washed over the hand he had been dragging in the water, smiling widely. His jacket sleeve was soaked to the shoulder.

Just then Dad said "A heron!" As he pointed, a bird flapped its huge wings, very wide in relation to its body, slowly along the lake in the wind. Time slowed down as the wings cut the space.

"It's a blue heron," said Dad. "I wish your Mother were here to see it."

Ellie came down to the dock to find them.

"Did you bring any matches?" she asked Dad.

"Probably," said Dad. "I'll come and look."

Mother and Dad looked high and low in the big camp kitchen, but there were no matches to be found, and no way to light the big gas stoves. The buildings were cold and felt damp. No one had used them all winter.

The kids stood around in their coats and scarves and watched Mother and Dad, wondering what to do.

Mother threw up her hands. "I'll go make up some beds," she said. She did not look happy. Line and Ellie went with her.

At last Dad found a hot plate he could plug in to cook the beans and wieners. At least the electricity was on. As Marty and Paul watched, he touched a paper towel to the hot plate and it burst into flames. "That's it," he said. He carefully lighted two gas burners on the big iron stoves and found pots to cook in. "Set the table, Marty," he said. "Looks like supper's on." Paul wouldn't leave his side, mesmerized by the growing warmth and the blue flame.

Marty found blue enamel plates and cups and flat knives and forks and set them at one end of a big table in the dining hall. They ate supper in their coats as it was still damp and cold, but Mother was relieved that they could cook the food they brought.

At one end of a long dormitory room, Mother, Ellie and Line had taken the mattresses off the bedsteads, and made two double beds on the wooden floor as there weren't enough blankets. Mother and Dad took Paul into their bed, and Marty, Line and Ellie slept in the other one. The air was damp and the mattresses smelled of mildew, but their bodies soon warmed up the bedding.

Marty curled beside Ellie's limp body so she didn't have to sleep on the crack between the mattresses. She felt sorry for Ellie, who always seemed alone. "Are you happy?" she asked.

"I'm okay," said Ellie. It was hard to get anything out of her, but she hugged Marty to show that she was grateful for her concern.

In the morning it was indeed raining, and the next day too, and the day after that. They explored the whole camp, but there were no fireplaces, so they couldn't build a fire and make it cozy. Campfires were held outdoors. They spent the first day reading and playing games in the dining room, but Line was restless.

"I wish we could go outside," she said the next morning at breakfast.

"I wish it would stop raining," said Paul.

"Don't complain," said Mother. "Many people are much worse off than you are. We are all safe, we are together and we are fine," she said flatly.

Dad told them to put on their coats, and they raced through the rain over to the chapel. He found the lights for the choir stall near the front of the chapel, and they settled down in the wooden pews in their damp coats and kerchiefs while Mother read. Hour after hour, she read from children's classics, paperback books of *The Five Little Peppers* and *Hans Brinker, or The Silver Skates*.

Marty, who was cold and wished she were home playing with her dolls, fell under the spell of Mother's voice, and the story of a poor family, the Peppers. Five kids and their widowed mother managed to be happy in their little brown house, but were then rescued and educated by a rich family. The odd thing was that they looked back at the times they had in the little brown house as more happy and wonderful than when they were well fed and clothed!

Marty didn't know any rich families except the Arnesons, who lived on a big wheat farm just outside of town and were involved in politics. The Mikkelsons weren't poor enough to be rescued by anyone. They lived in a nice house with lots more to eat than potatoes and mush!

Marty looked around at her brother and sisters, huddled in the choir stall pews in the dull light. In the distance, she could hear Dad moving around, looking at the altarpiece in the darkened chapel. Mother too wore a light wool coat and a scarf wrapped around her brown curls. Marty smiled to herself, thinking she looked like a hen with a flock of little chickens. Perhaps Mother and Dad weren't having a very good time either in the cold, gloomy Bible camp in the rain, but they had found a way to "improve each shining hour" with books.

Eileen was probably in Chicago. Marty pictured her on a sunny park bench near a bandstand listening to a concert, in a pretty dress with a dog. Or maybe if it were raining, she was in a department store trying on shoes. The Mikkelsons preferred "God's country," as Dad called it, where there were birds, weather, lakes, deer and great, dark pine trees. A little rain couldn't stop their fun. Marty guessed she liked nature better than cities, but she would have liked to experience both.

5

Line loved recess, but she loved it most when the high school kids came out and gathered everyone into a game. She especially loved Gary Breiland, the instigator. Line watched but she couldn't figure out how he did it.

Though he was a senior, he wasn't very big, more feisty and funny. But when he came out, everyone noticed and gathered around.

It was October and the leaves of the cottonwoods in the schoolyard drifted down in thick yellow piles. Line loved the waxy, pliable leaves, almost heart-shaped, with serrated edges and a neat little trough at the end of each stem. She wandered over and made a bouquet of the beautiful leaves, but, oh! There was Gary and a pack of high school kids. Line ran to join them.

"Red Rover," declared Gary. "Girls against the boys." The girls lined up in front of the school steps, the boys thirty feet away. The rest of the schoolyard emptied out, with most of the little kids joining the game. Long, ragged lines of kids faced each other, firmly holding hands, a few more in the girls' line. Bigger girls stood next to little girls in the hopes that they could hold hands tight, even if the little one let go. They wore jackets or coats, and scarves against the fall wind. Line hated her calico scarf, but if she didn't wear it, her ears ached.

Across from her Line saw Paul, standing staunch toward one end, with other little boys. He was a little young for first grade, but no one could hold him back and he loved school. Line worried about him, but at school there was nothing she could do. Paul would hate it if his older sister followed him around. No big kid would pick on a little kid anyway. It wasn't sporting. The only thing that made him different was that Dad showed up at lunch and they went into the principal's office to work on stretching Paul's leg.

"Rover, Red Rover," called Gary, "Let Helen come over." Helen was Ellie's best friend, a seventh grader. She knew where to run. She raced toward the boy's line, her dark hair flying, and broke through the tightly held hands of two second graders. She got to pick one of the boys to come back to the girls' line. He stomped on back, his fists in his pockets, not wanting to be there, but having no choice. He was fairly won.

The girls conferred and decided to choose Clyde. Recess was short, so they must choose carefully. The line with the most kids at the end of recess won. "Rover, Red Rover, let Clyde come over," sang out Helen.

Clyde was too proud to break through a weak link, but he ran with such force that he easily broke through between a high school girl and the third grader she was desperately trying to hang on to. Line felt a tap on her shoulder. Clyde chose her to go over to the boys' line. She was thrilled to be the only girl on the boys' line.

Gary decided to get serious. He broke up the boys and linked little ones with big ones. The line looked impregnable. "Rover, Red Rover, let

Patsy come over!" Patsy's father kept the tavern downtown. Line had seen her ride her white horse right between the swinging doors and into the tavern.

Patsy charged the boys' line, ponytail swinging. The boys she tried to break between fell over backwards, along with the boys on either side! But the line held. Gary whooped! "Atta way, guys." He grabbed Patsy's hand meaningfully, dragging her into the boys' line.

Line was near the end of the line, holding firmly to Clyde's hard farmer hands on one side, her wrist held so tightly by a high school boy on the other she was afraid it might tear off. But her eyes were shining. She looked toward the girls' line to see where Marty was. Marty stood between Helen and a high school freshman, who wore bobby socks, saddle shoes and a red flared skirt with a white poodle on it. Line wondered how she dared wear that skirt out to recess, but on the other hand, most of them didn't topple over.

All too soon the bell in the school tower rang. It didn't sound like the church bell, which was much bigger. But its insistent clapping ring meant that everyone must be back in their seats in five minutes. Kids rushed through the big doors and into the halls, the high school kids hanging back. It didn't matter whether the boys or the girls won the game. It was just fun to run around outside, getting hot and sweaty in the cold air before going back to their books.

As they hung up their coats on hooks in the narrow, dark cloakroom which ran the length of the school room, Line whispered to Marty, who was in the same room that year, "Who's that girl with the poodle skirt?"

"I heard someone call her Cathy," whispered Marty. "I got to touch it. It's felt!"

After school, Marty and Line found Paul outside the door waiting for them. They walked across the street and down the sidewalk toward home, trying hard not to step on any cracks. "Or you'll break your mother's back," Line told Paul. The new sidewalk didn't have cracks, but most of the old ones did.

"Miss Onstead says I can bring the terrarium to school," said Paul. "She wants the other kids to see the turtles."

"That's great!" said Line, "Can you leave them there? I really want a cat!" She had been begging Mother for a cat for some time, but Mother was reluctant. Among other things, she said a cat might hurt the turtles.

Up ahead, they saw Ellie turn in at Helen Jorre's house with her friend. Helen's father died in the war, and her mother managed the hotel downtown. There was no one at home when Helen came home from school, and Ellie was allowed to visit until Helen went off to the hotel for supper. Mother didn't like it. She was afraid Helen and Ellie might be listening to the radio, exposing themselves to bad influences, but Mrs. Jorre was a church member, and they didn't want to prevent Ellie from helping.

According to the list of chores on the refrigerator, it was Line's turn to help with supper that night. While Mother made spaghetti, Line set the table. She explained that Paul would be taking the turtles to school, and could she please have a cat?

Mother's eyes twinkled. "Line, you're starting to sound like a broken record."

"I promise I would feed it and clean up the kitty litter. A cat is hardly any trouble at all!" She wasn't asking for a dog, after all.

"I'll think about it," said Mother, tantalizingly.

"A cat wouldn't bother you when I'm at school. It would just sleep in a corner," said Line.

"Yes, yes," said Mother. "Now, how is your arithmetic coming?"

"I have some homework, story problems," she wrinkled up her nose. Sometimes story problems were fun, but arithmetic was not Line's strong suit. I'll get Marty to help me after supper, she thought. Marty was good at everything. She listened to Line's fourth grade class and knew as much as they did!

Mother was about to boil the spaghetti, but suddenly she got distracted. "Where's Ellie?" she asked. "Did you hear her come in?" Ellie had not come while they were making supper.

"I'll go look for her," said Line, and she ran upstairs. Marty was reading to Paul in the living room, Dad was in his study, and upstairs there was no one at all. She came back down, shaking her head.

"Go ring up Helen's house," said Mother. She wasn't going to finish the supper until they were all there.

Line stood on a chair to speak into the telephone, a wooden box on the wall in the study, with an earpiece and a little black speaking cone. She took the earpiece off its hook, and wiggled the hook. When the operator answered, she said, "This is Line Mikkelson. Can you connect me to Mrs. Jorre's house, please?"

"Hello," said Iris, the operator, with her sharp voice. "And how are the Mikkelsons?"

"We're fine," said Line. Mother told her often to be polite, but not explain family business to everyone who asked.

After a bit Iris came back. "I'm sorry, there's no answer at that residence."

"Thank you, Iris," said Line, replacing the earpiece. "No answer," she said. Mother stood in the door of the study and Dad was listening too.

"Carl, I think you should go look for her," said Mother. Mrs. Jorre's house was only a block and a half from their house. It would be pretty hard to get lost.

"Yup," said Dad. He and Mother exchanged significant looks. He went out to the entry, grabbing a coat and hat and his car keys on the way. Mother and Line peered into the darkness from the dining room windows.

But Dad hardly got out the door, before Ellie crossed the street. She was not coming from Helen's house, however. She was coming from town. Mother breathed in heavily. Ellie came dreamily up the walk in her warm woolen coat.

"Ellie," said Mother. "Did you go to the hotel with Helen?"

"Yes," said Ellie, her head drooping.

Mother's voice grew more terrible. "You know I told you not to go to the hotel. It's fine for Helen, her mother is there, but you are the pastor's daughter, and you may not go to the hotel at night by yourself."

There was nothing wrong with the hotel. In fact Line remembered they had once eaten Sunday dinner there. Behind a lobby filled with heavy oak and leather chairs which smelled pleasantly of cigar smoke, the dining room was lined with sideboards filled with dishes. Lace curtains graced the windows and the table was laid with china and silver on a lace cloth. Mrs. Jorre managed the cook and those who cleaned the hotel, and she was a fine woman. But both Dad and Mother knew that she might pull out a glass of liquor for an important man down from the Twin Cities to purchase grain or to visit with Mr. Arneson, who was in the state Senate.

"Yes, Mother," said Ellie, her dreamy eyes going moist and her shoulders going round and falling in toward her chest.

Line wanted to stand up for her, but both she and Ellie knew they couldn't defend themselves when Mother's voice was that serious. There was nothing more to say. Line wanted to go to the hotel herself, but there wasn't a chance now. Marty got to go to the train depot. Line felt she was the last person to do anything. Her back stiffened, just as Ellie's began to droop.

"Have I made myself clear, Ellie?" asked Mother. "You may stop off at Helen's house after school, but after an hour you must come right home. You have homework and chores to do here."

"Yes, Mother," said Ellie.

"Come on, girls," said Mother. "Let's finish up the supper."

Dad helped Ellie off with her coat and she fled upstairs. Line knew that Mother and Dad worried that Ellie was listening to Frank Sinatra with Helen. They didn't want their kids to be superficial and the words of some of the pop music was positively un-Christian!

Line laid out the silverware, fork on the left and knife on the right, wondering why the fork went on the left, when they picked it up in their right hands. Even she used her right hand for eating. She drew with her left hand, and wrote with it also, but she liked being ambidextrous and ate with her right.

Ellie was back by the time they sat down to supper. Everyone ignored her, and talked about other things to give her the space to recover her good humor.

Mother asked them in turn what they were doing in school. They must each listen while the others talked. Dad said that there was going to be a basketball game on Friday night, a home game for the Bryson Bruins and they would all go. Line had never been to a basketball game. At last! Something she could do.

On Friday night it was very cold and Dad drove the black Ford the short distance to the Town Hall. It was a gym with a basketball court painted on the wooden floor, low bleachers on both sides and a stage at one end. The town used it for lyceums and VFW meetings, when seats were set up on the floor. Once in a while the whole school trooped the three blocks down to see a presentation during school hours.

The school kids could never resist peeking through the iron bars into the tiny room with the word "Jail" over the door at the back of the hall. The door and window on the cement room were open, barred with iron. They had never seen anyone in it, but the idea of jail loomed in their imaginations. Hopefully no one was jailed in the winter. A prisoner would freeze to death!

As the hall filled up, Paul stood between Dad's knees, and Line and Marty crowded on both sides of them, listening to Dad talk about the game. Dad wore a suit coat without a tie and the kids their school clothes. Mother and Ellie sat beside them on the low bleachers. Across the gym were people from the opposing team's town, Mayville.

The players warmed up on the floor, dribbling, throwing baskets. Line saw Gary Breiland, the leader of the rambunctious high school kids, his brown arm muscles visible in a blue basketball jersey with the number 11 on it. Bryson wasn't big enough for a football team, but they could field a basketball team. Erik Arneson, who was 6'3" and in Dad's confirmation class, played center.

On the stage the cheerleaders clapped and waved their blossoms of blue and white shredded crepe paper, among them Patsy Ninas, Line's favorite. They wore white sweaters, with a big "B" on them, short blue skirts, and tennis shoes. Line looked longingly at them, determined that one day she would be a cheerleader. They were moving all the time, standing, clapping, waking up the crowd.

"We're Number 1, hey hey" Clap.
"Under the sun, hey hey" Clap.
"As for you" Clap, clap.
"You're Number 2" Clap.

The players went back into their locker rooms at either side of the stage. Most of them looked determined, their faces set to ignore the noise. But Gary smiled at the cheerleaders, and Line saw Patsy blow him a kiss! The coaches followed the players, also ignoring the cheering crowd as if nothing was more serious than the game ahead.

"When I was in high school," said Dad, "I was a forward. The forwards try to get the ball away from the guards, so they can shoot. If you can run and shoot, it doesn't matter if you're small."

Dad was quite a bit shorter than Erik! Line remembered the blizzard last year, when Erik came with Dad in his jeep to get them at school. It was the only time she could remember not walking home.

"Did you play in college?" asked Marty.

"Nope," said Dad. "I didn't have time for sports in college. But I still remember the words carved in stone over the door of the gym at Wittenberg, 'Mens sana in corpore sano.' Do you know what that means?"

Line didn't know. It was Latin. There was Latin on the penny, the nickel and the silver dime, 'E pluribus unum,' meant 'Out of many, one,' showing that the thirteen colonies were one country, the United States.

"It means 'a sound mind in a healthy body,'" said Dad. "You can't have one without the other. When I was in college, I studied and worked, but I also ran track and swam. And I went for walks with your Mother," he smiled over at Mother. The two of them acted as if they shared a special secret whenever Wittenberg College was mentioned. "And of course I worked all summer, either with your Granddad doing construction, or hired out on farms. It was hard! I wished I could study!"

The cheerleaders stood up and motioned the crowd to stand as the players came out on the court.

"Stand up and cheer!" they shouted, waving their pom poms left and right.

"Let them know you're here!"

"Stand up and cheer!" shouted Line standing and clapping in time, her face alight.

"Let them know you're here!"

Dad smiled approvingly at Line. "Go Sparky!" he said. "Your gang's all here!"

Paul stood against Dad, clapping, a little blonde roostertail sticking up at the back of his head. It was sad, Line thought. He would never be a basketball player.

The referee blew a whistle and the game started with a jump ball in the middle. Erik wore a band around the back of his head to keep his glasses on. He caught the ball and passed it, the Bryson team racing to their end of the court. Gary, short and fast, was all over the court with the ball. The cheerleaders yelled, "We want a basket! We want a basket!"

Gary moved in, avoiding all the hands above him and did a neat layup at the edge of the basket. Swish, the ball fell through the net. The whole Bryson side of the gym was on its feet. Two points! The first two points! Line jumped up and down. A man hung a big metal "2" on the scoreboard at the top of the bleachers under Home Team.

The teams raced to the other end of the court. Erik looked nervous, concentrating on the ball. He was only a freshman, but he was so tall he was expected to be good at basketball. Suddenly Erik's big gangling foot was in the way of one of the Mayville players while he was shooting and the referee blew his whistle.

"See," Dad explained. "The referee rules that Erik made a foul. So the guy he fouled gets to try to sink a basket from the free-throw line." Line felt sorry for Erik, but Gary touched him on the back as they lined up and the Mayville player sunk first one and then another basket.

The man near the scoreboard put up a "2" under the Opposing Team sign. "Even up," said Dad. "Do you see that they can't run with the ball without dribbling?" The boys ran down the court to the opposite side, patting the ball onto the floor as they ran.

Shooting was quick on both sides, and by half time the scores were Home team 42, and Mayville 50. The boys went back to their dressing rooms, the cheerleaders came down off the stage, and people began milling around.

It seemed that everyone in town was there. Dad talked to the Ellingsons about the house they were building across the street from the schoolyard. Mrs. Jorre and Helen came over to Mother and Ellie and they all talked about the Smorgasbord they were going to have at the church. Line's eyes moved around looking for Clyde, but he wasn't there. Maybe his farm was too far out from town.

Dad and Paul struggled through the crowd toward the front, Paul lost among the tall, coated people. They brought back crackerjack for the kids, and a chocolate bar for Mother. Line and Marty hunted for the prizes at the bottom of the crackerjack boxes. Line found a little cocker spaniel, and Marty a tiny Indian in a headdress. Marty gave her peanuts to Line, because she didn't like them, and her Indian to Paul.

"I heard Dad talking to Mrs. Husvedt," Paul whispered to Line. "He asked her whether they had any kittens that wanted to come live in town!"

"He did?" Line was thrilled. "What did she say?"

"She said that the barn was full of them and that Joan would pick one out to bring next time they came in!"

Line clapped her hands.

"Don't say I told you," whispered Paul, and Line ran her thumb and first finger across her mouth, as if zipping her lips shut.

Line and Marty stood in line to get drinks of water at the fountain. Pieces of blue crepe paper pom pom littered the stage. Line wanted to pick them up, but she didn't have time. The cheerleaders were back.

Patsy trailed behind them, thin and a little apart. Line thought she was beautiful with her curled bangs and long dark hair. Patsy's short pleated skirt showed off her straight, tan legs. She lived with her father in rooms behind the tavern, keeping her horse in a stable out at Arnesons.

Line thought Patsy was tragic, her pride holding her aloof in the little, church-going town, but all the more romantic a heroine for all that. She had no mother to care about her, so she had to take care of herself. Patsy and her father didn't come to church, but Line watched her whenever she could. Marty learned from books, but not Line. She was much more attuned to people.

The cheerleaders stood up and began chanting so people would return to their seats.

"We're Number 1" Clap, clap.
"We're Number 1" Clap, clap.

Line yawned and clapped and Mother laughed at her. "Past your bedtime," she said. But it was Friday night and it didn't matter.

"Should have brought our bearskin rug," said Dad. "A Bruin is a bear, you know."

"Carl!" said Mother. "Thank goodness you didn't!" Dad was willing to be silly and make a spectacle of himself, but Mother wasn't.

The Bruins were behind as the second half started, but you could tell they were gathering their courage and didn't want to be beaten in front of their families and neighbors. All eyes were on the ball as it went from one side of the court to the other. Erik made a basket from five feet away, then modestly raised his big hands to guard the players as they raced to the other end. Gary ran from side to side, keeping everyone guessing. His confidence and sheer delight were fun to watch!

"Dribble it" Clap, clap.
"Pass it" Clap, clap.
"We want a basket," rhythmically came from the stage.

"Who is that kid?" asked Dad. "Sure has that come-from-behind spirit." Gary Breiland wasn't in their church either, so Dad didn't know him.

"He's a good leader," said Mother. "He encourages all the other players."

The scorekeeper wasn't quite as busy putting up numbers during the second half. The guards worked hard and the players ran from one side to the other without scoring. Erik was fouled and he missed his first free throw, but made the second one. Line was growing scared. It was the fourth period and the score was 74 to 70 in favor of Mayville.

"Five points!" Clap, clap, yelled the cheerleaders.
"Five points!" Clap, clap.

Line's heart surged with Gary as he ran down the court, evading his guards and doing one of his simple layups. "Yeaaaaah!" shouted the home fans.

"Blue and white, fight!" Clap, clap.
"Blue and white, fight!" Clap, clap.

Just then Erik managed to steal the ball. He turned around and headed for the Bruins' basket, stopping and making a shot from several feet out. The score was tied! But there was a minute to go and the Mayville players made another basket. A groan went up from the bleachers around Line. But the buzzer sounded. The game was over. Line felt the wind leave her sails. She had been so excited, but now she was as limp as a dishrag.

Dad stood up, "What a heartbreaker!"

Gary Breiland was unfazed. He shook hands with the players on the other side, smiling broadly. Line couldn't hear what he said, but he seemed to be thanking them! Erik hung his tall head, but the coach congratulated him on a great game.

Line watched the cheerleaders. They came down off the stage onto the floor and stood around in the mix of sweaty boys. Line wanted to go out on the floor, but Dad and Mother were gathering them up, helping with coats and mittens. Now Line knew why Dad had driven the car the few blocks downtown. He knew they would be too sleepy to walk home.

"Good sports, our boys," said Dad. It was just the first game of the season, but it was hard to lose by so little on your home court. "Do you see what I mean by a sound mind? Level headed, good sports. That Gary Breiland sure knows how to spark a team."

Line was tired as she buttoned the buttons on her coat and tied on her hated scarf. It was exciting to know the boys who were playing, to see how they felt as they tried so hard to win for their town, their friends and families. They were heroes, and Patsy Ninas was a heroine. Line vowed that one day, she would be a heroine too.

6

Paul loved to watch Dad getting ready for pastoral visits. One Saturday at lunch, Dad looked at Mother and said, "I have to go out to see old Mrs. Torkelson. Why doesn't Paul come with me? We'll stop by the pond on the way back and see if it's still frozen."

Dad's visits were sometimes difficult, involving counseling, illness, even high tension. But if he were offering to take Paul, Dad didn't expect a hard time. It had been a long winter and Paul never got out as much as he wanted. The spring winds were beginning, though, and it wouldn't be long now.

Dad dressed in a suit coat and a tie, a little white handkerchief sticking out of his breast pocket, his dark hair combed back. His newly-shaven face smelled like a fresh, clean woods after he slapped skin bracer on it. Most importantly, he carried a little case of tiny heavy-bottomed glasses in a metal rack. Dad served communion in them and carefully cleaned them after each visit. The wafers were thin white disks of bread. Paul had never tasted one. Lutherans didn't take communion until after they had been confirmed in their faith, around age 14.

Paul slicked down his blonde hair with water and put on the brown corduroy jacket he wore on Sundays over his school clothes. They both put on galoshes; puddles and slush were everywhere.

In the old black Ford, Dad and Paul drove into the endless fields on the little gravel township roads, straight as if they were laid out with rulers. Dirty snowdrifts tinged with black mud and gravel lined the roads.

"Looks a little uncertain," Dad said. "See those clouds? We're in for some weather." The clouds lay like a low ceiling on the sky, regular pillowy puffs, with the wind scudding below them.

They passed Highland church, Dad's country parish, eight miles out of town. Instead of a spiked steeple, it had a square bell tower rising above the white frame church. A few gravestones poked out of the grey snow in the lonely cemetery next to it. There were no trees.

Past the church, Dad drove toward a grove of poplars surrounding a large barn and a white frame house. As they turned into the drive, a pack of dogs burst out of the barn. There were only three of them, but two of them were bigger and heavier than Paul.

"Stand still," said Dad when they got out of the car. "Let them smell you."

Paul stood still as the big black retriever, and then a golden one came up to him. Behind them was a smaller collie with a white ruff around its neck, the wind whipping its long golden fur. The retrievers sniffed Paul. He tried to stay still as their big wet tongues touched his face, but he wished these dogs would leave him alone, so he could pet the little collie.

A woman with no coat came out on the steps in the biting wind. Wiping her hands on an apron, she called "Blackie, Russ, come here!" She extended her hand to Dad and bid him come in. The big dogs followed her and Paul stole a hand out to the little collie. Its sharp, intelligent eyes met his and his sympathies reached out to it, the little one who lived in the big dogs' shadow. He petted its thick coat before following Dad into the house. The wind took the crackling plastic-lined screen door and banged it shut. The dogs all stopped at the porch.

"That's Little Joe," said the woman to Paul. "He's become quite a favorite."

"How is Mrs. Torkelson," asked Dad as he took off his galoshes.

"You know, we're not expecting much," said young Mrs. Torkelson. "The doctor says it could be weeks, or days. I know she's anxious to see you."

"And where are the men?" asked Dad. The men were Mr. Torkelson and his two younger sons. The eldest son was killed in Korea, which was very hard on them. Still, the Torkelsons were lucky to have sons left to help on the farm.

"They're out in the south forty, looking at the wheat," said Mrs. Torkelson. The Torkelsons planted winter wheat in the fall, in stubble from the previous year. Winter wheat was protected from cold by the snow, and could be harvested earlier than wheat planted in the spring. "I'm glad you brought your son. Kids always cheer up old people, if they are quiet," she said smiling at Paul. "You go on in and I'll make some coffee." She held out her hands for their coats.

Paul and Dad went through an empty living room into a bedroom. The hushed stillness in the room affected their voices. A clock ticked loudly and the room was warm, though the windows shook in the wind. In the bed a little, shriveled up woman leaned against the white pillows, her hands stretched out across a dark quilt.

"Pastor Carl," she said in a struggling Norwegian accent, holding out her thin brown-spotted hands. "Så hyggelig å se deg." Paul could see that she didn't have any teeth in her tiny, gaunt face.

Dad opened his warmest, beaming smile to her. He took her weak hand in his strong ones and said the words he used so often in greeting, "Grace be unto you, and peace, from God our Father, and the Lord and Saviour, Jesus Christ. Hvordan går det, Mrs. Torkelson?"

"Oh, Jeg er dårlig," said the tight mouth which seemed to be all tongue. "Can't get to church no more." She looked around. "Sit down, Pastor, sit down. Is that your son with you?"

Dad motioned for Paul to come closer. Paul stood by the bed, giving the old lady his hand. Her skin felt like thin, dry paper. She put a hand up to touch his hair.

"A little Norske," she said.

"That's right," said Dad. "This is Paul, named for the Apostle. He's six, already reading," Dad said proudly. Dad brought a chair over toward the bed and Paul sat gingerly on the edge of a sofa as quiet as a mouse.

"I know you haven't been able to come to church. That's why I'm bringing Christ's blessing to you. I thought you might miss the communion of saints," said Dad warmly.

Paul listened as Dad read a few passages from the Bible. Then he asked Mrs. Torkelson if she would like to take communion. He opened the tiny black leather kit with the wafers and wine in it, blessed them and read the liturgy that evoked the sacrament. "Remembering, therefore, his salutary command, his life-giving Passion and death, his glorious resurrection and ascension, and his promise to come again, we give thanks to you, Lord God Almighty, not as we ought, but as we are able."

He poured wine for Mrs. Torkelson, holding the tiny glass to wet her lips. The small, gaunt face, already peaceful, sank back on the white pillow.

The younger Mrs. Torkelson came in and stood nearby with her head bowed as Dad read, "Now lettest thou thy servant depart in peace, according to thy word, for mine eyes have seen thy salvation." He made the sign of the cross with upraised hands over Mrs. Torkelson, smiling and powerful, the words he spoke becoming the acts of God.

Paul went over to the bed and took Dad's hand as Mrs. Torkelson thanked him. Dad looked humbled by the actions of the church he was called upon to perform.

"Tusen takk, Pastor," she said weakly. "Tusen takk." She looked out the window, her eyes on another world.

Mrs. Torkelson came over, saying, "Would you like some coffee, Mother? I made some coffee and cookies for the pastor."

"Ingen, ingen," old Mrs. Torkelson waved her hand. "Takk, Jeg er fin."

Dad and Paul went out to the kitchen where Mr. Torkelson and his two sons were just returning from the fields in their heavy woolen plaid jackets and thick boots. Paul didn't know them, because they went to Highland church. They pulled up chairs around the formica kitchen table, drinking coffee and eating the sandbakkels Mrs. Torkelson made. They were sugar cookies which were pressed into little tins and came out shaped like fluted diamonds and shells.

"How's it looking out there?" asked Dad. He sipped his coffee, which everyone called Norwegian gasoline. The wind was shivering the storm windows, but steam rose in the warm room.

"Oh, pretty near like it should. Good snow cover this year. It'll sprout pretty good," said Mr. Torkelson. "It's blowing up out there, though. You might want to get off the road as soon as you can." He poured his hot coffee into his saucer to cool it.

"I'm sorry about your mother," said Dad. "I'm glad you can have her here at home." Mrs. Torkelson stood over Dad holding the coffee pot.

"Didn't like the hospital," said Mr. Torkelson. "Betty takes good care of her, though." He gave his wife a baleful look.

Paul couldn't resist reaching for another of the delicate sandbakkels. The contrast of the big men in heavy clothes eating the tiny, sugary cookies with their hot coffee was odd, but the tall brothers were eating as many as he was.

"We'll see you tomorrow," said Dad, preparing to leave. He put on his hat and tipped it to Mrs. Torkelson. "Thank you so much."

"Thank you for coming, Pastor," said Mrs. Torkelson. She walked them to the door, where the dogs lay just outside. Paul scratched the fur on the little collie as the dogs followed them out to the car. It was just his size.

"Is she going to die?" asked Paul as they drove up the road.

"Probably. Sooner than we are," Dad smiled at Paul sitting upright in the passenger seat, his eyes just clearing the dashboard. "Just think, Paul. She's 90. That means she was born during the Civil War! She was a little girl when her family came from Norway."

Paul thought about it. He knew Norway was a skinny little country up north with a ridge of mountains up its back on the globe. He and his sisters spent hours putting a finger down on the globe, spinning it to see where their finger landed and insisting to each other that they would end up there. Norway was so far north the sun didn't set in the summer, and didn't come up in the winter. Paul couldn't imagine it.

The wind whipped around them, but there was nothing to blow, no leaves on the trees, even the dirt was too wet to blow away. Dad pointed to the south and Paul stood up at his elbow, looking left. Against a white ceiling, a dark grey cloud formed, making a thin shape which went all the way to the ground. It looked like it was making a little dust storm around it.

"A funnel cloud," said Dad. "It's a twister. I thought so, but it doesn't look too serious. I don't think we'll stop at the pond though."

Paul leaned on Dad, trying to see over his shoulder as Dad drove steadily ahead.

"Is it going to be a tornado?" asked Paul.

"I don't think so," said Dad. "But Mr. Torkelson is right. The quicker we get home the better." It was late afternoon, the light from the sky disappearing.

"Are we going to go down in the cellar?" asked Paul. He remembered stories of tornados passing over people's heads as they sat in their basements. There was a picture of a funnel cloud in his Boy Scout book. Dad didn't seem very scared.

"Nah," said Dad as the car pulled into town. "I'll keep an eye on it, but it doesn't look like much."

It was fun to see weather from the car. Bryson was in tornado alley, so storms were to be expected. Paul wondered if Line and Marty were watching. But when they got home, the girls were playing with Mittens, the new black cat with soft little white feet.

"We saw a funnel cloud on the way home," Paul said.

"Yeah, I've seen them too," said Line nonchalantly, stroking Mittens.

Paul went up and found the Boy Scout book near his bed and brought it down.

Ellie was pinning a paper dress pattern to a length of striped cloth on the dining room table, as Mother taught her. She pinned the arrows on the pattern along the weave of the cloth, parallel to the selvage, trying to keep from wasting the beautiful new cotton. But when Paul pointed to the black and white picture of the tornado in the old, worn *Scout Field Book*, she came over to tell her tornado story again.

"I'll never forget," she said. "It was the Fourth of July, and we were new in town. We went over to the schoolyard to watch the fireworks they were going to put on, but all of a sudden people started rushing around because the radio said a tornado was coming. It was apparently visible for miles, but I didn't see it. We walked home, kind of fast. Line was only three, and Marty was tiny, so Dad and Mom carried them. They don't remember."

"I do," said Line. "Dad kept us all down in the fruit room, but he was outside watching." She shuddered, but Paul knew it wasn't because of the tornado. He knew she was scared of the cellar because it was full of spiders.

The walls of the cellar were damp with sweat and mold in the summer. The fruit room still had shelves of canned fruit and vegetables in glass jars hung with cobwebs from people who lived in the parsonage before the Mikkelsons. Mother wouldn't use them because she was afraid of botulism, another way you could die in a lonely town far from anywhere. Mother liked to serve frozen vegetables instead.

"Dad saw balls of fire in the sky when the twister hit the power lines. He said a farmer saw his car picked up and thrown onto a cow. The farmer lost all his buildings, but the family was okay, because they were down in the cellar.

"Some people were killed though," Ellie continued, "and lots of people were injured."

Mittens climbed up on the table and investigated the tissue paper pinned to the cloth, but her claws picked up the paper and tore it. Ellie's back was turned, but when she heard it she yelled, "Get that cat off the table!"

Line disentangled Mittens from the pattern paper, giggling, and took her into the living room. Paul sat near her on the couch, petting Mittens' soft fur and picking up her feet to look at the tiny transparent claws. The wind raged outside, but everything was cozy and safe at home.

Spiders were a more frequent occurrence than tornadoes, but Paul never met a creature he didn't like. He liked the cobweb-draped fruit room, though he was not anxious to meet a black widow spider. With a red hourglass warning painted on its abdomen, and its reputation for eating the male after it fertilized the eggs, female black widow spiders were the worst. They could kill a person with their poison.

The Boy Scout handbook had everything in it, animals, trees, camping, first aid and tracking. Paul couldn't wait until summer when Dad said he could sleep out in the back yard. You couldn't be a Boy Scout until you were 11, and there wasn't a Boy Scout troop in Bryson anyway, but Paul could practice. He carried the Boy Scout handbook everywhere, pretending he was a tenderfoot.

Dad was trying to get Paul to learn Morse code. It was a requirement for a ham radio license. Dad had a license and wanted Mother to learn, and Paul too. On a world map on the wall of Dad's study, red pins showed all the places he had talked to people by ham radio.

Morse code was a language. Each letter was a series of taps by a brass key mounted on a piece of black plastic which made beep sounds. Tapping out letters formed words, and hooked to a radio transmitter, they were broadcast on radio waves reserved for amateur operators. Mother was good at it and got her novice license. To get your ham operator license, you must be able to send Morse code at five words per minute.

Stories in the Boy Scout handbook told of people being rescued when scouts picked up code signals they sent out. Morse code was also used during the war. Paul tried to practice sometimes, but tapping out words took forever. He was much more interested in camping and tracking.

That evening the Mikkelsons had bowls of chili for supper, the kids took their baths, and Dad wrote notes for the sermon he would give in the morning. No one was to bother Dad on Saturday nights. Paul loved it when he could take off his brace and stump around in his pajamas without any hardware. The wind was still roaring around the house, but inside the radiators gurgled and steamed.

In Marty and Line's bedroom, the kids listened to the crystal radio set Dad made. It was a thin, plastic cigarette case, holding copper wire wound around a cylinder to make a crystal. The wire was attached to the bedsprings on Marty and Line's bed for an antenna, with big black headphones which they put over their ears in order to listen.

Line tuned the crystal set by pulling a matchstick tuner slowly in and out to find a radio station.

"Here, I've got one," she said, handing the headphones to Paul.

Paul put the headphones on. Somewhere in the world a band played and someone sang a popular song, though the sound crackled and popped. It was strange that you could hear radio stations miles away on a bedspring antenna, tuning for them on this tiny radio.

"Do you know how an antenna works?" Paul asked.

"I think it goes out into the air and pulls out radio waves that are coming toward us," said Marty.

"Yeah," said Line. "But how do we get the ones we want?"

"Tuning, silly," said Marty. "The tuner picks out the right frequency. You know, like on the radio there's those numbers. And to find *Sergeant Preston* we have to pick the right number."

"Yeah," said Paul. "Dad said it has a cat's whisker detector." He imagined that Mittens gave up one of his whiskers to make the little radio, but Dad said it was a tiny wire, as thin as a cat's whisker. "I think that the little matchstick is tuning between all the numbers, except on the crystal set they're too small to see."

Paul handed the black, cumbersome headphones to Marty, who put them on and frowned, listening.

"It's not much use," said Line. "If only one person can hear it at a time."

"No," said Paul. "And it's staticky. But it might be a good thing if you needed to radio for help and everyone was far away. Or if the whole town needed help." That was one of the reasons Dad became a ham operator. The short wave radio was expensive, but Dad decided it might help in an emergency. Also Dad was fascinated by it. He installed a huge antenna by the side of the parsonage, 50 feet in the air. Not as high as the church steeple, of course, but taller than their two-story house.

"I think it's neat," said Marty, removing the headphones. "I like hearing other languages on the radio." They heard Dad say, "W Zero VQX calling. CQ, CQ, CQ," when he wanted to talk to someone. He found a ham operator in the town in Minnesota where Grandma Mikkelson lived, so he could get a message to his parents more quickly than a letter, and more cheaply than long distance.

On Sunday the weather calmed down. The wind cleared the air and the sun poured down, warming the earth and drying up some of the snow and slush. After church and Sunday dinner, Paul begged Line to ask Mother if the Sundeens could come over. They lived a block away, a big Catholic family in a red painted brick house. If they came, there were enough people to play cops and robbers. Without them, the kids couldn't play Paul's favorite game.

Paul and the gang crossed the street beyond the church and knocked timidly on the Sundeen's back door. The house was built right on the ground with no basement and an oil heater for heat. Little Davy came to the door and stood looking at them. Kids, dogs and noise filled the cheerful, steamy kitchen which smelled of sausage.

"Who is it?" called the voice of an older man.

"It's Mikkelson kids," said Little Davy, who was called little to distinguish him from his father.

"Well, open the door and invite them in!"

Line, Marty and Paul entered and stood tentatively on the linoleum floor in the kitchen. "Could you come over to play?" asked Line, politely. "We want to play cops and robbers and we don't have enough kids."

Little Davy looked at the rest of the family who sat at their ease around a big wooden table covered with an oilcloth. They looked tousled and comfortable over the remains of breakfast, as if they had just gotten up. Mrs. Sundeen wore a bathrobe around her nightie. If they wanted to go to mass, they had to drive to another town, but it didn't look as though they had gone that morning. Paul imagined how horrified Mother would be if anyone outside the family saw her in her nightie.

"Go ahead," said Mrs. Sundeen, brushing her hair out of her eyes and smiling.

"But we need more people," said Little Davy.

"We'll come! We'll come," sang out some of his older sisters and brothers. "We'll get dressed and come over." One of the girls was a year younger than Marty, and one of the brothers was a year older than Line. Though they lived close by, the families had little contact with each other until Little Davy and Paul became friends at school.

Line, Marty and Paul walked across the street and slowly back to their house. The sun felt warm on Paul's face, but the kids were still wearing their winter coats. Mother wouldn't let them change into spring jackets until it was definitely warm. Spring was a time for colds and flu, the weather changeable and wet.

The birds acted like spring was in the air, flitting about, calling to each other. Pigeons and mourning doves fluttered around the cupola on the barn across the street. In the garden the thicket of raspberries, so long buried under the snow, stood up in prickly canes and the strawberries were shaking their dead dry leaves. Paul crouched, his skinny leg in its brace sticking out in back of him. He put his ear to the dark, wet earth. It looked so alive, but he couldn't hear anything.

Pretty soon four Sundeen kids showed up, Little Davy, Connie, Larry and Ed.

"Should we have more cops, or more robbers?" asked Ed, sizing up the situation. It was nice of him to play with them, as he was almost Ellie's age.

"You girls should be the cops, and we'll be robbers," said freckle-faced Larry. That was fine with Paul. He never liked being a cop, but he looked to Line to see if that was fine.

"Okay," said Line. "The sandbox is jail. We'll count to fifty. And you have to stay around our house." A huge rubber tractor tire lay on the ground near the back door of the house filled with sand. A swing cut from a smaller car tire hung from the tree next to it. Paul loved swinging, especially when Dad pushed. He could make the swing go so high.

"Awwww," said Larry. "There's nowhere to hide here."

"Okay, you have to stay at our house or the church," negotiated Line. The three girls leaned against the back of the house, their eyes closed, their heads cradled in their arms, counting.

Paul and Little Davy slipped their small bodies under the long silver propane gas tank which fed the parsonage stove and refrigerator. As they watched from beneath the tank, the girls counted to fifty. They shouted, "Ready or not, here we come!" and ran in different directions. Marty ran around the house and Line and Connie sallied quietly out into the back yard.

Dad called the gas tank a pickle, since it was shaped like a long dill pickle, and Paul thought it was a good hiding place. But Line's sharp eyes saw the boys and they couldn't get out fast enough. She reached under the tank, tagging them both and shouted, "Off to jail!"

"That was too quick," said Little Davy, miffed. But he and Paul dusted the dirt and sand from their coats and slouched off to the sandbox to watch and see if the girls could catch the two older boys. Suspense mounted as Line and Connie crept around the garage. Connie was little, with stiff red braids, but she was feisty from living with all those boys.

Pretty soon, Marty came around the house with Larry, tugging him by his jacket sleeve so he couldn't get away. They were both laughing. He had been lying in a culvert and it was wet enough that he didn't mind being caught! That left only Ed.

"Did you look under the porch?" Line asked Marty.

"Yes, that's the first thing!"

"I'm sure he went over to the church," said Connie. "Come on!"

"Shall I watch the robbers?" asked Marty.

"Never mind," said Line, annoyed. "They can't go anywhere. We need you."

The three girls crossed the alley to the big white frame church, shaped in an L because it was made of two churches. There were lots of nooks and crannies outside, but because it was white, it was hard to hide anywhere.

Paul and Little Davy dug trenches in the wet sand with sticks, making bridges with Larry helping. They could see the girls running around the church.

Suddenly there was Ed, leaping over the edge of the high white steps and rushing toward them with all three girls in pursuit. He must have been lying unseen on the church steps, but when the girls ran around and found him, he got away. The girls were screaming and Ed laughed. They couldn't catch him, so he danced near them.

"Na, na, na na na," he laughed just out of reach, his face red and his hair wild.

Line and Marty lunged for him together and he let them tackle him. They lay in a heap, out of breath and excited, their cheeks red and their limbs tangled, kerchiefs dangling around their necks. Paul stood up in the sandbox, excited and proud of his sisters.

"Okay," said Ed, getting up. "Our turn."

"Count to one hundred to give us a chance," pleaded Line.

The released robbers lined up against the back of the house, hiding their eyes and counting while the girls whispered a strategy to each other. Paul was terribly happy. It was all very well to learn things, but playing wild games outdoors was the best!

7

Marty heard Line shouting, "Hurry, hurry! The circus train is coming." The morning train was rumored to be carrying Barnum and Bailey's circus to its next destination. Paul and Line's faces were pressed to the glass of the upstairs window, trying to see through the raindrops.

Marty ran through the hall and into the bedroom, crashing into the window wrists first. The window broke into big spikes of glass and one of them sliced into her wrist, blood spurting everywhere. She looked out the window, but the circus train didn't look any different than any other train, closed, slatted cattle cars and freight cars clattering along the tracks. Marty looked at her hand and was shocked at the bright red blood gurgling out of her wrist, but didn't know what to do about it. She just stood there.

"Dad! Mother!" Line rushed downstairs. They both came up the stairs, responding to the urgency in Line's voice.

"Whew!" Dad said. "You must have hit an artery." He held Marty's wrist, applying a towel with some pressure. Mother brought the hydrogen peroxide, which foamed white around the deep, long cut. Dad kept applying pressure, but the bleeding wouldn't stop. Mother eyes looked worried. Line's face was white and Paul's eyes were very wide, but Marty just felt weak.

"Marty," said Mother quietly. "Lie down. We don't want you to faint." Marty lay still on the bed on the towels Line put there to catch the blood.

Dad telephoned Edna Ellingson, who was a nurse and lived a few blocks away. He came back with some white adhesive cloth tape and a scissor at her suggestion. He cut notches into a piece of tape and carefully applied it to Marty's wrist, drawing the gashed flesh together while Mother held Marty's arm.

"Lie still, Marty," said Mother. "Just stay quiet." She felt Marty's forehead with her cool hands.

Dad wrapped white gauze around Marty's hand and wrist. It grew bloody, but he said, "I think it's stopping." Marty lay still, closing her eyes, her hand throbbing. Nauseous, she could feel her heart pumping. Dad's warm hands passed over her head and her chest, meeting her little chicken heart with his warmth. "Easy does it, Marty," he said. "You're going to be fine."

"You stay here, Line," said Mother, "And watch her. Edna's coming over." She and Dad retreated slowly, going downstairs.

Line lay down beside Marty, "Sorry I yelled so loud," she said. Paul climbed up on the bed on the other side of Marty. They lay on top of the old, pink cotton bedspread like three felled pirates.

Marty smiled, wanly. "It's a good thing it's my left hand," she said. She wrote with her right.

"Yeah," said Line, who was left-handed.

"I was really hoping to see a lion," said Marty. "Did you see any animals?"

"Nope," said Line. "It was just like any other train."

"Serves me right," said Marty. "Expecting too much."

"Don't be silly," said Line. "It could have happened to any of us. Are you okay?"

"Yeah, I think so." Marty looked at her hand. It was throbbing, but the blood stains on the bandage weren't quite so bright. They looked dry and brownish.

When Mrs. Ellingson came over, she pronounced Dad's butterfly tape sutures just fine. "Good girl," she said to Marty. "It won't hurt you to lose a little blood. Eat well, and you'll have it back in no time."

Dad lifted the wooden window sash out and took it down to the hardware store where Mr. Beltz could cut a new pane and seal it into place with putty. Marty wondered whether his son Michael, her sweetheart at school, would find out that she had cut her hand. She felt bad about the window. Dad had enough problems without having to pay for new windows.

When Mother called "Lunch time!" they all went downstairs. Marty felt shaky and a bit chilled, but she sat up and pretended she was fine. She didn't want to worry anyone, or cause any more commotion than she already had.

It was raining, a Saturday, and the kids stayed inside. Ellie was at the sewing machine, Marty lay on the sofa reading and Line and Paul were drawing. A lonely wet robin turned up at the window feeder, but the feeder was dirty and there was nothing on it but a small lump of suet. It would soon be taken down with the storm windows for the summer. Mittens slept with her white paws over her eyes beside Marty on the sofa.

"My hand hurts," said Line. "I can't draw." She put down her pencil and held onto her wrist with her other hand, smiling.

"Sympathy pains," said Mother, who was looking at a seed catalog. To Marty she said, "We are lucky that Edna was at home, and that your Dad has a strong stomach. You could have used some stitches, but it's a long way to Mayville and you would have been bleeding all the way."

Marty was feeling much better, but it was nice to be quiet. She was lost in a book about pioneer days, about Laura and Mary, who were traveling in a covered wagon across the prairie with their faithful dog Jack trotting along behind. Mother read it to them once already, but Marty liked it so much she was reading it again.

In the next few weeks, Marty's hand healed, though it was tender. When she couldn't do something, like washing dishes, she thought of Paul, and all of the things that polio affected. Now Paul was as strong and active as any of them, though he still wore his brace.

Dad dressed Marty's hand each day. He too was pleased with the butterfly tape sutures. "You'll have a scar," he said, "but we did stop the bleeding."

By the end of May, the brief warm summer of the north was in full swing. Long days of sun warmed up the trees and the ground, releasing greenery unimaginable during the snowy winter. Marty breathed deep. The sweet spring winds filled the air with the smell of sap rising in the trees and grass growing rampant. In the schoolyard, the cottonwood seedpods opened, letting fly the gossamer white puffs which carried their seeds far and wide.

Marty went without a bandage on the last day of school, picnic day, exposing the long white scar on the inner side of her wrist. She showed it to Michael, whose father had repaired the window. Michael and Marty had shared the top of their class ever since first grade. Michael didn't have to do farm work, and he actually studied. Marty didn't study. She just paid attention and always seemed to know the answers, even for the fourth grade class which shared their room.

"It doesn't look so bad," said Michael, squinting and adjusting his thick glasses. "It's on the bottom of your wrist, so no one will ever see it." The trouble with Michael, in Marty's eyes, was that he was too serious. He was just as smart in Sunday school, where he wore a suit coat and slicked down his neat straight hair with water. He believed that he and Marty would grow up, get married and take over the hardware store. In spite of this, Marty did love him. She did want to get married, but she certainly wasn't thinking about it yet.

On picnic day, it was recess all day and no one studied. A chorus of freedom rang out terrible words across the schoolyard. "School's out, school's out, teacher wore her bloomers out! No more classes, no more books, no more teacher's dirty looks!" Marty didn't dare say it, but you could hear it from kids swinging on the banisters, hanging upside down from the jungle gym.

The older kids chose sides and played softball in the back of the schoolyard. The younger kids played hopscotch, jump rope, marbles, and rode the teeter-totters and dangerous merry-go-rounds. Marty and Anne pumped themselves up on the swings, wooden seats on metal chains mounted on high metal poles. They stood on the seats, leaning back and then forward, using momentum to go much higher than the tire swing at home could. Anne pumped herself higher, her scuffed shoes planted firmly.

"School's out, school's out!" chorused Anne, swinging. No one cared what she said. It didn't really mean anything. It was just a rhyme.

68

Marty held tight to the chains and swung as high as she dared, watching the cotton puffs blowing across the schoolyard and the kids playing. It was warm enough that they didn't have to wear coats. It felt so free to wear only a dress. The boys could see their cotton panties under their dresses, but no one was watching. No one cared.

Marty played jump rope, taking turns twirling with Anne and Eileen. Marty watched Eileen's black patent leather buckle shoes as they hopped, one step ahead of the rope. Then it was her turn to jump into the middle, chanting as the rope turned, trying to miss the rope each time. "I'm a little Dutch girl, dressed in blue. Here's the things I like to do. Salute the captain (Marty saluted), curtsey to the queen (Marty curtseyed) and sail on an ocean submarine."

The teachers were relaxed, eating lunch and talking. Little kids and big kids mixed together wandered all over the schoolyard. All the doors and windows of the school itself were open, as if it too was finally free of the winter effort of keeping kids warm.

The third grade girls, Anne, Eileen, Melody, Geraldine and Marty sat in a row on the steps outside the school, eating bologna sandwiches and peanut butter sandwiches out of brown paper bags. Geraldine wore overalls over her tee shirt but the other girls wore dresses. Eileen, her plump fresh pink face framed by bobby pinned curls, drank a coke in a beautiful green glass bottle. "Let's play post office," she said when she was finished. She went to find some boys to play with them, and then led them into the school room. Only Loren and Jerome followed her.

In third and fourth grade, post office meant something different than it did in first and second. This year post office was a game in which a girl went into the long, thin cloakroom with hooks for their wraps, and waited. A boy was sent in after her, while the rest of the kids giggled. It was dark in the cloakroom, and the boy would try to kiss the girl, or she would try to kiss him.

Eileen sent Melody into the cloakroom first. Melody was taller than any of them, lanky and freckled. She was quiet and helpful and Marty liked her.

"You go, Loren," Eileen directed.

Loren, like Melody was thin and sandy haired. He was the farm boy who had a terrific aim and took many of Marty's marbles. In a moment they both emerged, bashful and refusing to say anything. Marty didn't blame them. She resented the bossy Eileen telling them what to do, making them all play the game she wanted.

"Okay," said Eileen. "I'll go."

"I think she wants you to come in after her," said Marty to Jerome. She wrapped her arms around her chest and watched while Jerome, a bashful smile on his impish face, went in the cloakroom. There were no warm winter coats now, so it wasn't very dark and you couldn't hide.

Jerome didn't come out and neither did Eileen.

"Come on," said Anne, tired of the nonsense. "Let's play marbles." She and Geraldine and Melody began rummaging in the wooden desks attached to each other with black painted iron in a long row, looking for their marbles.

But Loren came over to Marty and took her by the hand. "Baby stuff," he said. "I'll kiss you in the daylight." He dragged her into the first and second grade room across the hall and they sat down on the tiny chairs lined up in a corner. Afternoon sunlight was coming in the big windows. Loren kissed her on the lips. He tasted like root beer and his long sandy eyelashes brushed her cheek. Marty liked it, but butterflies danced in her stomach.

"What if someone sees us?" she said out loud.

"Who cares!" said Loren. He kissed her again.

Marty looked earnestly into Loren's eyes, which were brown with flecks of green, like Mother's hazel-colored eyes. She couldn't move, constrained by Loren's sweet presence, and by danger. The two of them sat there, not talking, Loren holding Marty's hand. Two high school girls appeared in the door of the schoolroom.

"That's Ellie's sister," said one of them. "They're kissing!" They left, but Marty was sure they would tell Ellie. In fact, soon Ellie and Helen stood in the door of the room, looking like twins in their cinched-waist skirts and ponytails, one dark and one light. Their shoulders rounded self-consciously around their newly-formed breasts.

But even then, Marty didn't budge. "That's my sister," she whispered to Loren.

"So?"

"So she'll probably tell on me," said Marty.

"So what do you care?" asked Loren. He leaned over and kissed her in full view of Ellie.

Marty felt hot, smashed up into the corner with Loren hiding her from view. She stood up and brushed off her skirt, ready for the worst.

70

Loren stood up too, his back to the door.

"I liked kissing you," said Marty. She didn't want him to feel bad.

"Any time," said Loren. "Have a nice summer!" He left, his hands jammed in his jeans pockets, looking up boldly at the taller girls as he passed them at the door.

Marty stood there, looking down, ashamed in the presence of her older sister. Helen smirked and Ellie giggled nervously as they came toward Marty.

"He wanted to," said Marty to her chest, her voice muffled.

"I won't tell," said Ellie generously, "If you promise never to do that again."

"Okay," Marty still didn't raise her head. Inside she wasn't sorry, didn't think she had done any harm, but she was a pastor's daughter, and it was embarrassing. She went over to the aquarium, where Paul's turtles had been living all year, and pretended great interest. She picked one up and felt its dry feet on her hand. It was so big that Mittens wouldn't even bother it. Behind her back she heard Ellie and Helen leave, tittering to each other.

It was mid-afternoon, and kids were still playing games and milling around the schoolhouse and yard. But Marty wanted to go home. School, the picnic, everything was over. She felt a hollow pit in her stomach. She thought of Michael, and hoped he hadn't seen her.

Ashamed of herself, Marty wandered out to the back of the schoolyard to see if she could get up in the Big Tree. The town stopped at the back of the schoolyard and gave on to fields past a gravel road. One of the cottonwoods which ringed the schoolyard was known as "the Big Tree". Its accommodating branches were low, wide and comfortable. But on school picnic day, kids were everywhere. The high school kids were still playing softball. There was nowhere to hide.

Marty went back to the school room, took her precious pencil box and the papers out of her desk, crossed the road and walked home by herself, losing herself in a book on the sofa as soon as she got there.

Line and Paul burst in an hour later.

"Where were you?" Line asked. "We looked everywhere." They had prevailed upon Dad to pick them up in the car and bring the heavy glass aquarium home.

"Here," said Marty. Sometimes it was nice to have so many brothers and sisters that you got lost among them. No one noticed her or said anything at supper.

Summer burst upon them in all of its glory. In the mornings the sun was up long before the kids and the doves and pigeons called from their home in the barn across the street. Marty went barefoot, feeling the dew in the grass under her feet. She picked strawberries in the garden, trying to wait until they got red enough, but often enough picking them before they were ready. Rows of carrots, radishes and beets were marked with a seed packet stuck on a stick at the end of the row. Marty pulled up tiny carrots and ate them with the dirt still on them. They needed to be thinned anyway. She didn't quite see the point of radishes.

Olga Arneson, the senator's wife, asked the kids to tea. Paul declined in favor of staying home to study trees and insects. He was pretending to give himself Boy Scout badges if he did what the scout handbook said was necessary. But the three girls put on school dresses and shoes and walked across the railroad tracks to Arneson's farmhouse, a mile out from town.

From the parsonage, the big farmhouse could be seen peeking out from an avenue of trees. Mr. Arneson was a rich wheat farmer and went to Bismarck to the North Dakota assembly. Their son Erik played center on the Bryson basketball team.

It was warm as the girls crossed the railroad tracks, looking carefully in both directions first. Marty trailed behind Ellie, who enjoyed practicing being ladylike, and Line, who knew that Patsy Ninas kept her horse out at the Arneson's farm. Their footsteps ground along the gravel road. The sun on Marty's back was hot and sweat dripped down under her arms. It was better when shadows came over them, made by the row of tall trees thick with leaves.

In books, tea time meant fancy china, cucumber sandwiches with the crusts cut off and perhaps nice cakes or cookies. Marty thought tea time was British, like Queen Elizabeth II who had been crowned last year. *Life* magazine was full of photos of her coronation and her children Ann and Charles. Charles was the same age as Paul. Marty wondered if they drank tea and if they liked cucumber sandwiches.

At home the china cups and their saucers edged in gold paint sat on the green cupboard, to be dusted but never used. Mother and Dad drank coffee and ate cookies or bars with it, but there was no formality. Just a coffee cup and a plate of cookies, on tables filled with work, magazines, books. Home was comfortable, but not beautiful.

The Arnesons' large white frame house was set in expansive green lawns bordered by lilacs, peonies and spirea, with a sunporch running along the length of the front. Spreading shade trees arched over the house, proving that it had been solid and established for many, many years. The farm buildings behind it were so neat and well-ordered that you didn't even notice that you were coming to a farm. And sure enough, cropping grass in front of the house was a saddled white horse on a picket.

Line went straight up to the horse. It was twice as big as she was. She patted its neck, talking to it, while Marty and Ellie stood back at a respectful distance. It wasn't as white when you got close to it. Marty could see the gray hairs in its hide.

"Bring me some long grass from over by the fence," Line directed. The poor horse could hardly get at the short grass on the lawn.

Marty pulled some of the grass beyond the fence and brought it to Line, who made her hand as flat as possible and held the long grass up for the horse to take into its big teeth. It was a beautiful horse, with a grayish mane falling over its neck, but Marty was scared to death of horses.

Mrs. Arneson appeared at the door of the sunporch and came over to them, waving a handkerchief that she carried in one hand. She was tiny, wearing a knit suit with a flowered blouse. Graying tightly curled hair circled her face. She wore lipstick and pearls, as became a state senator's wife, even on a weekday afternoon.

"Hello girls," she said. "Patsy is coming later and she'll let you ride the horse I'm sure." Her voice came from somewhere back in her throat, but she was smiley and active. Marty noticed how tiny she was compared to her husband and son, who were more than a foot taller.

The girls gave her their hands. "Hello, Mrs. Arneson," they said.

"Let's go and have some tea," she said, leading them into the sunporch, which was lined with wicker chairs made comfortable with chintz cushions. Shelves ran along the top of the room, holding china figures, plates, birds and flowers. Shrubs and trees pressed against the windows made the light inside dappled, rather more shady than sunny.

Mrs. Arneson arranged the three girls at a round table set with flowered china, cups and saucers and a plate of sandwiches, and sat down beside them.

"Now I'm sure you girls don't really like tea," she said. "So I made you some lemonade." She poured lemonade into their cups from a flowered teapot, and passed the sandwiches. Marty noted that the crusts indeed were cut off the bread, but they were only cold cuts and cheese, nothing special.

Mrs. Arneson was gracious, putting them at their ease. She was the sister of their neighbor Alfred, who let them come over and watch his new television.

"And what do you like to do?" she asked Ellie.

"Mother is teaching me to sew. I really like it."

"That's wonderful!" said Mrs. Arneson. "Such a good thing for girls to know. And how about you?" She turned to Line.

"I like horses," said Line, sitting straight up and flashing her big smile across like a light. "And I like drawing, and I want to be a cheerleader."

"Oh-ho!" Mrs. Arneson smiled at her. "You certainly know your mind."

Mrs. Arneson turned to Marty, but Marty was slow to answer.

"Marty's a bookworm," said Line.

"Oh?" said Mrs. Arneson with interest. "I love books myself." She held out the teapot and poured them each more lemonade. "What are you reading?"

"The Laura and Mary books," said Marty, surprised that her voice came out so cracked and breathless. She cleared her throat and said it again.

"Ah yes," said Mrs. Arneson, "I think a new edition of those is just coming out. Illustrated." She stood up and went back into the house. Marty looked longingly after her, wishing she could go into the big house. But she wasn't asked; Mrs. Arneson came back with a plate of sugar cookies.

"You know, I always wished I had a daughter," said Mrs. Arneson. "You girls help me see what it is like to have girls in the family. What fun it must be!"

As they ate their cookies, Patsy Ninas appeared, wearing blue jeans. She came from the barn, where she was cleaning the stall she rented for her horse. She didn't seem to notice her audience on the sunporch as she came up to her horse, released the picket and fed the horse an apple, patting its nose as the apple disappeared in one bite. Putting her foot in the stirrup, Patsy swung herself up. But Line ran out to say hello and ask if she could have a ride, and Mrs. Arneson and the others followed.

"Sure," Patsy told Line. She jumped down and showed Line where to put her foot. Then she boosted Line up in her dress, and Line was on the horse!

"His name is Star," said Patsy. She patted Star encouragingly. "Just give him a little cluck, and walk around a little. If you want to turn, you just pull the reins in that direction. That pulls his head around."

Line walked the horse past them, smiling broadly, the leather saddle creaking as they moved together. She sat straight, holding the reins, high above them, walking the horse with his huge rump and tail. Marty couldn't believe it. Line got exactly what she wanted, just by asking for it!

"Star," called Patsy, and Star flicked his ears, turned around and came back. "Do you want a ride?" she asked, turning in the general direction of Ellie and Marty.

"No, thank you," said Ellie, as Marty backed away. "Line's the one who is horse crazy."

Patsy laughed. "Me too!" she said. "At least I'm crazy about this horse." Patsy swung herself up, and waved as she rode off, her dark hair making a horse tail behind her head to match the horse's grey one.

The Mikkelson girls stood watching. Mrs. Arneson turned to them.

"Well, you girls greet your Mother and Pastor Carl," she said, showing them that it was time to go home. The shadows of the trees were longer and they could see their own shadows angling thin and long across the grass.

"Thank you, Mrs. Arneson," they all said. Marty felt like curtseying, as she did in jump rope. Mrs. Arneson was almost royalty, Norwegian royalty, but she was also rather ordinary. She waved her handkerchief at them as they walked down the driveway.

Line skipped and jumped, crowing. "I got to ride Star! And talk to Patsy Ninas!"

Marty plodded along thoughtfully beside her in the shade under the arch of trees, her arms linked behind her back. Ellie was in her own world, as usual. Marty wished the tea had been more formal and that the talk was more interesting, like in books. The reality of having tea at the Arnesons' wasn't what she hoped. She shrugged and skipped beside Line.

"I'm really glad you got to ride Star," Marty said.

Driving into what Dad called "the north woods," Paul was hushed by the spires of the tall pine trees reaching back as far as Canada, as far as you could imagine. In places, birches and poplars punctuated the pungent woods, as well as lush undergrowth. It was nothing like the flat, treeless plains along the Red River.

Their destination was a cabin on Lake Michigami that Dad rented from another Lutheran pastor. When Dad said they were getting close, Paul's eyes were glued on the woods. Overgrown two-lane tracks left the gravel road at intervals and Dad drove into the one marked with a wooden sign saying "Lande." When Paul got out of the car, the smell of the woods and ancient humus underfoot was intoxicating. It was July and at 6 p.m. the sun was still high in the sky.

The first thing the kids did was go down the steep wooden steps to the lake below the cabin. To their left, the sun made the fluffy clouds shine golden at the edges. The lake was smooth, the surface undulating softly in rhythmic waves, making shushing sounds as it lapped at the rocks on the little beach. Paul was so thrilled he could not say one word.

Eventually they went up to the cabin. There was a room for Mother and Dad, and one for Grandma Bakken and Aunt Rose, who would be coming the next day, but the kids would sleep in the bunkhouse.

The kids took the cardboard boxes they had packed with a few clothes, toys, books and papers, and claimed a bunk. Pastor Lande had bought the whole bunkhouse from a Bible camp and dragged it into the woods. The thin mattresses with their blue and white striped covers smelled of mildew and sagged on the bedsprings. The screen door shut with a long "sprunnnng", but there were no mosquitoes inside.

In the morning before anyone else was awake, Paul sneaked quietly down the wooden stairs to the lake. Luckily there was a wooden handrail he could hold as he swung his weak leg down without a brace. Paul was growing and the shoe his brace fit into was tight and uncomfortable. He limped around without it as much as he could, but Dad and Mother usually told him to put it on. "We're going to have to get you down to the clinic before school starts," Dad had said. "You need to get fitted for new shoes and a new brace."

A mist rose along the edges of the lake, but the limpid air was full of the light of the sun. The water was silky smooth and a shining path on its surface came from the sun directly to Paul. A pair of birds with black heads and black rings around their necks swam lazily near the dock. One of them upended, tail in the air, going underwater to fish. The other began a melodious wail which started low and grew louder. It echoed across the early morning lake, and was followed by a series of gabbling hoots.

"The sound of the north woods," said Dad, who appeared behind Paul on the dock. "The common loon. It's the Minnesota state bird." Staring into the water, they saw a school of tiny minnows, the sun on their backs making them flash silver as they swam.

Finally Dad tore himself away, "I have to get some water," he said. "Want to see how to prime the pump?" The iron pump was halfway up the path, drilled into the soil, with a wooden landing beside it. A pail of water stood next to the pump. Dad took a cup of water from it, and poured it down the pump's throat, then pumped the handle in a slow rhythm, increasing the force until fresh water splashed out into another pail. "Not too bad," said Dad. "And the more we use it, the easier it will get."

Dad carried the bucket of fresh water up so Mother could make coffee. Mother was looking in cupboards, trying to figure out what dishes and cooking pots were available.

"What do you think, Lois?" said Dad, conspiratorially, grinning at Paul. "Don't you think Paul could go without his brace this week?" He had noticed that Paul was barefoot.

"I think you're right," said Mother to Dad, her eyes smiling down at Paul. "The kids will be in the water a lot, and I don't think a week would hurt. But you better keep up the stretching exercises."

Paul held his breath, listening to the conversation. Heaven was surely a place where loons echoed across a shining lake and he didn't have to wear a clumsy brace!

"Don't worry," said Dad. "We won't forget. Come on Paul, let's find a good place to do them." His hand grazed Paul's blonde hair as it came to rest on his shoulder.

When Aunt Rose arrived, she brought colored pencils, drawing pads and books. She was a grade school principal who had been a teacher. Big and cheery, she was very specific about everything she loved, from the insects Paul showed her, to the cup of coffee she drank in the morning on the dock, to the wide blue-green lake itself. She lived with Grandma Bakken, who was concerned that everything be done properly. But at the lake, even Grandma Bakken relaxed and enjoyed the natural world.

Mother and Aunt Rose did most of the cooking, but Grandma Bakken brought rolls of refrigerator cookie dough that she sliced and baked for an afternoon snack. If the kids were going exploring, Mother packed sandwiches for their lunches. Everything was easy at the lake, except for carrying heavy buckets of water up the hill. All the kids took turns doing it except Paul. He had enough trouble getting up and down the stairs.

The kids spent a lot of time in the lake. Stones made it tough to walk into the water from the shore, but if you jumped off the end of the dock, it was lovely and sandy. It wasn't deep either. Line and Marty could walk a long way out before they got to a place where, with their noses in the air, their feet didn't touch the bottom. Paul used an inner tube to float. They all dog-paddled, but no one was learning to swim.

Early in the morning, before they riled up the water swimming, Paul helped catch the lovely silver minnows in an improvised seine Dad made from a piece of gauze. Paul and Line held the seine on either side, letting the side which was weighted with soft pieces of lead drag in the water. When schools of minnows swam into it; they lifted the seine into the air and the unsuspecting minnows were dropped into the minnow bucket.

The tin minnow bucket was full of holes big enough to let in water, but not so big the minnows could get out. A Styrofoam collar kept it floating in the lake to keep the minnows alive until someone went fishing. The bucket had a hatch on the top which prevented the minnows from getting away. Minnows were precious.

At the edge of the lake was a footpath, once a deer path or an Indian path, but now used by people on the lake to visit their neighbors. Most of the buildings on the lake were summer cabins. So many were owned by pastors that a spit jutting into the lake to the east was called Preachers' Point. Pastor Lande helped this influx by renting his cabin to Lutheran pastors by the week.

On one side of the cabin a creek ran from deep in the woods beyond the road down into the lake. In the winter an aluminum boat was kept in a little house with no floor built over the creek. In this direction a pastor's family was living in a tent on land they had just bought. Mother and Dad met the family, and their kids sometimes swam off the Lande dock with the Mikkelsons.

On the other side of the cabin was a huge piece of land heavily forested with pines owned by "the trolley car man." Many years ago he had moved a large trolley car onto the land as a place to live. The trolley car man was reputed to be mean. He refused to sell his land to Lutheran preachers and didn't want kids on it. None of this stopped Line.

"We have to go," Line said as the kids put on their pajamas in the bunkhouse. "He's hardly ever there. And even if he is, I'm sure he would like us." Line turned out the light in the bunkhouse. It was totally dark and the air smelled of warm linoleum.

"But what if he is there?" said Marty. "And what if he doesn't like us?"

"Well what can he do?" asked Line. "Just ask us to leave, I guess." Each of them tried to imagine what the trolley car man would do if he wanted to get rid of them.

"Come after us with a rake?" suggested Paul.

"Hold one of us hostage, so Mother and Dad have to come and ransom us," suggested Marty, who read too many books.

"We can run faster than any old man," said Line, looking at Paul to see whether he thought so. "When would be the best time to go, do you think?"

"Maybe before he's awake," said Paul. He didn't like the idea of going into hostile territory one bit.

"We won't tell Mother and Dad," said Line, looking around to make sure Ellie hadn't come from the cabin yet. Ellie was spending the week writing Helen long letters and reading magazines. Mother despaired of her being interested in nature, or in swimming, or in anything. She was sulking and not much fun to have around, but she did sit with Grandma Bakken and listen to her stories.

"Not tomorrow," said Marty. "Dad's going to take us fishing, remember?"

"Okay," said Line. "We'll do it the day after. It can't be that far away."

In the morning Dad organized a boating party. Mother made a picnic, and Dad sorted heavy kapok lifejackets and fishing gear. He wasn't going to fish seriously, as he did with the men of the church when they went up to Lake of the Woods and spent days doing nothing but. He just wanted the kids to get the idea. He put his pole and tackle box in one end of the boat.

The minnow bucket went into an outer tin pail to hold the lake water. By this time, Paul was sad to see that a few minnows were floating with their white bellies up in the bucket, dead.

The lake, although not as calm as it was in the early morning, was gently rolling. Dad held the boat close to the dock while the kids stepped in carefully.

"Crouch low," said Dad. "Keep your weight low, and move slow." The boat skittered on the water whenever they moved. Mother slid onto the seat at the back of the boat.

There were three wide seats, and a small one in the prow of the boat for Paul. Under Paul's seat was a heavy iron anchor and the ropes used to tie the boat. Dad put the oars into the oarlocks at the sides of the boat and, after everyone else was in, got in and pushed them out with an oar. Ellie waved as they moved away from the dock. She was staying home with Grandma and Aunt Rose.

"You steer by rowing more with one oar than the other," said Dad. He rowed with the left oar, leaving the right one hanging and they began to go in a circle on the water. "If it's windy, the wind's going to push you around too. But today looks good. I don't think we'll get whitecaps and we'll stay close to the shore."

Paul knew that the fetch of the wind across the lake could whip the green water into frothy whitecaps at the top of each wave. It was fun jumping in the whitecaps when they were swimming, but the wind was cold. Paul was glad it was calmer today, the sun strong, the lake reflecting the big expanse of blue sky.

They were sunburned already. Their noses were red and the tops of their arms especially. Mother washed their skin with baking soda, but they wore tee-shirts today, as they would be in the sun in the middle of the day. Paul got lots of mosquito bites, so he was covered with dots of calamine lotion to dry them up.

Dad carefully switched places, letting Marty and Line take the rowing seat while he sat in front on the seat near Paul. Mother sat in the middle in the back, clutching the sides of the boat. She didn't want to be pitched into the lake, even if it was shallow! Line took one oar and Marty the other. Paul noticed that they weren't facing the direction they were going. Apparently, in order to pull the oars you leaned back. That meant that he might have to be the lookout, since he was in the front of the boat.

"Pull together, girls," said Dad. "See, you want to go that direction, so Marty has to pull more." The boat was heading straight for the shore. "Marty, pull! Line stop rowing." Paul could see that the oars in their oarlocks were clumsy, and that Marty was struggling. She tried to lift the oar out of the water until it was in back of her, and then pull it while it was in the water, just as Line did.

"Can I try?" said Paul.

"Wait a minute," said Dad. "Let the girls figure it out." Marty dipped her oar in, but it was at the front and they started going in a circle again. "That's not what you want right now, Marty."

Line rowed backwards with her oar, and the boat straightened out. The girls watched each other, trying to get in rhythm.

"One, two, three, pull," said Line. "One, two, three, pull." Finally they got it. The boat began to move along the shore, slowly but surely. The girls' slight bodies moved the heavy boat with the cumbersome oars, leaning into each stroke. Paul tried not to worry about them. He would get his turn. Looking up at the trees along the shore, he saw a piece of the grey metal roof of what must be the trolley car.

"Good!" said Dad. "Keep it up, keep up the rhythm." Marty and Line brought the oars up, dropped them in the water and then leaned back, pulling on the oars. "It's like swinging. You girls are good at swinging, using your bodies. You can do it with rowing too." The Boy Scout handbook must have lessons on rowing, thought Paul. He had never been in a boat before.

After the boat started moving more confidently, Paul looked into the water beneath them. He could see the ripples on the light sand below, the schools of minnows, rocks, seaweed. A thick brown leech undulated by like a snake in the water. The girls were afraid a leech would attach itself to their legs when they were swimming and suck their blood, but Paul found them interesting.

Mother watched the shoreline, looking for interesting birds. They passed a thickly wooded shore and then a place where the lake indented, making a little bay. The beach was sandy and cabins came almost down to the edge of the lake. "This must be Preacher's Point," said Mother. Docks stuck out into the water with fishing boats and motorboats attached.

"Head to the left, Line," said Dad. "See those reeds. There's supposed to be a channel into the next lake there." Line stopped rowing and the boat headed left, past the sandy beach.

"Could we stop for lunch here?" asked Line. She was tired, and Marty was too. As soon as she let up on the oars, the boat started to drift with the rolling ripples on the water.

Dad looked up at the sun and back toward Mother. "Let's keep going into the channel. I'm sure there will be shady places to stop there," said Dad. "It's not quite lunch time anyhow. You girls row to the channel, and then Paul and I will take over."

Paul's heart leapt up. He couldn't wait to row the boat! He faced the front and watched as the boat headed into a narrow space between tall green reeds.

But the oars got tangled in the reeds. Marty gave up. "I can't do it," she said dejectedly, letting go of her oar. The boat stopped moving, stuck in the forest of reeds. Dad shifted his weight, low in the boat, and moved onto the rowing seat, letting Marty and Line take the seat behind Paul.

"What we need is a canoe," said Dad. "So much easier! You can steer a canoe with one paddle. And we could get through these reeds in no time." He expertly maneuvered the heavy boat into the channel. Trees lined the banks, below them a fine sandy beach. There was no wind and the water was very still, slipping under them into the lake.

It was like the chip boats in the spring, Paul thought. There was just enough space for a boat, but they needed a little help to get around obstacles, like the submerged log Dad was negotiating. They were going upstream, but the water was hardly flowing.

"This is supposed to take us into the Bucket lakes," said Dad, "There's a Little Bucket and a Big Bucket."

"This is beautiful," said Mother. "Let's stop here." Dad ran the prow of the boat onto the sand under a shade tree at the edge of the channel and the kids clambered out. Marty and Line flopped on their backs on the sandy bank, pooped from rowing. Dad laughed at them, but Mother got out the sandwiches and fruit.

Paul stood with his feet in the water, eating his sandwich, and squiggling his feet in the soft yellow sand. On a half sunken log, a huge dark turtle was sunning itself. In the shadow of the fallen log Paul thought he saw fish, small green ones with stripes on their back. He showed Dad.

"Perch," said Dad. "Kind of small, but maybe." The sun filtered through the birches and poplars at the edge of the channel, dappling the people on the shore with light. It made Paul's eyes feel sleepy and lazy. He wanted to stay on that sandy bank with the water flowing by forever.

"Want to row, Lois?" Dad asked, when they got back into the boat.

"Not here," said Mother. "When we get back into the lake, I'll row." The channel was wider at this end, not clogged with reeds.

"Come on, Paul," said Dad. "Sit here by me." Dad sat a little more to the middle of the seat, to even out their weight, but Paul put his hands on the oars as Dad pulled the boat out into Little Bucket. This lake was a small circle, surrounded by reeds. "Must have been Paul Bunyan's toe," said

Dad. The 10,000 lakes of Minnesota were supposed to have been made by the footsteps of Paul Bunyan as he walked across the state many years ago.

"Look," said Mother, "A beaver lodge." She was pointing to a heap of reeds and sticks on the surface of the little lake. "The beaver has the door of his house under the water, to protect himself from enemies, but he sleeps in a comfy den up out of the water."

"Enemies?" asked Marty.

"Probably wolves, maybe coyotes or bear," said Dad, "depending on how big they are. Beavers can chew down trees. In fact that beaver lodge probably has some trees at its base."

The water on the little lake was smooth, the sun warm and Dad let the boat drift. Marty and Line trailed their hands in the warm water. "Shall we put a line in?" Dad asked.

"Do beavers fish?" asked Paul.

"No, I don't think so. They eat plants."

There was only one fishing pole, but Dad showed Paul how to thread a minnow onto a hook through its mouth and out the gills. "Be careful of your fingers," said Dad. "A fish hook in your finger isn't much fun." He attached a red and white plastic bobber to the line and a soft lead weight near the hook.

Paul wondered about the minnow, but it was still alive, swimming around once he lowered the hook into the water. He couldn't see deep into this lake. It was full of algae and dirt and things falling off the trees. He sat quietly; they all did in the sleepy, quiet lake, watching for birds and animal life.

In a few minutes Paul felt a tug at his line and the red and white bobber dipped under the water. "Wow!" said Paul. The tug of something live on his line was exciting. He pulled it up and there was a small perch.

"Big enough," said Dad. He took the hook out of the perch's mouth and attached the perch to a metal stringer, so the fish would still be in the water. "A fish's skin protects it. If you handle it too much, it will die. The fresher the fish, the better it tastes!" Paul watched the fish swimming, not knowing it couldn't go anywhere and would get eaten for dinner. It was the way of the world. Big fish ate minnows, and people ate big fish.

Paul passed the fishing pole to Marty. She caught a string of seaweed when the line tugged. When it was Line's turn, she caught a small perch. Paul caught two more.

"I thought there would be more fish in Bucket lake," said Dad. "You'll have to clean them when we get back. I'll show you. If you take life out of the wild, you better make sure you eat it. Otherwise it's a terrible waste."

"We will," said Paul. He could have sat on that peaceful little lake all day, but Line was restless.

"Could we go swimming?" she said.

"How about back in the channel," said Mother. "We don't know how deep this lake is. Have you guys done enough fishing?"

"Sure," said Dad. "I just wanted them to try it. And we will each get a bite of fish tonight, no more!" He laughed.

Paul remembered when Dad came back from Lake of the Woods with several great northern pikes. Mother dredged them in flour and cooked them in butter. Nothing was so delicious. Real fishermen went out in the late evening when the fish were feeding, and knew where to find them. Lake Michigami had fish in it, but they were unlikely to find any in the middle of the day.

On the way back Paul rowed with Line and then Marty. His strong arms could keep up with them, though he was shorter and skinnier. The wind was at their backs now, so rowing was easier, but they had to keep at it or the boat went sideways into the troughs of the small waves.

When they neared the Lande's dock, Mother took the oars. She was a good rower and snugged them up close to the dock. Dad got out and tied the ropes. She took the picnic remains up to the cabin, but the kids stayed down with Dad to clean the fish.

The kids watched while he showed them how to cut the heads off, slit open the fishes' bellies and clean out the organs. They each took turns cleaning one, and then, with the scaling tool, scraped the transparent scales off the sides of the perch. Paul's hands were slimy and full of sticky scales.

"I wish Mittens were here," said Line. "She sure would like a tasty fish head."

Dad said the fish were too small to fillet. They would have to remove the backbone when they were eating the fish, and try not to eat the bones.

Mother cooked the fish like the big northern pike. When they were shared out, each of them got only a bite full of bones, but they were delicious. Paul noted where the bones were, running up the back and making a cage around the organs to protect them. Like his own bones, he knew from transparent pictures in the medical encyclopedia at home.

After supper the kids went down to the lake and sat on the dock in the growing darkness. It was too early for stars in the bright sky and no one seemed to mind if they sat out late. Tomorrow was the last day they could stay at the lake. Line was still thinking about the trolley car.

"I really want to see it," she said, intensity in her voice. "It's a mystery, right in front of us, and we can't go home without figuring it out!"

Marty began to agree with her. There was never any question of Line going by herself. They would all have to go. "Okay, tomorrow morning. You can wake us up and we'll come." She looked at Paul, who resigned himself to fear and said nothing.

"I'll sneak in and grab some bananas and bread in the morning, and no one will know a thing until we get home," said Line.

"Hmmmmm," said Marty, doubtfully. "I guess that'll work."

"Don't worry," said Line quietly. "I'll wake you up early."

When they went to bed, Paul shut his eyes, but he couldn't sleep. What he liked best was lazing around the sunny dock in the mornings until Mother called them for breakfast. But he didn't want to be left out of an adventure. And he admired Line. It wasn't that he was afraid, either, he told himself. He did plenty of things that would scare kids his age. He just didn't like the sound of skulking around in a place you didn't know, with the threat of being found out and punished.

Paul woke to find Line shaking him silently. He put on shorts and a tee shirt and carried his handed-down sandals outside. The trees were damp and dripping with moisture. He did not want to go bother the trolley car man. It was like going to physical therapy. You had to do it whether you wanted to or not. Paul and Marty went down the wooden steps to the lake, but Line sneaked into the kitchen.

The sun was already hot on the dock, as Marty and Paul lay face down, looking into the still, glassy surface of the water. Sounds carried very far on the water. They could hear a man dropping fishing equipment into his boat way up the shore. When Line came down the steps she chivvied them.

"Come on, you guys," she whispered. "Pretend we're Indians." They took the path along the lake to the right single file, Line in the lead, then Marty and then Paul dragging his skinny leg along in the rear.

The path was obscured in places by thick drifts of long red dried pine needles. Line climbed over fallen trees and around rocks through the columns of tall trees. These were not Christmas tree pines, with spreading branches down to the ground. These were Norway and white pines whose long needles and pinecones began far up the tree. They kept the sun out, and prevented undergrowth. It was easy to see, but dark, somber and forbidding underneath them.

Paul was ankle-deep in pine needles, but he kept going. Marty looked back to see that he was coming. Scouting silently, Line kept her eyes on the hilltop to see whether anything was moving.

Soon they saw a line of dull grey metal along the top of the hill. Line began slogging through the pine needles, heading for the top. The trunks of the trees were straight and tall, close together. The kids steadily climbed, not very quietly, Paul dragging his skinny leg up the hill. More and more of the trolley came into view, the little row of windows at the top of the roof, and then the car. Nothing moved near it.

"I'll go around," said Line quietly when they got close, "To make sure." Marty and Paul stood in the silence, listening as the shushing wind moved in the pine boughs.

"I don't see anyone," said Line, coming around the side of the trolley. "There's no car or anything." They all moved closer to the closed grey trolley, which looked like an old sleeping car from a train without any wheels. How did it get there?

On the side farthest from the lake, some steps led to a door. Line peeked in the window and motioned to the others.

Paul was relieved to see that the car was empty. A purple carpet covered the floor and dirty little blinds hung at the windows, but everything was dusty and there was no furniture. A wood stove stood at one end, with a stove pipe pushed up into the roof.

"I guess no one's going to come out and chase us away," said Line, a little disappointed. She tried the door, but it was locked.

"No one's been here for a long time," said Marty. "What is everyone so worried about?"

"Well he does own the land," said Line. "We are on someone else's land."

"In the Paul Bunyan State Forest," said Marty, reasonably, as if she had never been frightened at all.

They walked around the car, looking for human touches. An old shovel stood against a wall, but it looked pretty lonely. An old train or trolley car stuck in the deep woods, owned by an old man who didn't like anyone. It was a sad story, thought Paul. The wind shushed in the long-needled pines high overhead. It was so quiet it felt like being in church.

"If we ever need a place to stay," said Line, "we could come here and figure out a way to get in."

"Like the Boxcar children?" asked Marty. "But there's no way to get food out here. And we'd have to chop wood to stay warm. Think of the snowdrifts! And the ice on the lake. I'd love to come up here in the winter and see it."

"Let's go," said Paul. "I'm hungry." He was imagining Mother and Dad having toast and coffee, talking to Aunt Rose and Grandma in the cheerful cabin. "Shall we tell them we were here?"

"Oh yeah," said Line nonchalantly. "Dad would probably want to know what we found out."

She turned out to be right. No one cared that they roamed around on the trolley car man's land and they didn't get in trouble. Paradise, thought Paul. This lake is paradise.

9

Marty and Line were supposed to be cleaning their room on Saturday morning, but instead they were arguing over a tee-shirt.

"That's my tee-shirt," said Line.

"You gave it to me," said Marty.

They had little enough to fight over. There was a drawer for each in the blue dresser, and the top drawer was divided in two for their socks and underpants. Clothes were important to Marty, and she hated having mostly hand-me-downs from her sisters and cousins. Line didn't mind looking like a gypsy or a hobo. They wore dresses to school, and took them off as soon as they got home, but their play clothes were old sweatshirts, tee-shirts and raggedy jeans.

Line folded the almost new tee-shirt in question and placed it firmly in her own drawer.

"Indian giver," said Marty bitterly. It was a lovely cherry color, pretty with her dark hair. She wanted to wear it with her brown pants.

"Aunt Rose gave it to me, and I don't remember giving it to you," said Line.

"You did," said Marty. "You said I could have it if I did the dishes that one week."

Line took the tee-shirt and threw it at Marty. "All right, have your old tee-shirt."

"Meanie," said Marty.

"I am not a meanie," said Line. "I look out for you all the time. You don't even stand up for yourself."

But Marty was already unhappy because she had to wear glasses and Line didn't. She liked being able to see things sharply instead of mentally pulling them out of the fog as she had done for a long time. But, "boys don't make passes at girls who wear glasses" was an established truth. Line's big eyes were beautiful in her school photograph, and Marty's were hidden behind the new glasses with the plastic rims. It was an insult that would last the rest of their lives.

"I do too stand up for myself," said Marty darkly.

"Prove it," said Line. "Tell me one time I haven't had to do it for you."

Marty put her arms around her chest and stood there. She couldn't think of one.

"Nah, nah, na nah na," said Line. "You can't think of one." She started to retreat. Marty was a pot about to boil over.

Marty followed Line as she left and went downstairs. Hurling a brown oxford shoe at Line, Marty was horrified to see it sail through the frosted window on the landing with a loud crash, missing Line. The window was old and surrounded by smaller panes of colored glass, but the large center pane was irrevocably broken.

Marty saw Line's shocked face looking up at her. Marty didn't say one word, but went into the long, low closet under the eaves and shut the door. She was miserable. Only last spring she had smashed into a window with her wrist when she ran toward the circus train. And now there was another broken one. Plus, Dad and Mother had to pay for her glasses. Marty was deeply ashamed.

Marty spent a long day in the closet, not coming out for lunch, thinking about her woes. She tried to be a good girl, so as not to have to deal with being in trouble. When she slipped a penny candy into her pocket at the grocery store once, she felt bad about it for a long time, and never did it again. She stayed in Line's shadow to enjoy the fun, but not get blamed for things. Mother teased her, calling her "the shadow" as in "the Shadow knows," because she was secretive and studied things intensively. Not that any of the girls ever heard the radio show called "The Shadow." Mother didn't want the kids listening to scary mystery programs just before they went to bed.

Marty admitted to herself that she was Line's sidekick in every sense of the word. She both loved and hated this position. She and Line knew they were equals with different strengths. But Marty felt as if she couldn't do what Line could. It made her both love and hate Line, and there was nothing she could do about it. Marty was part of Sparky's gang.

Also there was no getting around the fact that she broke the window. Marty, hidden back among the dolls and little camps they made in the closet, brooded. She couldn't hear anything happening in the rest of the house, but supposed everyone was having lunch and that they missed her. Line would be telling what happened, as Line spoke truths unvarnished, even by her own interest. Maybe Mother or Dad would come up and drag her out of the closet and make her give up her ten cents a week allowance until the window was paid for. Marty resigned herself to not having any sugar daddies, a caramel candy on a stick that lasted forever, in the near future.

After a while it seemed that lunch must be over. Marty still didn't hear anything happening in the house. No one came. She sat on the bear rug and pawed through some of the boxes of books left over from Mother and Dad's college days, reading the poetry in one of them until she was quite carried away. But still no one came and Marty thought it must be getting late. It was dark in the closet except for a lightbulb. She wondered whether the sun was still shining.

Marty emerged quietly from the closet. It was September, and the sun was receding. Marty poked her head out on the landing, and, lo and behold, the window wasn't even broken! It was no longer frosted glass, but clear. She could see through it to their neighbor's house. She went quietly downstairs. Ellie was leafing through the Sears Roebuck catalog on the sofa, Dad was in his study, and Line and Paul were nowhere to be seen. Mother was at the table in the breakfast nook, kneading bread she made from an Adele Davis cookbook. It smelled sweet and yeasty.

Marty was hungry. She got a bowl and poured herself some Cheerios. Mother's hands deftly turned and folded the bread, not seeming to notice Marty. Marty put milk on her Cheerios and ate them silently, watching Mother take flour from a canister and dust it over the dark, spongy mass. The thick book called *Let's Cook It Right* lay beside her on the table. Mother had made soup out of the book that year also, using their own garden vegetables.

At last Marty said, "I'm sorry I broke the window."

"Yes, we're sorry too," said Mother. "Dad spent his afternoon going to the hardware store and getting it fixed."

"I'll pay for it with my allowance," Marty said. "How much was it?"

"Don't worry about it, Marty," Mother said. "I think you've already punished yourself enough. But you and Line have to be friends. You will never have any friends as important to you as your sisters."

Marty hung her head. "Yes, Mother."

"Now go out and apologize to Line for throwing a shoe at her." Mother put her arms around Marty, holding away her floury hands, and kissed her.

Marty rested in Mother's arms, and tears came to her eyes. It wasn't often that she had Mother all to herself. She wept to be forgiven so easily, when she had made herself almost sick with shame in the closet all day.

"You girls," said Mother, releasing her. "You have so much: nice clothes, plenty of toys. I can't imagine what you find to fight about!" Mother had grown up during the Depression, Marty knew, but she had also been the baby of the family whom everyone felt sorry for, because her father had died. Her siblings were all older and she couldn't possibly feel as Marty did.

Marty reached up and adjusted the new plastic glasses, but she couldn't speak. She went outside. The sweet dry air took her breath away. What a goose you are, she said to herself, staying in the house all day on such a lovely day. She didn't hear Line and Paul anywhere. She sat in the tire swing and swung lazily. The air smelled of heat on the dry grass. Mother's favorite zinnias and asters were mauve, golden and blood red in the garden, lit by the low-angled sun.

Marty was thinking about poetry. School had started and she was memorizing a poem for the speech contest. Her teacher wanted her to learn "A Mortifying Mistake," which was a funny poem about a girl who couldn't remember what six times nine was. When the girl's sister told her to call her doll, "Fifty-four," she did. The only problem was that when the teacher next asked the answer to six times nine, she said "Mary Anne"!

It was okay. Marty could do that one. But she would rather have chosen a beautiful poem, like those in Mother's book. She swung a little in the tire swing, saying to herself, "How do you like to go up in the swing, up in the air so blue? Oh I do think it's the pleasantest thing, that ever a child can do." It was Robert Louis Stevenson.

Just then Paul and Line came around the corner of the white church half a block away and started toward home. Marty was surprised that she could see them clearly, and that they looked happy. Glasses were a good thing. Paul was walking well on his new brace, almost without limping, and Line held Mittens in her arms. Where had they been? What had they been doing? Marty left the swing and started toward them down the long ribbon of sidewalk.

"I'm sorry I threw a shoe at you," said Marty as quickly as possible to get it out of the way.

Line dumped Mittens on the ground and hugged Marty. "It was my fault, I suppose," she said.

"No," said Marty. "I didn't have to get so mad." It felt good to take the blame. The whole thing was washed away. "Where have you guys been?"

"We went over to Sundeens'," said Paul. "They were making a play, with a stage and a curtain and everything."

"They needed us," said Line. "But it isn't a very good play. It's kind of silly."

"When is it going to be?" asked Marty.

"Tomorrow," said Line. "You can come."

"Did Mother let you go?" Usually, they were not supposed to cross roads, but now that everyone went back and forth to school, it was harder for Mother to insist that they stay on their own block. She did like to know where they were, though.

"Yeah," said Paul, lazily. The sun was going down behind his head way too soon, thought Marty. Summer was over.

"I saved your shoe for you," said Line conspiratorially. "I didn't want you to get in trouble for that too."

"Yeah," sighed Marty. It was one of her new school shoes. She must have been blind mad! "Thank you."

The first two weeks of school were initiation for the few high school freshmen. The freshmen, dressed in burlap sacks and silly green hats, sang whenever the seniors told them to, "How green I is, how green I are, nobody knows how green I be." They carried the seniors' books, walking behind them, and one poor soul had to trace his foot in chalk, one behind the other, around the block of school sidewalks. Next year Ellie would be a freshman and have to do these things.

The school nurse arrived and set up a vaccination clinic in the basement. The kids dreaded it, but there was nothing they could do. They were all to be given diphtheria shots. The nurse was a tall, tough woman with a long man's face. She wore a blue jacket with an official insignia on it and a stiff white nurse's cap. Her voice was low and commanding, as if she was in the army. She inspired fear in all of the kids, especially in Marty.

When the third and fourth grade went downstairs, Marty stood in the middle of the line. If she were in front, she could get it over quickly, but Marty was too fearful for that. Michael was up at the head of the line, and so was Melody. Melody never seemed to be afraid of anything.

Marty stood just behind Eileen, quaking in her shoes. They had to take off their sweaters, or roll up their sleeves and present the nurse with their skinny arm so she could prick it with a needle. The principal, Mr. Newman, stood beside her, smiling kindly, and giving each kid a candy sucker, wrapped in plastic.

When it was her turn, Marty turned her head away so she didn't have to see the needle, or when they were going to stick it into her arm, or any blood. A sharp prick, a cotton swab with alcohol, a bandage, and a sucker. It wasn't so bad, Marty thought afterwards, sucking on the yellow, lemon-flavored candy. She trooped back upstairs to class with the rest of the kids.

"All right class, quiet down," said Mrs. Soderberg from the front of the room. "Fourth grade, let's run through your poems. Michael." They would recite in front of the school judges first, then the best students would go on to the County speech contest. "Now each of you, put some feeling into it. I would love to have one of my students win the contest!"

Michael stood up first, in his neat shirt. He was wearing glasses too. The year before the school nurse decided both he and Marty needed glasses so they could see the blackboard. They were both developing a squint, a furrowed forehead that might become permanent.

"The Highwayman," said Michael, "by Alfred Noyes." Mrs. Soderberg gave the poem to Michael because it was long and he could memorize it better than anyone else.

Marty listened, focusing on Michael as he used the rhymes to remember. But it was hard not to smile as he recited the passionate words in his conscientious, sing song way. Her stomach felt a little queasy.

"For the road lay bare in the moonlight,
"Blank and bare in the moonlight,
"And the blood in her veins, in the moonlight, throbbed to her love's refrain."

He finished the long poem and waited, relieved to have gotten through it.

"Very good, Michael," said Mrs. Soderberg, her pearls clicking against the buttons on her dress. "But remember, we are talking about life and death. Bess has warned the Highwayman, but lost her life. He is terribly angry. Imagine you are the Highwayman. How would you feel?" The kids in their seats smirked at each other, trying to imagine Michael on a horse brandishing a rapier, then dead on the highway with a bunch of lace at his throat.

Marty watched Michael. "Yes, Ma'am," he said, but Marty doubted that he would recite much differently the next time. He was just trying to please her.

"Okay," Mrs. Soderberg said, "Marty."

Marty went to the front, putting her hands at her sides and her feet together, but standing up made her feel dizzy.

"'A Mortifying Mistake,' by Anna Maria Pratt," said Marty, softly.

"A little louder," said Mrs. Soderberg from her desk at the front of the room.

Marty tried: "I studied my tables over and over,
"And backward and forward too,
"But I couldn't remember six times nine ..."

Marty was dizzy and prickles rose to her face. She felt cold and the life drained out of her face all of a sudden. She sank to the floor. Michael stood up and came toward her, but Marty didn't move.

"Come on," said Michael, gently. "Come and sit down." He took her hands. Marty shook her head, which felt like bees were buzzing in it, and struggled back to her desk. Mrs. Soderberg came over and felt her forehead.

"You're as white as a sheet," she said. "Lean down and put your head between your legs. The blood will come back."

Marty felt the eyes of the class on her, but she was too weak to protest. She leaned down and put her head on her lap.

"All right class," said Mrs. Soderberg. "I'll be right back." In a moment she returned with Mr. Newman, who took Marty by the shoulders and helped her into his office.

Marty shook her head, as if to get rid of the flies buzzing around it. She was surprised to find herself sitting on a chair in his office, but she felt better.

"Has this ever happened to you before?" asked Mr. Newman. He had a kind face, graying hair and wore a dark suit. "Have you ever fainted before?"

Marty didn't know what it was. She had never felt her head to be dizzy and woozy or lost control of her stomach and limbs.

"I'll bet it was those shots," said Mr. Newman. "Scared the daylights out of you, didn't they. Just sit here for a minute."

Marty felt a stab of fear when the school nurse appeared in the doorway with him.

"Silly kid," said the brusque, manly voice of the nurse. "Scared of a little blood." She felt Marty's forehead with a thin, cold hand. "You'll be fine. No whimpering now." She talked to Mr. Newman as if Marty weren't there. "There's always one in the bunch. A scaredy cat who faints at the sight of blood. Maybe she just wants attention."

Marty looked up at the sharp, hard face, stricken. The last thing she wanted was attention! She wanted the nurse to go away and leave her alone. But she didn't dare say anything.

Mr. Newman went back to the classroom and got Marty's coat, and asked Ardell, one of the high school boys with a car, to take her home. Marty felt humiliated. Things were not going well. Mother and Dad, who were getting ready to go to Ladies' Aid, told her to go up to her room and take a nap.

Marty had been branded a fainter, scared of the sight of blood. She would never make a nurse, or a doctor. But that was okay, because she would rather be a poet, she thought as she slipped into sleep.

Sunday morning Marty heard Dad getting out of bed very early to go and study his sermon for the day. Marty was wakeful, listening as Dad made coffee in the kitchen. She wrapped a blanket around herself and went downstairs. Dad stood in the kitchen, slicing himself a thick piece of the whole wheat bread Mother made.

"Good morning," said Dad, putting his hand on Marty's sleepy head and tousling her hair. "I was just thinking about whether it was cold enough to start up the furnace."

Marty looked up at him. He looked so strong and warm and loving in his old khaki pants and a faded sweatshirt.

"Should I slice one for you?" Dad asked.

"Please," said Marty shyly. "Thank you." Dad put two pieces of toast in the toaster and caught Marty and her blanket up in both arms, lifting her so she sat on the table level beside him.

"And what woke you up so early, my girl?" asked Dad, taking a sip of the hot dark coffee.

"Oh, nothing," said Marty. "I wanted to see the sun rise, like in the poem."

"Which poem?" asked Dad.

"Something about 'I stood upon the hills, when heaven's wide arch was glorious with the sun's returning march.' I remember it because of the rhyme," said Marty. "It was in one of your college books."

"Ahhh," said Dad. "You know, I wanted to be a poet once. I'll show you my poetry notebook some time." The toast popped up and a rich, honey sweet smell rose in the air. Dad put the thick slices on plates. "Here you go," he said, handing one to Marty. "I can't understand how anyone would want to put margarine on this wonderful toast!" They sliced pieces off the cube of butter and let them melt on the toast.

Mother had bought margarine in a package with a little dot of red dye in one corner because according to the magazines it was healthier and probably cheaper. Marty and Line took turns squishing the bit of red dye around in the plastic to color the margarine. But after buying it once, Dad put his foot down. "Life is too short to eat this stuff!" he said. They were all glad. None of them liked the taste of margarine. Mother tried making Adele Davis "better butter," a mixture of butter and oil, but Dad was unconvinced. He liked the taste of butter. "I'd rather die early," he insisted.

"Well, I better go study," Dad said, taking his cup of Norwegian gasoline with him. He paused in the doorway as he left, saying to Marty, "You know why I gave up poetry? I met your Mother and began to live it!"

Marty smiled. She climbed off the table and adjusted the blanket around her shoulders. Taking her plate, she slipped out onto the front porch. The screens were too thick to see through, so she went out on the steps, where the view across the railroad tracks and the fields to the horizon was uninterrupted. She didn't have her glasses on yet, but she didn't need them to feel the air or hear the birds beginning to wake up.

The toast was no longer warm, but tasted sweet, buttery and yeasty. Marty took small bites, trying to make the toast last. Across the tracks, the fields were dark and stubbly after harvest, but the blue sky was alive.

A train sounded in the distance, its long metallic whistle preceding it. Not stopping, it coursed along in front of Marty to a regular beat. She knew that Line and the others were probably sleeping right through it, but she felt the noise pounding through her. The train was long, and Marty wanted it to be gone! She was afraid she would miss the sun lifting itself over the rim of the horizon.

When the caboose swung along at the end of the train, Marty waved out of habit. She wondered if they saw her, wrapped in a blanket, eating toast on her front steps before the sun came up. The caboose was a blur without her glasses.

And then it happened. All of a sudden the sun cracked the lid the sky kept on the world, a few golden rays straying across into Marty's eyes. Soon it was intense and dark and Marty couldn't look in that direction. Looking at the sun burned holes in the back of your eyes.

Marty thought about Dad's life, wondering if it was poetry. This house full of chaos and kids, this town, the church? None of it was perfect. But Dad loved nature, as they all did. Nothing compared with stepping outdoors and being immersed in the weather, being one of God's creatures in the sun and wind and rain. Marty couldn't remember the rest of the poem, but she thought it was something like "if thou wouldst have a lesson to keep thy heart from fainting, go to the woods and hills". She knew what fainting felt like now, Marty reflected.

The sun's march across the fields steadily warmed Marty. In a few days night and day would be the same length, the equinox. Dad would certainly be starting the furnace in the mornings. The pigeons and mourning doves coo-ed in the dovecote across the street, "too hoo, toooo cu cu." The sweet toast, with its lovely butter, was gone. This might be poetry, she thought, but when would she know? She was too young to know. There was too much future and too much world ahead of her.

10

Line carried the picnic plates out to the table near the brick fireplace Dad had built in the backyard. It was chilly and the sun was very low in the sky, but Mother and Dad agreed they could squeeze one more picnic out of the short fall days.

"Wait," called Marty, running after her. "I want to put the tablecloth on." She spread a red and white oilcloth, patterned like a railway man's pocket handkerchief, over the table. Line put down the bright colored plastic plates. They were grooved so potato salad and baked beans didn't have to touch each other and there was room for a hot dog. The ingenious table was made from a tree stump cut just where the tree branched. Three spreading branches were sawed off to hold planks for a table. Smaller stumps made seats.

Paul combed the backyard for twigs. Line saw him lay a large stick against a tree and jump on it with his entire weight to break it, a serious look on his face. As she watched, he built a tent of twigs over crumpled paper in the base of the brick fireplace. Striking a match, Paul lit it and began to carefully add sticks to the flame.

Line stood next to Paul watching the flames, smoke rising all around her. Dad looked proud as he whittled the ends of willow sticks to sharp points. Paul could make a fire by himself now. He was becoming a regular Boy Scout. Paul wouldn't leave the fire, tending it, poking the logs together as they became glowing coals.

Ellie brought potato salad out to the table and Mother a tray of pickles, mustard, catsup and Bisquick dough. While Dad threaded wieners onto sticks, Mother wrapped a strip of Bisquick dough around them and pinched it together. The dough would cook over the fire while the hot dog was roasting.

Line didn't want to burn her hot dog, so she waited until there was more room over the crackling fire. The rest of the family stood around the fireplace with their sticks, trying to find the place over the coals that would roast their hot dog just right. The smell of wood smoke and burning meat hung around them in the twilight.

Line singed her fingers as she tried to keep the Bisquick wrapping from falling into the fire. She bit into the juicy meat. "Why does food always taste so much better outdoors?" she asked.

"It's because we come from cave men," said Marty, who always had an answer. "We just like being around a fire!"

"I sure do," said Paul.

Mother went in and got the tray that held marshmallows, chocolate Hershey bars and graham crackers. Paul put his marshmallow right in the fire and it burnt to a cinder, but Line roasted hers lightly and pulled off the light brown skin. Licking the hot sugar off her sticky fingers, she put the lump of marshmallow that remained back in the fire to brown.

The sky darkened and Dad turned on the light in the garage, so they could see better. He plugged in the radio and tuned it to the serial they listened to, which came on at 6:30 p.m. Why not? Electricity was everywhere.

One Man's Family dramatized the problems of rich people, but it made Line think of their own family, having a picnic out in the dark by the fire, and of the Ellingsons, who had just moved into a new ranch house with three adopted kids. How strange to have a brand new family all at once! Bruce was in Line's class, Julie two years younger, and Craig in first grade, almost matching the ages of the Mikkelson kids.

Line made a little sandwich of graham crackers and four small squares of chocolate. She roasted another marshmallow to melt the chocolate in the sandwich. It was called a S'more, because you always wanted some more! She stood shivering next to Marty near the fireplace, close to Ellie on the other side, their fronts warm and their backs growing cold. It was Friday night and there was nothing to worry about. Line was glad.

"Time to go in," said Mother, finally. "Everyone take something with you."

But Paul burned a stick in the fire. Pulling it out, he drew a sweeping, glowing shape against the night sky.

"It's like sky writing!" said Line. "I want to try." And she seized a stick and let its tip become a bright red coal. Pulling it out she watched the afterglow as it slashed across the dark.

Mother laughed. She and Ellie carried in the trays, leaving Sparky and the gang to their games, while Dad stayed to make sure the fire was out when they left.

That year Line escaped Mrs. Soderberg, who didn't like her, and went into Mrs. Tannenbaum's room. Clyde was still in her class, and so was Miss Perfect Carol, the daughter of county workers, with her new sweaters and perfect hair. But Line's ear was particularly tuned to Bruce, the new kid who was adopted by the Ellingsons.

Bruce, Julie and Craig came from the Lutheran orphanage where Mother worked long ago when Ellie was a baby. Just before school started, Adrian Ellingson, who ran the grocery store downtown, and his wife Edna, a nurse, adopted them all so they could stay together. The rumor floated around school that Bruce had caused so much trouble in a foster home that the three were sent back to the orphanage.

"Why did he cause trouble?" Line asked Mother, who was browning hamburger for dinner. The Ellingsons were important members of their church and Mother must know the whole story.

"I don't know," said Mother. "Unless you have walked in someone else's shoes, you don't really know how they feel."

"I'd like to talk to Bruce, but he doesn't say much," Line said.

"You help those kids get to know people," Mother said, a little gruffly, as if she cared a great deal. "They've a tough row to hoe, and you have it easy, Line. If anyone can reach out to those kids, you can."

Mother arranged with Mrs. Ellingson that Line, Paul and Marty go over to the Ellingsons on Saturday afternoon. Michael, Marty's squinty-eyed boyfriend who lived nearby, was already there. The living room was covered with acres of new carpet. A long low sofa and beautiful drapes made it look like the photographs of houses in magazines. Mrs. Ellingson ushered them into the kitchen and served cherry Kool-aid and Toll House cookies.

No one seemed very comfortable or knew what to say when Mrs. Ellingson left them to themselves. Drinking Kool-aid around the table, all six kids were quiet. Marty saved the day. "Is that a television set in the living room?" she asked rather timidly.

"Yeah," said Bruce. Bruce was dark-skinned, with his hair cut very close to his head. He looked wary, Line thought. His faced was closed, and his glance shifted around as if he expected something bad to happen.

"Do you watch *Disneyland?*" Marty asked. The kids knew about the program because their neighbors, Alfred and Alma Christianson, asked them over to their house to see it on their new television.

"We watched *The Ed Sullivan Show*," said Julie. "That's the only show we've watched." She was as tall as Marty, with thick blonde hair which came to a little widow's peak on her dark forehead and was pulled to the side with a barrett. Her direct, impassive gaze seemed to say, 'Do what you will. You can't hurt me.'

The little boys, Paul and Craig, started burping, and giggling. Craig was smaller than Paul, dark-skinned with his hair shaved close to his head. He was wearing a new cowboy shirt and a new pair of jeans, while Paul's clothes looked worn and his shirt was torn at the elbow. Sticky Kool-aid spilled on their clothes. Why did Paul act like such a little kid, wondered Line. When he was with her, he was much more grown up.

"Want to see my erector set?" asked Craig.

"Sure," said Paul, and they ambled off down a long hall to where the bedrooms must be.

Line could see that Bruce and Julie didn't know they were the hosts, or didn't know what hosts were supposed to do, so she passed the plate of Toll House cookies.

"These are my favorite. Did your Mom make these?" she asked. "Or did you make them?"

"I helped," said Julie. "She measured things and I ran the mixer."

Line wanted to ask if Julie and Bruce called Mrs. Ellingson 'Mom', but she knew that impolite questions didn't tell you what you wanted to know. It was better to watch people and learn from their actions, at least until you knew them better.

"Our Mom said you have a good place to rollerskate," said Line, "So we brought our skates." She leaned forward and fingered the skate key she was wearing on a cord around her neck. Their aluminum skates clamped onto their shoes in the front and were strapped around the ankle. In the summer, they skated up and down the new concrete sidewalk alongside their house.

"Are you guys part Indian?" asked Michael, pushing up his glasses with his finger in his usual serious way.

"Part Indian!" said Line, her ears perking up. That might fill in some of the puzzle of these adopted kids. "How exciting! I'd like to be part Indian."

"You wouldn't like it if you were," said Bruce. "Our Dad's father was an Indian. Everyone thinks Indians are either lazy, or stupid, or drunk."

"Not Tonto," said Marty. "Tonto is smarter than anyone."

"I just wanted to know," said Michael.

"No one is going to think bad things of you here," said Line. "The whole school sticks together. We had the best basketball team last year." She turned to Marty. "But what are we going to do without Gary Breiland? He was the best."

"Bruce can really throw a pitch," said Michael, squinting behind his glasses. "A lot better than me."

"Too short for basketball, though," said Bruce.

"Dad was short," said Line, "and he played in high school. He was a forward. You never know."

"May I have another cookie," asked Marty, her hand poised above the plate. They were so good, as good as Mother's. "I love chocolate chips." As no one objected, she took one.

"Down the basement is where we can skate," said Julie. "There's nothing down there. They haven't finished it off yet."

Line and Marty, Michael, Bruce and Julie trooped down the stairs to the basement, a big space of cement that you could rollerskate all over.

"Where's the furnace?" asked Marty, strapping on her skates.

Line lent the skate key, so Marty could tighten the clamp. Michael and the Ellingsons knelt down to put on skates also.

"It's electric, I think," said Bruce. "In there. What do you care?" He came up and tagged her and ran away. "You're it!"

Flushed, Marty followed him, but she couldn't catch him. Line steadied herself at one of the pillars spread throughout the room which held up the upstairs. "Girls against the boys," said Line. Three girls could match two older boys. They were all flushed and excited when Mrs. Ellingson came down to the basement to tell them Mother had called them home.

That year many people began to get television. If the Mikkelsons were invited to someone's farmhouse for Sunday dinner, everyone ended up sprawled around the living room on couches and hassocks, the kids on the floor, watching a quiz show or *The Ed Sullivan Show*. Dad sat with them, trying to talk to the men of the family. In the kitchen, Mother gathered with the other women, talking and washing up.

At school, Line was invited to join the Young Citizens League. YCL met after school, so country kids like Clyde couldn't stay. Farm kids took the bus home and did chores, but several town kids were at the meeting, including Bruce, Carol, Ellie and Helen Jorre. Mr. Newman, the principal, advised. The president, Linda Halvorson, was an eighth grader whom Line had never noticed.

Linda made an authoritative president, standing up in her red cardigan sweater and calling the first meeting of the year to order. "I will be running the meeting by *Robert's Rules of Order*, so we can learn parliamentary procedure," she said. "There will be time for discussion, and then motions will be made and seconded, and we will vote on them. If you haven't been here before, listen and see how we do it."

Mr. Newman nodded to her, as if to say, 'very good!'

Linda then called the role and asked Helen Jorre, the secretary, to read the minutes of the previous meeting. Line wasn't sure what they were trying to do, except earn money for school supplies and books, and promote school spirit.

A solemn eighth grader named Mark Amundsen read the Treasurer's Report from a little bound book full of figures. The leftover money from last year, $1.59, was carried forward.

"Is there any unfinished business?" Linda intoned. "If there is no unfinished business, the floor is open for new business." She stood waiting. People seemed to relax and shift in their seats, looking around. The club was for fifth through eighth graders. Its most active members had gone on to high school. Line watched, fascinated, as the remaining club members seemed uncertain as to who should speak and what about.

At last Ellie, flushed and intimidated by the presence of her bright sister, said "I think we should have a pep club for basketball games. We could wear the school colors and sit together."

"I second the motion," said Helen, immediately.

"No one has made a motion!" said Linda from the front of the room. "This is just the discussion part! The floor is open. What do the rest of you think?"

Helen bristled a little, but didn't say anything more. No one could really argue with the idea of having a pep club.

Line raised her hand and Linda called on her. Line could sense Mr. Newman watching her. "I just wanted to ask, what is a citizen? I mean, what does it mean to be a citizen here, in our school?"

Linda looked blank. She turned to Mr. Newman. "Could you answer that, Mr. Newman?"

Eyes followed Mr. Newman as he stood up in the back of the room. "Thank you, Linda. And thank you, Line, for asking. I think you are asking what the purpose of this group is. That is a fair question."

Line relaxed. He didn't think she was silly. How wonderful to hear that it was possible to discuss something she wanted to know about!

Mr. Newman went on. "If you were born in the United States, you are a citizen of this country. In that sense, you have all the rights the *Constitution's Bill of Rights* asserted for its citizens, but also all of the responsibilities. It won't be long before you are voting, when you turn 21. Your vote is your voice. Now, I know you are learning these things in your classes, but here we are putting them into practice.

"Parliamentary procedure, which is used by every group in the world, allows everyone to speak, and resolutions to be made based on what has been discussed."

He turned to Line and spoke directly to her. "Now, Line, you are wondering what it means to be a citizen in your home town. Participating in meetings is an act of citizenship, learning what your fellow citizens think. Some of them have different experiences than you, and believe the things we need to accomplish are different than what you think. Every opinion is valuable."

"But this is such a small place," said Line. "Don't citizens do things that are important out in the world?" It was what she had been thinking for a long time. She was tired of playing and pretending, practicing for being an adult.

"Believe me, Line," said Mr. Newman. "This is the world. North Dakota has been making history since it became a state in 1889. Even with our small population, the Non-Partisan League accomplished a great deal against corruption, which carries down to this day. This isn't the place for a history lesson, but I want you kids to understand that you, each of you, are citizens, and everything you do contributes to being a good one or a bad one. What you do on the playground, is citizenship.

"I know this isn't what you want to hear, Line. You want to take on some big cause and do something about it. We can do that too. We can study what is going on in congress and write letters to our congressmen. But we can also stand up for our school and our town, and expect the highest performance from our friends. And that leads to pep clubs!

"Now, I've been talking too long. This is your club. We form clubs because groups have more effect than one person by themselves. So I welcome you all. Say what you want to say, and let's get things done! I trust

Linda here to direct you all towards action. Thank you." Mr. Newman sat down.

Line felt deflated. It was always the same. People were always telling her to wait, to think, that her time would come. But she did see that groups might be useful. She realized that she wanted to be president. She would keep her mouth shut, and learn how Linda did it. And that was all she could do right now.

Linda, from the front of the room said, "Okay, we are open to discussion about having a pep club. Is there further discussion?"

Helen and Ellie smiled at each other, vindicated by Mr. Newman's words.

Mark, the treasurer, stood up. "We might need money to buy pom poms, or something. We need to make some money."

Line was full of ideas and could hardly keep her mouth shut. "I like the idea of buying library books that we don't have. Maybe we should earn money for that."

"That's not the question on the table," said Linda. "We are discussing the pep club right now. In fact, I am going to name Helen, Ellie and Mark as a committee to research the pep club. Next month you can come back with a report on what we need and any ideas you have on how to make some money."

Next month seemed a long way off to Line.

"Can I have a motion from the floor regarding the pep club?" asked Linda.

Ellie, a club member for three years already, said "I move that we have a pep club this year, and that a committee be appointed to research it."

"I second it," said Mark.

"It has been moved and seconded that we have a pep club," said Linda. "All in favor say Aye!"

A chorus of "aye!" came from the fourteen kids who sat in the desks in the seventh and eighth grade classroom. Line looked around. She and Bruce and Carol were the only new members. Bruce sat still, looking down, doodling with his pencil. Carol's mother and father drove ten miles every day to the capital of Traill County and worked in the courthouse. Carol was sure that she was the most important girl in their class. In fact, Line didn't really like any of the girls in her class. She liked Clyde and Bruce. Her best friend was her sister, Marty.

Linda said, "Okay, more new business. Like library books. Do we want to do that again this year?" The year before, the club contributed $6.00 to a library fund, which helped purchase new atlases for each room.

Carol now stood up, in her flared green skirt with its fashionable cinch belt. "I think we should sell cookies at lunch. Everyone has an allowance, and people would really like a homemade cookie after lunch." Line realized she should have waited to talk. Now Carol's ideas seemed more sensible than hers.

People seemed to like Carol's idea. Line knew that not everyone had an allowance, however.

"We could make them ourselves, or our mothers could make them," Carol went on.

"Let's just sell them on Fridays," said Helen. "Then people would know when to bring in their allowance. It would be too hard to do it every day."

"I agree," said Carol, sitting down.

Linda seemed a little uncertain as to what to do with all these ideas, but Mr. Newman stood up. "May I make a suggestion, Linda?"

Linda nodded, and Mr. Newman went on. "Brainstorming is a technique for helping people decide things. People put all the ideas that come from a group on the blackboard and then prioritize and discuss them. Now, you have a good idea for making money. Why don't you set a committee to get this going. Next month we could have a brainstorming session about what the group wants to accomplish this year."

Linda brightened. "Thank you, Mr. Newman," she said. "Carol, and Line, why don't you be on the cookie committee, and how about Becky, who has been on committees before." Becky was a popular seventh grader, jolly and smart. Line liked the idea of working with her, but Carol? Line realized she would have to make the effort.

"May I have a motion from the floor that we sell cookies on Fridays?" said Linda.

Becky moved and Carol seconded, and that was the end of it.

"Next month," said Linda, "everyone bring ideas about what we should do this year and we'll try brainstorming, like Mr. Newman says. Meeting adjourned!"

At dinner that night, Line repeated what Mr. Newman said about citizenship. She couldn't say how she had fumbled her attempt to participate in YCL, as they were not allowed to complain at mealtimes, but she would tell Marty later. Marty knew how she felt about Miss Perfect Carol.

"This is just right for you," said Mother to Line. "You're used to being the big cheese at home, but you need to learn how meetings work, and how everyone contributes!" She looked over at Paul. A little pile of green beans sat on his plate, uneaten. "Paul, finish your vegetables."

When Ellie's turn to talk came, she agreed that Mr. Newman gave them great reasons to be in Young Citizens League. "He liked our idea about a pep club," she said. Line suspected that Ellie and Helen wanted to be cheerleaders, and that starting the pep club would lead in that direction.

"Mr. Newman has a good head on his shoulders," said Dad. "You kids are really lucky. When I was going to school, there wasn't money for anything. I want to tell you a story, though." Dad pushed back his empty plate. "When I was in high school, I started wanting to go to college. An insurance man told my parents that life insurance would cost the same as a pack of cigarettes per day, and that you could borrow against the insurance money to pay for college.

"I got it into my head that if I didn't smoke, I could go to college!" Dad said. "My folks didn't have the money for life insurance or cigarettes, or college, for that matter. But when I saw my friends smoking, I refused, and saved the money. And it did help a lot!"

Dad seemed to be looking toward Ellie, whose face grew pinched and sullen under his gaze. "I don't want to see you kids ever spend money on cigarettes. You might as well take a dollar bill and light it!"

"Don't worry, Dad," Line said. "I hate the smell, and it looks like a dirty habit."

"It is a habit," said Dad, "hard to quit. And so many people waste their time and money on it." Line suspected that Helen and Ellie had tried smoking, trying to be like the high school girls they would join next year. But Dad didn't need to fear that she would smoke. It looked ridiculous.

"But what about all the poor kids in Africa? And orphans and poor kids in cities?" Line said. Everywhere she looked she was reminded that many kids didn't have the food and shelter that she did. "Why should we be spending our money on a pep club, when so many kids don't have things to eat or books for school?"

Mother smiled at Line's bright, earnest face. "You and Ellie are both right, Line," she said. "It would be shameful not to enjoy the wonderful life God has given us. We celebrate it with good food and nice clothes and our neighbors. But we also give part of our resources to help those who don't have what we do. That's the idea of the tithe. Ten percent of all you earn goes to the church, which uses it to help others."

"You have an allowance. You can choose what to do with it," Dad said. "Put some of it in the offering plate on Sundays!"

Mother leaned over and hugged Paul, who had finally managed to get his green beans down. "That's my boy, a member of the clean plate club!"

Line sighed. She was so far from grown up, and her little allowance of 10 cents a week didn't go very far. She was impatient, and people wanted her to slow down. She resolved to find some way of helping though. She wondered what Bruce, so recently an orphan, thought.

Once again, it was Marty who had ideas for Line. "There's a part of the United Nations that is for kids all over the world," she told Line. "It's called UNICEF. I saw in the *Weekly Reader* that some kids collected money on Halloween instead of treats, and sent it to UNICEF. I'll show it to you."

"What a great idea!" said Line. Halloween was over, but there was no reason some of the money from the cookie sales couldn't go to UNICEF. "Thank you, Marty! I can't wait for the next YCL meeting!"

11

Paul was mesmerized by *Davy Crockett* on television. The Mikkelson kids went to Alfred and Alma's house next door to watch each of the three episodes on Sunday nights. Alfred, an elfish old man with a red nose, whispy white hair and a wry sense of humor, loved the kids. He and his wife had left the hard work on their farm to their children and moved into town.

The television was in the dining room and the kids sat on the floor, up close, to watch it. Alma provided cookies and lemonade. Afterward, they put on their coats and rushed out into the cold, snowy night to their own warm house, spellbound by the heroism of the woodsy, plain-speaking freedom fighter and congressman.

Paul woke up with pictures of Fess Parker in a coonskin hat floating across his eyes. In school, his friend Davy Sundeen was just as excited by the story as Paul. Davy's father bought him a coonskin cap, and he wouldn't take it off until Miss Onstead insisted that even David Crockett courteously took his hat off around women.

"Do you think he was killed at the Alamo?" asked Paul. The question bothered him.

"Sure he was killed," said Davy. "But he got a lot of Mexicans before he died."

"It didn't show him getting killed," said Paul.

"He was," said Davy. "My brother said so." Davy's older brothers were serious boys who were already fishers and hunters, taught by their avid father.

"I don't think he died," said Paul. "I think he got away, and wandered out into the woods and was never seen again. 'Raised in the woods so he knew every tree.' " The ballad of Davy Crockett, sung by Fess Parker, was so infectious Paul already knew most of it.

After school, Paul asked Line whether she thought Davy Crockett died. "Davy Sundeen said he did."

"Let's look it up," said Line. She went over to the *The Book of Knowledge* set Mother and Dad bought from a traveling salesman. It was full of pictures, history, things to do, stories and poems. It wasn't in any sort of order and the pictures were old and black and white. It was usually more fun to look at magazines, but the kids used *The Book of Knowledge* when they needed to write a report for school or were trying to figure out what an insect or flower was called.

Line pulled out the index. "You have to look under his last name," she said. She found Crockett, David. "It doesn't refer us to anything. It just tells about him right here." Placing her finger on the text, she read to Paul, "He served in the war between Texas and Mexico and was one of the six survivors in the defense of the Alamo. With the other five he was shot after the Alamo fell."

Paul hunched his shoulders around his arms, not saying anything. Line looked up at him. "That terrible Santa Anna," she said, naming the Mexican commander who took the Alamo, the villain of the story. "He killed one of the best."

"Yup," said Paul, completely unable to separate the legend from the historical figure. He didn't expect Dad to buy him a coonskin hat, but he vowed to redouble his efforts to learn tracking and slipping through the woods without making any noise that summer.

Mother and Dad brought home "The Ballad of Davy Crockett" on a record from Grand Forks. Paul put the record on the little 78 rpm record player day after day, until at last Marty begged him to stop. "I know that song by heart," Marty said. "It plays in my head when I wake up! Do you really need to keep playing it?"

"No," said Paul sheepishly. "You're right. I don't need to." He turned the record player off.

"Come and help us choose the color for the new car," said Marty, dragging Paul off to look at the color brochure Dad brought home. The car was to be a two-tone Studebaker Conestoga station wagon. The family had never had a new car before. The kids stared at the printed pictures showing the sleek-looking new car. When all the opinions were in, Mother and Dad cast the deciding vote for a grey car with maroon trim along the windows. Dad ordered it from Indiana.

"I bet the car company made up the color maroon," said Line. It was a dark purplish red, not in the big box of 56 crayola colors.

"A conestoga wagon was a kind of covered wagon," Dad said. "I reckon it will be a good car for hauling all of us around. You can come with me, Paul, when I go pick it up in Grand Forks. We'll drive the old car in and come out with a new one!"

Paul couldn't wait. "When will it come?"

"Oh, it will be a couple of months yet," said Dad. "About the time school is out."

Paul must settle down and wait. When he told Davy about it at school, Davy said, "Why doesn't he just get a Ford?" Ford and Chevy were the two main car manufacturers, advertised in all of the magazines.

Paul didn't know why Dad wanted a Studebaker. When he and Dad went out to burn trash in the burning barrel in the alley near the garage, he asked.

"We don't have to do everything everyone else does," said Dad. "Your grandfather thinks Studebaker is a great car manufacturer and he owned cars long before other people did. He has a knack for picking good ones. The old Ford we're driving now came from him. The Studebaker people have crafted the Conestoga very well. It will be good for all the driving I do."

Paul thought of Grandpa Mikkelson, who almost never spoke. He was quite deaf, so he couldn't hear what the kids said. He sat reading most days, or he worked in the garden. He liked playing Chinese checkers with the kids, his thick, worn carpenter's fingers moving the marbles slowly across the board.

"How did Grandpa tell you?" Paul wondered. He pushed grapefruit skins in the burning barrel about with a stick. Trash must be burned every few days, but Paul didn't mind. He loved watching different things burn: paper, chicken bones, bits of plastic.

"We write letters!" said Dad. "But there is another reason too. Mr. Arneson's uncle has a Studebaker dealership in Grand Forks. So of course I'm going to buy a car from someone I know! Helps me, helps our friends."

The snow was beginning to melt, leaving dirty ridges and slushy places where car tracks drove up the alley. "You are getting pretty tall, Paul," said Dad, measuring him against the rusty barrel. "We're going to have to see about that leg of yours again soon."

Paul nodded. His shoes were starting to pinch again, and his brace wasn't fitting. "The brace is getting too small," he said, mournfully. There was something else he was worried about too. His toes were curling up and getting tight. He couldn't put his feet flat on the floor any more, and it was harder to run around and play. It was embarrassing, and he didn't want to tell anyone. He tried to walk lightly on his feet, imagining he was Davy Crockett and every step in the woods counted. Davy would not have complained about pain either.

"Yup," said Dad. "You're growing out of it. We'll drive our new car down to the clinic one of these days and get new ones."

That spring the American Legion bought drums and bugles and Dad agreed to organize all the kids in town into a drum and bugle corps. They would march in the Bryson Memorial Day parade at the end of June.

Practice started as soon as school was out. Dad brought home a couple of silver batons with rubber ends and Marty and Line were out practicing every day. They were awkward at first, but they got a little better as they moved the shiny batons in circles around their arms, twisting their wrists. Ellie was given a snare drum and sticks to practice drumming.

For Paul, Dad produced an old military bugle from a box in one of the closets. It was a simple piece of gold, shiny metal, with only one dent, but it was big compared to little Paul. Paul worked on finding the notes by moving his lips, as Dad showed him, but it wasn't easy.

"There are only five notes," said Dad. "Keep trying. Bring up the air from down in your diaphragm." Dad could play several bugle calls. "The

Boy Scouts use bugles to tell each other when it's meal time and lights out," he told Paul. "It's a good thing for you to learn!"

Dad asked all the town kids to meet in the morning in the road in front of the church steps to learn to march together. There were twenty-five of them, from high schoolers down to the littlest kids. Each of them carried a drum, a bugle, a baton or a flag. Dad formed them up into lines with the little flag bearers in front, then the baton twirlers, then the drums with the buglers bringing up the rear. The sun was bright and warm, and everyone was excited to be out doing something important.

"First we have to learn marching, so just carry your instruments," Dad said. He got them started, saying "Left, right, left, right." When they got to a corner, he explained how the line must wheel around. If they were making a right turn, all the people on the right took tiny steps, while the ones on the left took large ones. They practiced going around the block. "Left, left, left, left," said Dad at every other step. Raggedy lines crept around the corner and then grew straighter as they marched down the street. Paul's feet ached as he lifted them high and put them down.

"Keep it straight, keep the lines straight!" yelled Dad. "The ones on the ends are responsible. Work with them!" He moved the older kids to the ends of the lines, and the smaller ones to the middle. Round and round the block they marched.

"Okay," Dad said, "All the drums, over here. Bugles work on your notes over there with Ed, and batons, let Patsy work with you."

Patsy Ninas was the drum majorette at the head of the parade. A twirler in another school before she came to Bryson, she could throw her baton up in the air and keep twirling it as it fell into her hands. "But I can't always do it when I'm marching," she said soberly. Paul knew Line and Marty wanted to be like her. "Come on girls, don't stop!" she said, her baton flashing in the sunlight. Line's wide smile shone as she turned and twisted.

Ed Sundeen was the leader for the bugles. He taught them "Reveille". "Just say, 'I can't get 'em up, I can't get 'em up, I can't get 'em up in the morning." He laughed. Ed would play "Taps," at the Memorial Day service, but in the parade, the drum and bugle corps would stop and play, or at least pretend to play, "Reveille". Paul blew, but it just sounded like a "honk" to him. He wished he could have a snare drum. It seemed easier. But then it would bump against his leg and it might be worse. He sighed. Every single thing he did was affected by polio.

After they practiced in groups for a while, Dad formed them up again and marched them around the block. The drum majorette gave the direction. If she pointed left with her baton, they went left. When Dad blew his big silver whistle, everyone's eyes must be on Patsy and follow her. Finally, the sun was high overhead and Dad said, "Okay! Time for lunch. See you back here tomorrow morning, bright and early. Try to practice your instrument this afternoon."

Paul sat down on the church steps and let his aching legs rest, the bugle hanging from his fingers. Line and Marty came over. They danced around, excited, throwing their batons and letting them bounce off the rubber ends. Dad and Ellie headed toward home.

"I wonder if that bugle was his brother's," said Marty.

"His brother?" said Paul. He turned the bugle over in his hands.

"Yeah, his younger brother Marshall was killed at the end of the Second World War, in France. I think that bugle came from the war."

"He never talks about it," said Line. "But you know, at Grandma's house there's a photograph of the cemetery where Marshall is buried in France."

Paul didn't know, but the girls had spent more time at Grandma and Grandpa Mikkelson's house than he. "Show me," he said, "the next time we go there."

"I'm glad Dad didn't have to go to the war," said Line.

"It's ten years ago," said Marty. "Ten years since the war ended. Maybe that's why Memorial Day is going to be a big celebration this year."

"I think we have to march a mile out to the cemetery," said Line. She looked at Paul.

"A mile! Well, I guess a mile isn't very far," he said, but he was drooping a little.

"It's twelve blocks," said Marty, pushing plastic glasses up on her sweaty nose with a finger. "I think we did that today! If we march around the block three times, that's a mile."

The new Studebaker station wagon came before Memorial Day. It was a great day for Paul. School was out, so they could all have gone to Grand Forks to get it, but Mother thought it would be fun for Paul to go with Dad. She didn't care about motors or drive shafts, and she doubted that the girls did either.

The automobile dealership in Grand Forks was spanking clean with beautiful, shining cars parked right inside the building. The windows came right down to the sidewalk and the sun flashed in on the bright new paint.

Paul ran his hand along the fender of one of the new cars as he passed. He could smell the new upholstery.

Dad turned the keys to the old black Ford over to Mr. Arneson, who would sell it as a used car. Then they walked all around the new Conestoga station wagon, built in Indiana. Mr. Arneson showed them how to fold down the back seat, so the back became a long flat carrying space. Half of the back door flipped up, and the other half, the tailgate, flipped down.

"This will be great for vacations," said Dad. Paul imagined all of their boxes and luggage, and the four kids spread out in the back with their pillows.

"You can seat three in the front," said Mr. Arneson. He wore a suit and ran his hands through his salt and pepper hair, enthusiastically. "It's got a lot of power and drives very smoothly. You don't have to use high octane fuel. You're going to love it."

At last, Dad finished signing papers for the car and he and Paul got in, sitting on the smooth, shiny seats. Paul's legs stuck out when he pulled himself to the back of the seat. He held his breath as Dad put down the clutch, moving his feet between the brake and the accelerator. Dad's arm muscles moved as he shifted the gears and pulled the big wheel around, gliding into the traffic. It was so exciting! Dad pressed the blinker lever and a light on the outside of the car showed which direction he was going.

Dad smiled widely at Paul. "Don't have to worry about whether people saw my hand signal any more! Don't have to worry about that nasty headlight going out on the old black Ford, or the tires. It's a whole new ballgame!"

Everything smelled new, the carpet and the smooth upholstery. They could see perfectly out the clean windows. Dad drove out of town. When they were heading straight on the long highway home and there was no car up ahead, Dad put his foot down heavy on the accelerator. The car vroomed ahead, passing the telephone poles and the white dashes on the highway at record speed. Paul watched the needle on the speedometer twist up to 90 miles per hour.

Dad grinned rakishly. "Just testing," he said to Paul, as his foot relaxed and they settled down to the more normal speed of 60 mph.

When they turned off the big highway and headed west toward Bryson, Dad asked, "Think they can hear me yet?" He honked the horn experimentally. It made a pleasantly loud noise. At the railroad tracks, Dad started honking steadily in short bursts, his warm smile betraying his pride in the new car. Paul rolled down the window. Heads turned in their direction and Mr. Ellingson came out of his grocery store. Dad waved. Every man at the post office that morning had known Dad was going to get a new car.

At home, Dad didn't drive into the alley where he usually parked. Mother and Line and Marty and Ellie were all out on the front steps watching and waving.

"Hop in!" Dad called to them without getting out of the car. Mother opened the passenger door and Paul slid over. The three girls got in the back, and they all drove out to the gravel pit at the back of town in the warm, spring air. Old dead willows, and a few live ones, their branches tinged green, lined the road. The gravel pit was a swimming hole in the summer and an ice pond for skating in the winter.

"What do you think, Lois," asked Dad when he stopped. Line and Marty hung over the back of the front seat, staring at the controls of the new car, but Paul climbed over Mother and peered out the window.

"Beautiful," said Mother. "This is just what we need, Carl." She slid closer to Dad and hugged him.

"Can we get out?" asked Paul. He loved the pond and could hear frogs croaking. The air was warm, with a green, wet smell. It seemed a shame not to stay and look around.

"I know it's just a car," said Dad, "but it is fun to have something new for a change! Just look at that odometer. 66 miles!"

Mother turned to Paul, "Ten minutes. Don't stay long. It's almost supper time."

Paul raced down to the edge of the pond and looked between the reeds. Tadpoles and newts with rudimentary legs swam close to the surface. The wet sand looked delicious and Paul longed to take off his shoes.

In no time at all, though, Mother called, "Come on, Paul. We're going home."

Paul got into the front seat beside Mother. She stared at the sand on his shoes being transferred to the floor of the new car and sighed, "Oh well, it was nice while it lasted." With a big family, nothing stayed new-looking for long.

Dad laughed, "Don't worry. I'll keep a whisk broom in the car and any time dirt or sand gets in it, we'll just whisk it out."

At home, Marty showed Paul a picture of a Conestoga, a great ship of a wagon with its canvas cover pulled tight. It was so heavy it needed a six-horse team. A man carrying a long rifle walked beside it.

"Do you think that could be Davy Crockett?"

"Maybe," said Marty. "Except he was a scout. He would be up ahead, finding a trail through the woods."

"Yeah, you're right," said Paul. But the new car, because it was called a Conestoga, and because his mind was full of Davy Crockett, became linked to his dreams of being a woodsman in fringed buckskin, carrying a rifle. There might not be many wolves or wildcats left around. The rifle might just be for show. But Paul really wanted to travel through the woods, knowing every tree and animal track.

Practice for the parade continued. The lines marching down the block became a little less ragged and the drums rattled together when Patsy Ninas raised her baton at the front of the little group. Paul carried his bugle by his side, manfully blowing into it when it was their turn to play, but it didn't sound very good to him.

Ellie was proud of her snare drum, which was held on by a white brace over her shoulders. She drummed on anything with her sticks, especially wood, which sounded musical. She held the sticks lightly, as if they were a knife and fork, flicking her wrists and letting them rattle against the lively snare top. Paul envied her. He tried to hold the sticks, but they were longer than his arms!

On Memorial Day, the drum and bugle corps formed up at the church. The marchers wore dark pants and white shirts, but Line and Marty, as baton twirlers, wore white shorts Mother made and red tee-shirts to match the colors of the flag. Alone at the head of the group, Patsy Ninas wore a uniform from her last school with a short skirt and gold braid on its front. Orland Gunderson, from the Veterans of Foreign Wars, passed out red poppies made of crepe paper twisted around a wire to put in people's buttonholes.

Two tall flag bearers followed Patsy, carrying an American flag with its 48 stars and a blue Naval Jack in holsters. The Naval Jack had seen action on a gunboat in the Pacific during World War II, as Mr. Gunderson told Paul and the kids standing near him. "The Star Spangled Banner means a lot to you if you've watched the sun come up during battle," he said. But Paul couldn't imagine a gunboat. A battle in his mind's eye meant Davy Crocket hunkered down beneath the adobe walls of the Alamo, picking off Spaniards with his long rifle Betsy.

Dad helped the kids form up behind the Mayor's sleek black car. He spoke to Patsy and blew his whistle. They all started marching down the street, stepping in time, following the car which went very slowly. "Left," Dad called out. "Left, left, left." He wore a dark suit with a red poppy in his buttonhole as he marched alongside the group. Once they got started, there was no stopping.

Paul, in the first row of bugles behind the drums and baton twirlers, watched Marty and Line, marching as straight as they could, their batons stiff at their sides, their hair shiny in the sun.

At the corner, Patsy raised her baton and pointed to the right. The rows wheeled around, the ones at the right marching in place as the ones at the left made long steps. The corps marched into the main street, parallel to the railroad tracks. Behind him, Paul could hear the snare drums beating a light "rat, tat, rat tat tat," and the booming of the bass drum, carried by the tall Erik Arneson, who beat it with big white padded sticks.

As they passed the gas station, the snare drums took up a more insistent beat and the twirlers started circling their batons under their arms as they marched. People stood along the street watching. When Dad blew his whistle, all of the bugles were raised and the clear sounds of Ed Sundeen's bugle soared out, sounding "Reveille." Paul, the smallest bugle player, hit the two notes that he could, but left the rest to the others.

The drum and bugle corps marched past the main street stores, turned left and marched out across the railroad tracks, following the black car carrying the Mayor and his wife. Behind them came the veterans, marching in whatever uniforms they kept from the wars in which they had fought. Then everyone else from town fell in, walking out to the cemetery behind the tiny parade. Red poppies were everywhere, and so were the flags, red, white and blue, fluttering in the sun. Paul wondered if Mother was walking behind him.

By the time they got out to the cemetery, Paul was limping, his feet aching with the effort of trying to place them flat. The Mayor and his wife got out of their car carryng a wreath. The townspeople formed a group around them. There was nowhere to sit, but Paul sank down on the grass, his stiff leg out in front of him. Everyone else stood respectfully, listening as the Mayor spoke, and then Mr. Gunderson on behalf of the veterans. Paul was miserable, but he could not stand on his leg any longer, brace or no brace.

Linda Halvorson, president of Young Citizens League, came to the front in a white dress and recited the short poem "In Flanders Fields." It was from World War I, a poem about soldiers resting in cemeteries far from home. The poem was the reason everyone wore poppies on Memorial Day. Paul knew the poem already. "In Flanders fields the poppies blow, Between the crosses, row on row, ... If ye break faith with us who die, We shall not sleep, though poppies grow, In Flanders fields." She finished and hands were raised to clap as she walked away, smiling.

Dad gave a short blessing and Ed Sundeen played "Taps" very slowly, the notes blown across the cemetery by the spring wind. Dad's brother, lying in a cemetery in France, would sleep today, remembered, Paul thought. Perhaps French people were putting flowers on his grave.

People wandered through the graves, placing flowers, and talking. Slowly, they began to leave. Dad walked around, patting his corps members on the shoulder, telling them they had done well. The drum and bugle corps wouldn't march back to town. They had done their duty. Erik Arneson left his big bass drum on the grass and came over to Paul, wearing the white webbing which supported it.

"Hey, Paul, the Mayor wants you to ride with him in his car," said Erik.

"Really?" said Paul, getting to his feet.

"Yeah, come on, they're waiting for you." Erik took him by the shoulder and pulled him toward the black car, the only one parked out at the cemetery. Paul looked toward Dad, who nodded encouragingly to him. The Mayor's wife smiled and motioned Paul into the car on the big comfy back seat beside old Mr. Edwards, the oldest of the veterans, who carried a small, ragged American flag.

"I see what war you been fighting," said Mr. Edwards in his thin, crackly voice. "You're a veteran too. Of the polio wars!" He leaned back, his body shaking a little in his ancient khaki uniform. "Yep. You'll beat it. Just like we did."

12

Line dreaded the summer. Everyone in the family was going different directions. Paul must have reconstructive surgery at the clinic in Minnesota and Mother would stay with Aunt Rose nearby. Ellie was going to the Luther League convention in San Francisco. Line and Marty would once again stay with their cousins, and Dad would go back and forth.

Ellie was the first to leave. Long before the sun was up, Arne and Nora Thorson, the Luther League advisors, met the teenagers who were traveling with them in front of the church. They would drive three days to San Francisco, attend the convention and then drive back. Dad had helped Arne plan the trip as enthusiastically as if he were going himself, spreading maps and travel folders from the American Automobile Association on the dining room table for weeks. Arne's travel trailer was packed with a big tent for camping. Arne knew the boys, Erik Arneson and John Halvorson, were good Boy Scouts, and Helen Jorre and Ellie would take care of each other.

Mother and Dad hugged Ellie goodbye reluctantly. She was only 14, but it was an opportunity for her. The convention promised to be inspiring and she would see a little of the world. Even Line felt sad to see her leave. San Francisco was a very long way away.

"Send us some postcards!" begged Line. She was envious, but her turn would come eventually.

"But, where should I send them?" asked Ellie. No one would be home anyway.

"Send them to Grandma Mikkelson's house," said Line. "Right, Dad? Renville, Minnesota."

"Yup," said Dad. "Or else just send them here to Bryson and I'll show the rest of you. That's probably the best."

Hands fluttered in the air as the car and its little trailer drove off. The Arnesons were proud of Erik, and Mrs. Jorre told Mother and Dad how happy she was that Helen had a friend like Ellie. The sun was just coming up when the families went home in the cool, grey morning air. The Mikkelson kids had scrambled out of bed before breakfast to send off the Luther Leaguers.

"You kids better start your own packing," Mother said. "D-day is tomorrow, you know."

They were better prepared than they were the last time Paul went into the hospital, but it didn't make it any easier. The kids delivered Mittens to Julie and Craig Ellingson to take care of while they were away. The garden would have to take care of itself.

"I wish you didn't have to stay in the hospital all summer," said Line to Paul as they packed things into boxes. "It's the best time of the year."

"It's okay," said Paul firmly. "No use worrying about it. I just have to do it." Dad would have said the same, thought Line.

The station wagon felt roomy when they assembled the next day. Line and Marty had their boxes, and Dad and Mother shared a large black leather Gladstone bag. They could put the back seat down and stretch out, if they wanted to, but the first leg of the trip took only half a day. They were in Renville, at Grandma Mikkelson's house, by late afternoon.

The supper table was set when they arrived, painted china plates on a lace cloth spread on the big oak table in a corner of the living room, against lacy window curtains. Line sneaked one of her favorite crab apple pickles from a cut glass dish on the table. They were sweet-smelling, spiced with cloves. Line bit the soft skins and fruit off the cores on the tiny apples. No one made pickles like her Grandmother.

The old-fashioned, heavy clock on the kitchen counter chimed the hour six times. Grandma hurried around the kitchen in a big apron and black lace-up heels, mashing potatoes and turning the meat. She didn't want any help. Line walked around the house, checking on everyone. Mother was looking at the flowers and vegetables in the garden, with its trellis of pink roses at the entrance. Grandpa Mikkelson sat on the sofa in an old plaid flannel shirt, his hearing aid turned up, talking loudly to Dad.

Line found Marty and Paul in the room called the study. "See," Marty whispered. "That's a picture of the cemetery in France where Marshall Mikkelson is buried." Beside it hung a photograph of Marshall, handsome and young-looking in his army uniform.

"How old was he?" asked Paul.

Marty squinted behind her glasses, calculating. "He was younger than Dad, and he died in 1945, so he would have been 23 or 24 maybe." She looked at Line for confirmation.

"I guess so," replied Line uncertainly. Marshall seemed unreal, no more than a photograph, since no one talked about him. "Grandma wants us to come to supper."

At supper, the kids were quiet, eating. Grandma Mikkelson was the only one who talked, to Dad mostly. She talked about the cousins and how they were doing in school, and complained that Hilda, Dad's sister, who worked for the county, wasn't making as much money as she should be. Hilda's husband died, leaving her with the care of her kids, April and Diane, who were almost the same ages as Line and Marty. The girls would stay at Aunt Hilda's house. Line sighed. It was going to be a long summer.

Grandma Mikkelson believed that kids should be seen and not heard, unless asked a question. So the kids cleaned their plates quietly and asked to be excused as soon as was decently possible. The twilight was long in Renville, and they stayed outdoors as long as they could, sitting on the front steps surrounded by sweet-smelling peonies, talking and planning.

Line put Paul in the middle between herself and Marty, not wanting to let him go. When it got dark enough, they saw fireflies.

Mother came out and called them in to bed. Grandpa was already in bed, and there was Grandma, standing on a rag rug in the hall in her nightgown and robe, brushing out the long grey tail which she braided and pinned to the back of her head during the day.

The light from a tiny night-light was low in the bathroom as Line brushed her teeth. The smells were different from what she was used to. And there, in a dish, were Grandpa's teeth, the entire set in pink gums, grinning at her.

Paul was tucked up on the sofa downstairs, but Line and Marty slept in one of the two upstairs rooms. The bed was pushed up under the eaves of the house, smack against the old-fashioned flowered wall-paper.

"You crawl in, Marty," said Line. "I want to be on the outside." The starched white sheets crackled under a light quilt, with lace made by Grandma on the embroidered pillowcases. A tiny open window looked down into the garden. Beside the dresser ancient photographic portraits behind glass in oval frames stared down at them from the walls.

In the morning the early sun laid flat squares on the floor, which moved to their pillows. The heavy clock downstairs chimed the hours reliably, letting Line know time would pass. Things would not stagnate forever. She got up and looked in the drawers of the dresser. Old fashioned games and toys were all she could find, but she got Marty to come and look. "I think this must have been Marshall's room," she whispered.

Mother and Dad slept in the other big, dark room, separated from Line and Marty's room by a closet with calico curtains for doors. A huge oak washstand with a mirror which bent in the middle stood in the corner. Mother and Dad didn't seem in any hurry to get up, so the kids went downstairs.

They ate breakfast cereal as if they were at home, letting Paul have the ancient blue glass dish with a photograph of Shirley Temple stamped on the bottom. Line led them out to the garden where they picked sun-warmed strawberries, eating them one after the other. Grandpa was already out, on his knees, moving stiffly, thinning the carrots with his thick fingers. He liked the kids, giving them tiny carrots to eat after he wiped them off on his pants.

Paul begged Line to lift him up so he could see the sundial from above. When the shadow thrown on the dial by the sun showed it was 9:30 a.m., they raced indoors to see whether the heavy old clock said the same.

Grandma was energetically making potato salad in the kitchen. It was hard to know why she didn't like them, thought Line. But perhaps she was mad at everyone. She was a Norwegian hired girl before marrying Grandpa. In her spare time she made rag rugs and lace and embroidered linens.

Unlike Aunt Rose, who fostered their imaginations with books, colored pencils and drawing paper, Grandma wanted them to learn practical things. As little girls, Line and Marty were given embroidery hoops and pieces of white linen stamped with light blue ink, which they traced to make featherstitches, French knots and daisies with different colors of thread. But they never picked up their needles unless someone insisted they should. Crochet hooks, which in Grandma's fingers produced lengths of white tatting and lace, were completely beyond them!

After lunch they went over to Aunt Hilda's big house. She came from work to talk with Dad and Mother, but then she went back to the courthouse. Her daughters splashed through a sprinkler in the back of the house in their bathing suits with friends. They did not come out and talk to Line and Marty.

Line hid in the back of the station wagon, barricaded behind some boxes and coats. She lay there a long time, waiting for Mother and Dad to finish talking to Hilda and leave. Paul got in the back seat of the car, pretending he didn't know anything about it.

"Where's Line," demanded Mother, as she hugged Marty goodbye.

"I think she's out back with April and Diane," said Marty.

"Go look for her," said Mother. "I'm sure she wants to say goodbye to Paul." Marty ran around the house and was gone a long time.

Dad opened the hood of the new car, checking on the oil. Mother spread out the Minnesota map on her knees. Line listened, her senses acutely tuned.

"Can we have a hamburger at the A & W?" asked Paul, stalling for time.

"Maybe," said Mother, "but I think Aunt Rose will have supper waiting for us. Where on earth is Line?" Her voice was becoming annoyed. Dad stalked around the car, kicking the tires.

At last Marty came back, her clothes wet from the sprinkler. "She can't come," she said evasively. "They're playing a game back there."

Mother got out of the car and stalked around the side of the house. When she came back she said to Dad, "This is ridiculous." She walked to the back of the car and opened the hatch. "Line," she said sharply to the foot Line hadn't been able to hide. "Come out this minute. You can't come with us, and that is all there is to it."

Dad came around and looked, as Line slowly untangled herself from the coats in the back of the car. Mother seemed to be handling the situation, so he allowed an impish grin to come over his face.

"We don't want to stay here," said Line. "They don't really like us."

"Who doesn't like you?" asked Mother.

"April and Diane," said Line mournfully. "They would rather play with their friends."

Mother went and sat in the front seat of the car, drawing Line and Marty with her. "April and Diane are family," said Mother. "They don't have to be your best friends. Dad and I decided the best thing to do this summer would be for you girls to stay here, at least until Ellie gets back." She looked up at Dad, who nodded.

"I am sure all of us would rather be at home," Dad said. "But we have to make the best of it." He grinned at Paul. "I'm sure Paul would rather do something else this summer. That's for sure."

"You are my own girls," said Mother. "I will miss you, but I expect you to be your best selves, help Aunt Hilda, and take care of each other."

"Yes, Mother," said Line. She felt stupid. She was eleven years old, after all. She didn't have to be talked to like a little kid. But she was kind of acting like one.

"Come on, say goodbye to Paul," said Mother.

Marty and Line hugged and kissed Paul goodbye solemnly, and then their parents. Mother put Marty's hand in Line's and closed the car door. "Write to me," she said. "I'll be waiting for your letters." The station wagon pulled out into the road, and the girls waved until they couldn't see it any more.

It was a long month. Renville was bigger than Bryson, but they didn't feel free to explore. Every morning they went to the swimming pool with April and Diane until Aunt Hilda came home for lunch. Line tried to learn how to swim, but she couldn't get comfortable with lifting her head out of the water to breathe properly. In the afternoons, Marty sat in a pile of comic books on April's bed, reading one after another. Line drew pictures of her, and of a shoe, and of the trees and flowers in the back yard. Some days Aunt Hilda gave them each a nickel and they spent it on sugar daddies, carmel suckers which lasted forever. April and Diane came and went, secretive in their own ways, doing what they wanted with no parents at home.

On rainy days, all of them played together in the big enclosed sunporch, putting roll after roll on the player piano, dancing and twirling in the middle of the floor. April and Diane may have had dolls or paper dolls, but they didn't show them to Line or Marty. They didn't have games. Line and Marty just didn't know where they were or what they were doing. So the girls got from one day to the next, trying to be good guests, but not knowing how.

At last, late on Sunday afternoon, the new Conestoga station wagon drove up with Dad and Ellie in it. Aunt Hilda, Diane, April, Marty and Line all piled in and they went over to Grandma's house for supper. More cousins were there, boys older than Line and Marty. Everyone asked Ellie about her trip. She loved it, but she wasn't very good at describing it, and she was very glad to be home. After supper they played ante-i-over the house with a softball. At last Line felt alive, running and yelling and trying not to get tagged by the older boys.

The next morning, Grandpa and Grandma Mikkelson helped them pack into the station wagon once more. Grandma gave them potato salad, sandwiches and pickles to eat on the road. "Don't you kids take any wooden nickels," she said gruffly as she hugged them goodbye.

They drove across the state, to the clinic where Paul was in traction after his surgery. Dad stopped at a Dairy Queen. They sat outside at a picnic table, licking the white, creamy whipped tops of the Dairy Queens while Dad explained what to expect when they got to the hospital.

"You know how Paul's muscles were contracting and he couldn't get his feet flat on the ground? The polio was making the tendons contract, and the muscles couldn't extend properly. So, the reconstructive surgery cut some of the tendons and spliced others to get the muscles to stretch out. Paul has casts on his legs, and they're in traction to keep everything extended. When it all heals, he'll need a lot of physical therapy, but we are also hoping he doesn't have to keep wearing a brace," Dad said. "He's growing so much now, and with luck and hard work …" his words trailed off.

Line wasn't too sure about this. "What do you mean traction?" she asked. "Can we see him?"

"None of this is contagious," said Dad. "So you can all go in and see him, but he is in bed with his legs hung up at a certain angle, and he can't move. You girls will have to understand how quiet he has to be. He's feeling pretty good, though, and he can't wait to see you."

Line felt ashamed of her unhappiness at Aunt Hilda's house. She at least could move around freely and stretch, eat what she wanted to. She couldn't imagine being immobilized.

Paul's face did look wan when they saw him, pale and peaked. They all tip-toed into the room, where he lay flat, his legs in casts, wrapped in slings which hung by pullies and ropes from a frame around the bed. Line wasn't sure she could touch him, he looked so delicate. But Mother motioned them in, smiling. The lines of her face lifted, though she too looked tired and sad.

"How's Davy Crockett," asked Dad, putting his warm hand on Paul's chest.

"I'm okay," said Paul, in a small rough voice.

"You're looking great," said Dad, with a heartiness he tried to transfer to Paul.

"Can I touch your legs?" asked Line. "Do you want us to sign your cast?" She wanted to get past the strangeness of the hospital, talk to the Paul she knew.

"You can touch them," said Paul. He seemed to have retreated back from his usual self, existing in a cave deep within.

"Does it hurt if I do this?" Line reached up to touch his leg, stiff and hard in its cast. "Why are they both in casts? I thought just your left leg had polio."

"It doesn't hurt much any more," said Paul. "I just can't move, can't do anything."

"Both legs had surgery," said Mother, "Polio affected both of them, and Paul's spine, but there is less surgery on his stronger leg."

"I brought you some strawberries from Grandma's garden," said Marty, producing a little wax container, the bottom half of a milk bottle, with several strawberries in it.

Paul dipped his limp hand in and ate one.

"He doesn't have much appetite," said Mother. "I'm glad to see him eat anything!"

In front of Paul on a little table was a catalog for the stamps he was collecting, and a magnifying glass Dad gave him to look at them, and beside him was the little phonograph they brought from home. Line looked, and sure enough, the record lying on it was "The Ballad of Davy Crockett." On the wall was a calendar for July, with big red "X"s marking off the days.

The solemn white room seemed a little less forbidding with all of them in it. Ellie relaxed too, in the immediate family, and brought out the gifts she bought for them in San Francisco. They were from Chinatown, intricate colored cut paper shapes, a small pot-bellied brass incense burner, tiny paper lanterns, and for Paul, a bright paper kite shaped like a bird.

"I'm sorry," said Ellie, spreading it out on Paul's white bed. "I know you can't use it right now, Paul, but soon."

"They're wonderful presents," said Mother. "Thank you, Ellie. You've made good choices!"

"It's really like you're walking down a street in China," said Ellie. "All the buildings look Chinese." But it was too hard for Line to imagine. Ellie had sent postcards, of the famous bridge across the Golden Gate, and of Chinatown at night. "It almost seems like a dream, now," said Ellie.

"Tell us about the convention," said Dad. Ellie had told him some things, but he wanted her to share it with all of them.

"It was so inspiring," said Ellie, "all these kids coming from all over to be in one place, singing together and listening to speakers. I'll never forget it."

Line chafed at this, thinking that if she had been to San Francisco, she would have more interesting things to say for herself.

"And what was the theme?" asked Mother.

"Soli Deo Gloria," said Ellie. "It means that we should give our whole lives to the glory of God."

"Ahhh," said Mother. "That is also the Wittenberg College motto." She looked at Dad and that complicit smile they always shared when Wittenberg was mentioned spread across his face.

"Your Mother and I live by that motto every day of our lives," said Dad. "To God alone be the glory. We can share in it, but it belongs to Him." He went over to Paul and put his arms around him lightly. "For instance, when we get this young man home, and walking on his own two legs, we will give that victory to Him." He smiled back at the circle of family standing around the bed, Mother and the three girls.

Line winked back tears. Such a fight it was for Paul just to be normal. But it also set off a little spark of anger. Why did it have to happen? Why were there poor people and sick people and hatred? It just didn't seem fair.

"You know, I almost forgot I have a present for Paul too," said Dad. He pulled a packet of tissue paper out of his pocket. As he unwrapped it, a tiny carved ivory figure emerged. A fisherman in a kayak with a spear in his hand, it was a simple but powerful-looking figure. "Aunt Mabel gave it to me." Aunt Mabel was a missionary to Alaska who worked in villages in the Arctic. "I went to hear her speak last week. I wished you were all with me. She showed slides at a church in Alexandria, and when I told her why you couldn't be there, she gave me this figure for Paul."

Dad looked over at Mother. "She's left Shishmaref and is moving to Sitka, to work with the native students at the high school. It's down on the islands near Juneau, much less arctic than the Seward peninsula."

Mother nodded. "That's good. I'm sure she must be feeling the cold more as she gets older."

"The Lutheran Daughters of the Reformation gave her a check for her retirement," said Dad.

"Wonderful," said Mother.

Dad turned back to the little figure. "Living all winter up in the Arctic, where they carved this fisherman, would be a little like being in traction. The sun hardly comes up and you are usually snowed in. So they spend their days carving things. This is from a walrus tusk, she told me."

"Can I see it," Line asked. She wanted to hold it in her hand, look closely at it. She picked it up, turning it over and over, then handed it to Marty. Aunt Mabel had shown slides of the Alaska missions at their church last year. Photos of igloos and Eskimos in fur-lined parkas.

Line remembered going out to a farm with Aunt Mabel so she could take photographs of pigs. Eskimos didn't know where bacon came from and Aunt Mabel wanted to show them. She gave them a wonderful Eskimo doll, made of skin and dressed in the same fur parkas and mukluks the Eskimos wore. She told Line she had to eat chocolate to keep warm in the snow, which made Line want to become a missionary!

"It's easier for me to imagine Alaska than it is to imagine the city of San Francisco," said Line.

"Yeah, me too," said Marty. "We've seen lots of snow, and we live in a village. It would be strange to be surrounded by people in a city."

"It was scary," said Ellie. "The streets were full of traffic. But at the convention hall, when everyone was together, singing, it was wonderful."

"I love being together," said Mother, "just our family, even if it is only for a little while. And I'm so proud of all of you. You are learning and sharing things. Paul and I have enjoyed your letters so much, and we think of you every day." She was going back and forth from Aunt Rose's house to the hospital, spending the afternoons and evenings helping Paul stay comfortable and reading to him.

Mother's words knit them together. Line knew that the small hardship of not being at home was the least she could do to help the situation.

"What's that blue 'D' doing on your calendar next Tuesday?" asked Line. "I see you are marking off the days, but what does 'D' stand for?"

"Done!" said Paul in his strongest voice yet. "That's the day I get out of traction and can move again!"

"D for Done! That's great," said Line. "We'll be home by then and we can imagine you walking around! Right, Dad?" She looked at Dad, who seemed to be in charge of what they were doing.

"Yup," said Dad. "We are going home. And we will think of you every day until I come and get you for good."

"I'll make a calendar at home," said Marty, "and it will have a blue 'D' on it for the day you come home."

"I'll tell Mittens all about you being in the hospital," said Line. "And if I see Davy Sundeen, I'll tell him you'll be home soon."

"Hope so," said Paul.

Line was heart sore again. There was lots of hard work ahead for Paul.

"Let's sing something, like we do in the car when we're driving," said Dad. "What shall we sing, Lois?"

Mother looked as if she would cry if she tried to sing, so Dad turned to Paul. "What shall we sing?"

"The poor old slave," said Paul. It was a silly song in the end, but it didn't start out that way.

"Okay," said Dad, beginning in his clear tenor, "The poor old slave has gone to rest…"

They all joined in, "We know that he is free, oh free free. His poor old bones they lie at rest, way down in Tennessee, oh see see."

They continued, adding vowels in the right places, stringing out the song and looking at each other as they kept going. Laughing with her bright eyes and singing, Mother joined them. At the end they grew louder: "The pickety, packety poor old slickety, slackety slave has gickety gackety gone to rickety rackety rest. We knickety knackety know, that hickety hackety he is free, oh free free!"

Line was pleased to see that Paul was laughing too, the little carved ivory fisherman rattling on the flimsy hospital table across his chest.

13

Marty held her hands behind her back as she put her face down in the washtub of bobbing apples, trying to bite one. Apples skittered away if you tried to get close to one. Finally she was able to get an apple stem in her teeth. She laughed as she sat up with the apple hanging from her mouth, water dripping down the front of her witch costume.

"Try to get it by the stem," she coached Anne, who knelt beside her, trying to get a purchase on an apple.

Anne leaned far enough over the aluminum tub to bite an apple pinned against the other side. She laughed too as she came up dripping, the smeared charcoal on her face wet and glistening. A hobo, she wore a ragged shirt and a pair of jeans with one leg mostly torn off and carried a handkerchief tied around a stick.

All the kids in town filled the brightly lit church parish hall. They had gone trick or treating for UNICEF, and were being rewarded by a party. Line and her Young Citizens League suggested it, but the Lutheran Ladies Aid and the Luther League helped. The whole town dug down to find silver dimes and gave them to the costumed kids who held up their cups and waxed milk bottles. At the church the dimes poured out, a rain of silver into another big washtub. The dimes with the winged head of Liberty were especially beautiful, delicate and shining.

Marty and Anne ran off to play games. In the bright fluorescent light people's costumes looked rag-tag, as if they were strung together with scotch tape and glue.

"Isn't this great?" yelled Line as she passed Marty. "More fun than going home and stuffing ourselves with candy."

But Marty's mouth was full of sticky caramel and she couldn't reply. She watched Line heading off toward the kitchen in an old cowboy hat, a plaid shirt and jeans. Line wanted to be a cheerleader, but Mother objected when Line proposed cutting off one of her skirts to make it very short.

Marty retreated to the side of the room. The caramel apple was more than she could handle. Watching everyone, her eyes composed little groups of figures. There was Michael, blindfolded, wearing a straw hat and a pair of overalls with some hay sticking out of his pockets, holding his arms out toward the people in the circle around him. There were Anne and Eileen, the hobo and the tiara-crowned princess, in a group playing musical chairs.

Paul was the best in a tree costume he made himself. He cut fir branches with Dad's help and tied them on to his brown trunk. He wasn't a Christmas tree; he was just a tree with a bird's nest attached to one of his arms. Davy Sundeen, in a coonskin cap and a fringed jacket, a tiny rifle slung over his shoulder, was Davy Crockett "followin' his legend out into the west." Davy and Paul ran up to people, confronting them with brilliant wax lips and wax fangs. Paul still looked pale after his summer surgery, but he was growing and getting stronger, and he wasn't wearing a brace.

Glasses are a kind of brace, thought Marty, but she was glad she could see. The room was gay and colorful, full of moving people. Dried corn shocks, hay bales and a glowing pumpkin dressed the corner. In the low window looking into the kitchen, Marty saw ladies in aprons making big steel urns of coffee and bowls of buttery popcorn. She straightened her black cardboard witch hat and smoothed the long black skirt Mother let her borrow. She wore a black crepe paper cape but no mask, and carried a broom.

Caspar the Friendly Ghost floated past. Marty knew it was Caspar because of the way the eyes were drawn on the sheet, but she wasn't sure who was under it.

"Talk to me," she said to Caspar, "so I can figure out who you are."

"Booo-ooo-ooo," said the ghost, drawing out his voice and trying to be scary. The ghost was taller than Marty, with its head sitting high like a hat. The eyes were slits in the sheet below.

"Caspar is supposed to be friendly," said Marty, who had been buried in comic books that summer.

But Caspar ran off, boooo-ing at someone else and Marty followed, dipping her hands into a bowl of candy corn and biting first the yellow part, then the orange part and last the white sugary base, as she went. A perfect Halloween party.

At school, Marty was in fifth grade, once again in a classroom with Line. Their teacher, Mrs. Tannahill, taught what she called "folk dancing."

She told Line's class to study, took Marty's class down to the basement, and played 78 rpm records of fiddle music with square dancing calls. Line had told her Mrs. Tannahill loved teaching folk dancing more than arithmetic and reading, and Marty was surprised by how much fun it was.

It was dark in the basement by the glowing, iron furnace. Wintry light came in at the small high windows. There was just enough room on the concrete floor for eight kids to make a square. Mrs. Tannahill paired up the boys and girls and explained the moves. She was a large woman in a print jersey dress, with tightly curled iron-grey hair, showing kids half her size how to swing their partner.

Mrs. Tannahill lifted the needle on the phonograph and moved it to the beginning of the record. "Put your little foot, put your little foot, put your little foot right out," sang a scratchy voice. Marty held hands with Michael, putting out one foot then the other, turning in a circle, waltzing. Michael wore his new khaki Boy Scout uniform with a red scarf, proud he was now in the troop and going to a meeting after school. A fiddle played in the background.

Marty moved in time to the music, turning and waltzing. Then Jerome took her by the hand and they did it all again. Dancing was easy, Marty realized. You didn't have to think about what to say to your partner. You just moved with him and stopped when the music stopped.

The waiting kids joined them for "The Virginia Reel," girls and boys facing each other in a line. The music was like a sailor's hornpipe, slow at the beginning, but fast when they got going. Greeting Loren in his plaid cowboy shirt, Marty do-si-doed around him. Marty grew breathless as Loren seized her hands and slide stepped with her all the way down between the lines. Sashaying, Mrs. Tannahill called it.

Loren's hands were tough and dry, farmer's hands, used to hard work. Putting up their arms Loren and Marty knit their fingers together, making a bridge for other couples to go under. Left at the end of the row, they ran through all the motions again, and then slipped under the bridge of hands made by Eileen and Michael.

Mrs. Tannahill stood by the record player, taking up the needle. "In this next one, the call is 'allemande left.'" She walked through the square, showing the kids how to go to the left and take the hand of your opposite partner, grabbing first Loren's, then Michael's hands, her wrinkled face spreading into a smile. Marty tried to imagine her as a young girl, pink cheeked and smiling at a barn dance. "Okay, ready?" said Mrs. Tannahill. "It's called 'Take a Little Peek'."

"Swing your partner," the man on the record called in a nasaly voice while fiddles sawed in the background. "Allemande left and do-si-do." The record was scratched and worn. You could hear the revolutions as it came around to the needle. Michael partnered Marty. His hands were soft and puffy, as he lived in town and didn't have to do chores, but he looked smart in his red Scout neckerchief. And Marty loved him. They were alike with their squinty eyes, glasses and good grades.

Marty wondered if being smart was so important though, watching the country kids dance. Melody and Geraldine flashed around in their cotton dresses, big smiles on their faces, swung by their partners. The country kids might be a bit more bedraggled, didn't say as much in class, but Marty suspected they knew things she didn't. Maybe there were other ways to be smart than reading and arithmetic.

It wasn't the sort of thing Marty could say to anyone, not even Line. It was more a feeling than a thought to be put into words. But at night in bed, Marty and Line snugged the covers up to their chins and talked softly about school.

"What does Craig say about folk dancing?" Marty asked. Line was sweet on Craig. She said his farm family didn't think school was very important, though.

"It's Craig's favorite," said Line. "If he thinks there is going to be square dancing, he'll come to school no matter what!"

"He likes dancing with you!" said Marty.

"Well, I like dancing with him too," said Line, stretching out her arms in her flannel pajamas in a yawn. It was one of their sleepier nights. Sometimes Line wore red socks to bed, pretending they were boots so she could be Bloody Dave, the pirate they had seen in a movie once. Or they pretended they were boys chasing girls, or even secretaries, using their pillows as typewriters.

"I wish there were Girl Scouts in Bryson," said Marty. She would have liked to get the merit badges shown in the Boy Scout book. Paul was still not old enough to be in Boy Scouts either.

"I'd rather be in 4-H," said Line. 4-H was for farm kids, helping them learn things they needed to know, like raising animals and cooking. "Head, heart, hands and health. You can have your old Girl Scouts." The cold moon came in their window, throwing a bright square of light on the bed.

Marty yawned. "I guess so. What are you going to wear tomorrow?" But Line's breathing changed. She was asleep. Marty turned her face away in the big double bed, and lay beside her, waiting for the Sandman.

That weekend it snowed, big feathers drifting down lazily. Out of the thick feathers came a bus carrying the Wittenberg College choir. The choir was on its way to an evening concert in Grand Forks and Mother and Dad asked the Ladies' Aid to serve them a meal. Mother asked Ellie, who would be going to Wittenberg in a couple of years, and Marty to help. Marty was there when more than fifty lively choir members piled out of the big, silver bus at the church.

Marty rushed out without a coat and couldn't resist stepping into the bus to see what it was like. Thick plush carpets covered the floors and big plush seats, two by two, lined both sides of the bus under tall windows. Tiny lights lit up the bus. It was just like a comfortable living room. The bus driver waited for her to look around, but Marty was freezing. She ran back into the dining hall.

Two long tables with white paper coverings stretched down the room. Ellie laid silver around the plates. The choir members stood talking and laughing with each other along the sides of the room, waiting for the food to be ready. They must be older than the high school kids Marty knew, but they didn't look like it.

Mother and Dad were talking to Mr. Duncan, a man of about their age, with an impish face and hair combed high into a puff on his head. Dad called Marty over and introduced her to him. Mr. Duncan was the choir director.

"She's taking piano lessons, but I wouldn't say she practices a lot," said Dad.

Marty hung her head. It was true. She had started taking lessons out of the red book, doing the finger exercises and playing simple songs.

"If you find you love it," said Mr. Duncan in a velvety treble voice, "you will surely practice. I played the piano from the time I was five years old. I thought it was my life."

"I promise to practice more," said Marty softly.

"I have a photograph of myself playing the piano in Berlin in 1945. It's one of my favorites!" said Mr. Duncan.

"I'll never forget hearing the story that you liberated a bust of Beethoven!" said Dad.

"Yes," said Mr. Duncan. "No one else could have loved it as I have. It's in my office at Wittenberg."

"Well, we'll be down there one of these days," said Dad. "These kids just keep on growing! No stopping them."

Mother motioned Marty toward the kitchen. "Put out the salt and pepper shakers, Marty, and refill the water glasses once the choir has been seated." Marty rushed up and down the tables, spacing out the little glass salt and pepper cellars along the tables. Ellie filled water pitchers at the water fountain. The pitchers were heavy, but Marty carried them carefully and together they filled all the glasses.

At last Dad could tell that everything was ready, big platters of food along the counter, the women standing in the kitchen ready to help. Dad led everyone to the tables and began a grace. Afterwards, Mr. Duncan raised his hands and Marty heard one of the girls hum a little to find a note. The most ethereally high voices began to rise in the room. "Praise to the Lord, the Almighty, the King of Creation. Oh my soul, praise Him, for He is thy health and salvation." Marty held her breath, standing to one side with Ellie, a pitcher of water in her hands.

Lower voices joined the high ones in wonderful, clear harmony. "All ye who hear, now to his temple draw near. Join me in glad adoration." Almost before the beautiful voices finished this phrase, the muscular men's voices joined them, singing "Praise to the Lord, the Almighty, the King of Creation" in a round. The voices rose and fell, carrying Marty up and then down with them. Mr. Duncan's arms marked the time, drawing sound first from one group, then another, as if the voices were a big pipe organ.

The phrases kept repeating and repeating, dashing over each other like water splashing on rocks. "Surely his goodness and mercy shall bravely attend thee." The men's voices created a strong beat and the women's voices floated on it, washing like a powerful waterfall over Marty's body. "Let the amen, sound from His people again. Alleluia!" The high notes lingered toward the end and trickled off into quiet.

For a moment Marty could hear a pin drop in the room, and then, all at once, everyone started to move and breathe again. They picked up their plates and formed a line to get their food, laughing and talking. The church women stood behind big platters of roast beef and mashed potatoes with gravy, tubs of carrots and peas, and green beans. The students spooned them up eagerly. Apparently that angel choir was fed by good earthy food!

Marty walked around, filling water glasses and listening to what people were saying. Wittenberg College lived in the stories her parents told of walking in the bluffs along the river, of the library, of the fire at Old Main, and in the photographs. Mother and Dad worked on the college newspaper, argued with each other and then fell in love, they said. Marty had never been to Wittenberg. But here were these college kids on a choir tour, headed up through North Dakota to Winnipeg, Ontario, stopping at churches along the way to sing.

"Aren't you excited about going to Wittenberg," Marty whispered excitedly to Ellie as they passed one another.

Ellie gave her a baleful look. "No," she whispered back. "I don't really want to go to college."

Marty looked at her, amazed. Why would anyone not want to go to college? But there wasn't time to ask her. It was time to pass the cake and ice cream. The Mikkelsons weren't going to the concert, as it was far away and wouldn't be finished until late at night. Even Mother and Dad didn't go. They just wanted to help the choir as they passed near Bryson.

At Christmas there was lots of singing, but none of it held a candle to the angel choir Marty heard that night in the church parish hall. New Year's Eve was Marty's birthday, her tenth. Early in the morning the kids went into Mother and Dad's room, as was their family birthday tradition. There was a small pile of presents beside the bed. Not many as Christmas was so recent. One was a small leather diary with a tiny key and lock on it. Marty clutched it to her chest, the perfect present.

"The biggest one is downstairs," said Dad. "It's so big we couldn't bring it up here. Go look on the dining room table."

Marty rushed downstairs with Line and Paul right behind her, but she couldn't see anything on the table.

"Look!" said Line. "Come closer. You don't have your glasses on."

When Marty got close enough to see with her nearsighted eyes, there was a tiny Lucite box on the table. Opening it revealed a silver ring circling a clear blue topaz shaped like a heart, her birthstone. She had longed for a birthstone, and guessed she might get one, but it hadn't come at Christmas. Marty put it on her finger and raced upstairs to thank Mother and Dad.

"We meant to put it in another box, and then in a bigger box, and then in a bigger box, but we didn't have time," said Mother, her voice stifled by lying in a cocoon with Dad under the covers.

Each of the older girls already had birthstone jewelry. Ellie's was an opal ring, perfect with her blonde curls, and Line's was an emerald-colored stone set in a locket, which complimented the reddish-gold glints in her hair. Marty wished hers were a ruby, as she was so dark, like "Bess the landlord's daughter, plaiting a dark red love knot into her long dark hair." But it couldn't be helped. She was born at the end of December. She did love the silver and topaz ring, the stone light blue, like water.

After supper there was a cake with chocolate frosting, made by Ellie, Line and Paul. Its top layer sagged over the bottom layer, but it was all chocolate, Marty's favorite. And the candles shone.

Line begged to stay up to see the New Year come.

"Go ahead," said Mother. "If you can!"

"You can come with me to ring the New Year in, if you're still awake," said Dad.

By ten o'clock Paul was asleep on the sofa, wrapped in an afghan, his arms sticking out. Ellie disappeared and Marty and Line played Parcheesi on the living room floor.

Dad popped his head in the room at 11:30. "Are you kids coming with me?"

"Yes!" said Line. She looked over at Paul. "I'll prop up his eyes with toothpicks!"

Marty struggled into her coat, boots, scarf and mittens while Line waked Paul.

"Dad can't wait," Line insisted. "The whole town would know it, if he was late!"

Dad was in the entry, zipping up his overshoes. He looked like a Russian in his fur cap with earflaps. He opened the door and the cold stung their faces. Line followed him, and then Paul. With Marty in the rear, they took the path across the alley to the church under the big, unpredictable sky. Snowflakes filled in the newly shoveled path. Wan streetlights marked the distant corners of the blocks. A naked bulb hung over the door to the parish hall. Marty put out her mittens and watched the wet clumps of snow land on the red wool in the light.

They stepped into the dark church, stamping to get the snow off their boots. Marty followed Dad, Line and Paul through the church in little pools of electric light made as Dad turned on lights. In a vestibule off the front entry, a stairway ran up to the steeple. Rough brown boards lined the walls as they climbed the steep steps. It was very cold. At the top hung a rope as thick as Dad's leg with a huge knot tied in its end.

"Don't get too close," said Dad. "Stay there, on that side of the railing."

Marty looked high up into the dark of the steeple. The great bell must be there, but she could hardly see it. Line stood at the top of the stairs, followed by the sleepy Paul.

Dad stood near the thick, rough rope in his double-breasted brown overcoat with its raggedy fur collar. He took out his pocket watch. "One more minute. Do you want to count?"

"One, two, three, four, five ..." the kids chanted, but Dad was looking at the watch. All of a sudden he pulled on the rope strongly, setting the wheel which turned the bell swinging into the clapper. The rope swung up and out of his hands as he let it go, the great knot swinging up into the bell tower. A full, deep sound resonated through them and out into the snow-covered town.

Though the bell reverberated through their lives, Marty had never been so close to it. When Paul was born, the first boy in the family, Dad rang the church bell to announce his birth to the little town.

"Happy new year!" yelled Dad. As the knot of rope came down, he jumped onto it with both feet. He swung up high into the air as the rope wound around the wheel, swinging the bell into the clapper.

"Dad," shouted Paul in fear. "Come down!"

"It's okay, Paul," said Marty, putting her arms around him from below. "He knows what he's doing."

Dad swung down and up again, the deep, powerful tones of the bell sounding through the cold air.

"Can I try?" begged Line, her arms reaching over the railing to where Dad stood.

"No," said Dad. "You kids are too little. It's too dangerous." Dad swung down and jumped off the heavy rope, batting the knot of frayed ends away from him as it swung up again, the bell tones continuing.

Dad came toward them and stood at the top of the stairs, awkwardly putting his arms around all three of them at once and squeezing them. "Did you like it?"

"Yeah!" said Paul, his face shining.

Marty was deeply happy as they stomped down the stairs, turned out the lights and walked back across the snowy walk to their own house. She was ten. Every year was better. But could it get better, really?

14

Paul stood in the tall grass at the foot of the Big Tree, looking up at Line and Marty. They rode the thick branch of a cottonwood as if it were the back of a swaybacked horse, one behind the other. The tree was at the back edge of the schoolyard, where they were allowed to play as long as they told Mother where they were.

"You can make camp, Paul," said Line. "We have to go for supplies. Look, Marty, there's a town over there. Let's go and see if we can swipe a chicken to roast."

Marty and Line were barefoot, scarves wrapped artfully around their heads, playing gypsies. Paul wore his most raggedy clothes and carried the old dented bugle, in lieu of a violin. In *The Clue in the Old Album*, a Nancy Drew mystery Line was reading, Nancy is captured by gypsies.

"It would make more sense if I went to get supplies," Paul grumbled, "and you girls made camp." It seemed to him that he had stood at the foot of this tree while his sisters climbed up forever. Two years ago he was too small and his brace too stiff. Last year he spent the whole summer in the hospital. He was growing, but the girls still couldn't boost him up.

Paul stomped down the long green grass, which reached up to his waist already, flattening a space for the gypsy camp. He spread out a small blanket and put out the brown paper bag of Hydrox cookies they brought. They also had milk in a thermos, but there was only one cup.

Circles of downy cotton carried the seeds of the cottonwoods through the air in early summer. Paul lay down and looked up at the grass seeds at the ends of the spears waving in the sun above his head. Cotton puffs floated across the blue sky. Far beyond them, were fluffy white clouds. In the hospital, Paul had imagined himself floating on the downy pillows of clouds that floated past the window. This summer, he was determined to be outdoors as much as possible.

When the girls climbed down from the tree, they shared out the cookies and milk. "Two for each of us," said Marty, taking off the top of a cookie sandwich and licking the creamy white frosting.

Paul took tiny nibbles. Knowing how many cookies he had made him savor each bite.

Line stood up and caught cotton fluff that sailed through the air. Holding a handful, she blew on them to watch them get away. "Where are you going, my pretties?" she said.

"They're like gypsies," said Marty. "Or pioneers floating across the prairies."

"They look for water," said Paul. "Along river banks. The wagon trains used to look for cottonwoods to see where the creeks and rivers were."

"I want to stay here forever," said Line, stretching her arms wide.

"Me too," said Paul, looking up. The afternoon sun shone in the wisps of her red-gold hair. Line was twelve now. He could see that she was changing, growing away. She liked being alone more now, but so did he. He loved being with Line and Marty, but he also liked it when no one knew where he was. Outdoors, though. He didn't ever want to go inside.

"We have to be home for supper," said Marty. "We should go." She stood up, and the sun lit her too from the back, the edges of her dark hair glowing.

"Pull me up," said Paul, reaching up his hands. The two girls grabbed his hands and pulled him until he was standing. No one could see that one of his legs was skinny and one thick under his pants. Paul knew he might have to have more surgery, but for the time being, he felt great.

At home, Ellie and Mother were bringing in stiff cotton shapes off the clothesline and folding them into piles. The dining room table was full of clean-smelling piles of towels, sheets, and tee shirts. Dad was in his study, working on his sermon.

"Go ahead and brown the hamburger, Line," said Mother. "Set the table, Marty. We're going to have chili." Line pulled out the heavy cast iron skillet, lit the stove and began mashing the hamburger with a fork. When the meat had begun to sizzle in the fat, she opened a package of Lipton's dried onion soup and sprinkled it on the hamburger to flavor it. Marty put bowls, spoons and crackers on the built-in table in the kitchen.

Paul watched the comings and goings from the dining room table, pretending to tap out the Morse code he was supposed to be learning so he could get an amateur ham radio license. When Ellie and Line briefly stood next to each other, he mentally measured them, guessing there was at least four inches difference in height between them. When they all sat down to supper, he confirmed that Ellie's head was higher than Line's.

After supper they were supposed to be quiet so Dad could study. Paul collected the garbage and took it out to the burning barrel. He set the cardboard cereal boxes upright, pretending they were a fort. Like an Indian, he threw flaming matches, or rather arrows, at them, trying to burn it down. As the cardboard caught, the garbage began to burn, and glowing red sparks flew up. The sun was slow to go down at this time of year. While it blazed it was hard to see the fire. Burning garbage was more fun in the winter.

When Paul came in, reeking of burnt scraps and cardboard, Mother and Line were folding church bulletins. The printed side of the sheet was sent out from the national church office. For the other side, Mother typed up Bryson's Sunday service and weekly church activity information on blue stencil paper. Dad inked up the mimeograph and ran the bulletins against the stencil. When they were dry, Mother and whoever was available folded them, making a neat stack for the ushers to pass out in church the next morning.

"Take your bath," said Mother. "Ellie just finished." There wasn't enough water for each of them to have clean bath water, so Paul bathed in Ellie's water. Since they didn't have a well, a water truck arrived each month to pump clear, fresh water into a cement cistern built into the basement down beside the furnace. Marty and Line would bathe after him, sharing their water.

It felt nice to be clean on Saturday nights, in clean pajamas, blown dry in the sun. Sometimes the sheets were clean too, but not every week. Paul was still sleeping in the "youth" bed in Ellie's room. He climbed into bed with his Sunday School book and tried to memorize the Bible verse for tomorrow.

The sun was a glowing red ball just behind the church, casting a reddish light into the room. The Bible verse was John 3:21: "But he that doeth truth cometh to the light, that his deeds may be made manifest, that they are wrought in God." He wasn't sure how one "doeth truth", but he did like being in the light. He wasn't sure about the rest of it either. He would think about it tomorrow. When Mother came up to kiss him goodnight, he was thinking about how to get Ellie to help him.

Sunday wasn't the day, though. There was too much to do. Dad got up very early and drove out to preach at the Highland Church. He came back during Sunday School and got ready for the service at Immanuel, the white church just across the alley from the parsonage where the Mikkelsons lived.

Paul, wearing a light summer shirt with his dark cotton dress up pants, and Line and Marty, wearing the Christmas dresses Aunt Rose bought them that year, joined Mother in the third row in the nave of the church. The service began after Sunday School, which took place in circles of chairs in the parish hall, each grade with its own teacher. The kids were old enough now to behave quietly. Line was mischievous in church, passing notes and smiling at the others. But a holy hush descended upon Paul when the church was filled and quiet, the organist playing softly.

Above the altar at the front, a painting of Christ was set into a wooden altarpiece carved with ornate crosses. The painting depicted Christ ascending into Heaven in a shaft of light with the disciples looking on from below. Today was Pentecost, the day the church celebrated the gift of the Holy Spirit given to the disciples. A red silk scarf with golden embroidery glowed on the wooden altar.

Dad came out of a vestibule beside the altar, wearing white robes over his dark gown and a red silk stole embroidered with gold around his shoulders. He nodded to Mrs. Thompson, the organist, and she began to pound out the chords of the hymn Martin Luther wrote to celebrate the church, "A Mighty Fortress Is Our God." Everyone opened their hymnbooks and as they sang, the choir, including Ellie, processed up the aisle in its blue robes and filed into the choir loft, singing loudly. Paul offered up his high little voice as well. "Did we in our own strength confide, our striving would be losing. Were not the right man on our side, the man of God's own choosing."

Dad's sweet tenor sang most of the liturgy, but Paul felt Dad's warmth most from the pulpit as he talked in his own voice during the sermon. After the sermon, communion was served because this was a festival Sunday. Line, Marty and Paul sat in their seats, watching as row upon row of church members went up to the front and knelt on the velvet pads which cushioned the step built against a railing around the altar.

The bottoms of people's shoes pointed out toward the church as they pressed their knees together. Mr. Gunderson, leader of the VFW, had a hole in his left shoe sole Paul noticed. Line looked at him significantly. She smiled when he looked at her, knowing he saw.

The kids were not yet confirmed in the Lutheran faith so they could not take communion, but Ellie was. Paul watched her come down with the rest of the choir, and go up to the railing. Dad circled along the inside of the railing, giving each person a white wafer, the body of Christ. "Take, eat," said Dad's voice, quietly representing Christ. "This is my body, given for you."

Dad then came around again to give each person a tiny glass of wine. "This is my blood, shed for you." He circled again with a silver tray, each person putting their tiny glass back into the holes cut for them. Ellie's face, surrounded by a white satin collar, didn't show anything as she filed back into the choir stall facing the audience. But then you could never get much out of Ellie.

By the end of the long service, Dad's voice was husky as he said the Benediction. Paul closed his eyes and lifted up his face to feel the rays of the Lord's face shining down on him. "The Lord bless thee, and keep thee: The Lord make his face shine upon thee, and be gracious unto thee: The Lord lift up his countenance upon thee, and give thee peace." It was Paul's favorite part.

No one ever said so, but Paul knew that he was meant to follow in Dad's footsteps. Girls couldn't be pastors and he was the only boy. Some day he would serve communion and give the benediction, invoking blessings and peace upon his own congregation, just like Dad.

The Mikkelsons were invited out to Ellingsons' farm for Sunday dinner, along with Adrian and Edna and their newly adopted kids. Pete and Adrian were brothers, with Pete running a wheat and soybean farm, and Adrian the grocery and dry goods store in town. Both brothers were doing well and had built new ranch houses. Paul and his family visited Pete and Annie's farm often. Paul loved to go because Pete's operation included sunflowers, a few dairy cows, chickens and bees. Livestock of any kind was hard work, and both Pete and Annie worked hard, especially as they had no children.

The kids wore their church clothes, but after a big dinner of Annie's fried chicken, mounds of mashed potatoes and coleslaw, biscuits and gravy, Pete put on his overalls and some mud-crusted boots and Paul and Craig followed him out to the barn to look at the new calves.

The barn was an airy space on two levels, with a haymow up above, and a grain silo beside it. Sunlight filtered in from the open doors. The barn smelled of sweet hay, and in some places of manure. Pete pitched hay down to the cows in their pens from the haymow. Concrete troughs in the floor helped him keep the cows' pens clean. Dried up cowpies had never bothered Paul. They were just piles of grass that went through a cow's four stomachs with some digestive juice in them. He guessed wet manure was the same.

Most of the cows were in the grassy pasture near the barn, but the three cows with new calves rested in their stalls, their calves beside them. One of the calves was only two days old. He stood on spindly legs beside his mother, nosing at her side as she chewed her cud, then turning his black face and big ears toward Paul. His soft eyes were mostly black with hardly any white part, and his body was white, but covered with big black patches. Paul reached out to touch the white patch on his face which spread down toward his pink nose.

Pete brought a wooden milking stool and sat beneath the mother. He pulled at the teats attached to the cow's full udder, filling a little silver pail with milk. He dipped a cup into it and gave it to Paul. Paul tasted it tentatively with a tiny sip. He was used to cold pasteurized milk from the store, and this was warm and tasted like grass. Craig made a face when he took a sip and Pete laughed at them.

"You boys don't know the first thing about farming," said Pete. "But you can learn if you want to. Do you want to try?" Paul did. Everything about plants and animals excited him. He sat down on the stool and put his small hands around the soft teats. They felt like hollow fingers.

"Pull," said Pete. "Pull hard. She doesn't know your hands, but she might try." The cow edged away from Paul's hands, as if he were an insect she was trying to get away from. "It's okay, we've probably bothered her enough today. Come on boys," said Pete. He stroked the cow to reassure her.

An orange barn cat jumped down from the beam of the haymow as they left the barn. Pete picked him up and stroked him. "How are you doing?" he said to the cat. "Caught any mice today?" A farm with wheat and sunflowers needed a few good mousers in the barn.

The bees lived in two towers of white square boxes near the sunflower field. It was a very active time for them and they didn't need anything, so Pete and the boys just stood aside and watched as bees traveled in and out of the boxes. Paul could almost see yellow pollen on their legs.

"They're like apartments," said Craig, who once lived in a city.

"Yup," said Pete. "They managed pretty well this winter. Never know how it's going to be, but this was a pretty easy winter for them."

"How do they stay alive all winter?" wondered Paul.

"Well," said Pete. "I don't know. A heavy fall of snow keeps you from freezing, you know, like an igloo, and they're up off the ground. I'm pretty sure they just sort of hibernate and eat some of their own honey."

Paul resolved to figure this out when he got home. They ambled back along the gravel road toward the farmhouse. The flash of a bright red wing from the phone wires to the top of the fence signaled a redwing blackbird, screaming his rough "con-cor-eeeee" to his friends. Paul spied some of the wild pink roses that Mother loved, growing in the ditch. Bees were crawling in the blossoms.

"Can I take some of those roses to Mother?" he asked Pete.

"Sure," said Pete. "North Dakota state flower. Plenty of 'em. The bees won't mind if you take a few."

Paul picked a few of the wide open pink faces with a single row of petals, their stamens studded with pollen in the bright sun. A meadowlark with a yellow breast warbled its sweet tones from a fence post and cicadas rubbed their legs together in the still heat.

"So what are you boys up to this summer?" asked Pete.

"Swimming lessons," said Craig, scuffing his shoes along in the gravel. After a year of living with the relaxed Ellingsons, he was a little less pinched and anxious. Mrs. Ellingson was driving Bruce, Sandy and Craig every morning to Hillsboro, the county seat, for lessons.

Pete looked over at Paul, who said, "I'm supposed to be learning Morse code, so I can get my ham radio license."

"Yeah, your Dad is quite the ham, isn't he!" Pete laughed. Dad's license plate for the new Studebaker now showed his call letters, "W Ø VQX." Everyone in town knew how enthusiastic Dad was about electronics.

"I'd rather be outside, though," said Paul, a little cloud passing over his face. He wanted to please Dad, but that part of science didn't interest him. He liked living things better. Radio waves and frequencies were part of life, but he couldn't keep the ohms and the volts straight. He still didn't know a capacitor from a transistor, and he just didn't care enough about it. Dad noticed, and didn't ride him too hard, but Paul knew that Dad still wanted to share his excitement with Paul.

"Hmmmm," said Pete. "Maybe you have the makings of a farmer. We need farmers, you know."

"Maybe," said Paul. The future was a long ways off and he didn't want to think about it.

When they got back to the farmhouse, Annie was cutting up a sheet cake and serving it with ice cream. Paul presented Mother with the wild pink roses and she asked Annie for a jelly jar so she could put them in water.

Dad was explaining to Adrian that he'd been spending a lot of time at the electronics store next to the grocery.

"We're going to rent one of his Sylvanias," said Dad of Mr. Mitchell, who ran the store. "Lois wants to watch the political conventions this summer. Should be interesting."

This was news to Paul. He dipped his spoon into a bowl of ice cream and ate some of the yellow cake and frosting with it. A Sylvania was a television.

"Don't think there'll be much to see," said Adrian. "Same as last year. Stevenson can't touch Ike."

"It's a chance to see some of our politicians," said Mother. "They don't come here because there are too few voters. But I'd like to actually hear some of them speak."

Pete and Annie watched their television at night, especially in the winter when the nights were longer and they weren't so busy. Paul had watched their television with them.

"Yup," said Dad. "We won't have to keep bothering you folks when we want to see something!"

"You're not a bother, Pastor Carl," said Annie. "We love having you come over. And the kids too!" She wore a bib apron over her print church dress. "More cake?" she asked.

But the kids knew to say "no thank you," politely. One piece was enough.

The next morning, Paul slipped out of bed early when everyone was still asleep. He toasted a piece of toast and made a bowl of cornflakes with milk and sugar. He put these on a plate, and pouring a glass of orange juice, carried them carefully upstairs to the bed where Ellie was just beginning to stir, her blonde head turning on the pillow. Paul stood beside her with the plate and glass, smiling.

Ellie sat up, and giggled. "What are you up to, Mr. Smartypants?"

Paul handed her the plate and glass. "I want you to come with me for a minute this morning, and I figured you would go if I did something for you," he whispered. He didn't want to wake anyone else up.

Ellie sighed but she was smiling. Paul was pretty sure she would do it. "Oh, all right," she said.

Paul was dressed in a second. "Meet me downstairs," he whispered. In the kitchen, he made himself a peanut butter sandwich. He drank some milk and waited until Ellie came down the stairs dressed in shorts and a sleeveless shirt.

"Come on," Paul said urgently. He was desperate to get away before anyone else came down.

They went out the back door and down the sidewalk toward the schoolhouse. Mourning doves were calling from the dovecot across from the church. "You're taller than Line and Marty, and I think I could get up in the Big Tree if you boosted me. They can almost do it, but not quite," Paul explained.

Ellie giggled. "We look like Mutt and Jeff," she said, watching their long shadows moving ahead of them in the early morning sun. Hers was much taller than Paul's, who stumped a little when he wanted to move quickly.

Cotton puffs still sailed across the schoolyard. When they got to the Big Tree, the flat place where the kids made their gypsy camp was matted down, the long grass wet and dewy.

Ellie circled the tree. She had never spent much time in it. "If I boost you up, and you fall and break your leg, it would be my fault!" she worried. "Haven't you spent enough time in the hospital already?"

Paul tried to reassure her. "I'm sure I can get up. My arms are really strong and I'll pull myself up. I just need a boost!"

"Okay," said Ellie doubtfully. "Just remember, I'm not so sure about this."

"Ellie," said Paul. "I'll tell them I begged you. Anyway, I'm not going to break my leg!"

Finally Ellie found a spot. "Look here, Paul," she said. "There's a knot. If you put your good foot here, I'm going to boost you and you see if you can get your arms around the trunk and climb."

Paul's stomach wavered a little. It was awfully high up.

"Come on," said Ellie. "I can't stand here all day."

Paul stretched his foot onto the knot which was as high as his hip. Ellie pushed him up from behind and he reached for a small branch with new green leaves on it, pulling himself up the trunk and laterally onto the wide branch everyone used as a horse. Paul crawled carefully out onto the thick branch and hung his legs over. Its bark was smooth it was used so much. Paul tried to get used to the feeling of being so high off the ground.

"Are you okay?" asked Ellie from down below.

"I think so," said Paul in a quavering voice, but he was smiling.

"Can you get down by yourself?" asked Ellie, "or do you want me to stay."

"No," said Paul. "I'm sure I can get down. And I won't fall. I want to sit for a while, now I'm here. Can you hand up my sandwich?"

Ellie handed up the brown paper bag. "You're sure you're okay?" she asked. "You promise not to get hurt?"

"Yup," said Paul, his voice strong. "I promise. I'm on top of the world!"

"Ok," said Ellie. "I'm going to leave you." She started back to the road, swishing through the long grass.

"Thank you!" yelled Paul as she left. "Tell Mother I'm here." It was just what he wanted, to be up in the tree with no one around. Now that Ellie showed him how, he was sure he could get Line to boost him up also. The summer was looking fine.

From his high perch, Paul watched the many shades of green as the new cottonwood leaves shook in the breeze, light flashing on their waxy leaves. He looked out across the fields at the edge of town and imagined being an Indian brave, scouting ahead for his tribe from the top of a tree. He could move around a little on the thick branch, hang his legs in different directions, lean against the truck. It was just as he always imagined, a perfect place. When a man came out of the house across the street and went into his garage, Paul wondered whether he saw him. But the man didn't look up.

After a while Paul heard voices. Laying down along the big branch, he looked to the front of the schoolyard. Sure enough, it was Marty and Line. They had suspected. Or maybe Ellie told. They came straight for the Big Tree through the long, swishing grass.

"I see you, Paul," said Line when she reached the bottom of the tree. "Congratulations on getting yourself up!"

"It's great up here!" said Paul. "I can't believe it!"

"Dad went to get the television," said Marty. "Don't you want to come home and see it?"

Paul considered. He supposed he did, though it was more fun to be up in the Big Tree, invisible. "I guess so," he said without conviction.

"I'm coming up," said Line. She hitched her arms around the trunk and started climbing with her knees, reaching for the thick branch. "Stay where you are," she told Paul, as she pulled herself up. "This tree can take all of us." She looked down at Marty. "Come on! Let's all get up here."

Paul looked apprehensive. He was furthest out on the limb, after all.

"Don't worry," said Line, climbing over him as Paul hung on for dear life. She was agile and at home.

Marty reached for the knot and the small branch of green leaves and pulled herself up. She climbed out on the smooth limb too and they sat in a row with Paul in the middle. "Three little monkeys," said Marty. "Sitting in a tree. See no evil, hear no evil, speak no evil. Which one are you, Line?" she asked.

"Well I do speak evil," said Line, grinning wickedly. "So I must be hear no evil, since you're the one who can't see."

"Okay," said Marty. "Paul's speak no evil. He doesn't either, does he. Put your hand over your mouth, Paul." She put one hand over each eye.

Line put her fingers in her ears. "I wish someone saw us," she said. "Dad would love it if it were true."

Paul laughed through his hands, which covered his mouth.

"Paul!" said Line. "I guess laughing isn't evil," she conceded.

Paul giggled again. What silly sisters!

15

Mother watched most of the Democratic and Republican conventions that summer on the rented television. Dad popped his head in now and then, and Marty and Line sat with her also, but speeches didn't interest Marty. She was much more excited that Mother was pregnant with a baby to arrive next February. Paul, the last baby, was born more than eight years ago, when Marty was too young to remember.

In November, when Eisenhower had been re-elected, the snow was heavy and people didn't get out as much. Marty settled in front of the television on Sunday afternoons with the rest of the family, watching news programs. Hungary was in revolt, students demonstrating, the statue of Stalin in Budapest toppled. Stalin was dead, but Soviet Russia would not give up the country.

The Hungarians declared their freedom, but only ten days later, wave upon wave of Russian tanks and troops entered the city. Line was incensed, but what could they do about it? The television news showed tiny people next to huge, lumbering armored tanks on caterpillar tracks, a long gun protruding from the front. Marty had never known how big a tank was before.

The moving pictures brought the Cold War into their lives as nothing else had. Soviet Russia was the enemy. Khrushchev, the new Russian leader, ordered the tanks in to quell the revolt, bringing the Iron Curtain crashing down around Hungary.

Though the stark black and white images on television came right into the Mikkelsons' living room, the reality was far away. Knowing the films had been made last week, and seeing people throwing stones at the tanks on the streets of Budapest helped Marty imagine them. But, the frost on their own windows, Mother's growing tummy, the leafless trees, the peaceful little town buried in snow were what she knew.

One day, Dad came home with a big cardboard box of used ice skates. He dumped them out on the floor and invited the kids to try them on, to see if any of them fit. There were high white leather lace-up skates for women and black ones for men with thick silver blades. All of them were a little scuffed up, but Marty, Ellie and Line began rooting around among them. Paul stood aside.

"I'm lucky I can walk," he said, sturdily. "I don't need to skate."

Mother stood back too, her swollen stomach enough of a reminder that she wouldn't be ice skating either.

"They've made the swimming hole into a skating rink this winter," said Dad. "I think we should go try it out on Friday. Paul, you can sled down the snow banks onto the pond, if you want." He looked excited, picking up one skate and then another, trying to find ones that fit.

"Here, Marty. These are the smallest ones," Line said, handing Marty a pair with its long grayish shoelaces knotted.

"I can't wait!" said Ellie happily putting on some skates. "All the other kids have been talking about ice skating and I really want to go! Thank you, Dad, for finding these!"

"These would work if I wore a couple of pairs of socks," said Line. Tying the laces, she stood up carefully on the kitchen linoleum, holding onto a chair, the silver blades sharp and dangerous under her feet.

Marty's were a little big, but they would certainly work. Marty was afraid she wouldn't be a good skater, but that wasn't going to stop her.

After an early supper on Friday, Dad put the sled in the back of the station wagon. The girls wore their skates tied around their necks by the laces. They were all dressed as warmly as possible.

It was a cold, clear night, the moonlight intense. A few tall lights, streetlights, were spaced around the front edge of the pond, but the far edge was lit only by the almost-full moon. The near part of the ice had been cleared of snow. Toward the far side was a sled run. Dad took Paul with his sled over to have a look and see how safe it was.

Marty's teeth chattered as much with fear as with cold, as she laced up her skates on a bench under a light.

"See where you warm yourself up?" asked Line. She pointed to a little house with smoke coming out of a stovepipe. She was already laced up and dancing on her silver toes, ready to leave. "Have fun!"

Marty shivered. She had rollerskated, but these skates were more dangerous. She stood up, walking gingerly in the snow down to the pond. It looked like wonderful fun, though. People circled the shoveled part of the pond, alone or in groups, laughing and calling to each other. They sailed into a dark spot and then emerged back into the light, twirling and sliding, cutting the ice with a loud schussing noise when they stopped near Marty. She stood near the warming hut, watching as people trooped past her.

Finally Marty put her feet out on the ice and starting walking around the edge. She wasn't balanced enough to glide, but slowly, as she got more comfortable, she could slide a little with one foot, then with the other, holding her arms out in case she fell. She was ashamed of how stupid she looked, but she must start somewhere.

Lots of the people on the ice were grownups. Patsy Ninas skated up ahead, making three rounds while Marty made one. She wore a green circle skirt and a short jacket, her dark ponytail streaming behind her as she came into the light. Line was doing a little better than Marty, sliding along, sure of herself. But it was wonderful to see Ellie. She and Helen Jorre skated together, hands clasped with a boy in the middle who was shorter than they were. Was it Bruce? The three circled lazily, their matching legs moving perfectly together.

On the far side of the pond the moon lit up the sled run. Marty stopped for a moment to watch. Sleds came down a little hummock, getting up speed enough to move out into the snowy ice. Dad climbed onto the tiny sled with Paul, lending his weight to give Paul a good run.

But as Marty watched, Dad waved to Paul and went back to the benches so he could put on his skates. Paul and the other boys dragged the sleds to the top of the rise and lay down on their stomachs. Two at a time, they went down, leaning with their bodies so the sleds went further.

Marty circled the pond, trying to catch up to Line. Patsy Ninas' legs flashed in front of her as she skated backwards. Patsy didn't even live in Bryson any more. Every move she made was beautiful. Every once in a while, she skated out into the middle of the ice and tried a figure or an experiment, some circles or a figure eight.

Dad came up to Marty on his skates and took her hands from behind, gliding with her. He was slow, holding her up and showing her how to move. "It's all about your weight," said Dad. "Let yourself sink into your feet. Let yourself go." And Marty did relax, feeling her body swooping into the steps. "There you go," said Dad. He let go of Marty and her balance faltered, but she kept moving, leaning into her legs.

Marty watched as Dad moved into the center of the ice. He was short and wiry and you could see how comfortable he was. He put one leg behind him and made a figure eight, then sailed around the cut he made in the ice with both skates, his legs wide.

Marty's toes were cold. When she passed the warming hut, she walked up onto the snow on the broken path. Inside the hut there wasn't much light and steam fogged Marty's glasses. It smelled like wet wool and kerosene. Marty squeezed in on a bench between Line and Julie. "Cold toes," she said.

Mrs. Sundeen stood over the stove warming her fingers. She was a large woman, but she seemed happy on skates. "How's your mother doing?" she asked.

"She's fine," said Line. "She stayed home."

"I should think so," said Mrs. Sundeen. She had a bunch of children herself, Davy the last one. She opened the door and went out into the snow.

"It's so nice in here," said Marty. "But I like skating too. Could you skate with me, Line? I think I do better holding hands."

"Sure," said Line. "I wish I was better too. Did you see Patsy?"

"Yeah," said Marty. "Maybe there's a skating rink where she lives."

"Come on," said Line. "Are you ready?"

"Yeah," said Marty slowly. The coziness of the warming hut was hard to leave. They opened the door, the air in front of their noses steaming up as soon as they got outdoors. It was easy to walk on the crunchy snow. When they got onto the ice they took each other's hands, crossing them in front as they saw others do, and stepped together.

"It is better for me with someone else," said Marty, when they got their legs synced up. "Dad showed me."

"He's good!" said Line. "I didn't know he could skate." They slid around the edge of the pond, following the other dark figures in big coats as they all circled. Dad came up behind them and then flashed on past, speeding low on his skates.

"Is that Bruce Ellingson with Ellie and Helen?" asked Marty.

"Yup," said Line.

"But he's three years younger!" said Marty.

"They don't seem to care!" said Line. It made her mad though, Marty could tell. Bruce was in Line's class and she tried to be nice to him, as he was adopted. "I think he's a little fast," she said low to Marty.

"It's all so beautiful," said Marty. "If I weren't cold, it would be perfect."

"I'm not cold when I'm moving," said Line. "In fact I'm perfectly warm." They were coming around the far side of the pond. "Let's stop and see if Paul's okay." They scanned the moonlit rise. A few boys were dragging sleds through the snow, and one of them walked with Paul's stumping gait.

"He looks like he's having fun," said Marty. "And you can't go up there with skates on. You'd just mess them up."

"You're right," said Line. She let go of Marty's hands. "Ok, bye!" She skated off confidently.

Marty followed her more slowly. She was happy. The circles were mesmerizing, plenty of room for everyone to go at their own pace. High school boys took over the middle, running with a hockey stick, chasing a small dark puck. One of them fell hard. Marty stopped at the warming hut again. Her frozen toes could not get warm in the cold leather skates, but water dripped off her mittens onto the floor.

Dad popped his head in. "Come on," he said. "I think we've had enough. Paul is back at the car with his sled."

Marty followed. She found her boots near the bench and changed into them, her frozen feet happy to walk on solid ground. Looking over her shoulder, she headed for the car, taking a last look toward the pond where the skaters circled under the light and the round silver moon shone in the background.

When they got home, the kids stood around Mother, who sat on the couch, their cheeks red and their coats wet and steaming. Marty leaned against a radiator in the living room, not wanting to take off her coat, her feet prickling as feeling returned to them.

"It was wonderful," said Line. "Dad can really skate!"

Mother laughed. "I know he can," she said. "There's hardly anything he can't do!" She looked happy, her eyes looking off as if she were remembering something. She pulled Paul toward her. "Did you have fun too, my little pioneer?"

Paul's eyes were bright. "Yes! The moon shone on us. And there was a rabbit. We saw his shadow in the moonlight!"

Marty's cheeks were rosy and her arms and legs felt radiant too. The radiator was burning hot, but her body was prickling hot and cold and it felt like her toes would never get back to normal.

Christmas passed in its usual happy blur, but all of them were beginning to sense the immanent arrival of a new family member. They talked as if the baby were already there. Next Christmas it would be.

When Grandma Mikkelson sent the Christmas lefse and klub, Mother fried up the klub in butter, but wouldn't eat any of it. Klub was sausage made with flour and blood and fat, and bits of barley. The kids loved the sweet, dark taste, but none of them wanted to watch Grandma make it. Dad told them enough. Lefse was a flat Norwegian bread, baked lightly on a circular griddle. Spread with butter, and sometimes sugar, and folded into triangular pie-shaped wedges, it was a great treat.

In February there was a blizzard. Marty listened to the radio in the dark morning and sure enough, the announcer said the snowstorm would continue. Schools, the depot and the post office would be closed. "Snow vacation!" Marty cried happily into the bedrooms. "Everyone can stay in bed!" Snow fell for two days before the sun finally came out, clear and bright. Deep drifts lay around the house. Snowplows scraped the roads, clearing space for people to drive.

Dad was worried about Mother, but the hospital was nearby in Mayville, and they left when it started to look as though Mother was about to have the baby. The kids were so excited that they couldn't go to bed. The question was, would it be a boy or a girl?

Late that night the phone rang and they all rushed downstairs into the study. Ellie lifted the receiver. "You have a little sister," said Dad, loud enough so they could all hear. "Her name is Kristen, but we are trying to decide on her middle name. It will be either Mary or Esther. Are you all there? How many of you vote for Esther?"

A little flurry happened around the phone. The kids said softly "Not Esther!" "We like Mary." Esther was an Old Testament name, but Mary sounded better, Kristen Mary Mikkelson. They were glad she would have a Norwegian name to begin with.

"None of us wants to name her Esther," said Ellie into the phone. "We like Kristen Mary."

"All right," said Dad. "Sounds unanimous. Mother likes it too, so I'm going to tell them for the birth certificate. Go to bed now, kids. Everything's fine. I'll be home after a while. God be with you."

The winter wind howled around the house as Marty snuggled down into her covers, but she couldn't go to sleep. A little sister! What would she be like? Of course, Paul probably wanted a brother, but God saw fit to send another girl. This one is mine, Marty thought to herself. It had been hard for her to penetrate Paul and Line's strong bond. But Kristen was for her. A baby in the family was more than she could have wished for.

The bulletin board in the dining room was covered with congratulatory cards when Mother and Dad brought Kristen home a few days later. Presents for Mother and the baby piled up on the dining room table.

Mother put Kristen on the bassinette and pulled off the blankets. She was a tiny red thing with a barrel chest and a bandage around her middle. Kristen lay on her back, tiny hands clenched next to her face, oblivious to her brother and sisters who crowded around. She didn't have much hair, and her skin was mottled red and pink.

"Look at her perfect little toes," said Paul, touching them with a finger. "How did she breathe when she was inside of you?"

"Her oxygen and food came through the umbilical cord," said Mother. "That's where she was connected to me. It will fall off soon. You know, where your belly button is. We can take the bandage off when it dries up." She changed Kristen's diaper and wrapped her in a blanket. "You can hold her if you sit down somewhere. I'll bring her to you."

The kids sat on the sofa and carefully passed the little bundle from one to the other, awe on their faces. For the first few weeks, Mother did most of the baby care, but as Kristen's flesh turned pink and rosy and she appeared more sturdy, all of the kids learned to take care of her.

Baby bottles were sterilized in hot water on the stove and Mother made the formula. The filled bottles were kept in the refrigerator. If Marty were going to feed Kristen, she heated one in warm water. She tested the milk by shaking a few drops from the nipple onto the inner part of her wrist, as Mother taught her. It should be just warm to her wrist, not cold and not too hot. Picking up Kristen, she sat in the old rocker, the bottle cradled at the right angle so Kristen could suck it. Afterwards, she lifted the little bundle against her shoulder and patted Kristen's back, so she could burp.

Marty was there, front and center, whenever Mother needed help with Kristen. She bathed the little naked body in the folding bassinette made of oiled cloth. Then she pulled up the soft stretched oilcloth table on the top and laid Kristen on it. She fitted the tiny arms into a white cotton tee shirt, pinned on her diapers, and wrapped her in a series of blankets.

Marty gently jiggled the little body as she walked, as she saw Mother do. She loved holding Kristen when she was sleeping. Kristen smelled of sweet baby skin, her downy hair soft, a soft spot on her skull where the bones could grow bigger. A baby was a marvel. How had it learned to breathe when it came out of Mother's tummy all of a sudden?

In March, Mother and Dad, Paul and Baby Kristen drove down to Iowa. They stopped at the clinic to see Paul's doctor and visited a church and its parsonage in Montauk, Iowa. When they returned, they announced that the family would move to Montauk that summer. Dad had received a call from the Lutheran parish and he was going to take it.

The girls were in shock. Leave their school and their friends? But Dad and Mother liked the new parish. It was close to Grandma Bakken and Aunt Rose, to Paul's clinic and to Wittenberg College, which Ellie would soon be attending. There was a town church and a country one, and a big parsonage at the edge of town. The town was set into a little bowl with hills all around it. The Turkey River ran through it. It sounded very different from Bryson. What was it like to live near hills?

Marty and Line quizzed Paul. "What was the house like?" asked Marty.

"It's the same as this one, except much bigger. It was covered in snow, but there is a big evergreen tree in front, a weeping willow and cedar trees all around it," Paul said.

"Trust Paul to know all about the trees!" said Line. "Did you go in? How many bedrooms?"

"I don't remember that stuff," said Paul. "Ask Mother."

"Did you see the school?" asked Marty. She lifted Kristen onto her shoulder and stood up to walk around. She had missed her baby sister when she was gone, and took every opportunity to hold her.

"No, we drove by some places, but I didn't know what they were. The church is downtown. And there's a park, a block from the house, a square block of park with a little bandstand in the middle."

"I think it's exciting," said Marty. "I like new places."

"I don't want to leave," said Line in a mournful voice. "I was going to be in 4-H next year." Marty suspected what she didn't say, that she didn't want to leave Clyde. "And what about Mittens?"

Ellie too was morose. She walked around the house as silent as a stick, her shoulders drooping and her forehead tight. The kids didn't try to help her. She would have to work it out for herself. There was no possibility of her staying in Bryson. She would have to finish her last two years of high school in their new town.

Winter was long, with snowstorms into April, but the house was warm and having a cuddly baby in the house made it even more cozy. In the early morning, Marty went into Mother and Dad's room and checked to see if Kristen was awake. If she was, she pulled her out of the crib and took her downstairs so Mother and Dad could sleep longer. Kristen was fat and chubby now, and could sit up in the high chair if you propped her up.

After changing Kristen's diaper, Marty got herself a bowl of cereal and found a little jar of baby apricots for Kristen. She sat spooning them into Kristen's mouth, while eating her own cereal.

"Line, will you make me a piece of toast?" Marty asked, when Line came down, dressed for school and dragging the French horn she played in the school band in a slightly battered case. It was a used one, but quite beautiful Marty thought.

"Sure," said Line. She poured herself some orange juice from a carton in the refrigerator and put two pieces of bread into the toaster.

Paul came down too and found himself some cheerios. He poured milk on them and brought them over to the table.

"Should I make the lunches?" Line asked. "There's some bologna in here." When it was cold out, the kids took the hot lunch, but now that it was a little warmer, they brought their lunches in paper bags. Line lined up slices of bread on the counter and spread them with mayonnaise, putting a piece of bologna on each one. She wrapped the sandwiches in waxed paper and put them in brown paper bags for each of them. "Apples?" she asked.

Marty was flying a spoon around Kristen's head, watching her eyes move. "She's watching me," she said. "She's smiling!"

Paul stood beside them, looking closely at Kristen. "She doesn't have to do anything but grow!" he said.

"Make her a bottle, Paul," said Marty. "I need to go get ready for school." She was still in her pajamas.

Ellie was nowhere to be seen. Since Mother and Dad decided to move, she spent even more time than usual with Helen Jorre. She left early in the morning to have breakfast at Helen's house and walk to school with her.

Marty rushed upstairs and put on a school dress. It was warm enough now to skip the pair of corduroy pants she wore under it during the winter. She put on socks and shoes and met Line as she came up the stairs with baby Kristen and her bottle. Line would lay Kristen in the crib in Mother and Dad's room and prop up the bottle with a blanket, so Kristen could suck on it. Mother and Dad stayed up late, working in the quiet house after the kids went to bed, so they didn't get up until later.

"Come on," hissed Marty from the stairway. "We've got to go." The kids put on their coats, grabbed their books and lunch bags. They wore galoshes because the sidewalks and roads were wet and slushy, the snow not quite gone.

"I can't wait until we don't have to wear all these clothes," said Paul. "It's coming. Summer is a-comin'." He dragged a stick as he trailed behind Marty and Line.

"I wonder if they'll have band in our new school," said Marty. She was taking piano lessons, but she thought she might want to play an instrument.

"Of course they will," said Line crossly, burdened by the heavy French horn. "They'll have everything. Dad says they have basketball for girls, even! I am excited about that."

Everything the kids did now felt odd, like the last time. Mother and Dad packed every day while the kids were at school. When they got home, Marty and Line took care of Kristen. Mother complained about Ellie being gone so much, but it was getting harder to talk to her. She was 16, after all, and less amenable all the time. Marty could see that Mother was starting to choose her battles.

On May 1, the kids gave out May baskets. Marty and Line, and Paul too, made theirs from thick paper samples in an old wallpaper book. The paper, in pastel colors and flowered patterns, made beautiful cones and ingenious woven baskets. They taped handles on them and filled them with candy. May baskets were filled with soft mints, salted peanuts and chocolate eggs left over from Easter. Spring candy was different from Halloween candy. No caramels and orange and yellow candy corn now.

A May basket was hung on someone's door, leaving them to guess who sent it. But, as with valentines, the Mikkelson kids were sensitive to fairness. They only gave baskets to kids in their own class, putting them on their desks at school. Everyone got equal shares, just as Mother and Dad tried to make sure things were fair between them at home. Their friends could tell who had made each basket even without names on them. This was important because a May basket required a kiss in return. May was full of chasing and catching, and kisses for both boys and girls.

Marty thought that Michael was treating her differently than usual. His hair was cut short in a crew cut that he made stand up with glycerine. When Marty tried to catch him and kiss him, he wouldn't let her. He easily caught her, of course, rushing up and pecking her on the cheek when she wasn't looking at lunch one day. But whenever she got close to him, he raced away so quickly she couldn't get him back.

Finally, one Saturday in May, Michael, Julie and Craig came over to roller skate. It was a breezy day with high clouds. The grass was so tall and thick it would soon have to be mown and new leaves had popped out on the trees overnight.

"Here's Mittens," said Paul, putting the cat into Craig's lap as he sat in the tire swing, rocking back and forth. "He doesn't need much. Just in the winter, you have to have a litter box because it's too cold for him outdoors."

Line was upset that Mother wouldn't let them bring Mittens to Iowa, a cat who had been a member of the family for years now. Line had become stubborn, and wouldn't have anything to do with finding Mittens a home. But Marty and Paul were worried, and hoped that Craig and Julie's mother would agree to take Mittens into their house.

Line and Julie made dandelion bracelets, their fingers covered with milky, sticky liquid, while Marty pulled up fortune-telling plantains. "Where's Bruce," asked Line, innocently.

"He's with Father at a Boy Scout leadership meeting in Grand Forks. Father wants Bruce to get more involved in the troop," said Julie looking up with veiled eyes beneath her smooth, dark forehead.

Marty and Line knew what she wasn't telling them, that Bruce was worse than Ellie, that he didn't want to go to school and do what he was told. But he was only 13. He was too young to be on his own. Michael was in the troop and knew Bruce better than they did, but he didn't say anything either.

"How many kids will you have, Michael?" asked Marty. The plantain she pulled up had three long white strands sticking out and one short one. "Four!"

"Fie upon that," said Michael. "I say fie. That's just silliness."

Michael kneeled down, fastening his skates with a skate key so they would stay on his shoes, and Marty did the same. She pretended to be uninterested in getting close to him, so that he would get comfortable and forget that she still planned to kiss him.

They skated down the smooth sidewalk that connected the Mikkelsons' house with the church, sailing up and down the ribbon of grey concrete in which there were no cracks.

"I'm going to miss you," Michael finally said, seriously, pushing up his glasses with one finger.

"I'll miss you too," said Marty. "You won't have any competition for the best grades any more!" She flailed down the sidewalk, holding her arms out. She was hardly better at rollerskating than ice skating, but it was less frightening.

"Yeah," said Michael. "You were it." None of the other kids in their class were even interested in school. They were just there because they were supposed to be. "I'll write to you if you'll write to me."

"Oh, that would be fun!" said Marty. She remembered all of a sudden that mail could be used to talk to other people. "I've never had people to write to before. Except relatives."

"You'll never know what having Mrs. Wheeler for a teacher is like," said Michael. "And I guess neither of us will get to do 'The Virginia Reel' again. But I'll write you and tell you about it." Mrs. Wheeler's room was reputed to be no-nonsense. She thought students should learn history, English and math.

Michael was a better skater than Marty. He kept going toward the church, but he was looking away, watching a car pass, when Marty saw her opportunity. She rushed toward him and bumped into him, pushing him down onto the soft, thick grass. Firmly she planted a kiss on his cheek as she tumbled on top of him. "There, I got you," she said.

16

"This place looks like a cyclone struck it," said Line, arriving home on the last day of school. Wooden apple boxes packed with magazines and brown paper boxes of books crowded the dining room. It would be another month before the family moved, but boxes of things they didn't need until then were accumulating.

Mother wrapped china in pages torn from old magazines and packed it in an orange crate. Beside her were stacks of bone-colored china, a ring of blackberry briars and leaves painted around each piece. There were plates, saucers and bowls, but most of the cups had broken, shivered off their hooks in the cupboard by rumbling freight trains.

In the distance, they heard a little cry. Line ran into the other room and lifted Kristen out of the dingy baby buggy. After a nap, Kristen was sweet and a bit soggy, her eyes, hidden in plump cheeks, opening slowly. She smiled at Line as if she was satisfied with herself, but she didn't smell good.

"I think a little girl needs changing," said Mother, as Line held Kristen up for a kiss. She smiled at them.

"I'll do it," said Line. She laid Kristen on her back on the bassinette and took off her diaper, wiping the tiny bottom with a damp wash cloth until it was clean and pinning on a new diaper with big safety pins with plastic heads. "Want to go outside?" she said to Kristen, as if Kristen could answer her. "Come on, let's go outside and see if Marty or Paul are home."

Paul was in the garden, turning over the leaves of the strawberries to see whether any of the berries were turning red. There was no point in planting anything this year, as they would not be there to tend or eat it. Line sat down beside the garden in the thick, new grass, crossing her legs so Kristen could sit in the little bowl they made. Kristen couldn't sit up by herself very well yet.

"What was your last day of school like?" Line asked Paul.

"Okay," said Paul, evasively. Line knew he didn't think about people. He cared about plants, animals and stars, maybe not in that order. Stars were his latest hobby. He went out even when it was cold and looked up, especially if the moon wasn't bright, learning the constellations. The stars would be the same in Iowa.

"I hate it too," said Line. "I hate listening to people say they will miss me and stuff. I'd like to just disappear." There were lots of goodbyes left to say. The church farewell would be a big one.

Behind them, an afternoon train rumbled through. Line jumped up. "Come on, Paul!" she said. "Let's go count the cars and show them to Kristen. She won't grow up next to a railroad like we have." She lifted Kristen up and Paul followed them to the front of the house. Car after car passed with the familiar metal music of steel wheels on steel, ka-chung, ka-chung.

"Remember when you tried to learn to read by reading the names?" said Line. She was already missing her childhood, which was thrown into relief by the impending move. She hated to leave Mittens and she couldn't even talk about Clyde. She knew she would never see him again and that he would never write. He was already driving the tractor in the fields at 13, and smoking like his father. Leaving Bryson would be leaving some of her precious life behind.

But Paul would have none of it. "This isn't the last train you'll ever see," he said, matter-of-factly. "There are trains everywhere."

"Oh, all right," said Line. "You're no fun. Is he, Kristen?" she put her face in Kristen's tummy and snuffled, making her laugh. "He's no fun."

As the month wore on, every day was full of activity. The phone rang and rang, as people in the congregation asked the family out to dinner one last time. It helped, as then they didn't have to cook. Mother was worried about the Pastors' Convocation, a meeting of pastors from the neighboring towns. The group convened two or three times a year and this time it would be at the Mikkelson parsonage, which was in a state of shock. Dad told Mother not to worry about it. It could happen to any of them. The pastors and their wives would understand.

But hospitality was important to Mother, being Scandinavian. She wanted the house to be spotless and beautiful, her children to be clean and well-mannered, and to serve delicious food. It was a potluck, so they didn't have to cook too much, but there was no time for spring cleaning. The convocation was to be on Sunday afternoon, after the pastors held services in their own churches.

The Saturday before, Mother marshaled all the kids and gave them jobs. She trusted Ellie to clean the bathrooms and the kitchen, and asked Line to dust and vacuum downstairs and sweep upstairs, while Marty looked after Kristen and helped her hang out clothes. Paul must help with the trash and clean the play room, which was in a big mess because no one knew where to put anything. Mother herself would spend the morning washing clothes.

"Now, don't stuff things away," she emphasized to Paul. "Pack as you go. We don't have time to pull everything out again later."

Line sang as she vacuumed: "Give me your tired, your poor, your huddled masses yearning to breathe free!" Mrs. Wheeler played the song for them at school, the words on the statue of liberty in New York set to music. "Send these, the homeless, tempest-tossed to me. I lift my lamp beside the golden door." Her voice soared toward the end, as she imagined no one was listening.

Line pushed the vacuum up and down on the rug in the living room, not worrying about the corners. Soon the furniture would be moved, the room empty. "I lift my lamp beside the golden door." The music wasn't too high for Line. She could hear the chorus in her head. Line imagined herself working for the United Nations, surrounded by needy children after the war. She passed out food and candy and warm clothes. She was saddened by the dirty, poor children who crowded around. They seemed not to know that things should be different.

Whoops! The vacuum stopped all of a sudden. Line had pulled the cord right out of the wall socket. She stopped and took a break. Ellie wandered through with her usual hangdog expression, headed for the kitchen. Line was worried about Ellie. Ellie told her and Marty, "I just want to be normal. I don't want to move. This is ruining my life." But she wasn't openly rebellious to Mother and Dad.

Line went down to the basement where Mother stood at the washing machine, feeding clothes from the hot rinse water into the wringer, which she turned with a crank. She was about to ask Mother whether she needed to sweep the porch, but Mother's eyes were red. She was crying.

"What's the matter?" Line was frightened. She never saw Mother crying.

"It's my birthday," blurted Mother. "And there's so much to do."

Line was aghast. They had forgotten! Mother did so many nice things for them on their birthdays, and no one remembered hers! It was terrible! "Happy birthday," Line gave Mother a hug. It was the best she could do at that moment.

Mother stopped, wiped her eyes and blew her nose on a piece of Kleenex she pulled out of her sleeve. "Oh, well, I guess there's no rest for the wicked." She smiled at the joke through her tears. Then she continued wringing out the clothes, her hands red and blotchy from the water.

Line rushed up the stone staircase. In the back yard, Marty reached up to pin towels and sheets to the clothesline with carved wooden clothespins, Kristen in a playpen near her. The sunlight shone and the wind blew through the clothes. It was warm enough that they didn't even have warm clothes on. A cotton tee-shirt was enough.

"Marty, we forgot Mother's birthday!" said Line. "I feel terrible about it. What shall we do?"

Marty looked stricken. "That is terrible," she said. Thinking for a moment, she added, "I think we should ask Dad."

"I should have remembered," said Line. "Dad could have reminded us. But no, I'm old enough. I should have known." Line remembered that Mother was the youngest and half an orphan, pampered by her older brothers and sisters as much as the Depression had allowed anyone to be. Only since she married and had so many children did she have to work hard.

"Well, ask him what to do about it," said Marty. "He's over at the church."

"Do you think I should interrupt him?" asked Line. None of them bothered Dad when he might be working. But confirmation classes were done for the year. He might just be organizing something.

"When it's time for lunch, you could go get him and ask him," said Marty.

At noon, Line went to get Dad for lunch. Mrs. Arneson, representing the altar guild, fussed over the altar, dusting it and putting up new flowers. Dad changed the paraments, the colored silk hangings on the pulpit and the altar, to green. They would be green for most of the summer.

Dad looked up at Line, "Lunch time?"

"Yes," said Line. "I'll wait for you." She didn't want Mrs. Arneson to overhear her problem.

Dad looked at her quizzically. She wouldn't usually wait. But he was ready in a minute. They walked out the door together, waving goodbye to Mrs. Arneson.

"We forgot Mother's birthday," whispered Line on the way out.

"Whew!" Dad said. "I think you're right. I forgot!"

"Well, what shall we do?" Line had no idea how this situation could be saved.

"We'll have to take a rain check," said Dad. "Let's not say anything about it, and you kids make some cards for her. We'll give them to her tonight and tell her we'll celebrate when we get to Grandma Bakken's house."

"What's a rain check?" asked Line.

"It's when you have tickets to a baseball game, and the game gets rained out. They give you a rain check so you can get into the next baseball game free. Put the words 'rain check' on the cards," said Dad. "We'll celebrate later. There's just too much going on right now."

"Ok," Line said. She liked it. They could have a real celebration when they got to Grandma's house, and a little one tonight, just to let Mother know how much they loved her. It was the best they could do. Mother wasn't poor, or homeless. But she was certainly tired and a little tempest-tossed. Line got right to work, whispering to Marty, Paul and Ellie about the cards.

Supper was a hurried affair that Saturday night, bowls of canned baked beans with wieners cooked into them in the breakfast nook. The house was reasonably clean and stacks of clean clothes were put away, though packed boxes lined the rooms. Mother and Dad were silent and everyone ate quickly. Afterwards Line and Marty cleared the plates and scurried around. Ellie had saved the day by making a pan of Rice Krispie bars without Mother noticing and hiding it in a cupboard. Line dug candles into the sweet sticky bars and Marty rushed upstairs and gathered up the homemade cards.

"Happy birthday to you," they sang as they carried the candle-lit pan of Krispie bars toward the table where Mother, Dad, Ellie, Paul and baby Kristen in her high chair sat. Mother's eyes grew wet again and she brushed at her cheeks with her fingers.

"We did forget," said Dad. "But you will get two birthday celebrations. I'm sorry, dear." He looked at Mother kindly.

"You are all my presents," said Mother. She pulled Kristen out of her high chair and set her in her lap, kissing the top of her soft head. "And this is the sweetest one."

"Look at the cards," said Line urgently.

Mother opened the cards. Line's was a girl under an umbrella walking in the rain. The words "rain check" hovered above her. When you opened the card there was a rainbow inside with a pot of gold at the end labeled "Grandma Bakken's house."

"Grandma Bakken's house?" Mother questioned.

"We'll celebrate your birthday there," said Dad. "We'll consider today rained out!"

Mother laughed, but she looked at Dad questioningly. There was a lot to do before they got to Grandma Bakken's house!

Line had spent a lot of time on the rainbow with colored pencils, looking in the *Book of Knowledge* to see what the order of the colors should be. The pot of gold was also good. Line looked admiringly at her picture. It was the best she had ever done, she thought.

Marty's card showed three little heads up on a branch of the Big Tree, with Ellie holding a baby standing below. It said, "We all wish you a happy birthday, Mother!" The figures were a little stick-like, but the faces, hair and eyes were better. Mother leaned over and kissed Marty on the nose. "Thank you, Marty."

Ellie's card was a poem in her handwriting, which she loved to practice. She found the poem, which featured a bee and some flowers, in the fat literature book Mother often read from. "That's beautiful," said Mother. "And your handwriting is good!" Ellie looked down modestly, but Line could tell she was pleased. Ellie might think she didn't want to be in their family, but she was and she wasn't a bad sort either.

Paul's card was filled with recognizable colored birds, a bluejay, a black-capped chickadee and a downy woodpecker, the birds they saw on the winter feeder. "Oh, Paul," said Mother. "You have captured them perfectly. All our favorites. I didn't know you could draw so well." Hugging Kristen to her, she leaned over toward Paul and put her arms around him. Paul squirmed, beaming.

"Thank you all," said Mother. "It has been a wonderful birthday after all. What richness we have!" She looked appreciatively at Dad.

There were no real presents, thought Line. But Mother was happy. What did Mother want anyway, she wondered. Mother kept a small blue book by the side of her bed called *The Imitation of Christ* by Thomas a Kempis. Mother was trying to be a better person, just as they all were. Line had looked at the book, especially the parts which were underlined. They stressed unselfishness and putting aside the vanities of this world.

The next few days the weather was unsettled. Low grey clouds hung in the sky, like the undersides of pillows. "Pocket clouds," Dad said.

They heard that a tornado was coming, and then that it touched down in Fargo, about sixty miles south of them, carrying destruction across a wide swath of the sizeable town.

Dad brought home a newspaper. The picture on the front showed what everyone feared from tornados. Homes and buildings destroyed, debris picked up and carried for miles. People had been evacuated as they knew it was coming, but ten people died, and it would be a long time before the town could be rebuilt. The Mikkelsons didn't know anyone in Fargo, but the church took up a collection for the victims.

The tornado was sobering. Dad said their new home was in the rolling hills next to the Mississippi. Tornados were unlikely, as it wasn't flat enough. But there might be other hazards. No place was free of weather-related disaster.

A week before the Mikkelsons planned to leave for Iowa, Immanuel Lutheran and its sister parish out at Highland, held a farewell party for them on Sunday after church. People got up to say what they remembered about Dad, gently ribbing him. Line loved their farmer voices. Norwegians like themselves, their voices were rough and dry, as if they didn't use them as much as Dad used his. They wore their Sunday suits and ties, but farmer tans showed which ones wore ball caps in the fields, their faces red and weather-beaten below white foreheads, and which ones wore cowboy hats.

People told of the fishing trips the men of the church took up north to Lake of the Woods, of how Dad energized the young people through Luther League activities and events. One of the Torkelson kids, Ed, described moving the heavy bell from the old brown church to Immanuel Lutheran. He was in college now, home to help in the fields for the summer.

"Four of us were up on scaffolding wrestling that heavy bell across a 4x4 with a pulley. We saw it wasn't going to hold and put another 4x4 in there. But there we sat, watching that iron bell slowly go down onto the ground. We didn't know Pastor Carl was there behind us. Myron said, 'Jesus Christ, it's good to see that bell down on the ground.'

"Then we all froze, because here come Pastor Carl's voice behind us. 'I'd say that's one way to state the case,' he said." Ed laughed. It was a story from when the brown church building was put on rollers and moved down the street to form the parish hall at Immanuel. Line was too little to remember it.

Mr. Ellingson, who was now Bruce, Julie and Craig's father, said, "There was a Sunday when Pastor Carl couldn't remember the gospel he was supposed to read. He stood in the pulpit, paging through the Bible for many minutes, before finally we heard Lois' voice from the pew below. 'I think the gospel is John 13, verse 4,' and Pastor Carl smiled down from the pulpit and read the story of when Jesus washed the feet of his disciples."

Mother and Dad laughed at these stories and thanked the congregation. A table in the dining hall was full of presents and cards, including some for Kristen. It was clear how much the people loved Mother and Dad. But the churches were calling another pastor, who would move into the parsonage with its closets under the eaves, its outdoor fireplace and picnic table that Dad built. It was sad, thought Line. But they had known for months they were leaving.

After the farewell party, Line collected Mittens in her arms and went down the block to sit in the long grass near the alley where they sometimes played. She stroked Mittens, crooning to her like a baby. Mittens had often consoled her for the shortcomings of people.

Deep within herself, Line didn't have much use for the church. She liked people, but not the surfaces everyone presented. For church, parents and children dressed up in their best clothes, acting as if they never yelled at each other or hit each other, were never bitter or mean. They were quick to judge others, but less clear on their own faults.

Even Dad, whom everyone loved, was not above yelling at or slapping his kids. Line knew his anger well, much as he tried to control it. She herself was stubborn, but at least she knew it. Mother would say, "Line got my stubbornness. Her Dad still has his!"

Most damning, in Line's eyes, was the fact that she was told that animals didn't have souls. Line had been working on this question in her mind for a while. That's just not right, she thought to herself. But if they're not right about that, how could these Christians be right about anything?

Line knew no one but Christians, however, and she desperately wanted to be good, to be of use in the world. She had no patience for hypocrisy, for people who presented themselves as good, yet harbored mean and unclean thoughts. Marty was quite capable, Line knew, of pretending. When Mother came up after bedtime to see what the racket was about, Marty lay down in bed and pretended she was a good girl, when in fact she had been dancing around or talking as loudly as Line had.

Line deplored this craven behavior. She wanted to get to the underside, to find goodness in people, and it was surprising how often she found it under a crusty, sardonic surface. Like Clyde, who was a sweetheart, though he was flippant and even cruel to people who he thought weren't worth his trouble.

Line vowed their new town would be a clean slate. She would become a better person. Less selfish, more concerned for others. And she would watch her sharp tongue. She was sad to leave Mittens behind, but Mittens was independent, smart and resourceful. She would go live with the Ellingsons when the kids moved away. "Animals don't have souls, humpf," Line said to Mittens, putting her face into Mittens' beautiful fur. Maybe she would ask for a dog when they got to Montauk.

The last week in Bryson was hectic. Mother sent the kids out to their friends' farms, so she and Dad and Ellie could finish packing and loading the moving van. She kept Kristen with her, as Kristen didn't need much watching yet, and taking care of her was a rest from packing.

The kids went out to the Husvedts, who lived in the basement of a ranch house they planned to finish as soon as they got the rest of the money. Everyone was scared of Mr. Husvedt, who didn't come to church and didn't let Joan stay in town to play with them. But the day they spent at the farm, playing in the haymow and down by the creek, they didn't see him.

Mittens came from this farm long ago. They visited her brothers and sisters, cousins, nieces and nephews, barn cats all. Joan and Stevie showed them their favorite places and Mrs. Husvedt let them take sandwiches and lemonade down to the creek for lunch.

In the willows by the creek, Stevie and Paul skipped rocks and played with chip boats, while the girls made flower dolls of hollyhocks. They used the buds for small heads, sticking them onto the downturned flowers with toothpicks, and put another toothpick through them for arms. The resulting dolls wore long pink and lavender dresses. The seed pods were round and filled with small seeds next to each other like slices of bread. This became food for the hollyhock ladies.

It seemed to Line that she was too old to play with dolls, but so was Joan. They didn't know what else to do anyway. It was nice under the willows, talking, but Line felt forlorn, as if they had been sent away and couldn't go back.

In the evening when they got home, the house was full of cardboard boxes and orange and apple crates. The furniture was piled in corners and the empty wooden floors creaked. The mission barrels and everything else in the storage closets under the eaves came out. The kids had already packed their few possessions, but somehow Dad and Mother found things stuffed in the garage and in the basement, all of which must be packed.

The weather was good and the sun stayed up late into the evening. Line wandered aimlessly through the house. There was nothing to do and nowhere to sit. They ate hotdish sent by Mrs. Ellingson for supper. Line and Marty did the dishes, while Mother rested in the big old plastic-upholstered rocker with Kristen.

"I wish we would just go," said Line, handing Marty a glass to rinse. "It's like we're just waiting around for the slaughter."

"I'm excited!" said Marty. "It will be fun to have a clean, bare house."

"Huh," said Line. "We'll have to make new friends. Ellie's probably going to kill herself. But you seem perfectly happy and Paul just wants to explore the hills!" The new town, Montauk, was in the bottom of a bowl formed by hills around it. Paul had seen them when he went to look at the town with Mother and Dad.

"You won't have to be in the same class as Miss Perfect Carol next year," said Marty.

"Yes, I guess so," Line said, bitterly, allowing there was some consolation in this. There would be no more YCL either, but Carol had spoiled it anyway by pre-empting Line's participation. "Do you always have to be such a Pollyanna?" She poured the dirty water out of the dishpan.

Marty didn't disagree. She just smiled and hung up the dishtowel.

"Of course, you'll spend all your time writing to your boyfriend Michael," Line said in a voice laced with sarcasm. She envied the locket Michael gave Marty, clear heavy glass with a red carved rose in it, the word "Love" engraved on the back in gold letters. It came in a white box, laying on a piece of cotton fluff. No one gave Line a present like this.

Finally the moving van came. The furniture went into it, the boxes of books and dishes and winter clothes and Dad's ham radio equipment. It took all day to pack the van and the house echoed when they walked around in it, the floorboards creaking. That night they slept on the living room floor in a few old army sleeping bags. They didn't have to worry about Kristen, because there was no place for her to fall!

Line was tired. She lay down with her head on a folded sweatshirt and was dead to the world.

The next day they got up so early the sun wasn't up. They went next door and Alma served coffee and milk with cinnamon rolls. Everyone hugged goodbye and tears struggled down Alma's pink papery cheeks. Helen Jorre stood out by the car in a sleeveless blouse and shorts, waiting to say one last goodbye to Ellie.

"Hey, kids," said Dad, as heartily as possible. "Let's get this show on the road!" And the Mikkelsons got into the Studebaker station wagon and drove over the railroad tracks and out of town. Line watched the tiny town recede on the western horizon, the elevator in the distance the last thing she could see.

17

"That's my red-winged blackbird," Marty heard Paul shout from the tiny space carved out of boxes and suitcases in the far back of the station wagon.

"Yup, I see it," said Marty, her head swiveling back to look. The Mikkelson kids were playing a "three thing" game as they drove south into Minnesota. The first to see a redwing blackbird, a John Deere tractor and a screened-in porch won. Claiming an item required the confirmation of one of the other two players.

Marty had found two of the three items, but so had Line and Paul. The next person who found something would win. Only sharp eyes caught the red crest on the wing of a blackbird on a fence post at 60 miles per hour, but the Mikkelsons were up to it. Marty could see well through her glasses.

Up front, Dad drove steadily down the two-lane highway. Mother sat beside him, holding Kristen. The windows were cracked open, and the breeze brisk, but moisture and heat dampened Marty's skin as she sat between Ellie and Line in the middle seat. Her bare sweaty legs stuck to the leatherette seat and prickled. Paul, in the back, must be even warmer, thought Marty.

They had started early, but the sun was now high. They would soon be at Grandma Mikkelson's house, where they would have lunch. Marty hoped there would be crab apple pickles, or watermelon pickles or any kind of pickles. She loved the sweet cucumber gerkins Grandma made. Her mind wandered just long enough to miss what Line saw out in a field.

"That's my John Deere tractor!" yelled Line. Her eyes were the sharpest, though Paul's were almost as good. Line was also in the window seat. Marty had traded with Line when they stopped for gas. Neither of them wanted to dicker with Ellie for her window seat, as she was in a gloomy mood.

"I see it," Paul's voice was small, coming from the back. "You won, Line."

That was it. The game was over. Marty felt deflated. She wanted to beat Line, or Paul to beat Line! Line was older and she won too often. But it was too late now.

A freight train came toward them from the other direction, its whistle sound changing as they passed the engine. It was long, but moving so fast it was gone in a few minutes. Then again, farmland stretched out in every direction, green fields of corn with golden tassels just forming, low green fields of soybeans, black and white cattle in pastures. Clumps of trees hid white farmhouses set in lawns beside large barns with windmills to pump water. Rusty, abandoned farm machinery lay about some of the farmyards. Sometimes there were pigs crowded around a water tank.

"Can I see the map, Mother?" Marty asked. She spread the big map out on her knees. The paper was torn into slits at the folds. Marty watched to see the name of the little town they were arriving in. "Watson" said the small green sign. The road went right down the main street of Watson. Dad slowed and stopped at an intersection. He didn't mind. He liked smaller highways, even the county roads, where he could look at things.

Marty found Watson on the map. They had traveled south for most of the morning, but now they headed southeast. Dad didn't really need the map because he made this trip so often. This was the country where he had grown up.

"I'm thirsty," said Line's voice.

Marty smiled at her. "You're thinking about that red jug of cold water in Grandma Mikkelson's frig, aren't you?"

"How did you know?" Line's laughing eyes looked at her. Dad just kept driving, if he was even listening. Probably not. With so many kids in the car, he didn't stop for anything unless it was absolutely necessary. They had already had a rest stop.

Marty added up the miles they still had to go from the little red figures on the map. If Dad drove at 60 miles per hour, it was easy to figure out how long it would take. "We're almost at Grandma's house!" she announced.

"How long?" asked Line.

"Less than half an hour," said Marty. On the other side of her, Ellie sighed. She was off in some private dream world, her bangs damp on her forehead, her head leaning on the glass.

"How are you doing back there, Paul?" Mother turned around to ask. He sometimes got car sick, but he was also the smallest and could shut his eyes and put his head down on a pillow.

"Okay," said Paul, his voice muffled by the things packed around him.

Out of silliness and boredom, Line tried to twitch the map out of Marty's hands, batting it and laughing. But she was right behind Dad and pretty soon the map was bumping into his head.

"Girls!" came Mother's stern voice. "Don't bother Dad when he's driving." She lifted Kristen to her shoulder.

Line smirked at Marty and turned toward the window, keeping her hands to herself. Marty folded up the map into its proper folds with the Minnesota cover in front. They wouldn't need it until after lunch.

"I bet you would like some lunch, wouldn't you." Mother nuzzled Kristen, who gurgled in response. "Marty, can you hand me a bottle?" Mother asked.

"Shall I fix the nipple?" Marty.

"Yes, please," said Mother.

Marty dug into the small cooler at her feet and pulled out one of the glass baby bottles Mother prepared for Kristen. She unscrewed the cap that held the nipple and inverted it, so the nipple was available, and handed the bottle over the seat to Mother.

Kristen finished her lunch as they pulled into Grandma Mikkelson's house. No cousins were there to greet them as they would be leaving right away. They must drive many miles before they got to Montauk, Iowa, that night. The moving van was also making its way across Minnesota and Dad and Mother wanted to get there before the movers tried to unload.

It was wonderful to get out of the car and stretch. Marty breathed deeply of the cool air in the shade of the dogwood tree Dad planted long ago at the front of the house. At lunch, they sat around Grandma's big oak table with its lace cloth. There were indeed pickles and plenty of cold water, and Marty and Line got their fill. But then they all went to the bathroom, one after the other, and got back into the car.

The afternoon part of the trip was shorter, but they must still drive across the bottom of Minnesota, which was long. Marty spelled Paul in the back, and sat with her legs cramped, surrounded by boxes. She rooted around until she could get her legs up in the air, making a little lounge seat for herself. It was hard to look out the window from this position, but she also got headaches if she tried to read a book while the car was moving. So, like Ellie, she gave in to her current favorite daydream.

In it, she was in a train, being taken to another city to be tried as a spy. Cameras followed her but she modestly tried to avoid them. She was wrongly accused, of course, but people wouldn't learn that until the trial. In the photograph that appeared in *Life* magazine, her face, beautiful and sad, looked out from the train as it passed through a station.

It was hot in the back of the station wagon. Marty felt sticky and sweaty all over, and sleepy. Dad stopped for gas in a small town and then at the Dairy Queen. They sat outside at a picnic table along the road, licking the cool, white whipped cream in a sugary cone. Dairy Queens seemed to be everywhere.

It was past suppertime when they finally reached the town Grandma Bakken and Aunt Rose lived in. The Mikkelsons stumbled sleepily out of the car, Mother carrying Kristen.

Aunt Rose greeted them with a big bowl of grape lemonade. She took cans of frozen grape concentrate and frozen lemon concentrate and mixed them up with three cans of water each. She added ice cubes and ladled it out of the bowl into glasses. Marty drank as much as she wanted, happy to be liberated from the car where she was folded into a pretzel.

Aunt Rose was a grade school principal. But she was also a good teacher and understood kids, especially boys who didn't want to go to school. She had told Marty about a boy who came to her office every morning to talk to her, before he got the courage to go to his own class.

In Marty's eyes, Aunt Rose and Grandma Bakken's little townhouse was the opposite of Grandma Mikkelson's. At the Mikkelson house, built by Grandpa and Dad a long time ago, the oak furniture was old and heavy, and many things, like the linens, quilts and rag rugs, were made by Grandma.

The Bakken's two-story apartment was tiny, the furniture light and modern. There was nothing extra, only what Grandma and Aunt Rose needed. Aunt Rose's oil paints and drawings were in a basement below the apartment and upstairs were two bedrooms. In the living room was a rocker in which Grandma Bakken sat most of the day, eating little but graham crackers and Postum, the grain drink she used instead of coffee. She was delicate, straight-backed and a little shaky, but she told a story with wry humor that made you want to listen.

Marty saw that each of her grandmothers had their own idea of how things should be. Grandma Mikkelson, Dad's mother, was a practical peasant woman who worked hard and liked to do everything herself. It was hard to help her, and she judged people by how independent and resourceful they were. She had worked as a hired a girl before she was married and she wasn't interested in books.

Grandma Bakken, Mother's mother, on the other hand, was a school teacher. When she married a Danish Lutheran pastor, she helped him write his English sermons. All of her children were educated and became teachers and writers themselves. She had an aristocratic sense of herself and a great respect for the life of the mind. At her house, Aunt Rose did most of the work these days.

Both of Marty's grandmothers were born in America, but they spoke Norwegian and their parents came from Europe. There were so many Norwegians and other Scandinavians in the places they lived, that they carried their northern European ideas seamlessly into the lives they lived in America. Norwegian was spoken in their churches until the early part of the century.

Mother and Dad could understand Norwegian, but they spoke it rarely. They were American, especially after the two European wars, which brought all races and emigrant nationalities in America together to fight and to do relief work afterwards, helping those who were wounded or displaced by the wars.

Marty would never be anything but American. But she could see in her grandmothers what it would be like to have one foot in Europe. At least Grandma Bakken hadn't lost any of her children fighting the war.

Aunt Rose, like Mother, used recipes from magazines. For supper Aunt Rose made a potato salad with cubed ham and cut up sweet gherkins in it. There were delicate white dinner rolls with butter and a large platter laid out with cold meats, cheese, carrots and radishes. Because there was no place to sit in the tiny dining room, they made up plates of food and juggled them on their knees. The kids took theirs outdoors and sat on the cement steps.

Afterwards, Aunt Rose brought out a birthday cake for Mother! The cake was a beautiful chocolate layer cake, frosted with butter cream. "I'm so happy you are going to be closer to us," said Aunt Rose. "This is a homecoming cake as well as a birthday cake." She lighted the candles and they all sang "Happy Birthday."

Tears came to Grandma Bakken's eyes and her hands quivered as she brought out the presents they had wrapped for Mother. There was a lovely scarf and pin from Aunt Rose and Grandma, and Dad asked them to buy the big "Birds of America" book, with its paintings by John James Audubon, as a present from the family. Mother was a bird watcher. It was another thing that wouldn't change when they moved to Iowa. Birds were everywhere.

But Marty felt like a guest at Grandma Bakken's house. There was nothing to do, nothing to play with and nowhere to go except up and down the sidewalk outdoors. At the back of the house there was no garden, only garbage cans and clothes lines. She took Kristen and sat outside on the front steps of the house with Line. Ellie stayed inside, listening to the grownups catching up, and Paul searched through a book he found on the shelf about dogs.

Dad came out and stretched his arms wide. He was tired too, from all the driving. "Run around a little, girls," he said. "We'll be leaving soon." The sun was going down, which meant that it was late and they should all be going to bed. But they must still drive several hours before they would get to sleep. The air was cooler, though. It was nice to drive at night.

Marty hoped someone else would go into the back of the station wagon for the last leg of the trip. Paul was sleepy, so he did. They headed south and soon it was dark, the bright lights of oncoming cars shining in their eyes. Dad dimmed his lights and so did the other cars. The air was damp and fragrant with smells, cut grass and hay, occasionally the smell of manure.

Dad started singing in the dark, "Tell me why, the stars do shine." Mother's sweet alto took up the harmony, "Tell me why the ivy twines, tell me why the sky's so blue, and I will tell you, just why I love you." Their voices together were the most beautiful thing Marty could imagine.

Line and Ellie took up the tune, and Marty sang harmony with Mother. From the back they could hear Paul's little voice. "Because God ma-ade the stars to shine, because God ma-ade the ivy twine, because God ma-ade the sky so blue, because God made me, that's why I love you."

Soon Mother was sleeping with Kristen in her arms and Marty felt Line's head slip down on her shoulder. Ellie's head was on a pillow smashed against the window. Marty was excited. It was up to her to talk to Dad and keep him awake. She let Line's head slip down and sat forward so she could talk softly into Dad's ear. A sign along the road said that they were entering Iowa.

"Iowa!" said Marty. "I've never been to Iowa. Do you want me to look at the map, Dad?" she asked.

"It's okay, Marty," said Dad. "We're just going to go south about an hour on Highway 63 here, and then we'll go east when we get to Highway 18 and that will take us right home. You can help me watch for Highway 18. I don't want to miss it."

"We need to watch for it in about an hour?" asked Marty. She didn't have a watch. "Can I have the map?"

Dad handed over the map and a flashlight and Marty hunted to find out what towns they would be going through. "If we get to Fredricka, we've gone too far," said Marty. "There aren't many towns."

"It's all farms," said Dad. "Cornfields and hogs. That's what Iowa's known for. You kids will like it. The high school is new and it will be much bigger. More opportunity for you."

Marty knew why Dad and Mother wanted to move. Montauk was closer to Wittenberg College, closer to Paul's clinic, closer to Grandma Bakken. Family reasons. Marty tried to think about what she wanted to ask Dad, now that she had him all to herself for once, but she couldn't think of anything.

"Are you tired, Dad?" she asked. "Do you want me to talk about something?"

"No, Marty," said Dad. "I'm fine. Here I am, driving my carload of kids, my family through God's country on a beautiful night. What could be finer?"

There wasn't much traffic on the road. A few big semi trucks hauled down the highway, a few cars. The highway they were on became Highway 18, so they didn't have to worry. Soon they were headed due east, though it was so dark you couldn't tell.

"Does your ham radio license change when you are in a new state?" Marty asked, trying to think of something that would interest Dad.

"Nope, same as before, W Zero VQX," said Dad. "Just have to get some kind of antenna up. And I guess we'll have to change our car license plate. We'll be Iowans soon!"

Mother stirred and waked up when Kristen did. Kristen was so little that she didn't take up much of Mother's lap. She lay in a ball, like a kitten. Marty wished that she could take her, but Mother thought Kristen was too little to sit with the kids in the car yet. They were too jumpy.

Marty was exhausted when they got to Montauk. It was 2 o'clock in the morning. She was awake enough to look around as they drove through town, but all she could see was a little main street of brick buildings lit by street lights.

"That's our house on the right," Dad said, as they drove up behind a white frame house with a big porch. It looked much bigger than their house in Bryson, but everything was dark.

"Come on girls," Mother said. "We're home. Take your boxes with you." The kids piled out of the car in a driveway leading up to a brick garage, and Marty opened the hatch of the station wagon so Paul could get out.

No one was there to greet them, but the light over the back door was on and no one locked their doors. Dad turned on more lights as they walked through a big kitchen and then into a dining room and a living room. The rooms were empty except for carpets on the floor. It will be a little softer than last night, thought Marty. She was way too tired to care where she slept.

In the morning, they again woke up on the floor when the moving van came. Big squares of sunlight came in through the uncurtained windows. After some sleep everything looked more interesting.

Marty marched up the grand staircase, her hands on the smooth banister held up by delicate, carved wooden spindles. She walked through the empty bedrooms and up a tiny hidden stairway to the attic. The exposed wooden timbers of the attic were old, dark brown with nails sticking out. The windows, one on each side of the huge uninsulated room, weren't meant to open. The air was stuffy, melting with the heat of the summer. In a pile in a corner were boxes, trunks and furniture.

Marty went to the front window and looked down into the yard. A big pine tree rose up in the corner, a weeping willow tree close to the front porch. Across the street there was nothing but trees, the back forty of a house at the edge of town.

From the other windows, Marty saw houses on the street to one side, and to the other, one small house on half a block with a big garden and orchard behind it. At the back, only their own garage and a brick shed with a big garden beyond. One whole half a block appeared to be their own yard.

Marty raced downstairs. The family sat at a rough wooden picnic table in the yard. Tall cedars surrounded the edge of the space, giving it privacy. "Is this whole half a block ours?" she asked Dad.

"Yup! It's like a little farm at the edge of town. You just wait," he said. "We'll have vegetables on every square inch of that garden. And you kids will have to help!" He had gone downtown to the grocery, and brought bananas, milk and tiny boxes of cereal you could cut open and eat right out of the box. There were plastic spoons because no one knew where theirs were. Marty poured milk into her tiny cereal box, impressed. Breakfast in their new home!

Hills rose up behind the house. A field of sorghum, a corn-like plant used for sweetening by the pioneers, lay next to their neighbors' house. Standing in the summer sun, a sweetish smell rose from the tall canes. Behind it was a mill where the sorghum canes were crushed and boiled up. It certainly did seem as though their new home was on a farm.

The moving van rolled over the front yard and up to the porch, where the men laid a ramp over the steps and began to unload boxes. Dad helped, directing where to put the furniture. Mother and Dad, with Kristen's crib, moved into the front bedroom, Marty and Line took a large room and Paul was given his own room. Ellie moved into the small bedroom at the back, once the maid's room.

This parsonage was built during Victorian times, with a back stairs for a servant to creep down to the kitchen. The back stairs had been boarded up, as it was too steep and dangerous, creating a closet off a tiny hall outside the room. The attic staircase ran up from the maid's room. Marty loved these quaint extra spaces. She imagined that the little hall and closet would make an office. But she had never had her own room, and probably never would.

Marty and Line's bed and their boxes went into a large, west-facing room. "Do you want the left or the right side," asked Marty. Radiators under the windows prevented the bed from going there. The bed must be on the opposite wall.

"You can have the left. Then you can keep your precious things nice in that corner," said Line. There were no closets in the room and no wardrobe. "We could make a row of apple boxes for shelves when the china is unpacked."

"Okay. Thank you, Line." Marty was glad Line was interested, at least for the moment, in putting things in order. Line was messy, leaving things around as she moved from one thing to another. Marty loved having a neat row of books, loved her clothes to be folded, so they looked nice when she put them on. The room was much larger than their old bedroom so it would probably be nice in the end, but she envied Ellie that back room.

Marty unpacked Jewel, her best doll, but there was nowhere to put her. She wanted to keep Jewel for her children, but she was getting too old to play with dolls. Jewel sat on a cardboard box in her best dress, her lustrous curly plastic hair surrounding her delicate waxen face.

Marty's favorite "new" thing was the beautiful Kodak camera Aunt Mabel gave Ellie. It had an accordion front which extended the lens when you opened it. Ellie didn't seem to know how to use it, didn't care, might never ask for it back, so it was among Marty's things.

Marty lifted the black leather camera from her box. She had shot a roll of film on it before they left Bryson, photographing the rest of the family against the back door, next to the garden, by the picnic table and fireplace. When she got to the end of the 12 pictures on the roll, Dad helped her roll the film back onto its spindle in the camera and put it in a sealed envelope. They would have the negative developed when they got to Iowa, he said. Marty didn't dare ask about it until the house got more settled.

The town of Montauk was primed for the arrival of this big new family. In church Marty met the kids who would be her class. Most of them lived on farms and came in to school on buses. When she was introduced to people, Marty felt large and special, the new pastor's daughter. But this feeling quickly wore off when she realized she didn't know a thing the kids were talking about and didn't know what to say to them. Then she felt small and insignificant, especially when she couldn't remember all the new names.

Few kids lived in their immediate neighborhood. Marty, Line and Paul spent the rest of the summer exploring the hills and the creek near their house. They climbed the path past the sorghum mill up the hill, Paul limping a little. He still didn't do well on hills.

"Who does this belong to?" wondered Line, surprised they could walk on the land freely.

"I think it's a cow pasture," said Marty.

"But we didn't climb over any fences," said Line.

"You're right," said Marty. "And there aren't any cow pies, either. Maybe the town just left it like this for people to walk on."

The kids sat in the grass in a fold of the hill, under an ancient oak, looking down on the tiny town spread out below. A truck with a load of sorghum canes pulled up at the mill. Crushing had started, and the smell of the sweet syrup which was boiled off the canes filled the air. In the mornings, steam rose up from the boiler chimneys.

In the distance was an iron bridge over the Turkey River, though the river itself was nestled in trees and Marty couldn't see it. The white steeple of a tiny Presbyterian church built in the exact middle of the country by its benefactor could be seen. Past the little town and the river, another tree-covered hill rose up.

Marty looked down in wonder at how beautiful a place could be when seen from above, its human edges blurred. She thankfully put off the looming problem of not having any friends until school started. Before she got too absorbed and she stopped noticing, before she had habits, it was a lovely place.

18

After her initial jitters, Line loved junior high in Montauk. Every night of the first week of school, the Mikkelsons took time for a leisurely meal in the dining room. Mother and Dad wanted to hear everything that was happening to their kids. By Friday, Line could see how it was going to go.

Paul was in fourth grade at the old Larrabee school, a big brick building with wide marble staircases and large windows. It was built as a model, right next to the school Marty and Line went to, with a big playground out back. But Paul didn't want to talk about it.

"What did Miss Vasby talk about today?" asked Mother. Miss Vasby was ancient, a thin, upright woman in a lawn dress with a sweater, her hair done up in a braid. She was smiley, she liked kids and she had been teaching as long as anyone could remember. She was an institution.

"Mmmm. Lots of things," said Paul.

"Tell us one," said Mother.

Paul appeared to be racking his brain. Line piped up, trying to help, "You told us you were going to study Iowa history."

"Let Paul talk," said Mother. And they all sat quietly, waiting, eating the macaroni and cheese with frozen peas that Mother made for supper. Kristen banged her spoon on the wooden tray of the high chair.

Finally Paul said, "She told us about Governor Larrabee, and the house he built up on the hill, and how he built the school. His daughter lives up there now. He was Iowa's 13th governor."

"Good!" said Mother, taking Paul off the hook and turning to Marty. "And how is it going for you, Miss Bookworm?"

"It's okay. I like having different teachers," said Marty. "English, math, science in the morning, and history and P.E. or band in the afternoon." Moving from room to room for classes was a new thing.

"So you're carrying around school books all the time?" asked Dad.

"We have lockers for our books, but there isn't always time to go to your locker. I have to get P.E. clothes, blue shorts and a white blouse." Marty did not look happy about it. Line knew Marty didn't think she was good at sports.

"You too, Line?" asked Mother. The junior high had its own gym, and now, instead of recess, there were physical education classes. There were 96 kids in the newly consolidated junior high, which used the old Montauk high school. Kids were bussed in from two other towns, and it was new to everyone. A new high school had been built between the towns.

"Yup," said Line. "We're going to play girls basketball! I can't wait! Mr. Farnsworth is such a good coach. The kids say that the girls team out at the high school is championship material!"

"He's teaching science also, I hear?" asked Dad.

"Both me and Marty have him for science. Then in the afternoons he goes out to the high school to coach," said Line.

"So you two have many of the same teachers?" questioned Mother, looking across at Marty and Line.

"I think so," said Line, looking at Marty. "We haven't had time to talk about it yet."

"I met Mrs. Brookhaven across the street today," said Mother. "Mr. Brookhaven is a history teacher out at the high school. They have a new baby and wondered whether one of you girls would be willing to babysit now and then. You could use some extra money, couldn't you, Ellie?"

"That would be great," said Ellie. Ellie was the real surprise of the week. She was glowing, her shoulders relaxed and her face pink and pretty with her blonde curls.

"And how about that new high school?" asked Dad. Before school started, Dad had taken them out into the country to have a look at the gleaming low building set into the hills, two miles from Montauk. It wasn't open, but they walked around, looking at the football field in front with its sets of bleachers and the leveled practice fields in the back. They looked into the glass front doors of the blonde brick building and saw the trophy case now shared between previous rival towns. Spacious and modern in every way, the high school was beautiful.

"I love it," said Ellie softly, but she wouldn't say why. Ellie took the bus to the new school with other kids from Montauk.

"What do you like about it?" asked Mother.

"It's just so new and clean. And the kids are nice. I think it's great." Ellie never had much to say. Something's happened to her, thought Line. Ellie wouldn't tell them, but Line decided she would figure it out. It was odd. She and Ellie were the most apprehensive about leaving Bryson, but they were the ones who were happiest about the new schools. Paul was retreating into himself, Line thought. She would have to find out what was bothering him. And Marty also clammed up. She didn't seem to be as sure of herself as she usually was.

But Line loved school. Powerful new cliques between kids from different towns formed quickly. Line didn't understand them, but she watched and listened closely and soon knew who everyone was.

Eighth grade science lecture was held in the assembly room, with sun shining in the huge windows, the kids sitting at old-fashioned wooden desks attached back to front with black ironwork. Mr. Farnsworth took on all fifty kids at once.

"Come on up, Line," he said, responding to Line's bright face as he stood beside a Van De Graaf generator. "It won't hurt you."

The wooden floor creaked as Line came and stood beside him, turning the crank and watching static electricity crackle like lightning across the arc between two metal balls.

But Mr. Farnsworth didn't need fancy machines and electrification to get the eighth grade attention. He was short, with wiry curls clipped into a tough crew cut and he spoke quietly with great authority. If he went across to the window to adjust the shade, the kids followed him with their eyes, wondering what he would say next. He didn't seem to care as much about science as he did about them, teaching them psychology as well as science.

Line didn't understand static electricity, or any other kind of electricity. She could understand magnets, just not electromagnetics. But she loved Mr. Farnsworth and learned the answers to questions so she could get good scores on tests.

And she hoped, like many of the other girls in her class, that next year Mr. Farnsworth would consider her for the basketball team. There was a junior high girls basketball team which played a handful of games. This was where the top girls clique was made. The top girls got A's in school and were also good athletes. Line had little trouble getting good grades, but she wasn't fit. This surprised her, but she tried hard to stay on the team, practicing with them day after day.

The difference between girls and boys basketball was that there was an extra player, three guards and three forwards. They didn't cross the midcourt line so girls didn't have to run up and down as much. Line got Dad to put a basketball hoop on the garage above the driveway and begged Marty to practice with her.

"Now you're a cheerleader, I know you don't care about basketball," jibed Line, "but could you please shoot a few baskets with me?"

"Cheerleading is important," said Marty. "I need to hem my skirt today, and make my beanie." The school colors were purple and white, and the cheerleaders wore short circle skirts made out of purple corduroy, with purple beanies. They each made their own outfit. "You wanted to be a cheerleader. I remember. What's wrong with it now?"

"They didn't have girls basketball in North Dakota! That's what's wrong with it. Who would want to cheer, when you can do the real thing?" asked Line, reasonably.

But that was not a good tactic with Marty. "You don't need me to shoot baskets," she said firmly. "I need to finish my skirt."

Line went and got a couple of Macintosh apples from the bushel basket up in the attic, where they stayed cold and crisp. The apples came direct from an orchard, bought at a roadside stand on a trip the family took to see the Mississippi River. Line dangled the apples in front of Paul, who was watching a program on television about Sputnik, the satellite the Russians had put into space.

"Come out and shoot baskets with me?" Line wheedled. "I promise to come out and look at stars with you tonight."

"Oh, all right," said Paul, hauling himself up from a prone position on the couch. The October nights were clear and cold, perfect for stargazing.

In the middle of the day the sun was warm, but Line and Paul wore sweatshirts over their Saturday clothes. Paul was short and gimpy in the leg. He shot baskets gamely, but didn't care about it. They took turns doing layups, dribbling and running in to shoot, or shooting from an imaginary free throw line. But you couldn't dribble well on the broken concrete, and when an airplane flew over, they both stopped and watched the four distinct little white puffs streaming out of its engines against the stark blue sky.

"I really want to be up there," said Paul. "I want to fly."

"Some people do," said Line. "But where do you want to go?"

"Nowhere," said Paul. "I just want to fly."

"What's with you and school?" Line hazarded. "Are the kids treating you okay?"

But even with Line, Paul was evasive. "Yeah, I think so," he said.

"Tough to be a new kid?" she asked.

"I won't be a new kid forever," Paul said.

Line sighed. He was too adult, too stoic, taking the long view. The mills of God might grind slowly. They were much too slow for Line. "Let me know if you want me to beat someone up," she said firmly. "I would do it! You know I would!"

But that seemed to be just what Paul was afraid of. "I'm fine," he said. "Don't worry about me." He squared his small shoulders and wandered off toward the house.

Line ached for Paul, but there was nothing she could do. She stayed a little longer, shooting baskets up at the orange rim, listening for the swish of the ball through the white net. She heard a tractor coming up the road. David Berglund and his dad were taking a wagonload of sorghum canes to the mill to be made into syrup. David drove, standing up to wave at Line. He was in her class, and went to East Montauk Lutheran, Dad's country church. Line watched them. The sorghum mill belched off steam, and the sickly sweet smell of boiling syrup hung in the air.

The country kids were different in Montauk, Line thought. In North Dakota they had less money than the town kids, but here in Iowa, they ruled the roost. The town kids she met seemed to be poorer, like

Louise, who lived at the end of the street where her dad ran a mink farm. Line liked tall, tan David. He was independent and smart and didn't have to be like everyone else. Farm kids might be more physically fit from the chores they did, thought Line. She and her sisters helped cook, clean house and take care of the baby, but these things weren't very strenuous.

That night after supper, Line and Paul dragged the army sleeping bags out into the yard. They had looked at constellations in the summer, but the sky wasn't as clear. Now it was too cold to lie on the ground very long. It was hunting season and ducks flew south. Days were short, with darkness falling as soon as they got home from school.

Line thought it was cute that Paul's favorite things were his flashlight, which he used to look at a star map, and his jackknife. He had his own room now, and it made all the difference. He was all boy, but he still liked company.

They chose the most open part of the yard, back behind the garden where there were no trees obstructing the view. The lights of town were some hindrance, but they could see the Milky Way as it drifted across the middle of the sky, and pick out the Big Dipper and the Little Dipper with Draco, the Dragon, slithering down between them. The moon was waning, so it wouldn't be up until after midnight.

"I don't get it," said Line. "I just don't see that the stars revolve around the North Star." It was the star at the end of the handle of the Little Dipper. Two of the stars in the Big Dipper pointed to it. Early travelers navigated by the North Star.

"Well, we'd have to stay here all night to see it happen," said Paul. "Do you want to?"

"No," said Line. "Not tonight." Or any night, she thought. Maybe in the middle of summer.

"That's Casseopia, that looks like a W," said Paul.

"Yeah," said Line, "I see it."

"So now there's a little Sputnik up there somewhere," said Paul. "We'd need a telescope to see it."

"What's it for?" asked Line. She really preferred not to think about it.

"Exploration," said Paul. "It has instruments in it and they radio back information."

"I don't get that either," said Line. But it was clear that President Eisenhower wasn't pleased. If the Russians could put up a satellite, they might be spying. "It could be a weapon," she said.

"Nah," said Paul. "They just want to know, just like we do."

"But Krushchev said he would bury us!" said Line.

"Maybe," said Paul. "But don't believe everything you hear."

Paul might have been right, a little nine-year-old boy with a flashlight. And the question of security seemed very far away to Line. It was up to Eisenhower, and the United Nations. They lived in the middle of the country, far from factories, cities and atomic tests. They heard about them, especially since there was a television in the house, but it made Line cold to think about it.

"Come on, Paul," she said. "It's freezing out here!"

Paul got out of the bag he was snuggled into and rolled it up. "Don't worry, Line," he said. "God will take care of us. He promised."

When she was warm and tucked up in her bed beside Marty, Line lay there thinking about the world. Paul was right, of course. There was nothing to worry about in a cosmic sense, nothing they could do about it. Though she didn't think much of church, Line was as sure as Paul was that God held the world in his hands.

What she thought about were the many things she was doing. She liked basketball, but she was also enthusiastic about band and should be practicing her French horn more. She was taking confirmation classes from Dad on Saturday mornings, in order to be confirmed in the Lutheran faith. (On Mother's advice, Line tried to keep her mouth shut in class.) She took the babysitting jobs that Ellie didn't want. She still liked to draw in her free time, and at last, there was 4-H!

When Line finally became a member of 4-H club, she couldn't believe she had invested it with such romance in the past. Girls took turns hosting the meetings and serving dessert afterwards to those who attended. Usually mothers were there to help out and give rides. An adult leader from the state Co-op Extension education program coached the girls, and at each meeting someone gave a practical demonstration. They also had county fair projects. The country kids raised animals for projects, but the town kids made furniture or entered something they baked.

For her first demonstration, Line was paired with Louise because she lived close by and they could practice. Louise was a skinny, dark girl, her French Catholic family unusual to Line. Louise was already helping raise and feed the mink on her dad's farm. Line had seen the long, low mink houses at the end of their road, but she didn't want to think about the poor mink inside, grown for their beautiful fur.

Louise came to Line's house to practice making baked custard.

"I hate egg custard," Line whispered, conspiratorially. "It makes me gag."

Louise giggled, but she didn't say anything. Margaret, the lady from the Co-op Extension, wanted the girls to demonstrate how simple making custard was, so they had to do it whether they wanted to or not. Louise was ready to do whatever she needed to make her way in the world.

Mother bought the tiny Pyrex custard cups they needed. Line set them in a baking dish and put on water to boil. She scalded milk on the stove until it was just barely boiling. Louise beat the sugar and egg together with a hand-turned eggbeater. The tricky part was adding the vanilla and scalded milk. Louise kept beating while Line added them slowly. Then Louise carefully poured the custard into the cups. Line poured the boiling water around them to make a water bath, dusted them with ground nutmeg, and put the whole thing in the oven without spilling anything.

"Good! Now you will have to describe what you are doing as you go," said Mother. "Let's try again and talk your way through it."

"Again!" Line was aghast. "But we just did it!"

"Well, pretend then," said Mother. "You are going to have to explain each thing as you do it. That's the point of a demonstration. And because there are two of you, you have to know who is going to talk. I would like to be proud of you, Line."

Of course Mother was right. Louise and Line tried mocking up the demonstration. Louise didn't want to say anything. She just wanted to beat the eggs. But Mother encouraged her.

"Why don't you explain why you have to add the milk slowly," said Mother.

"So it won't curdle?" said Louise tentatively.

"Yes," said Mother. "So explain that as you go. Let Line start talking, and then Line, you turn to Louise and set it up so she can talk about the custard curdling."

It was exhausting, and it wasn't much fun to work with Louise. Line knew she should be more open-minded, should be more interested in this person who was so different than she. But she wasn't. Louise was as flat as a doormat around Line and was clearly not important in the junior high school hierarchy.

When the day of the 4-H meeting came, Marty had to remind Line to iron her 4-H uniform. Marty wore one too. They were a blue-green color, with white piping around a sailor collar and a white scarf tied under it.

They met in the dining room of a nearby farm. The room was filled with chairs with a small table up front for the officers. Line and Louise brought everything for their demonstration in a grocery bag. Mrs. Johnson showed them where in the kitchen they would do their demonstration and they sat down among the other girls.

The meeting opened with the 4-H pledge, "I pledge my head to clearer thinking, my heart to greater loyalty, my hands to larger service and my health to better living, for my club, my community, my country, and my world." Line put her hand on her heart, pledging with her whole self. She wanted nothing more than to be a good person. But she couldn't relax until the demonstration was over.

After the meeting, Louise and Line put aprons over their uniforms and stood at their station in the big farmhouse kitchen near the stove. The members dragged their chairs in to watch.

Line took a deep breath and said "I'm Line Mikkelson and this is Louise Dufresne. Today we're going to show you how to make baked custard. All you need is milk and eggs and sugar and your whole family will love it." She smiled with just a hint of wickedness at the people in the rows of chairs. Only a very sharp person, like Marty or her Mother, would have caught her true feelings about custard. She didn't dare look at them.

Once again Louise beat eggs, sugar, vanilla and salt, and Line added scalded milk slowly as Louise beat the mixture. Line described everything they were doing, asking Louise questions as she went. Louise poured the results into the custard cups and Line topped them with nutmeg. Line lifted the heavy pan and put it in the oven to bake.

"Any questions or comments?" asked Line.

"Was the milk boiling?" asked Janet, a sweet serious girl from Marty's class.

"I know you couldn't see it," smiled Line, "but the bubbles at the edges were just starting to form when I took it off the stove."

At last Margaret, from the Extension, stood up. "Good job, girls," she said. "Your speech was clear and natural. Good delivery. The only thing

I would say is that you should use more precise measurements. Teaspoons from your table service aren't necessarily always the same size. Use measuring spoons in the future to make sure of your results. Thank you."

Line looked at Mother, who looked chagrined. Such a criticism reflected on Mother too. Line hadn't even thought about measuring spoons. But everyone clapped and that was the end of the demonstration. Line sat down with relief.

Marty helped pass the cookies afterwards and she let Line take an extra one. Line was free until she heard the timer on the stove buzz. She took the custard out of the oven and set it out to cool. With luck, she thought someone else might want it. But no one did. They would have to eat custard again for dinner tomorrow. Line sighed.

Everything Line did seemed to involve competition. In band, she was the last of the French horns. She didn't mind, because the others had been playing longer. But it was hard to be placed in back of two seventh graders. Line vowed to practice more. She loved the sounds her French horn made and the way it felt in her hands. But she was lazy and had too many ideas for her free time.

The band didn't sound good. Poor Mr. Greenway stood up in front of them and, using all of his compassion and his best humor, tried to get them to play the correct notes in the correct time. It was only junior high. They all had a ways to go, but Mr. Greenway still looked pained.

At her private lesson with him, Line did her best, and Mr. Greenway nodded enthusiastically. "Very good, Line. You have the makings of a good French horn player. You understand the music; you must just find the notes! Now take this exercise for next week and please, practice!"

It home, Line played Beethoven's "Ninth Symphony" on the record player, listening for the French horns. Marty came in and listened too. She had taken up the oboe, though she practiced the piano more, because of her amazing teacher, Mrs. Jorgenson. But band was fun, and Marty wanted to be in it. In high school, they would get uniforms and play in the marching band.

Ellie was not in band. She wasn't in anything, so they didn't learn much about high school from her. She was hopeless, just as dreamy as ever. Line couldn't figure out what Ellie found to make her happy in Montauk, but she thought it must have something to do with boys. Ellie often stayed after school to help the home economics teacher and Miss Carney gave her a ride home to the parsonage in the evenings.

Line and Marty tried to spy on her, to find out what she was up to, but it was impossible. At home she was a cipher, helping Mother, taking care of Kristen, making clothes for herself, putting up her hair in pincurls, doing homework. And then she was gone. She went off to high school and that was that.

Alone, Line loved drawing most. There was no one to teach her, no one to help her, and that made it more her own. Aunt Rose gave her books showing how to draw figures, animals, and landscapes, but Line was teaching herself.

Before they left Bryson, Marty took photographs of the family with the Kodak camera Aunt Mabel gave them. Marty was thrilled by the resulting photographs, of Dad by the outdoor fireplace; of Line, Paul and tiny Kristen in front of the raspberry patch; of Mother holding Kristen. They were sort of grey and sometimes out of focus.

"But what do you expect?" asked Marty. "It's the first time I tried."

"They're beautiful," said Line. "I'm going to draw them." Line penciled in light places and dark places, sketching the round sunny faces, the little wrinkled blouses and pants, the tricycle in the picture, Dad in his khaki trousers. She tried them small first, and then bigger. No one said anything about how she was doing, how she could do better or told her to practice. She didn't show her sketchbook to anyone. As in 4-H, her motto was, "To make my good better, and my better, best." Only when she was drawing, the ideas were all her own.

19

When Mother and Dad took Paul to the clinic in the spring, it was only a one-day trip. Dr. Cousins seemed pleased when he examined Paul.

"You're growing, Paul. You're doing very well, putting a little muscle on that leg," said Dr. Cousins.

Paul smiled, but he held his breath to see what else the doctor would say. He could not forget the weeks spent in traction, with months of physical therapy afterwards, three years ago.

"Your toes are still curling in, however," said Dr. Cousins. "You'll need another surgery. But not this year." He consulted his charts. "I think we'll wait until next year. Give those muscles and bones a little more time to grow."

Paul breathed a sigh of relief. Time felt a lot different when you had something like this hanging over you. Any time you were free was a good time, and Paul could get around pretty well. He just couldn't really run. One leg was skinny and the other leg thick, but he didn't have braces. He felt like a normal kid.

"Looks like you are keeping up with your therapy at home?" Dr. Cousins looked at Dad.

"You bet," said Dad. "We're lucky. With my work it is easy to schedule it."

"How often?" asked Dr. Cousins. He hadn't seen Paul for a year.

"Three times a day," said Dad. "Regular as mealtime. Good little wrestler, this one. After therapy, we wrestle, if there's time." Paul loved wrestling, down on the floor with Dad. It was the best part of having polio!

Walking out of the clinic, Paul breathed a big sigh. Nothing to worry about for another year! Mother seemed happy too.

Paul might have felt normal, but the kids at school didn't treat him that way. At recess, the boys in his class ran to the back of the schoolyard, playing baseball and sometimes football. They ignored Paul, who was left with the fat, sickly kid Arnold, and the girls. Paul was new and strange, and the boys' ancient rivalries and friendships took precedence. The boys seemed to understand polio, but they didn't want to know anything about it.

Paul was by nature sociable, and it was painful to be treated this way. He felt shunned, as if he had something contagious. It opened his eyes, though. He stopped talking unless someone talked to him, and he found that the effect of that was to make him see interactions between people very clearly.

Dad came at lunch and did therapy with him in the principal's office. Dad poked his head into the schoolroom too, but Miss Vasby was old-fashioned and shooed him away. She didn't want any disruption or special treatment going on in her class. Finally, in the winter, when they saw that Paul was stoic, didn't ask sympathy, and was smart and funny, a few of the boys in his class welcomed him into their group.

Paul's social difficulties made his home and his sisters very precious. They knew him intimately, knew what he could do and couldn't, and didn't worry about it. Marty especially was a life-saver that year. At the back of her school's assembly room were shelves of books to borrow. They both liked the science fiction books of Robert Heinlein so much that Paul begged Marty not to read them without him. *Farmer in the Sky* was about a father and son who emigrated from earth to a colony on one of the moons of Jupiter. It wasn't the sort of thing Mother read to them. These books were just up from comic books, but Marty and Paul couldn't get enough. The special words used in the colony on Ganymede became a secret between them.

Paul was fascinated by the idea that a planet or moon could be made habitable for human life, that he could take off on a weightless journey in a space ship (where polio would be the least of your worries), and live where few men lived.

Galileo discovered the moons of Jupiter. It was said you could even see them with high-powered binoculars under certain conditions. The Russians had put a satellite into orbit around the earth. It seemed likely that in Paul's lifetime there would be men in space, but the idea of people living on other planets could only be explored in fiction.

There was no need for terraforming that summer, however. The earth's biosphere was just fine in Paul's eyes. The big garden attached to the parsonage was ready for farming! Dad asked Mr. Berglund to come out with his tractor and plow up the big garden as soon as it was dry enough, at the end of May.

Earth clods big as spades and black as night lay in the field. The kids, including Ellie and Kristen, hoed up the clods and raked the field smooth. Kristen was over a year old now. She took off her shoes and went barefoot in the dirt with someone keeping an eye on her.

Raking the field with his feet in the dirt, summer stretched out precious in Paul's sight. Several months of heat and sunlight in the warmth of his family, without worrying about social pressures or more pain than usual. Paul loved the black earth, loved being out in it barefoot. When his hoe accidentally chopped an angleworm in half he was miserable. It was said that both halves grew into new worms. Paul wanted to test this, but if you took worms out of the soil they dried up, and Paul couldn't bear to make the worms doubly unhappy.

Dad laid out long straight rows with strings and the kids planted beans and peas, carrots, beets and radishes from seeds. They hoed up "hills" and planted five seeds of corn in each a few inches apart. They also cut potatoes around their "eyes," planting two eyes per potato hole. Dad bought tomato plants at the hardware store and set them out, giving them plenty of room.

At the back of the garden, Dad found asparagus spears, odd finger-shaped green growths coming right up out of the soil. Marty loved them, and enthusiastically cut them off just under the soil with a knife to have for dinner, but for some reason, Paul hated the taste.

One weary evening Paul found himself sitting long after everyone else had left the table, facing down a plate of slimy asparagus which he must finish. Late in spring when no one was looking, he went out and stepped on the asparagus spears! Paul enjoyed this secret wickedness, but he noticed they were going to seed, the spears rising up into frothy trees. It wasn't the end of them after all.

Dad bought and planted apple trees. There were lilacs too, smelling sweet and purpley, like those in North Dakota. But the most precious tree was a gingko in the square of space at the back of the garage with lovely little fan-shaped leaves. Line told Paul the gingko was the last of a whole phylum of plants that no longer existed. It wasn't much taller than Paul and he loved it.

In the hedge which separated their house from the Sherwoods, Mother found nests of chipping sparrows with tiny birds in them. She told the kids to stay away from them, and hoped that no cats were near enough to notice. The Sherwoods were an older couple whose small house, garden and large orchard took up the other half of their block.

Except for Ellie, the whole family seemed happy that summer. Paul saw Ellie in a different light these days. He saw that the closeness between Line, Marty and himself put her at the edge of the family. She was older, with different preoccupations and there wasn't much he could do about it, but he did understand. Ellie had started drooping again. Who knew what she was thinking.

As the Mikkelsons expanded into the ancient parsonage in the warm weather, they found lots of odd spaces and places to explore. Line was delighted to hear that the pastor before them had kids who were known as "holy terrors"! The girls were older and a little fast. One of them had left a pile of belongings in the attic. Between the cracks of the floorboards in his closet, Paul found penciled notes. He showed them to Line, who said they must have been passed in school. They were just notes about a boy liking someone.

A shed with several derelict spaces in it was so full of old junk that Mother and Dad didn't try to do anything about it. One of the rooms was an outhouse with two holes in its seat, which now held gardening tools. Another held a pile of old magazines which Line and Marty sifted through, looking for interesting things.

Line found a magazine dedicated to James Dean, an actor who died a few years before in a car accident. She took it up to her room and showed Paul the photos from his movies. Dean looked both tough and vulnerable, full of deep feeling, but Paul was a little surprised and disgusted that Line should take to someone like this, clearly a rebel and troublemaker.

One of the back entries to the kitchen was boarded up when the kitchen was modernized. It was empty and useless, a shed attached to the house. Paul adopted this unused place as if it were his office, filling it with apple box shelves in which he kept tiny boxes of dead moths and butterflies, dead crickets and other insects, like the June bugs which flew thickly after dark in June. Marty especially was terrified of getting them in her hair. But Paul found them clumsy and interesting.

In the front yard were a weeping willow you could hide under and a large pine tree you could climb, if you didn't mind the sap. The branches of the cedars at the sides of the yard came all the way down to the ground, making secret spaces under them.

Under the cedars Paul made gypsy camps and Marty and Line were not above helping. They laid out campfires with stones and twigs and hung over them little aluminum cooking pots which they fashioned from foil. The most precious item, which was traded back and forth several times, was a set of grey lichens which looked like cups and dishes. Butter was a particular gold stone they found in the road. Cedar seeds were food for tiny dolls and rubber animals. Paul buried an orange juice can in the dirt and surrounded it with pebbles to make a well.

Enclosed in the corner of the cedars was a tire swing and a sandbox, which Kristen enjoyed. Paul liked playing with Kristen. She was a tiny human, watching his every move. She didn't talk, but he could see what she was thinking. He dug little ditches and made walls in the sand, driving tiny cars through them. Kristen's downy blonde hair smelled sweet when you kissed her. She was so much younger than the rest of them that they were all careful of her.

Dad and Mother must have been feeling optimistic that summer, because they bought a freezer made by people at the Amana Colonies, four feet high and six feet long. They filled it with frozen meat, vegetables, cookies and pies. They also bought a tall milk cooler in which cans of milk were stored. The kids lifted a handle whenever they wanted and cool milk flowed down a tube. The big airy farmhouse kitchen was big enough to hold both of these things, as well as a table with benches for eating.

Still, Mother and Dad wouldn't buy just anything. Dad reminded the kids he had made his own toys when he was growing up. When bright colored plastic hula hoops began to be seen everywhere and could be bought cheaply, Dad just laughed.

"Come on, Paul," he said. "Let's go to the hardware store."

Dad was a little less loyal to the hardware store in town as it wasn't owned by a member of his church, but he still shopped there. Everyone in Montauk fiercely supported the little town. Dad went to the post office every morning to hear the news and pick up mail. A tiny library building was sometimes open, and so was a sad, dull dry goods store with almost nothing in it. Paul and his sisters only went downtown to buy groceries and cleaning supplies.

On Saturday nights the farm kids came to town with their folks. The Mikkelsons didn't get to go "over town" on Saturday nights, but in Sunday School the next morning Paul heard the whispers at the back of the class about what had happened. There was no drive-in or even a drugstore where you could get ice cream. The farmers and their wives met in the Masonic Lodge and the taverns, but Paul guessed the kids must stand out in the street.

At the hardware store, Dad bought thick black plastic tubing, the kind used for protecting electric wires. He looked at the hula hoops and Paul tried one out, so they could see how big they were supposed to be. Paul was now 4' 6". The hula hoops came up a little higher than his waist, with a diameter of 28".

"Ok, now," said Dad. "That's about right."

At home in the garage, Paul watched as Dad sawed the tubing into lengths. "I'll make these a little bigger, since you guys are growing," he said. He sawed the tubes with a hand saw at 32" and cut little slices out of the end of the tube. Then he stuck the sliced end into the other, and taped it with electrical tape. There it was, a heavy-duty black hula hoop. Paul rushed out into the yard to show it to Marty and Line while Dad made two more.

Marty giggled, "Just like Dad. He doesn't realize that the colors are part of the fun!" But she tried it, wiggling her middle to try to make the hula hoop stay up and not fall. Pretty soon all three kids, Line, Paul and Marty were twisting their bodies in the hula hoops, while Kristen watched, jigging up and down on her little feet and crowing. Mother came out to see them and laughed, but interest in the hula hoops didn't last very long.

Paul found it was getting harder to collect his sisters to play. Line lay about her bedroom listening to "Top 40" songs on the radio and reading the pop magazines she found in the shed. Otherwise, she was out shooting baskets so she could get a suit on the basketball team in the fall.

Marty was hard hit by an article in *Life* magazine about Anne Frank. Anne Frank wrote a diary about the years she spent hidden in an upstairs annex in Holland because she was a Jew. During World War II she and her family were betrayed, rounded up and put in concentration camps. Though she also enjoyed Robert Heinlein, after that article Marty got lost in the life of Anne Frank.

Mother and Dad didn't pay too much attention to what the kids were doing, as long as they did their chores. A list on the refrigerator for each week showed who was to watch Kristen, make lunch, wash dishes, burn the garbage, clean the bathrooms. Rotating chores made them as fairly divided as possible. Toward the end of the summer, Dad had to badger them to weed the garden, as everyone lost interest. But they picked peas and tomatoes for dinner and the corn started to ripen.

Early one August morning Line and Paul walked out to the creek. Paul carried a worn Bible wrapped in plastic. Going east on the road, which became gravel as soon as you left town, they walked into the sunshine. Halos of light hung around every tree, behind the grasses, and touched the gravestones at the Catholic cemetery. The lowering sun made the sky darker and it felt like summer would not be with them long. Redwing blackbirds and meadowlarks still sang from the fences, however.

Paul and Line slipped down a grassy path skirting a farmyard. The sound of water flowing over rocks reached them as they squeezed through willows and there it was! Shining, clear as drinking water in the sun, it passed over sand and pebbles, frothing and gurgling as it narrowed and passed between larger rocks. In seconds, their shoes off, Paul and Line were wading in the sandy water. Most of it only came up to their ankles.

"I think I see more birds when I'm with Mother," said Paul. "We saw an indigo bunting last week."

"She's looking all the time when she's outdoors. She doesn't miss anything that moves!" said Line. She bent down, looking at the minnows in the clear water.

"I hate it that summer's almost over," said Paul, scrunching his feet down deeper into the soft sand under the water.

"Yeah," said Line. But her eyes were sparkling. "It'll be better this year," she said. Paul knew she was talking about school. She was going out to the high school this year. Paul would only be in fifth grade.

"Maybe," said Paul. He was no longer expecting anything of school.

"Let's pretend we're on an alien planet," said Line, intent on cheering Paul up.

"Okay," said Paul. "I want to put this Bible somewhere so hobos can find it."

"But what if they don't speak English," asked Line.

Paul considered. "Well, they would take it somewhere to find out what the words meant."

"Even if they found out, would they know what the Bible was talking about? Remember, we're on an alien planet. There might not even be people," said Line.

Paul got out of the creek on the far side and walked barefoot up the bank. "Come on," he said. "I know where I want to put it." The path was lush and overgrown. Iowa was hot and damp in summer, with thunderstorms. Paul took the path to a place where a large dead tree lay on its side.

Line followed him, watching.

"Have you seen any hobos around here?" asked Paul. "They might need to know about Christ's love."

"No," said Line, giving up on the make-believe alien planet. "I haven't really seen any, but there might be some on the river or by the railroad." The kids didn't go to the Turkey River on the other side of town because of this wonderful creek a couple blocks from the parsonage. The Rock Island railroad line ran through the far side of town, but the kids didn't even hear it.

Paul put the Bible wrapped in plastic in a knothole he had noticed on a previous trip to the creek. "I'll come back in a week or so, to see if anyone has used it."

Line said nothing about Paul's idea. She ran back to the creek, her feet splashing in the sandy water. Paul followed. He had delivered the Bible. It was now in God's hands. He yelled after Line, "Hey, wait!"

At the end of summer came Dairy Days. It was a week of circus in the park one block from the Mikkelson's house. The park was so full of trees it hardly ever got any sun, so the kids didn't spend much time there. A tiny gazebo in the middle was occasionally used for high school band concerts.

Paul was amazed to see how the circus stuffed itself into the tiny park, with a large ferris wheel and a tilt-a-whirl spilling out onto the roads at the edges. There were kiddie rides and booths to win stuffed animals if you could shoot straight, or hammer hard enough for a weight to come up and ring a bell. Vendors sold cotton candy and ice cream. It felt sort of cheap to Paul, but, like his sisters, he did not want to miss a single one of the nightly shows on the tiny stage.

Every night after supper, Line, Marty and Paul left Kristen with Mother and gathered in front of the stage where a ringmaster called out the dog show, the magician, the clowns and the acrobats. Electric lights strung around the stage lit up the darkness. The people on stage were so close Paul could see the emotions on their faces, their muscles and the details of their clothes.

The circus dogs were a family of smart black terriers who knew how to climb steps, sing for their suppers, dance on their hind legs and jump through hoops. Paul ached for them, following each other across the stage in their little red sweaters and hats, getting treats after each trick. People could usually say "no" to demeaning nonsense, but dogs didn't have much choice. The littlest dog stole the show by being reluctant to do anything.

The magician was okay, and the clowns were fun, but the real reason they came was to watch the acrobats, several of whom were their own ages. It was a family, of all heights and sizes. There were two grownup brothers, the wife of one of them, and three kids, the amazing Leoni Family. They made pyramids, jumping and tumbling, with the tiniest one, who was only five or six, confidently climbing up the others onto their backs. Paul watched the young boy, who was about ten, climb up his father and stand on his powerful shoulders.

"I wonder if he has to go to school," he nudged Line. But Line was watching with her hands in front of her mouth.

While the clowns danced around the stage, the Leonis set up a rope which drooped in the middle. One of the grownups walked into the center of this slack rope. His wife, on the ground, began tossing him clubs, which he juggled while balancing on the rope. The two juggled six clubs back and forth between them. On the ground, the boy rode a unicycle and the girl, who was only a little taller, stood in her aqua leotard, her hands raised to point to the others.

Then the young girl got up onto the slack rope, balancing with a pink parasol in her hands. She walked across the rope, the muscles in her strong legs tense as they tried to find balance. She curtseyed and bowed while the rope swayed, holding up her little parasol. Paul didn't think that Line was even breathing.

When the girl jumped down, she tossed a bouquet of flowers into the audience and ran lightly in her soft little ballet shoes off the stage. The boy on the unicycle came to the edge of the stage and bowed. Then the whole family, who had put on velvet capes, came to the front of the tiny stage and bowed to the audience, the six-year-old kid doing handsprings and backbends in front of them.

As the kids watched, the Leoni family walked out into the darkness, probably to a trailer they lived in.

"What I wouldn't give to be going with them," said Line. "Traveling all over, seeing places."

"You'd really have to practice then," said Marty darkly. "I bet they have to get up on that rope even before breakfast!"

The show was over. Paul hung onto Line as they walked through the crowds, stopping to watch someone shooting at a target. Line spent some of her babysitting money on a pink cotton candy, and they all ate bits of sweet fluff off the cone she carried. It was late, and there were fewer little kids around. The whole park was alive with weird, garish light and color.

Marty grabbed Paul and pointed. "Do you see, up on the ferris wheel? I think that's Ellie!"

It was Ellie, with a boy, and her blonde head was leaning on his shoulder, going around the big wheel in a little gondola. She was wearing a dress, and the boy was smiling. He was good looking with big shoulders.

"Wow," said Line. "So that's the secret she won't tell anyone."

"She gets letters," said Marty. "I've seen them, and they aren't all from North Dakota. Some of them are from a place called Elk Creek, Iowa."

"That's the town on the other side of the high school," said Line.

Paul watched as the wheel hung for a moment, the gondola with Ellie and the boy at the top. They kissed each other, maybe thinking no one could see them. Then the wheel dropped down a little, letting each gondola stop at the bottom, so the people could get out. The kids hung together in the dark, watching, mesmerized, as Ellie and the boy got out and walked toward them, completely oblivious.

Marty tugged Line's and Paul's hands. "Come on," she whispered. "Don't let her see us!" Ellie walked past them as if in a dream, but this time a real dream with a real boy.

When they had moved away, Line said, "I wonder if Mother knows."

"Probably," said Marty. "She's seen the letters when Dad brings them home from the post office."

The kids walked home, running into the front room where Mother was watching a drama on television with Kristen in her arms. She turned the sound down and hugged them. "I see you've all had fun," she said, looking at their lively faces.

"Ellie was on the ferris wheel with a boy," said Paul.

"Oh?" said Mother. But she kept any further comments to herself. "You kids better get to bed. Tomorrow is another day, you know." It was, thought Paul, and he felt his heart constrict. Only one more week until school started and the family would all go in different directions again.

20

Marty flew down the hill from her piano lesson on Mother's old bike, with its crooked brown-painted frame. Dad had told them that if they could learn to ride it, they could ride any bike. It was the only one they had anyway, and it was the fastest way for Marty to get to her lesson early in the morning and back in time for breakfast and school.

Marty was hungry. She could see her breath in little clouds in front of her. Tree branches and their last leaves were rimed with frost in late October. Icy white crystals formed on the withering grass, the bushes and the gravel road. Touched by the early morning sun, the frost was dazzling, but the atmosphere of cozy darkness pervading the Jorgenson house on the hill followed Marty. Dark woodwork, the ebony grand piano covered with signed photographs of Dinah Shore and Doris Day in glass frames, cozy velvet-covered furniture.

Mrs. Jorgenson, an older woman with gray curly hair and cheeks blushed with tiny pink veins, encouraged Marty. She liked the way Marty's fingers formed a delicate strong arch over the keys, "like a little barn." She praised Marty's sensitivity and worked with her on pieces by Debussy and Mozart.

Dad had bought a beautiful new blonde spinet piano, but Marty was the only one left taking lessons. She still didn't practice enough, playing because she wanted to please Mother and Dad, and, of course, Mrs. Jorgenson. She tried to analyze the chords in the Lutheran hymnbook as

Mrs. Jorgenson suggested, figuring out which were minor chords and which major, but she was only going through the motions. She did not understand music at any deep level and she didn't care. Marty did not think the piano was her life as Mr. Duncan did.

But none of it mattered after today. Mrs. Jorgenson and her husband were leaving that week for southern California where they spent the winter. Marty didn't have to practice until next spring when they returned!

Marty had never known anyone like the Jorgensons. Even in Montauk, which had many more kinds of people than Bryson did, the Jorgensons were unusual. They wrote novels together in the 1920's which were reputed to be risqué. Marty found a ragged copy of *The Circle of Vengeance* in the public library, and tried to find the juicy parts, but she didn't dare to actually borrow the book.

Sometimes tall, thin Mr. Jorgenson popped his head in and told Mrs. Jorgenson he was going to the post office or the store. Where did they live in southern California, with Mrs. Jorgenson giving music lessons to stars? Marty could not imagine. Hollywood was as far away as the moon.

Steam rose off the sorghum mill boiler chimneys and the sweet smell hung in the chill air as Marty dumped her bike in the garage. In the house, she got a bowl of cornflakes and poured milk and sugar on it. Line had left long ago to take the bus to Valley High School. Paul too was nowhere to be seen. Dad was in his study, but Mother and Kristen must still be asleep, as Mother often stayed up late.

A rush of heat entered Marty as she left the house, anger at her latest skirmish with Mother over the crinoline petticoat she wanted. Last night, Mother said that no, she couldn't have one. They didn't have the money and she didn't need a "can-can," as they were called.

As Marty stomped off to school, the mood of delight in the frosty October morning and the coziness of the dark Jorgenson house completely disappeared. She needed that crinoline, she huffed to herself. All the other girls wore them. The petticoats were made of tiers of crinoline net that made your skirt stick out like a bell. Most especially Barb Odegaard, the reigning queen of the eighth grade, had one.

The school year had begun well enough. Marty now knew everyone and was less confused. She loved the beautiful old school and liked her classes, except for the dreaded physical education.

When Marty arrived at school, Marlene and Barb were getting off a bus which picked them up at the end of their farm roads. Marty watched, chagrined, as they patted down their skirts in the wind. Fluffy white tiers of net and lace peeped below them.

"Hi!" they shouted to Marty in the crisp air. Marlene, the chattiest girl in their class, remarked on the weather. "Finally getting cold out! I put my hood up walking against the wind this morning!" All of their thick winter coats, even the one Mother made for Marty, had big cloth hoods, though these usually hung down their backs.

The girls hung their coats in their lockers, and rushed up the wide stairs to Mrs. Easler's mathematics class. Marty didn't think she was good at math, but Mrs. Easler showed them how it was used in the real world. She asked them each to choose a stock or two to purchase with imaginary funds. Each week they looked at their stock in the newspaper. Since they knew how much they "purchased" it for, they could figure out how much it was worth, plotting its value over time on graph paper.

Looking up from the *Des Moines Register* Mrs. Easler brought in, Rodney crowed, "Hey, I made some money since last week." Barb and Marlene crowded around the newspaper, but Marty waited. The stock market pages were in such tiny print that she needed the paper all to herself to see whether the blue chip stocks she chose, half in General Electric and half in 3M Corporation, did well over the weekend.

"Marty," said Mrs. Easler. She was older, with crimped graying hair. A tick in her face made her wink every few sentences, but she was so sharp and intelligent she didn't seem old to Marty. "Can you stay after school tonight? I need help correcting papers."

"Sure," said Marty. Mrs. Easler paid her 40 cents an hour. Marty's quick mind wondered how many hours it would take to buy a can-can. At least nine or ten, she thought. But maybe that would persuade Mother. Mother was quite willing to pay for piano lessons, but not for things that were merely fashionable, like petticoats.

What drove Marty crazy was that Mother wavered. A week ago she sounded like she might let Marty buy one, but last night she said that Marty didn't need such a thing just because all the girls in her class wore them.

Marty peered at her stocks in the newspaper and wrote down the points they had moved up or down. She figured out the values and plotted them on the green graph paper Mrs. Easler provided. They were learning lots of things at once. It was the first time Marty ever liked math.

When the bell rang, Rodney followed Marty out, teasing her, "Give me a good grade on my test, Marty. I need it!"

"I only check seventh grade tests," said Marty modestly. They both knew that Mrs. Easler asked her because she lived in town and could walk home. Few kids lived in town. Rodney took the bus back to Elk Creek, and then another bus to get home to his farm.

The kids streamed through the halls, stopping at their lockers to pick up books or drop some off. Marty went to English and then science. Hot lunch was served on plastic trays, hamburger hot-dish, vegetables and fruit cocktail, which they picked up in the cafeteria and carried into the gym. The tables would be folded up and put away after lunch. Marty put her tray down beside Cathy and Janice, not the popular girls.

"Did you hear that the Gunderson kids can do 100 sit-ups without even trying," asked Cathy. In physical education, they were being tested to find out how many pushups, sit-ups and other things they could do.

"They walk five miles down the hill to the bus every morning, and five miles back up at night," said Janice. "Even in the winter."

"Ugh!" said Cathy. "I can't even do 10 sit-ups without getting tired." She wasn't any more interested in athletics than Marty. Marty had been to Cathy's house, where her very own large bedroom was papered with posters of film stars and musicians. Cathy's family was poor, but she made herself happy in spite of it. She was smart enough, just not interested in the serious things Marty was.

"They can do more than anyone in the school. And they're not even tired after 100!" said Janice.

Marty sighed. P.E. was her nemesis. After a brief time as a cheerleader in seventh grade, she decided she couldn't keep up. She started band, playing oboe because she loved the rich, mordant sound it made. It was a difficult instrument, with a tiny reed that you babied into just the right wetness to play. But she felt bad that she wasn't better at physical things. It was why she was reluctant to put her tray down at the popular girls' table. They were smart and basketball players too.

"What's all this testing for?" asked Cathy.

"It's the President's Council on Physical Fitness," said Marty. "They're trying to decide whether we would be prepared for a war. I bet they care more about the boys' scores than the girls'."

"Fine," said Cathy, flatly. "I'm glad I don't have to go."

Janice looked solemn. Her sister was training to be a nun. Janice was gawky and serious, but she and Marty sometimes got together to do homework as she too lived in town. "We could be nurses," she said.

"Not me," said Marty. "I faint at the sight of blood."

But willy-nilly, they all went to P.E. that very afternoon. In the locker room, the girls changed into white blouses and blue shorts. They ran laps around the gym, as Mr. Johnson decreed. They did jumping jacks and sit-ups and push-ups. Marty was miserable. She could barely do one push-up. *And these are the arms that carry Kristen around constantly,* she said to herself! Girls' pushups, in which they could keep their knees on the ground, were easier. Mr. Johnson blew his whistle.

"Keep practicing, girls," said Mr. Johnson, his voice echoing in the large space of hardwood floors and cement bleachers. "We're going to have another test in a couple of weeks to see whether you've gotten better. Okay! Let's have some dodge ball!"

The girls chose up sides. As usual, the last girls to be chosen were Marty and Janice. Marty was quickly sidelined. She wasn't quick enough to avoid being hit by the soft soccer ball. Marty knew her mind was considerably sounder than her weak body, but it made her sad. She wanted to be good at everything.

In the evening before dinner, Marty took a moment to confide her troubles to her diary. Since reading *The Diary of Anne Frank* after a *Life* magazine article appeared with a photo of Anne Frank's winsome face on the cover, she had started a notebook, addressing her entries, "Dear Anne." The article in the magazine, accompanied by drawings of Anne's life in Auschwitz and Bergen-Belson, described her death and that of her sister three weeks before liberation of the camps in 1945, the very year Marty was born.

Marty treated Anne as if she was a friend with the same interests as herself. She didn't describe her most crass desires and anger. She imagined that, like Anne's diary, someone other than herself might someday read it. But it was a comfort, and when she looked back at what she had written she could see the feelings roiling below the surface of the words. She wrote that she felt she had two personalities, one bright and sociable, and one dark, ambitious and quiet. She called them Kathy and Kim, and sometimes told Anne which persona she was writing from

At supper the talk came around to Ellie's plans. Dad chivvied Ellie about her application for Wittenberg College. "The sooner you get it in, the sooner we will know about next year," Dad said, smiling. "You have good grades and you will surely get financial aid, since you are the daughter of two alumni."

"Going to college is the most important thing you can do with your life," said Mother, gently. "It enables you to be a cultured person and teaches you to appreciate books, music, and art. I was lucky that, even though I was a girl, my family thought it was important to send me to college."

"The girls in my family didn't get to go to college," said Dad. "And no one could really help me financially."

Ellie, as usual, hung her head. "I'll work on it," she mumbled.

Marty and Line looked at each other. They knew that Ellie was in love with Bruce, whose father was the janitor at Valley High. Line had discovered that Bruce helped his father sweep the halls and the gym floor and empty wastebaskets after school. So that was why Ellie stayed after to help the home economics teacher, Miss Carney!

Line told Marty she liked Bruce, who was handsome, but quiet and industrious. He was polite to everyone and worked hard in school. Line wasn't sure why he fell for Ellie, but, she confided, they were perfect for each other. Bruce didn't do athletics or band because he was reputed to be too poor, and because he was saving money to go to college. Since Line liked Bruce, she and Ellie had become friendlier. Ellie needed allies at home.

But problems weren't usually solved at the dining room table.

"I saw Ellie and Bruce holding hands in the corridor today," whispered Line to Marty as they cleared the table after supper.

"She's wearing his class ring on a chain around her neck," said Marty. "She didn't care if I saw, but I'm sure Mother doesn't know." Ellie, as the oldest, tested the waters of many things for Marty and Line. Ellie listened to pop music long before they were interested in it, and she had had a few fights with Mother about clothes herself. Marty watched Ellie become a woman, growing breasts and having her period. No one talked about these things beyond the minimal education girls needed.

"They don't want her getting serious so young," continued Line in a low voice as Marty ran water for the dishes. "Plus, he's a Baptist!"

"Yup," said Marty. She was in confirmation class now, and had learned from Dad that Baptists were not on the right track. "At least he's not a Catholic," she said. "That would be really bad."

According to Dad, Catholics believed that the bread and wine of communion were changed into the body and blood of Christ at the time the host was elevated during the service. Baptists, Methodists and Presbyterians believed that the bread and wine only represented the body and blood, while Lutherans believed that they simply were the body and blood of Christ in the mystery of the sacrament.

"She's almost 18," said Line, speculatively.

"I don't think it matters," said Marty. "In this family, you're not on your own until you get out of college," she said carelessly.

Line laughed, "I hope that's true."

But Marty wasn't going to worry about Ellie long. "I don't see why you love Mr. Farnsworth so much," she said. "He's giving us too much homework. And he's never going to even look at it!" She didn't like science anyway.

"He's a great coach," said Line. Girls basketball didn't start until football was over, but Line was hoping to get a suit on the girls team.

"Yeah, that's why he doesn't care about teaching," said Marty. Mr. Farnsworth was young, and he tried to hypnotize the class into feeling his personal power. It bothered Marty.

"Oh, yes he does," said Line. She looked up to see Paul in a white sheet painted with a huge black spider, a red hourglass on its bulbous belly.

"How do you like my Halloween costume?" he asked.

"It's good," said Line. "A black widow spider?"

"I'm an arachnid," said Paul. Line and Marty were too old to go trick or treating, but Paul wasn't.

"At least you're not Zorro," said Marty, scrubbing plates in the sink. "Every kid and his brother are going to be Zorro this year."

"I have to learn how to move," said Paul. "Like an arachnid. Spinning my web."

"First one long leg and then the other?" said Line. But Paul went into the living room where Mother was reading a picture book to Kristen.

"I don't see why you need a silly can-can," taunted Line, turning back to Marty.

Marty flushed. "And I suppose you don't think how you look is important, now you're in high school?"

Both of them were pin-curling their wet hair at night. Line's lovely red-gold hair waved, but she tried to train it by pin-curling it. Marty's dark hair was straight. Dad cut their hair short, layering it up the back in a shingle and giving them bangs in front. Pin-curls helped the bangs and sides fluff out around their faces, but the bobby-pins dug into their heads at night.

Mother told them, playfully, "You have to suffer to be beautiful, girls," which made Marty mad. She just didn't believe it. Ellie kept her blonde hair long, wrapping the ends in squares of toilet paper and curling them in tiny pink plastic curlers. Her hair hung down with tight curls at the bottom or swung about her head in a curly ponytail.

"Of course how you look is important," said Line, "but you don't need a can-can to look nice." She left the dishwashing pantry and went to put dishes up in the cupboards. "You just want to look like Barb Odegaard," she taunted loudly.

"I do not," said Marty, ruffled. But to herself, she admitted that Barbara Odegaard, popular, pretty, smart and athletic was exactly who she would have liked to be, at least in her Kathy incarnation, the outgoing part of her personality. "It's just the fashion right now." She was scrubbing a pot with a scouring pad, her head down.

"I think that you are a conformist," said Line, coming back to the pantry. The look on her face showed she knew she was trying to get Marty's goat.

"I am not!" said Marty emphatically, turning to her. "Just because you want to look fashionable does not mean that you are a conformist! Conformity means that you think the way everyone around you does, instead of standing up for your own values. Like smoking when you don't want to, just because everyone else does."

"Yeah," said Line. "But a can-can isn't much better than smoking. It's entirely unnecessary and you just want one because everyone else does. I think Mother isn't as worried about the money, as about you wanting to conform."

Marty looked at her, incredulous. Maybe Line was right. She hadn't thought of this before. But she couldn't let Line have the last word. "If you want to be a rebel just like James Dean you're just as much a conformist as I am."

Line tossed her head. "Maybe," she said. She hung up the wet dishtowels. Just above her, in the metal cabinet, they both knew there was a package of chocolate chips. "Do you want a chocolate chip?"

Marty did very much. They could take snacks whenever they wanted, but chocolate chips were hidden, kept for making cookies. She nodded. She was glad Line was more daring than she was.

"I'll just see if they're open," said Line. They were. She poured a few out of the package into Marty's hand, taking a few for herself.

"If I get started on these, it's all over," said Marty. Nothing tasted as good as chocolate. But she also knew that if she ate chocolate, she would see the results on her chin in the form of pimples. She sighed. Eating a few made her want to eat more. The two girls wandered out to the living room where Mother sat with the sleeping Kristen.

"I heard you girls arguing," said Mother. "You know that you will never have better friends than your sisters, don't you?"

"Yes, Mother," said Marty. She smiled at Line, softened by the chocolate. She didn't want to bring up the crinoline petticoat again. The fierceness of her desire for it and arguments about it wore her out.

At the end of October, the Sears' Christmas catalog came in the mail. Magazine subscriptions and catalogs found the Mikkelsons wherever they were.

Marty waited until Paul and Line got sick of the Christmas catalog and stole up to her bedroom with it. She lay on her bed under the electric light, turning the thin pages. They were filled with beautiful dolls, but she didn't even look at the dolls any more. Mother said they could pick their Christmas dresses out of the catalog this year, so Marty was hunting for the perfect dress. It was her once-a-year chance to have a dress that wasn't hand-me-down or home-made, Aunt Rose's Christmas gift to each of them.

After much shopping through the catalogs, Marty picked a white nylon blouse with a soft collar and a grey flannel jumper trimmed with black braid. It was understated, and thus tasteful, but also folky and feminine.

On a Saturday afternoon in November, Mother said, "We'd better get that order in so your dresses get here before the Christmas program!" The wonderful aroma of apple pies Ellie had just pulled out of the oven wafted through the house. The pies, made of Betty Crocker pie crust sticks rolled out and filled with sliced apples, sugar, cinnamon and butter sat on the top of the stove, still bubbling.

"Why don't you make out the order, Marty," said Mother. "Write down what each person wants on the order form, and I'll check it afterwards. That is also a good use of arithmetic."

Marty sat at the dining room table, writing up the order with a newly sharpened pencil. The corners were turned down on the pages where the chosen dresses were shown. Marty looked up the catalog number for each item, its description and size, and put them on the lines of the order form. Quantity was one, and at the end was the price. There were dresses for Ellie, Line, the blouse and jumper for herself, and a shirt, sweater and a pair of pants for Paul. For Kristen Mother selected a little golden brown pleated linen dress with a white collar, to match the red-gold hair that stood out in soft curls around her head. It had never been cut.

"She'll be the prettiest little girl!" Marty said to Paul, who sat at the other end of the table looking at star maps sent from *National Geographic*. She totaled up the costs on the right, and wrote the sum at the bottom. Then she figured out the tax and the shipping costs, and made a grand total.

"I'm finished," Marty said, bringing the catalog to Mother, with the order form tucked into it.

Mother looked over the order. "You know, Marty," she said. "I bet that crinoline would look nice under that grey flannel jumper. Do you still want to buy it?"

Marty looked at her, her spirits soaring. "Yes!" she heard herself almost shout. She had given up on getting a can-can.

"Do they have the one you want in the catalog?" asked Mother.

Marty knew the exact page the petticoats were on. She turned to them and showed Mother the one she wanted, tiers of fluffy white nylon net gathered into an elastic waistband.

Mother looked at it closely, reading the print underneath. "Well, I guess that's not too bad. You can put it on the order. Just erase your totals and re-total everything, and then I'll look at it."

Marty looked at her, her eyes sparkling. "Thank you, Mother! I promise I will take good care of it and I'll never ask for another thing!"

21

That spring Paul was not very anxious for summer to come. It was creeping up, the days lengthening and growing warmer, and with it his next surgery. By this time, he couldn't imagine that his skinny leg and the foot on which the toes curled inward would ever get better. But Paul was stoic. How could it be worse than spending several weeks in traction, as he did four years ago? He willed the days to go slowly.

On the last day of school, Paul slid down the giant silver tube that was the Larrabee school fire escape with the other kids. They were allowed to slide down on Fridays, even in winter if they wanted to, when the tube was cold as ice, and you couldn't touch it with your naked skin. This time it was warm from sitting in the sun. Paul swooshed down and didn't stop to play. He walked home, taking his time along the cutoff which angled across an old baseball field, and under the trees of the quiet residential streets. There were cicadas in the grass, but Paul just looked closely at them. He only collected dead things.

When he got home, Paul went straight to his "office" at the side of the house, the closed-off entry where he kept his collections. The smell was musty and comforting. His dried plants and insects mostly survived the ice and snow in little cardboard boxes Paul amassed in previous summers. But molds of various kinds clung to the corners of the room and the wooden apple box shelves.

Paul sat on a box, thinking. He could either get rid of all the moldy boxes and start over, or he could just leave them like a museum, a science experiment to see what happened. That was the most likely. He wouldn't have time to collect anything this summer.

He was also thinking about a dog. Dad and Mother said a dog would have to be tied up in the summer so it wouldn't get into people's gardens. But they said that Paul could have one next year, when he was free to take care of it. He was already dreaming about what sort of dog it would be. He knew that when he was ready, when they put the word out next spring, the right dog would be born somewhere and would find him.

Paul finally got hungry enough to go look for a snack. But first he peeked at the chipping sparrow nest in the hedge. Three little sparrows lay naked of feathers, keeping each other warm. The nest was lined with Paul's blonde hair! Dad put hair clippings out under the apple trees and the sparrows found them.

Watching from a distance, Paul saw the tiny yellow beaks of the baby sparrows open wide when their parents returned with food. The nest was so low any cat could have found them. Paul whispered, "Grow, grow!" It was a race against time, the sparrows needing to grow up and fly away before they were found by a neighbor cat.

Lilacs bloomed furiously by the back door of the house. Paul went in expectantly. Usually something was going on in the big farmhouse kitchen, his sisters milling about. But no one was there. Paul opened the top of the Amana freezer and rooted around for the frozen plastic bag of chocolate chip cookies. He pulled two cookies out, and re-clipped the bag with a clothespin. At the cooler he pulled down a handle and cool milk flowed out of a rubber tube into his glass. He sat down at the kitchen table, listening to see where the activity in the house might be, and enjoying the taste of the cold chocolate bits buried in his cookie.

Kristen toddled into the kitchen with Marty right behind her. She was talking now, and running all over the place. Luckily one of her many older brothers and sisters was assigned to watch her.

"What's everyone up to?" asked Paul. Marty must surely know.

"It's graduation night for Ellie," said Marty. "We're going out to Valley High School to see it."

"Wow," said Paul. "That'll be neat."

"Cookie," said Kristen, reaching up toward Paul's cookie.

"Can she have one?" Paul asked Marty.

"No," said Marty. "She already had one. She has to wait until supper. But she could have some milk if she wants it."

That night they watched Ellie in a blue gown and a cap with a tassel on it walk across the stage and pick up her diploma.

Afterwards, she stood at the end of the gym with her boyfriend Bruce and his family, and shyly introduced his parents to her family. Paul had met Bruce before, when he came to pick Ellie up for the senior prom.

"And what are your plans," Dad asked Bruce.

Bruce took the mortarboard off his head and brushed his hand over his glistening hair, relaxed and engaging. "University of Iowa next year. My uncle works up in the Twin Cities, at 3M Corporation. He thinks there's room for me up there, if I get a business degree."

His father, Mr. Morland, laughed. "This boy's known what he wants for a long time. Thinks he wants to be a city boy." Paul couldn't imagine this man in a blue suit and tie as a school janitor. He looked like a teacher, or a farmer or grocer. Mrs. Morland also looked ordinary in a print dress with a light blue jacket.

Dad and Mother laughed too. "You do sound certain about all this!" said Mother. "Not everyone has life all planned out when they graduate from high school!"

Marty seemed to be bursting at Paul's side, as if she wanted to say something, but wasn't sure if she should. "What is it Marty?" asked Dad.

"I tracked the 3M stock this year in my math class. It did very well. I could have made some money on that stock!" Marty said.

"Hey!" said Bruce. "Maybe I can find a place for you up at 3M!"

But Marty smiled and looked down shyly. Paul knew, as she did, that Marty was expected to be a teacher, as he was to be a pastor. Business was the world of mammon, not for people in their family. Christ threw the moneychangers out of the temple and wished to save their souls, not their bodies. In the Mikkelson family, the emphasis was on the soul.

The Mikkelsons piled into the station wagon and went home to celebrate with ice cream and cake. Mother brought out cards from relatives she had collected. Line brought two brand new beautiful suitcases out of a closet where they were hidden. One was a train case, with a little mirror in it to hold necessities, and one was the matching suitcase in which to pack your clothes. Ellie would need them when she went to college.

The day that Paul went off with Mother and Dad to the Mayo clinic a week later wasn't quite as happy an occasion. They all knew that Paul was in for another tough summer. But there was nothing that could be done about it. The doctors planned to do reconstructive surgery, transferring some tendons and fusing bones in his foot so that he could use it. They were experts by this time, since so many kids had polio at the time Paul did. Little kids didn't get polio any more, though, as most got vaccinated against it.

Because they now lived close to the clinic, it would be easier to see Paul while he was there. Mother planned to stay with him the first week, leaving Kristen in the care of her sisters, and Line would stay with Paul the second week. They would live in a rooming house and come to the hospital during the day.

The clinic felt normal to Paul by this time, but even he was unprepared for what he found when he woke up from the surgery. He was in a cast up to his hips. Open wounds on his feet were held together by stitches and he was in acute, nonstop pain, moderated only every four hours by a morphine shot. After the shot he would be in la-la land for a little while, resting. But then the terrible pain would slowly build again until he began to beg for a hypo.

"I can't wait until 4 o'clock," Paul said, looking at the wristwatch Mother brought.

But he must wait. The nurses would not give him any extra pain medicine. He lay there miserable, unable to concentrate on anything. Mother read to him, trying with her whole spirit to lift him out of his body and into a place of the imagination. But Paul couldn't focus. He receded into himself, like the yoke of an egg, resting after each shot, and then accepting the growing pain until it was time for the next one.

At night Mother left to get a few hours of sleep. The ward was quiet. There were three other beds in the room, but only one had another kid in it. His name was Roddy, and he had surgery a few weeks before Paul. At night Roddy slept, but Paul lay in the same tough pain as during the day, until the night nurse gave him a hypo and he could rest a little.

Doctors and nurses came and went, days became nights and then days again. Mother helped feed Paul and nurses washed him and helped him use the bedpans. But the pain stayed. At the end of the week, Dad arrived with Line. Mother had told him by telephone not to bring Kristen, Marty and Ellie. Kristen shouldn't see Paul in so much pain, she said.

Dad and Line brought the outside world in, fresh recruits to the war which Mother and Paul fought. Paul looked like a little wizened old man and Mother was exhausted as well, her peaceful features haggard and worn.

Dad brought cherries flown in from California and a transistor radio. The dark fruit glistened in the white hospital room like something from another planet. Paul bit into the dark sweet, crisp bing cherries and remembered that pain wasn't the only thing going on in the world. It would some day be over. He was exhausted. The cherries were the first thing he could enjoy. He ate them slowly, as if they were the last cherries in the world.

Line was subdued by seeing Paul like this, but she watched and listened. They came on Friday so Dad would be there when Dr. Cousins made his rounds.

Dr. Cousins looked sympathetic. "The cast will come off in a few weeks," he said. "Healing is happening all the time. You should be feeling a little better in the next week, Paul, but you will keep getting pain medication."

Dad stood by the head of Paul's bed, smoothing his warm hand across Paul's pale forehead and holding one of his hands. "Watch and pray, Paul," he said. "I hate to leave you here, but God is with you. We are all with you in spirit."

Line assured Mother and Dad she could watch over Paul. "I'm 15 already, and I can call the nurses if Paul needs them," she said. "Go ahead, Mother, you need rest too. We'll be okay, won't we Paul." She looked to Paul for confirmation.

Paul nodded. He still didn't like to open his mouth because he was afraid a cry or a whimper would come out.

Slowly, reluctantly, Mother and Dad kissed Paul goodbye, winking back tears. "We'll come next week, and bring the other kids," said Mother.

Line looked excited, however, ready for battle. She came over to the head of Paul's bed and whispered, "I brought *The Red Planet*. Marty found it for us at the library."

When supper came in on a tray, Line tried to help Paul, and ate whatever he couldn't eat. After supper it was time for a hypo and Paul relaxed a little while Line fiddled with the radio. The air was warm and sticky.

"There's a game on tonight," Line said. "I've been listening to the Minneapolis Millers and the St. Paul Saints games. Which one are you for, do you think?"

"I don't know," said Paul, his voice sounding thin. "Which one are you for?"

"The Millers," said Line. "They beat the Montreal Royals last year in the Minor League Series, and I'll bet they'll be good this year too. You want to listen?"

"Sure," said Paul. He didn't care what happened, as long as the days past.

Line found WCCO, a station out of Minneapolis, and they listened to the announcer describing the game between the Millers and the Havana Sugar Kings. "Hey," said Line. "I thought they were having a revolution in Cuba. I didn't know they could still have baseball!" The game was being played in Minneapolis. Paul listened wanly as the familiar pain in his legs began to kick in.

It turned out, though, that Line's enthusiasm for everything did help Paul. She played checkers with him, read to him from *The Red Planet* and the newspapers she managed to find. She spied on the other kids, the doctors and nurses in the ward. In some ways, it was easier to have her around than Mother, who was so distraught when he was in pain. Line was sympathetic, she could listen, and Paul didn't feel he had to keep quiet. He could tell her things and she wouldn't come apart. When he couldn't focus, she just waited until he could. And that time increased every day.

At the end of the week, when the rest of the family came up, Paul looked a little better. The bones in his face weren't quite so prominent, though he was still wan and feeble.

"Can I please stay another week?" begged Line. "I am really helping Paul, I think, and I love doing it!"

Paul watched as Mother and Dad looked at each other. He would soon be moved into a bigger ward with more kids, but he hoped Line would stay with him as long as she could.

"Okay, Line," said Dad. "I think you are good medicine. Looks like you've been coaxing some food into this kid." Dad ran his warm hands over Paul's head and chest, trying to send some of his lively spirit into him. "I've been missing my little wrestler," he said. "Don't know what to do with myself!"

Mother beamed at Paul and held Kristen over him to kiss. "Paul," she said shyly, sticking out her small fingers at him. "Paul. Come home?"

Paul's heart went out to his little sister. She was missing him too. "Pretty soon," said Paul weakly. He had no idea when it would be.

"How's *The Red Planet*"? asked Marty.

"It's good," said Paul, but talking was hard for him, especially when there were so many people standing around. He couldn't get up the gumption to make long sentences. "You tell her, Line," he said.

"We loved it, Marty," said Line. "We really liked the Martians, how they are imagined. We liked imagining 'water brothers', and Willis!"

"I brought you another one I found," said Marty. "It's called *Tunnel in the Sky*. I liked this one even better! It's about being pioneers on another planet, without all the technology we have. It's great!"

Paul listened to his sisters. They were trying to save him once again. And he was doing pretty well. Time was his enemy, the long, long nights. But he was getting through them, sleeping a little more. Imagining yourself on another planet was helpful.

"Tell Dad about the Sugar Kings," Paul said to Line. He was surprised to find that Line's enjoyment of baseball captured his imagination as well.

"Oh, guess what we've been listening to on the radio," said Line. "Baseball! The Millers are playing so well! They played the Havana Sugar Kings from Cuba. I thought the Cuban revolution would cancel all that."

"It's canceling a lot of things," said Dad. "Cubans are escaping to the United States, that's for sure. Castro says he is an anti-imperialist. But I guess baseball is still fair." He laughed.

The summer wore on. Paul was weaned off the hypos and transferred to a bigger ward once he was out of the cast. He privately celebrated every victory over the pain, over his immobility and being indoors. The best thing was getting out in the sun. Paul knew the clinic well and he was again using a wheelchair to get around. As soon as he could he wheeled himself out onto the sunporch so he could look out.

Soon after that, he could go down a ramp onto the sidewalk at the back of the building. He sat near a bank of peonies in the sun, smelling them and feeling the sun's hot rays on his skin. A row of tall pines shadowed the lawn. He was going to beat his enemies, pain and time. He would make time his own.

It turned out that knowing something about baseball was a good thing on the big ward. Because he had a radio, several of the boys crowded around when it was time for a game on WCCO.

One morning the ward was hopping with talk about the game their very own Rochester Red Wings played in Havana. The boys weren't able to hear it on the radio, but it was discussed in the sports page the boys passed around until it fell into tatters. It was the end of July, and the Red Wings went down to Havana for a ball game. They were in the 11th inning, when gunfire broke out. Cubans were celebrating the anniversary of the beginning of the Cuban revolution several years before. But gunshots got into the stadium! Stray bullets caught the Havana shortstop and the third base coach of the Red Wings. They weren't badly injured, but the Red Wings immediately stopped playing and took a plane home, refusing to play the last game of the series.

It could have been the end of minor league play for the Havana Sugar Kings, but as the story developed in the next few days, the boys were excited to hear that Fidel Castro intervened, promising that visiting teams would be safe. Castro loved baseball and the Sugar Kings were having a good year. He wanted them to keep playing and they did.

Paul got to know the players on the Millers team, Lu Clinton, Red Robbins, Ed Sadowski and especially the voice of the radio announcer, Halsey Hall. The boys said he got his gravelly voice from smoking cigars. Paul loved to listen to his stories about the players. He made baseball interesting.

Paul also hung around the chess corner, a spot in the cafeteria where some of the older kids had an almost permanent game going. He remembered when he had first been in the hospital, so short he could hardly see over the wooden pieces. But now he could follow the game well. It turned out Roddy, who had surgery just before Paul did, was especially good at it. He explained the moves to Paul and let him play.

One day two young doctors worked over Paul with pliers to pull out the stitches that held together the wounds from his tendon transfers.

He held onto a metal bar above the treatment bed, yelling out at every single stitch, unable to keep silent. The two young doctors just said, "Don't jerk!" and kept talking to each other. Paul thought he must be bending the metal he held on to. The doctors had hundreds of kids to pull stitches out of, Paul thought. He hated yelling, but he couldn't help it.

Once that was over, Paul again could rest. Not long though. He would soon start physical therapy, to regain the use of his flaccid muscles and weak tendons. Dr. Cousins showed him how his foot could now flatten on the ground.

"You might not be able to run like everyone else," he said. "But you will be able to walk as much as you like."

A faint light of hope illuminated Paul's face. Perhaps he would be able to choose a life for himself after all.

"Just got to grow those muscles," said Dr. Cousins. "We've done the best we can. Now it's up to you."

What a relief. If the ball was in his court at last, Paul could do something with it. He resolved to work hard. Inside himself he had wondered whether the reconstruction surgery was worth the pain. But Mother and Dad wanted the best for him and they, together with the doctors, were making the decisions.

Through the rest of the summer, the Mikkelsons spent Saturday afternoons with Paul. Therapy was slow, but he showed them each week the progress he made. Again he moved from a wheelchair to crutches and finally toward the end of the summer he was getting around on his own. But he couldn't leave the clinic, the hot whirlpool baths that helped him heal and the physical therapists who knew how to work his muscles and what was happening with his nerves and bones.

The Mikkelsons brought fruit and books and magazines, and their own lively interests. Alaska and Hawaii became states that year and Line brought Paul a new flag with fifty stars on it. It was tiny, but he flew it over his bed. The United States also chose seven astronauts. Marty collected anything she could find about them in magazines for Paul, bringing it with her to the clinic. Before long he had a box of clippings about space.

It was hard for Paul to talk about his feelings in the big weekend family gatherings. But one day Mother and Dad took Ellie and Kristen with them to do some shopping for Ellie's college venture in September. They left Line and Marty with Paul at the clinic. The kids were overjoyed to have time for their old camaraderie, which went underground unless they were together.

The girls followed Paul on his crutches out to the edge of the lawn at the back of the clinic. They sat under Paul's favorite tree, a long needled pine like those in the North Woods, and ate ginger cookies Line had made.

"I guess I'll never be an astronaut," said Paul. "They're all from the military, from the Air Force and the Navy. I thought someone like me might be a good choice, because I'd be good at being weightless. But they're all in top physical condition. So many people are competing to be astronauts."

"You don't want to be in the military," said Line. "I won't let you."

"Nah," said Paul. "I don't really want to either."

"Be a writer, like Heinlein," said Marty. "Wasn't *Tunnel in the Sky* wonderful? It's my favorite book!"

"Mine too," said Paul.

"Yeah," said Line. "Rod Walker is an ideal guy. A leader, and smart. Not just smart about books and learning either. I picture him like Dad. You know, Dad knows how to do so many things. You just mention something, and pretty soon he's figured out a way to make it or do it."

"Wow, Line. And you don't even get along with Dad that well," said Marty. "I'm glad to hear you say that."

"Dad grew up in the Depression," said Paul. "They didn't have anything. They did everything themselves, like he keeps telling us. Compared to him, we're rich!"

"I really liked how Rod acted when he came back to earth, to all that plenty, and they just brushed him off!" said Marty. "But he figured that out too. That's why he's such a great guy."

"I'll be glad when I can get back home," said Paul. "You guys know me best. I don't like having to tell people things all the time."

"No best friends here?" asked Line. "How about Roddy, the guy who was in your room when I stayed with you? Remember he tried to get me to play chess?"

"He's gone. Guys are always coming and going. I turn around and there's a new one in the bed next to me. I like them, but then they're gone," said Paul. "We help each other. We all have to do physical therapy. Roddy taught me to play chess before he left. It's great. And we're still having wheelchair races! I'm in them!"

"I'm so glad you're better," said Line. "It was so hard to see you in pain. You don't look like a little old man any more."

Paul's eyes went dark and looked back. It was still pretty close, all that pain. He hadn't expected it, had never been in that kind of pain before. But now he knew. He had been held by it, wracked by it, thought it would never come to an end. It was like a journey, a place he had gone Marty and Line didn't know about. But it was over, at least for now.

"I think I have to start school here," Paul said. "They say I have to stay through September."

"Aw, you won't miss much," said Marty. "You'll still be at the Larrabee school. It'll be just the same if you start in October." She was going out to the high school with Line this year. Paul could see her face light up just thinking it, though she didn't say so.

"You guys are so far ahead of me!" wailed Paul all of a sudden. It was true. Their little band was breaking up. Paul felt like one of them, but they were hurtling into adulthood much faster than he was.

"There's no rush about anything," said Line. "We've all got plenty of time."

"It does look as though I'm going to be okay," said Paul. "I don't think my legs are going to stop me any more."

"That's great," said Line. "What do you want to do?"

"Learn tracking," said Paul. "I want to go to our newest state, lay low and track wildlife."

Line and Marty stared at him. "You've always wanted that, haven't you?" said Marty.

"More than flying through space?" asked Line.

"Yup," said Paul. "More than anything." It was a long way off and lots of things could happen along the way. But at least he was pointed in the right direction.

22

One Saturday when the Mikkelsons returned from a visit to Paul at the clinic, they found the house filled with food. Hundreds of ears of corn were piled along the shed like logs. It was called a "pounding," a way congregations helped their pastor by anonymously giving him food.

Line looked at Mother. How did she feel about being gifted with so much food? In the old days there were pounds of flour, sugar, potatoes and so on, but now it took many more forms. The counters and kitchen table were covered with grocery store items, cans of soup and bags of pasta and rice. Glass jars of home-canned vegetables, pickles and jams stood on the counters along with bags of potatoes and onions.

The most overwhelming thing was the rows and rows of sweet corn. This was Iowa, after all, the state best known for its corn. A pounding wasn't the custom in North Dakota, so the family was surprised by it. Mother said nothing, but simply began to put the food away. There were baked goods too, cookies and pies. Even with their big family, they could not eat all of it quickly enough. Some of it would have to be frozen.

"Okay, girls," said Mother finally. "Monday will be sweet corn freezing day. No buts, and no excuses. That means that someone should wash the plastic bags today."

Line and Marty washed all the plastic bags they could find and hung them in the sun on the clothesline. Plastic bags were precious because they kept food fresher. They came from the store with fresh produce, especially fruit. The translucent bags looked funny dripping on the line, inside out so they could dry.

Early on Monday, Line walked barefoot in the dewy grass. The sun always seemed darker in August, coming up a little later. Regret coursed through her. Where did the summer go? How quickly the warm days slipped away. She hadn't practiced basketball at all that summer. In her freshman year she got a suit for the team, but she only played a few minutes of two games. She wasn't a bad guard, but not very tall. She knew she was the last girl on the team. Line sighed. She would never be as good as Mary Hallborg, their star forward, or even Sylvia Hanson. She ought to have a basketball in her hands at all times, practicing dribbling, running, just feeling it. But she was too dreamy, too lazy.

After breakfast, Mother set up an assembly line for freezing the corn. Dad helped Marty with the husking outdoors. After the green husks and the silky tassels which clung to the corn were pulled off, the cobs were brought into the kitchen in a tub.

Mother stood over the stove with a long tongs, fishing the parboiled cobs out of a huge kettle of boiling water. She put them on platters and handed them to Line and Ellie, who stood at the kitchen table, cutting the kernels off the cobs and scooping a meal's worth of kernels into plastic bags, folding them over tight and shutting them with clothes pins. These were popped into the big Amana freezer at one end of the big kitchen. The atmosphere was merry in the big light-filled room with everyone working.

All morning Line stood at the kitchen table with steaming platters of corn cooling in front of her. She cut the kernels off cobs of the hot wet corn, trying to get down to the core so nothing would be wasted. She had learned in biology that the endosperm in the middle of each kernel was where the best food was. Her hands got puckery from the milky liquids in the corn and the corn slid everywhere.

Kristen's job was to bring cobs from where they were piled along the wall of the shed and give them to Dad. Some of the cobs had smut on them, a dark fungus which ate into the kernels, but Dad just cut that part off. The corn was called "sweet" because it was different than the hard field corn, which was left to dry in the fields and used to feed animals.

"Shut the screen door," yelled Line, as Marty held it open with her foot to let Kristen come in after her with a cob of corn. "The flies are getting in!" Kristen was funny, running unevenly on her short legs, carrying a cob of husked corn that seemed bigger than she was.

A big lazy fly hovered over the kitchen table. Line grabbed the fly swatter and shooed it into the entry, where she could swat it away from the food.

At lunch time, Mother cooked a platter of sweet corn a little longer and took it outdoors. Line brought dark bread and butter and cold meat and sliced tomatoes, and Ellie a tray of glasses of milk. They sat around the wooden picnic table surrounded by green husks, eating the delicious corn.

Line put butter and salt on three rows of corn and ate them without looking up, making sure to eat the little endosperms. It was easier to get them with your teeth than cutting them. It was messy, but it didn't matter outdoors. Then she buttered the next three rows and ate them to the end, as if she were a typewriter. "Wish Paul were here," Line said. "I wonder if he gets sweet corn at the clinic."

"Probably," said Dad. "But not fresh out of the field."

A day did not go by in which no one mentioned Paul. He was in therapy every day now and using crutches to get around. He would start school there. The doctors wanted him to get the full benefit of reconstructive therapy before he left the clinic.

Line had made the dark bread herself a few days before, heaping wheat germ, powdered milk, and light and dark flours into a yeasty mixture with salt and melted butter, kneading it and letting it rise. She made six loaves at a time. Some of them were put in the freezer too, but a loaf of bread went quickly in their family.

Line looked up and there was Kristen, holding a cob of corn for her to husk. Line laughed, "That's not my job, Kristen. I have to go back in and cut kernels." She took the cob of corn from Kristen and picked her up, hugging her and burying her nose in Kristen's sweet-smelling chubby neck. But Kristen struggled to get down and Ellie picked up the dishes. The row of cobs along the shed was shorter, but there were still a lot to go.

As soon as they went back into the kitchen, there were platters of cobs cooling, ready for kernels to be cut. Line and Ellie went back at it, cutting and scooping, putting the finished bags into the freezer. By the end of the afternoon they were all tired, but the rows and rows of corn by the shed were converted into food for the coming winter.

"Good work, girls," said Mother. "I'm so glad that's done!" After dinner that night, she made chocolate sauce and served it on ice cream for a treat.

When the whole family wasn't together, however, Line brooded. The beginning of a school year in September felt more momentous than the year that began in January. This was her chance each year to remake herself, to become the bright star she longed to be. Line mentally chalked up her wins and losses, willfully deciding a course for the coming year. She would follow it doggedly, at least until she began to feel like she couldn't do much about things, that everything, as usual, was decided for her.

What excited Line most about the coming school year was, unexpectedly, Speech Club! The previous year, she and her classmates prepared speeches about any topic they wanted to and then gave them to each other. They weren't exactly debates, but often lively question and answer sessions followed the speeches. Their advisor, Mrs. Schneider, chose one of them to go on to a state contest.

Most of the speeches were about current events. For instance, that summer someone proposed a fleet of hospital ships be dispatched around the world from the United States, helping in disasters, famines and wars around the world, "The Great White Fleet." Teddy Roosevelt had sent a fleet around the world in 1907 to show the world the power of the US Navy, but this proposal was for a fleet of ships for peace, painted white with red crosses on them. Line imagined herself making a speech in favor of this proposed white fleet and its humanitarian efforts.

World affairs thrilled Line. She wanted to be someone special, to do something great, to make a difference in the world. She followed events in Cuba, as Castro seemed to be turning toward Communism. This meant a Communist presence in their very own hemisphere, an ominous turn of events. Though her parents were still Republicans, in favor of Eisenhower,

Line was excited by the young John Kennedy, who was going to run for president next year. The main fear about Kennedy was that he was Catholic, that he would do what the Pope in Rome told him to do.

The affairs of Montauk, Iowa, looked pale to Line compared to the excitement of world events. She didn't mind being an outsider because she had just moved to town. In fact she preferred it to being a staid Iowan who would go on to become a farmer or a farmer's wife. She was much less interested in 4-H when she figured out that its intent was to educate young people toward the betterment of their future farms. David Berglund, the boy she liked best in school was a farmer, a tall, tan Swede who worked for his dad and proudly wore a blue corduroy jacket embroidered with the golden emblem of the Future Farmers of America. But Line couldn't see herself staying in Iowa.

Line had survived Dad's confirmation class and was confirmed in the Lutheran faith that spring. One of her best efforts at diplomacy was not to challenge Dad during the two years of Saturday morning classes studying Martin Luther's catechism. Mother helped her, reminding Line that she could ask questions, but she should keep her personal thoughts about Dad's less than perfect character to herself. For all of their sakes.

What bothered Line about the church was hypocrisy. If people said they were going to do something, they should live by their words. Perhaps because she was so close to him, and things she said rubbed Dad the wrong way, Line was especially sensitive to his faults. When she was little she had been slapped by Dad, as he tried to quell her stubborn unruliness. While she loved him, she could not forget it. She wasn't sure what she wanted from Dad.

Line was less worried about her own wickedness. She said what she thought plainly, without worrying whether it hurt others. When it did she was just as able to say how sincerely sorry she was. Conflict made Paul nervous and Marty retreat into platitudes and pandering. It didn't bother Line one bit.

On Sundays Line listened to Dad's warm tired voice at the end of the service repeat "Lord, now lettest thou thy servant depart in peace, according to thy word: For mine eyes have seen thy salvation, Which thou has prepared before the face of all people; A light to lighten the Gentiles, and the glory of thy people Israel. Amen." Line prayed for peace too. No one was without sin. They were all in need of God's grace.

One afternoon Line half-heartedly practiced basketball at the hoop above the broken concrete driveway to the garage. Marty came around the corner with Kristen on her hip heading for the garden. Kristen could walk perfectly well, but Marty still liked carrying her, her body hunched to the side. Line came over, happy to be diverted.

"I'm so glad you're going to be out at Valley this year," said Line.

Marty knelt in the dirt, turning over the bean leaves looking for the long green beans hanging under them to pick for supper. She looked up. "Me too!" she said.

"We can walk home, you know, if we want to," said Line. She had done it a few times, though not in the winter. It was two miles, a long walk on a gravel road, but trees next to the road made it shady and cool.

Kristen stood on her little legs holding a stainless steel bowl into which Marty picked beans.

"I'm thinking of not going out for basketball," said Line dramatically.

"You are?!" asked Marty, surprised. "What about your undying love for Mr. Farnsworth?" Mr. Farnsworth tried to help Line. He even dropped her off at home after practice last year, as he lived in Montauk.

"You'll see when you get out there," said Line, discouraged. "Mary Hallborg walks around school like a goddess. There's no one like her. I'm the last one on the team, I'm sure of it. And I'm not getting any better."

"Well, it's up to you," said Marty. "You still like band, don't you? I'm so excited about marching band!" Last year Line had regaled her with tales of dance routines for the football games.

"Yes," said Line. "Band's great. Actually, I can't wait for school to start! But Marty, I don't think I'm an athlete!"

"Don't worry about it," said Marty. "You can't do everything. Everyone acts like we should be good at everything, but I don't think it's true. You'll do the best at what you like best."

Line considered. "I'll think about it," she said. "But thanks, Marty. You're going to love high school."

Marty stood up and took the bowl from Kristen. "Yup. I guess so. I like when it's just our family, but school will be fun too." She smiled at Line hopefully.

"You mean that can-can hasn't made you the most popular girl in school?" teased Line, wickedly. But she regretted it when Marty's face darkened. Marty just picked up Kristen and headed to the kitchen with her bowl of beans.

It was just the family when they took Ellie to Wittenberg College at the end of the week for her first year, minus Paul of course. They had visited the beautiful campus with its vast lawns surrounded by buildings before, but never gone into them. Lovely old trees skirted the lawn, and only a few people walked around campus. It was a week before school started, but part of Ellie's scholarship was a job in the registration office, as she took typing and stenography in high school. She was asked to be at school a little early to get used to her job before classes started.

Ellie was assigned a room with two other girls in the new women's dorm, Brandt Hall. Dad knew where Brandt Hall was, so they parked nearby and entered the dark, beautiful lounge, full of big couches and coffee tables and tall lamps.

Line was awed at the plush carpets and furniture, but Ellie was as diffident as ever. Ellie moved like an automaton, doing what she was supposed to do. When she got her room number from the house mother, a pleasant older woman named Mrs. Larson, she carried her train case and Dad carried her suitcase down the hall.

Line was delighted by the new room with its blonde beds built into the wall, one slightly higher than the others with a little ladder up to it. A window with a wide ledge beneath it covered almost the whole of one wall. Two desks faced each other under the window, and there was another on the far wall. A pile of sheets and blankets lay on each uncovered mattress. Three dressers were the only other furniture, the blonde wood much nicer than anything at home. Shelves were built into the sides of the desks for books and there were three closets.

"I guess you will have to choose your bed," said Mother. "You're the first one here. Line and Marty, why don't you make the bed for Ellie, while she puts her things away."

Line unfolded the sheets and she and Marty stretched them over the new bed. When they were done, Line lay down on the clean blankets.

"Oh," she said. "What I wouldn't give for a hard bed like this."

"I wonder if we were supposed to bring some kind of bedspread," Mother worried. "I didn't think of that." She sat in one of the wooden chairs, while Dad stood, holding Kristen so she wouldn't get in the way. "We'll bring you one the next time we come," Mother decided. Ellie moved awkwardly, trying to decide which closet was hers, which dresser.

Line was deeply excited, as if she were the one going to college. She could imagine herself free here, free to sleep if she wanted to, wear what she liked. Line watched Ellie hang her clothes in the closet. Ellie wore a plaid cotton dress with a full skirt she made in a flurry of sewing at the end of the summer. Her blonde curls hung down her back. She was pretty, but solemn, even a little dispirited. She did not seem to be a girl who was thrilled to go to college, though Mother and Dad would be making sacrifices to send her.

Ellie put her other things in the dresser. She put the notebook and pencils Dad bought her on one of the desks, but then there was nothing more to do. She would buy her books at the bookstore when they were assigned. Tomorrow morning she would report to the Registrar's Office to start work. Ellie hung her head in the middle of the room.

"Let's go over to New Main," said Dad, "So we can see where you might be working, and stop at the bookstore and the canteen. Then we'll all go out for a hamburger before we say goodbye."

Line was surprised. It was almost like leaving Paul at the clinic, another part of their lumpy family cut off, like a finger. She didn't expect to mind not having Ellie around. She didn't expect to even notice!

They walked across the wide campus, Kristen running ahead. She was wearing a little dress, as if she were going to church, and Marty and Line wore school dresses too. The air was warm and the late afternoon sun lay across the lawns like a blessing. Kristen's little shadow fell long behind her and Line ached with the beauty of the new. But it would be three years before it was her turn to go to college.

"Remember the night Old Main burned?" Dad asked Mother. "I'm not sure why I was here. I had already graduated, but that night was unforgettable."

"Yes, I remember hearing about it. I was working at the orphanage," said Mother. "It was quite a shock!"

Dad showed Ellie the door of the Registrar's Office. It was locked, but at least she knew where to go in the morning.

In the bottom of the New Main building was a bookstore. Line watched Marty, excited by the piles of books. Labels for the classes which assigned them were attached to the shelves. Ellie didn't know what her classes would be. There were piles of Wittenberg College sweatshirts, navy and white. The school's colors were Norse blue and white, and its teams were Vikings.

"Now where is the canteen?" wondered Dad. He went up to the man running the bookstore and asked.

"It's in those old barracks buildings they dragged in after the war, over there on the other side of the highway," said the man. "They're working on a new student union with a cafeteria over there below the bluff. Should start construction in a year or so."

"Hmmmm," said Dad. "That's quite a ways away. Let's go over there and have a look."

They hiked over to the canteen. It wasn't so far from Ellie's dormitory, just a long way from classes.

"At least you'll get your exercise," said Mother. "Maybe you can pack a lunch and take it with you. Lots of working people do that."

It was all new to Ellie. She looked nonplussed.

"Maybe there's a hotplate somewhere in the dorm," said Dad. "Or a kitchenette. You girls could heat up some cocoa for breakfast maybe." Everyone was trying to put themselves in Ellie's shoes, imagining what living on campus would be like.

Line was exhilarated. She would know how to make a life for herself at college, she thought. She couldn't wait.

The canteen was a low, dark building with windows along one side. Signs on the door of the canteen noted the hours of breakfast, lunch and dinner. "Freshmen must wear beanies at all times," the sign said.

"Where do you get a beanie?" asked Marty.

"Oh the joys of being a freshman," said Dad, stepping inside the canteen. "Probably get one when you're registered at college."

Inside the canteen were tables and chairs, and an industrial-looking row of stainless steel tables against the wall where the food was laid out. It looked pretty much like the hot lunch areas in high school, thought Line. But what if you couldn't get any snacks, she worried. She looked at Ellie, but Ellie was as flat-faced as ever, following along behind Dad.

"It looks like it will be fine," said Mother reassuringly. "Make sure you get good solid meals with plenty of vegetables." She put a hand around Ellie's waist. "You're my good girl," Mother said softly. "How I will miss you. But you're going to have a wonderful time."

The staff was organizing supper for the few students who were already on campus. But Dad had said they would go out for a hamburger, so they walked to the car, parked along the road beside Ellie's dorm. Line was a little subdued by the fact of Ellie going off by herself. She would be 18 in a month, however, and one had to grow up sometime.

Dad drove to an A&W stand he had seen on the way in, and they each ate a hamburger and drank a root beer. Line loved root beer, loved the sweet dark-tasting liquid at the back of your throat and how it felt in your nose.

They drove Ellie back to Brandt Hall. Line and Marty hugged Ellie goodbye, and Kristen, who didn't really know what was happening, waved goodbye cheerily. Dad and Mother kissed Ellie on the sidewalk, releasing her into her new life.

"You'll be glad you came early," Dad said. "By the time the other kids get here, you'll know where everything is and be way ahead of them."

"Write to us!" said Mother. "Let us know how registration goes, and if you need anything. We'll be thinking of you every day."

It felt very strange to Line as they drove off. She was now the eldest and there were only three kids at home. Paul would be home in a month, of course, and they would slowly get back to normal, but Ellie might never be back except for vacations. She was planning on going to summer school because there was no place to work in Montauk, and it would be cheaper to work at the college and finish early.

The day after they got home, Marty moved her things into the little back bedroom that was the maid's, giving Line a room of her own for the first time in her life. Ellie had packed her things before she left and put the boxes up in the attic, so someone could move in with Kristen. Marty desperately wanted the room because of the little desk in the anteroom where the staircase once went down to the kitchen, which was fine with Line. A big old rocker allowed someone to rock Kristen to sleep or read her a book before putting her in her crib.

Line found it strange to have a room of her own. She and Marty fought over so many things because they were so different and shared a space. Now Line could shut the door, which meant that people must knock before entering. She could leave her things where she dropped them on the floor and no one would whine at her. And she could listen to whatever radio station she wanted.

She was still listening to baseball games on WCCO. The Minneapolis Millers were doing so well that they might win their league pennant. If they did, they would play in the Little World Series. Line listened to the gravelly voice of Halsey Hall, knowing that Paul was probably listening too.

In the middle of the week, Dad went up to the clinic and brought Paul home. Line and Marty were thrilled to have him back, and Kristen marched around chortling. Mother set a celebration table out in the dining room, and the number of place settings was back up to six! They were now pushing Kristen's high chair up to the table, so she could eat like a grownup, and she did try.

The Millers won the pennant. The Havana Sugar Kings came up to Minneapolis to play them in the Series, but it was terribly cold. Halsey Hall was upset that so few fans came out in the frigid weather, and the Cuban fans were louder than the Minnesotans! Line could hear maracas on the radio.

"They're moving the rest of the Little World Series to Cuba where it's warmer," Line said to Paul after dinner. "It'll be so exciting!"

But it wasn't as much fun as they hoped. The kids read the newspapers avidly, and saw pictures of the thousands of soldiers stationed around the stadium, young men with guns. The Cubans won the first two games, but the Millers battled back to win the next two. Things were tense. The players couldn't leave their hotel except for games, because no one knew what was going on.

Even Marty took an interest in the final game of the series. The kids crowded around the newspaper when Dad brought it home. In the last game Joe Macko and Lu Clinton, Paul's favorite player, hit home runs, putting the Millers ahead. But the Cubans came back, driving in just enough runs to win the game. Even though they had lost, the Millers were relieved and so were Line and Paul.

"What if Castro didn't keep his promise to take care of them?" asked Paul. He was worried about Lu Clinton.

"Castro's a dictator," said Line. "Everyone has to do what he says. All those soldiers answer to him."

"Hmph," said Paul. "I wouldn't want to do that."

"Me either," said Line. "I'm beginning to think I should become a diplomat. I'd like to work for peace."

"How do you do that?" asked Marty, reasonably.

"I have no idea," said Line. "I'm reading *The Ugly American*. I really want to do some good in the world, like Homer Atkins. He wasn't a diplomat. He just helped people on little projects. I think he was an engineer." Line's face was flushed.

"Those Minnesota guys were brave," said Paul, "going down to Cuba in the middle of a revolution."

Line looked at him. She didn't say it, but she knew she would have gone down to Havana and played in those dramatic games. She imagined herself walking down the steps rolled up to the door of an arriving airplane which she often saw on television. More than anything she wanted to ride in an airplane and go to another country. It would be nice to do something for other people, but most of all she wanted an exciting life.

23

Marty waited for Line on a chilly October morning, as they both took the bus out to Valley High School. But Line was late and her blouse was wrinkled. Marty hated to rush, so she left Line to her own devices, bundled up in a coat and scarf, and collected her stack of schoolbooks. She struck off by herself down the sidewalk. The sun was low behind the trees, throwing long shadows. If she blew out, her breath formed a little cloud in front of her mouth.

Marty's heart swelled as she walked along singing to herself, a song from high school chorus, "When you walk through a storm keep your head up high, and don't be afraid of the dark." The music was an anthem to her feelings. "Walk on through the rain, though your dreams be tossed and blown." So much ahead of her, she thought. So much to see and think about.

The bus dropped the kids from Montauk at the high school which felt spanking new to Marty, with its blonde wood, spacious classrooms, halls, gym and library. Because Russia was ahead in the space race, the school was given a lot of new funding. It was mostly for science and mathematics, but the library benefited. Marty's first period was a study hall in the library. She was thrilled by the wall of books at the back of the big room with its long modern windows looking out on fields.

But not by the science books! Her favorite was a book of poetry translated from the Chinese, a big orange book with printed paintings in it, scenes of girls in silk dresses dancing or sitting in a garden, contemplating lotus flowers. And the poems were so simple. Marty felt she might fall into the book, it was so strange and enticing. She picked it off the shelves and paged through it as often as she dared.

High school didn't leave much time for poetry, however. For Marty there was algebra, American history, English, home economics, biology and then band or chorus. She loathed P.E. classes as much as ever, but they were leavened by all the other exciting classes and music. She loved high school. It was football season, and the band put on uniforms and played at home football games, doing half time routines which they practiced over and over.

By seventh period, Marty was out in front of the school on the football field with the band. They had it to themselves as the football players were on the practice fields at the back. The late fall sunshine was still strong, but fading fast. Mr. Greenway shouted at them as they strutted along in their sections, playing marches, sweating. He wished they could play the songs by heart, but most of them used music printed on small sheets, clipped to their instruments with tiny lyres.

Marty carried a heavy pair of cymbals because no one could march with an oboe reed in their mouth. She followed Maureen, the other oboe player, a tall girl with very fair skin, who lifted her dark curls up on one side her head with a barrette. Marty was happy she could concentrate on the dance moves, her legs marching, trying to keep up. Down the field and into position they marched, lightly clashing the cymbals together in rhythm with the march.

The band marched into the shape of a tiger, the mascot for Valley High School. Once in the shape, they played the fight song. Ahead of her, Marty saw Line with her French horn, confidently marching. The trombones straggled, which looked bad because they were so visible. Mr. Greenway wiped his hand across his eyes. "Trombones! You must move faster! March! March!"

Marty giggled and looked at Maureen. Everyone was laughing. At least now, in practice. They wanted to look good at half time during football games, but it was comical now, with Mr. Greenway trying desperately to get them into shape.

Marty and Maureen were at the end of the tail with their cymbals. Mr. Greenway on the bleachers above them, shouted. "Good head," he said. "Good tail. Back up a little, you front feet. It should look as if the tiger is crouching." He raised his hands and his little baton. "And, one." The fight song crashed around them in the open air with nothing behind them to concentrate the sound. But that was what a marching band sounded like.

Most of the band knew the music and the routine from last year. But Mr. Greenway was creating a new one. He wanted them to become a train and chug it down the field. He gave them each a copy of the sketch he made. Marty and Maureen were to be up at the top of the engine, where the smoke would come out, crashing their cymbals lightly through the march. They were visible, and important. Everyone changed the music on their lyres to the new "Colonel Bogey" march.

First they walked through it, finding their positions. Then they played the march standing out in the sun, their long shadows at their feet. "Sounds good!" said Mr. Greenway from the stands. "Now keep your positions and march down the field. Horns, face forward, but when we come to the horn section, every other beat flash your horns toward the audience. It won't work unless everyone does it. Okay?"

It was impossible to tell how things looked from the stands if you were a band member like Marty, marching forward, trying to stay in position. She thought Mr. Greenway was asking a lot of the band, but it was definitely as much fun as Line said it would be!

Mr. Greenway shouted "Good horns! Try again. Listen for the beat and follow Steve! He's got it right." He was getting hoarse from shouting.

The band played, the familiar melody whistling cheerfully as the woodwinds carried it. Then the more raucous horn section began. Marty was too far forward to see whether the horns were flashing together. Line must be in that mix. Marty marched forward. It was easy for her. But Mr. Greenway wanted her to learn the piccolo. The only piccolo player was a senior and would be leaving, and he needed piccolos for Sousa marches.

At last, Mr. Greenway called it quits and let them go. They flopped off the field, band instruments at their sides, exhilarated by the activity, but tired. The sun was going down and the chill coming up from the cold, grassy ground. Marty and Maureen rushed back to school and gathered up books to catch the last buses back to town. Marty was very pleased to have a friend in band. She and Maureen now shared their problems with their reeds and many other confidences as they sat together, though Maureen was a year ahead of her, in Line's class.

Marty chose the oboe because she loved Sonja's theme, the duck in the "Peter and the Wolf" symphony by Prokofiev. The oboe was exotic, with a lovely, mournful sound. She thought it appropriate that Line's instrument, the French horn, represented the wolf, who almost got Sonja, at least in the dramatized Disney cartoon. Mother and Dad couldn't afford to buy a piccolo too, but Mr. Greenway said that the band owned one, and she should learn to play it.

Marty's life was full of music. Mrs. Jorgenson, her piano teacher, had left for the winter, but Marty was in two choruses as well as band. As she stumped along home at twilight, she was still singing "Walk on, walk on, with hope in your heart, and you'll never walk alone, you'll ne-ver walk alone." The trees stood against the sky like black lace, beginning to lose their leaves. She thought of the melancholy Chinese poems in the book in the school library, but she was singing a powerful American song, a song from a musical by Rodgers and Hammerstein, *Carousel.*

As if that weren't enough, that night Mother said "The Hubsch family would like you kids to sing at Grandpa Hubsch's funeral on Sunday. Do you have a few minutes to practice tonight?" Because they had sweet, resonant voices and were close in age, Marty, Line and Paul sang together for church now and then, for funerals and weddings.

They were outdone by the Gyer family, the largest family they knew, 15 kids, most of them girls and many of them part of their family singing group. They lived far out in the country and went to a different school, but Marty was fascinated when they sang in church. Siblings singing together in groups were very popular.

Mother didn't like to commit their free time, but it was hard to refuse a church member. Marty looked at Line, who could be moody lately, but Line agreed readily. They loved singing together.

After the dishes were done, Mother sat down at the little blonde spinet and turned the pages of the hymn book. Kristen, who could never stay out of the action, plunked on the keys at the end of the piano. "Let's try it," Mother said. "Just sing it through with the harmony."

Marty took the alto, and Line the soprano. Paul was ten, and his warm, sweet voice was still high, so he sang the melody with Line. "Help me the slow of heart to move, by some clear winning word of love." It was a quiet song, but Marty loved it deeply, especially the harmony. Little Kristen stood beside them, her mouth open as if she knew the words.

"Okay," said Mother. "Let's try it again, but Paul take the third verse as a solo, with you girls humming the harmony. Then all of you come back on the fourth verse." Paul's voice was true on the notes of the melody, "Teach me thy patience; still with thee, in closer, dearer company," and the girls joined him on the last verse: "In peace that only thou canst give, with thee, oh Master, let me live."

"That sounds wonderful," said Dad, coming out of his study to listen for a moment.

"Yes, you'll do just fine," said Mother. "Thank you, my dears." Her dark hair shone in the lamplight. She turned to Marty. "You'll take Kristen up?"

Marty nodded, putting her arms around Kristen and swinging her up on her hip. It was dark by this time of day at the end of October. The storm windows were up, but it was cold near the double paned glass. Dad had begun to stoke the furnace to heat the big frame house.

Kristen's favorite thing was climbing the big stairs and poking her nose out of the carved wooden banisters, so Marty put her down at the bottom of the stairway and let her climb, shadowing her from behind so she couldn't fall.

Upstairs she helped Kristen to the potty, washed her up and put a nighttime diaper on her. The two of them sat in the old rocker, looking at picture books while Kristen pointed to things and babbled about them. Then Marty read her Christopher Robin poems in a sing-song voice until Kristen's head fell into her lap, and she could put her in the crib.

Marty was surprised at how different the house was, now that Ellie wasn't there. Ellie was a silent worker, helping Mother with everything. She rarely said much, but her absence left big holes.

Line did not step in. She was always excited about things, rushing in one direction and then another, but Marty began to see a melancholy behind this. Nothing was ever good enough or exciting enough for Line. When she was free, Line spent her time mooning about alone. Marty thought she herself was the dark, brooding one, while Line was the bright light. But now she saw that beneath Line's piercing light was an equally strong darkness. And it turned out that Mother turned to Marty when she needed help.

Paul was home now too. It was a great relief to have him, but he wanted things to be ordinary, with no fuss. He and Dad were looking for a dog for the family. Mother wasn't very excited about it, but she agreed, if Paul would take care of it.

On Saturday there was a letter from Ellie. Mother read it to them at dinner. Marty found it funny to hear the inside of Ellie. They had never known what she thought. Ellie wrote that she liked her job, but that among her roommates, she was the odd man out. "I think it is because I am usually working," she wrote. "They are always doing things together, and they don't ask me to come with them. I don't like to go to dinner alone. When I get there, I can usually find someone to sit with, but I don't like it."

She didn't sound excited about her classes. She was taking Western civilization, English, biology and religion. She knew that Mother and Dad wanted her to take Latin from Dr. Haatvedt, the only one of their own professors who was still teaching, but Latin was the last thing Ellie wanted to learn! She was homesick and wished she were at home putting Kristen to bed or baking pies.

She also wrote that Bruce was doing well in Iowa City and loved studying, but that they missed each other. He was coming up the next weekend and she couldn't wait. Marty saw Mother and Dad's eyes meet when Mother read this. It was clear that Ellie would not meet a Lutheran boy at college. She would not get over Bruce. Mother sighed, but Dad smiled.

"Well, if you can't beat 'em, join 'em. At least in this case," said Dad, genially. "You know I don't always roll over like this, but Bruce is a fine young man." He looked around, not wanting to talk about it any more. He and Mother would talk it out privately, Marty knew. "How about a piece of that pie you girls made?"

But Mother's eyes were troubled. "I hope you kids value your college educations," she said. "Even if it doesn't lead directly to jobs, college is a wonderful chance to enrich your life and open your minds."

"Yup," Dad said. "They don't call it higher education for nothing! Your mother and I have always hoped that each of you could have the education you deserve. It wasn't a normal thing in my family, but I think I am happier than my sisters partly because of my education."

"Don't worry," said Line brightly. "We want to go to college! You won't get any lukewarm letters from me when I go!"

"I didn't think so," said Mother. "There's nothing lukewarm about you, Line. I'm sure you would be a little homesick at the beginning. That's normal. But I do hope to see some enthusiasm."

Paul didn't say anything, but his expressive face showed he agreed with Line.

"Couldn't we go visit Ellie?" asked Marty. "That would cheer her up." She stood up to go get the apple pie from the kitchen. "Do you want ice cream?" she asked.

"Just a little," said Dad. He and Mother exchanged glances. "We'll see about visiting," he said.

Marty felt the chill air rise as she opened the big freezer and brought out the paper carton of ice cream. She just wanted to go to the beautiful town of Cardinal, to visit the college. She couldn't get enough of it.

"Mmmmmm," said Paul. "The best pie. Thank you."

Marty carefully collected a combination of apples and cream with her spoon. The taste of cinnamon and sweet sugar with tangy Jonathan apples in a flaky crust was just about as good as anything she could imagine.

Mother got up, lifted Kristen out of her chair and turned on the television, where the champagne bubbles of Lawrence Welk's music began to play. The four Lennon Sisters sang in close harmony, while Kristen jigged to the music and Mother folded the mimeographed church bulletins she had typed.

Marty and Paul cleared the table. Paul, in his droll, serious manner, explained to Marty while they did the dishes that he wanted to teach her chess. Black and white plastic chess pieces were part of a collection of games they owned, but no one had used them.

"It feels like history," said Paul. "People have been playing it for so long."

"I think it will be hard," said Marty.

"Nah," said Paul. "It isn't that difficult. Roddy taught me at the clinic. You just have to get used to what moves each piece can make."

"Well, I'll just do my best," said Marty. "I'd like to play with you." Though it was unspoken, they both knew why Paul hadn't asked Line. A chess game might take forever, and no one expected Line to sit through it!

"Tonight?" asked Paul. Once he grew determined about something, little stopped him.

"Sure," said Marty.

When the dishes were done, Paul pulled out the game board and pieces, and set them up on the coffee table at the back of the living room, queen beside king, rooks at the end of the row. The television played in one corner of the room, so they could look over if they wanted to, but neither of them was deflected by polka music.

Dad popped his head out of the study, however, when Welk played an accordion polka. Dad frowned on television. To him it was a waste of time, but once in a while he came and stood at the back of the room to see what everyone else was watching.

Marty took the white pieces and Paul the black. It wasn't hard to figure out how the pieces moved. The hard part was keeping the whole board in mind, not missing a move your opponent might make with a piece you didn't notice.

Marty felt pleased to learn. Chess was a part of the medieval world in the movies of early England and Scotland they saw, movies about Mary Tudor, who fought to marry her true love despite her royal birth, and Rob Roy. Chess was romantic and powerful, evoking rooms with great stone fireplaces where women worked on tapestries and men played with tall wooden chess pieces in velvet robes trimmed with ermine.

She was also happy to share this avocation with Paul. When Paul looked up at Marty indicating it was her turn, his secret smile conveyed all the complicity of a moon now able to connect with its twin, while circling their common planet, Line.

Line hovered in the background, watching them. Finally, she mocked their serious intent, trying to disrupt them. "I don't suppose you two could interrupt your game to help me fold clothes," she said sarcastically.

Marty looked up, stricken. It was Saturday night and clean clothes must be put away, bulletins folded and Sunday School lessons reviewed. But Paul said, "Here. We'll leave the game right here and finish it tomorrow. Don't touch it," he admonished Line sweetly.

Line preferred any game in which she could move. She was much happier when Sunday night rolled around, with the high jinks of a Luther League meeting in store. Now that Marty was in high school, she could go to Luther League also. This was the week of the hay ride, one last outdoor party before the snow fell.

Dad drove the station wagon down to church, where a truck had pulled a hay wagon into town with bales of hay on it. The plan was for everyone to pile into the hay wagon and ride three miles out of town to the East church and have a bonfire with the Luther Leaguers from East. Dad liked to get the two church groups together. He felt he wasn't getting the evening participation he was used to in North Dakota. He attributed it to the fact that there were more animals on farms in Iowa. People were always rushing home to do chores, even in winter.

Barb and Marlene were among the girls who came to Luther League, wearing slacks and several shirts, sweaters and jackets, their heads tied up in scarves. Marty joined them on a hay bale. Soon there were 15 kids on the hay wagon, teasing and carrying on. Dad swung up into the truck, and it eased off down the street, moving slowly.

As usual, Marlene was the one who knew how to make small talk. Marty admired her for it. She had no idea how to do it herself. If it was up to her, she would have talked about Khrushchev's visit to the US, about the book she was reading, or about playing chess with Paul. But none of these things resonated with anyone else on the hay wagon. Marlene didn't care. She started talking about herself, about anything, and pretty soon she engaged the people around her and they were all talking.

Marlene's older sister worked in Mason City in an insurance office. There were no jobs in Montauk for young people, and if you weren't needed on your farm, or getting married, you left. Usually people didn't go far. Marlene's sister came home often, regaling Marlene with stories of movies she saw, theater nights and dates with friends.

"Carol was home this weekend," began Marlene. "She and her two best friends decided to go to New York to see *The Music Man*. Isn't that amazing?"

"Wow," said Barb. "Wouldn't that be expensive?"

"Of course," said Marlene. "But they want to do it. We're never going to get to see it here. And they're from Mason City, the original River City! They think they deserve to see it." Line had gone to the North Iowa Band Festival in Mason City in the spring, telling Marty about the parade of 25 high school bands marching down the street in their uniforms.

"They're probably right," said Marty. "I'd go see it, if I could." As with many Broadway productions and Hollywood movies, she heard bits and pieces of songs on television or vague stories about actors, but never saw the thing itself. Musicals from New York might arrive in the Midwest at some point, quite a while after they were hits on Broadway. This time, Mason City, Iowa, was being dramatized in New York. Meredith Willson, from Iowa, was the writer.

Marty pulled a bit of hay out of the bale and chewed on it as she listened to Marlene.

"They're going to take the train, and just book a hotel room, and then they'll come back. Easy as pie, Carol says," said Marlene.

"Don't you wish you could go?" asked Marty.

"Sort of," said Marlene. "But I don't like big cities. They'll be okay if they stick together, I guess. And I wouldn't like to take a train for three days!"

"Your Mom and Dad will let them go?" asked Barb.

"They can't say anything about it," said Marlene. "She's 20 years old now and no one can tell her what to do."

"Wow," said Marty. They were only 14, but it wouldn't be long now before they too came of age.

The hay wagon moved slowly on the gravel road, past the parsonage, the creek and the Catholic cemetery, and then a few miles out into the country. The boys crowded around the girls and pretended they must hold onto them to keep them from falling off. Marty slipped down onto the floor of the wagon, where it was protected from the wind. She hardly knew the boys in League.

Line tried to get everyone to sing, but even the irrepressible Line couldn't get the rowdy group to coalesce into one.

At the East church, a big bonfire was laid in the parking lot. There was hot coffee and cocoa in the church basement, and marshmallows on sticks. Marty was grateful for a mug of the warm cocoa. She took it out and stood by the fire, her front very warm and her back chilled.

Big logs burned down into glowing red coals in the middle and around the fire kids roasted marshmallows. There was no need to talk to anyone. The fire was a warm and friendly circle uniting them, crackling and spitting sparks in a comfortable conversation with itself.

Nearby Marty in the circle was Line, standing companionably next to David Berglund, his corduroy Future Farmers of America jacket open to the warmth. East was his church, and his farm was close. Seeing them, Marty understood Line's enthusiasm for Luther League better!

Marty had the disconcerting feeling that the fire wasn't much, though. She wondered what it would be like to watch a musical in New York, and what the people there would think of people like her, clustered around a bonfire in the country, miles from anywhere.

Dad didn't take much control of this social evening. Marty thought he just wanted the League kids to get together and have fun. But later, when the fire burned down to a low bed of red and orange coals, he offered a prayer and invited them all to sing. They all knew the words to "Onward Christian Soldiers" and "What a Friend We Have in Jesus," and Marty sang the harmony she knew, chiming in with Dad's sweet tenor, covering over the kids who didn't sing as well.

Across space filled with sparks dancing in the fire came Dad's tenor, building with power and love. "Oh Lord my God, when I in awesome wonder, consider all the works Thy Hand hath made; I see the stars, I hear the mighty thunder, thy power throughout the universe displayed." It was a song Tennessee Ernie Ford sang on his television show, and everyone chimed in on the chorus. "Then sings my soul, my Saviour God to thee, how great thou art, how great thou art!" Singing together was better than anything, thought Marty.

At last Dad began "Now the day is over, night is drawing nigh," a song from their own Lutheran hymnal. This one had simple chords and Mrs. Jorgenson had made Marty diagram them. "Jesus give the weary, calm and sweet repose. With thy tend'rest blessing, may my eyelids close."

"Peace be with you," said Dad, raising his hand in benediction. He had quietly gotten even these kids' attention.

"And with thy spirit," said Loren, one of the more serious seniors, in response.

The kids from town climbed into the hay wagon, which headed back. A few couples now held each other, and the others crowded together for warmth. Marty rested quietly at the bottom of the wagon, her head leaning on a sweet-smelling hay bale, social needs and ideas momentarily extinguished. She looked up at the half moon hanging above them, and the tiny pinpoints of stars "in awesome wonder" as the truck rumbled along.

<h1 style="text-align:center">24</h1>

Paul was so glad to be home he could not believe it was allowed, that he could wake up each morning and eat whatever breakfast he wanted, go to school in his own good time and fall asleep in his own room, with his parents and sisters sleeping near. The frost and the low-angled sun, the snowstorms that winter were magical and his feet, both of them, were cooperating.

One of Paul's legs was still skinny and the other thick and strong, but he could walk like any other person. It was a miracle, although Paul didn't quite trust it. Dad still put a mat down in the study after supper, and he and Paul worked on Paul's leg. "It's our chores," said Dad. But it didn't seem terrible when they missed now and then. Paul began to feel like a normal person.

On a snowy December Saturday afternoon, Paul went over to John and Alice Sherwood's house next door. He sat in Alice's kitchen and spooned up the thick brown betty she made, which she served with a creamy pudding. Mother's recipe for apple crisp used oatmeal, but a betty was made with breadcrumbs, Alice told him.

The Sherwoods were like grandparents. John was a skinny old man who wore an engineer's hat and a red neckerchief in the summer when he worked in his orchard and garden. The Sherwoods had more cultivated land than even the Mikkelsons. Alice was also thin and wizened, in cotton dresses, aprons and thick cotton stockings coming, Paul thought, from the previous century.

Paul loved the quiet, old-fashioned house in which Alice and John lived simply. Alice made quilts and rag rugs, and John sat with his books at a little desk in a corner of the living room. They didn't have music or television or seem to pay much attention to the outside world, though John read newspapers. John helped out at the sorghum mill during the fall and winter if they needed him, as he was related to the Appelmans. He was an engineer on the Rock Island Line for many years before retiring.

Railroads in Montauk were quite different in importance than they were in North Dakota. The town was not on the east-west lines run by the Burlington Northern and the Atcheson, Topeka and the Santa Fe Railroads out of Chicago. But the Rock Island Line had important runs all over Iowa and, in partnership with Southern Pacific, passenger and shipping runs from Chicago to Los Angeles. John knew everything about the railroads and loved to tell about it. When he heard the Rock Island train rolling through town, he signaled to Paul.

"Going south," said John, listening to the faint train whistle for the afternoon run. He told Paul about the huge railroad hub 30 miles south of them at Oelwein, Iowa, built for the Chicago Great Western at the turn of the century.

John also grew up in Montauk's heyday when the Larrabees and the Appelmans were active in town. Mr. Larrabee, once governor of Iowa, could trace his ancestry to William Brewster and Mrs. Larrabee traced her family, the Appelmans, to John Alden. Both Brewster and Alden arrived on the Mayflower and established the Plymouth Colony. Mrs. Larrabee saw her children as members of an elite class, hiring a French instructor for them and insisting they all speak French. The only one of the seven Larrabee children left was Miss Anna. She now lived alone on the farm on the ridge above town established by her father and planted with 100,000 trees.

The Larrabees were Methodists and so were John and Alice. The Larabees built the brick Union Sunday School with its huge pipe organ inside. At John and Alice's humble house, Paul realized that he and his family were newcomers, recent immigrants to a place where the landed aristocracy had lived in the country since the 1600's.

In the stories told by the Mikkelsons, so relentlessly Norwegian Lutheran, anyone outside their church carried the faint aura of the unredeemed. It wasn't that Dad and Mother thought Norwegian Lutherans were better than anyone else, Paul thought. It was just that they didn't really know anyone else.

At the clinic, there were all kinds of kids with polio. Paul felt bad for kids whose parents didn't come as often, or who didn't seem to care about them. But he talked with lots of them that were different from him, and most of them enjoyed their lives. The stories John Sherwood told also showed Paul that people outside of his family and the wider circle of the Lutheran church might be fine.

Paul admitted to himself it was nice to get away from the busy atmosphere of the parsonage. Just now, before Christmas, it was particularly charged. Ever since Thanksgiving, when Ellie and Bruce met with Mother and Dad behind closed doors, Mother had been sewing dresses for a wedding. She didn't seem happy about it, but she was doing it nonetheless, preparing the first wedding in the family. Paul got the news third hand, from Line and Marty.

Ellie was leaving college. She planned to get married and move to Iowa City to work and live with Bruce while he finished school. According to Line, Ellie became stubborn and didn't care any more what Mother and Dad thought. There seemed to be something more to it than just getting married, but Paul couldn't figure out what it was. Anyway, what did he know. He was only 11. Getting married was something people did far in the future. He was happy to get away from the dining room for an afternoon though, where Mother sat silently sewing with pins in her mouth.

The snow came down thickly, piling wet and soft around the houses. John and Paul sat companionably at the kitchen table as Alice whisked the apple betty plates away. In their lives, nothing was going to happen that day, except that it might stop snowing and John might go out to shovel the sidewalks. Paul liked the feeling that nothing might happen. He could feel his life most certainly underneath him, if nothing else was going on.

"What could I make for Ellie's wedding present," asked Paul. "Something useful, maybe?" The kids often made Christmas presents for each other, sometimes with Dad and Mother's help. Paul's tiny allowance didn't stretch to buying much. Line and Marty were frantically trying to embroider pillowcases for Ellie.

According to Marty, brides were supposed to have a "trousseau." A "trousseau" was a chest with the linens and blankets a bride needed once she was married. Mother still had a beautiful cedar chest in which she kept precious things. But it was all happening too quickly. There was no trousseau for Ellie, and she didn't seem to care either.

"Some jam or some honey?" asked Alice. "We could help you with that. Everyone needs them."

"A bird house?" asked John. He was famous for making wooden birdhouses. He looked around the spotlessly clean kitchen. "Or maybe a breadboard?" Alice didn't go in for knick-knacks. Everything in that room was useful.

"A breadboard!" said Paul. That would be perfect. "Could you help me?" he asked. John's tiny woodshop had an iron pot-bellied stove in it.

Paul loved the smells there when a fire was going. There was probably time to make a breadboard. Ellie and Bruce were still at school. They would be home a few days before Christmas and the wedding would be on Little Christmas Eve, December 23rd.

John agreed. "A breadboard is a simple matter," he said. "We will cut a piece of hardwood to the proper size and then you can sand it off and give it a light finish."

"That shouldn't take very long, right?" asked Paul.

"No," said John. "I'll pick the wood this week, and next week on Saturday you can come over and sand it."

"Perfect!" Paul said loudly. "Thank you! And thanks for the apple betty. I better go home now and see how things are." Paul put on his coat and boots and ran home, delighted that he could do something for Ellie.

Preparations for Christmas and the wedding continued. Choir practices, Advent services, and work on the Sunday School Christmas program vied with sending out Christmas greetings and school.

Marty and Line baked batch after batch of Christmas cookies and dusted off the manger scene which went above the piano. Christmas cards were taped up along the woodwork between the living and dining rooms and Dad and Paul brought a large fir tree home from town. Secret presents were stored in people's bedrooms and the house was full of Christmas music. Many hands around the house contributed to filling the house with light at the dark time of the year.

Mother too seemed to have worked through her gloominess. Vacation began and all the kids were home from school. In the morning, Mother opened the window in the dining room and brushed the snow off the bird feeder. She asked Paul to put out a dried sunflower and a piece of suet. Downy woodpeckers came up to the suet right away, chickadees flitted and nuthatches with their turned up tails followed. The cardinal was king, however. When it arrived at the feeder with its brilliant slash of color, the smaller birds fled.

Later Paul lay on the floor of the living room, listening to carols on the phonograph. The lights on the Christmas tree flashed on and off, reflecting the tree's needles in flickering shadows on the wall. Once again he thought how lucky he was to be at home with nothing in particular to worry about. It was the day before Ellie came home. Aunt Rose and Grandma Bakken were due to arrive the day after for the wedding.

That night, however, Dad got a phone call. He left after supper and a little later Mother called everyone into the living room. Kristen wasn't asleep yet and Marty was making sure she didn't knock things off the Christmas tree as she looked at the packages.

There seemed to be a commotion out in the entry. "Okay, Paul," Mother said softly. "Early Christmas present."

When the door opened, in rushed a tiny collie, golden with a thick white ruff of fur around its intelligent, sharp-nosed face. A red ribbon encircled its neck. Dad followed, a big smile on his face.

Paul put his arms around the little dog, so surprised! Kristen was entranced. "Dog!" she pointed. "Doggie!"

Paul looked into the little foxy eyes and felt under the dog's fur for what its body was like. It was a tiny dog with lots of fur! But its eyes were dark and showed excitement. "A girl?" he questioned Dad to be sure.

"Yup, it's a little girl," said Dad.

"What are you going to call her?" asked Line, right behind Paul, with her arms around the dog.

"She has foxy eyes," said Paul, full of wonder. "And a sharp, foxy nose." Other than the ruff and her underbelly, which were snowy white, her hindquarters were all golden fur.

"It's a Sheltie mostly," said Dad. "But Shetlands usually have more black. She's about six months old and she's been living in the barn at the Odegaards'. They have so many dogs, they thought they could let go of her. She likes lots of company, so it may take a few weeks to tame her down, but we have plenty going on here and she'll get used to us."

Mother wanted to lay down the rules right away. "Now, Paul," she said. "She has been an outdoor dog, and once she grows accustomed to us, she can spend a lot of time outdoors. She can sleep in the basement during the winter, next to the furnace. You'll have to be responsible for her."

Paul put his face close to the little sharp face. "I think I'll call her Foxy," he said. It was almost like having a little brother or sister, another member of the family.

"I've brought some food," Dad said, "but I think you should be the one to feed and water her, Paul. So she knows you are her master."

"Yes," said Mother. "We're going to have a big day around here tomorrow. Everyone must get ready for bed!"

Dad and Paul went down to the basement. Dad found a pillow to make Foxy a soft bed, and he brought down a couple of old bread pans for food and water. Foxy seemed to be happy with the arrangements, but Paul was loathe to leave her and go up to bed. Dad hung around too, loading coal into the furnace and watching.

Finally Dad said, "You know, Paul, I think if we close the door, she's going to know we're all upstairs. She has to get used to her home, and I think she's tired and will settle down to sleep."

Paul listened, imagining he was Foxy. The coal fire in the big iron furnace softly crackled, but they could also hear people in the rest of the house, climbing the stairs and shutting doors. He took Foxy in his arms once more and told her quietly he would be back in the morning and to have a good night. He and Dad went up the wooden stairs and closed the door to the basement. They stood listening on the other side of the door, but there was no yelping.

"You should get dressed first thing in the morning," Dad said. "So you can go out with her. Show her around the place and make sure she knows it belongs to her. It's her new farm."

"I will, I will!" said Paul, his eyes shining. "Thanks Dad! It's the best present!"

"You better thank your mother," said Dad. "She agreed to this, even though she has so many other things to worry her this week."

Paul thanked Mother, who was adding candles to a centerpiece on the dining room table for the wedding, and went up to bed, wishing Foxy could sleep with him. But, as Dad said, she was a farm dog. He fell instantly asleep.

In the morning, in the grey dark of the house, Paul didn't even think of the Advent calendar, which was slowly ticking off the days until Christmas. He remembered that for him, Christmas was already here! He jumped out of bed, put on his clothes and raced down to the basement to see if Foxy had only been a dream. But, there she was at the foot of the stairs, looking up expectantly. She "arfed" a couple of times when she saw Paul.

It was a new era, Paul thought. He had a friend. A friend who would follow him everywhere and look up at him hopefully, egging him on. Paul carried Foxy up the stairs as he thought her legs were too short, put on his coat, and they went out.

The snow was deep in the yard. Maybe Foxy wasn't used to so much snow, if she was only six months old. Paul showed Foxy the paths out to the garage and around the porch and the sidewalks. Foxy seemed equal to anything, skittering on her white paws in the snow behind Paul. Paul looked towards the Sherwoods' house, but it was a little early to bother them. As they walked toward the house, Paul saw Marty and Kristen in the window, waving.

Paul stamped his feet in the entry and picked up Foxy to carry her down the stairs to the basement. But he could hear Kristen calling, "Where's doggie? Doggie!" And Marty opened the door and let Foxy in.

Foxy's nails clicked on the kitchen linoleum. Kristen petted Foxy, but then Paul took her downstairs. He didn't quite dare let her run around by herself yet and dogs slept a lot in the winter, he reasoned. Nevertheless, as he ate his breakfast, his heart was spinning toward the basement, imagining Foxy down there.

The wedding was simple. Dad, in his pastor's robes, waited before the altar dressed with Christmas roses. Only Bruce's mother, father and grandmother sat on his side, and on Ellie's side, only Grandma Bakken and Aunt Rose. Line, Marty and Kristen, wearing the dresses mother made, were the attendants, and Paul stood up for Bruce.

Mother played the wedding march and Ellie and Bruce walked up the aisle to the altar, where Line, Marty and Paul were arranged along the railing. Kristen carried a little pillow with their rings tied to it, but she wouldn't stay in front. She gave the rings to Line and went and sat with Aunt Rose.

Afterwards, Dad said, "You may kiss the bride," smiling tenderly at his oldest daughter. Ellie and Bruce faced each other, and Bruce lifted the veil made of net and flowers off Ellie's face. Marty, Line and Paul came down to the organ and sang Ruth's song to Naomi, from the Old Testament, "Entreat me not to leave thee, or to return from following after thee; for whither thou goest I will go, and whither thou lodgest I will lodge; thy people shall be my people, and thy God my God." The melody wasn't that familiar, but the words were.

Aunt Rose took a few photographs, and so did Mr. Morland, Bruce's father. Paul stood beside Bruce, reaching to his shoulder. He was trying not to think about Foxy, alone in the basement.

At the parsonage, a cake with three white tiers stood on the green cupboard and places were laid for the grownups in the dining room. Paul went down to the basement to reassure Foxy. Kristen clung to the door at the top of the steps shouting "Doggie come!" So Paul lifted her up and carried her down to see Foxy. She was wearing her little linen dress.

Mother was nervous and people were milling about, preparing the meal for the reception. She sent Line down to ask Paul and Kristen to feed Foxy and let her be.

A card table was set for the younger people. Everyone took their plates into the kitchen where the food was laid out and served themselves from the dishes the girls had made. Mother was at her most gentle and gracious, but Paul knew she was anxious for things to go well. He had attended a few weddings, either to sing or because cousins were getting married. He was glad this one was small.

While Mother and Marty cleaned up, Dad whispered that it was a good time for Line and Paul to go out to the garage. Paul took Foxy out with them. Line put signs saying "Just Married" in big black letters in the windows of Bruce's old blue Chevy, one in the back and one on the side. She and Paul tied strings of cans to the car fender with sash cord. It was cold and snowy, and almost dark, but there would be a little bit of noise and fun when Bruce and Ellie drove out of town.

Foxy was delighted to be out in the snow with Line and Paul, but all too soon, Paul put her back in the basement. "Shhhhh," he said to her. "It'll be over soon and we'll go for a walk." Foxy's intelligent eyes looked back at him. He was sure she understood.

Upstairs, Ellie and Bruce were about to cut the cake. Ellie looked content, powerful and happy, more than Paul had ever seen her. She and Bruce held their hands together on a knife, cutting the first piece of cake together. With everyone watching, they fed each other a bit of the cake with their hands.

Then they sat down on the couch beside the little pile of wedding presents. There wasn't time to collect many presents. Paul thought Grandma Bakken looked a little shocked by the whole proceeding. But Bruce and Ellie looked happy. Afterwards, they packed up and put Ellie's things in Bruce's car, which looked festive in the snow, with the lights from the garage on it. Ellie and Bruce came back in to wish everyone goodbye.

Mother was crying and Dad's eyes looked a little moist as well, but to Paul it felt sort of normal already. He shook Bruce's hand and planted a little kiss on Ellie's cheek. They were going to a hotel, and then would spend the rest of Christmas vacation at Bruce's family's house in Elk Creek. The Morland house had more room.

Ellie caught Kristen up in her arms and lifted her up to kiss, and then she turned and left, leaving her old life without looking back. They would come back later to celebrate Christmas with the Mikkelsons.

Paul didn't stick around to hear the Morlands saying goodbye, or to listen to what Aunt Rose and Grandma Bakken thought. He put on his coat and boots and headed straight for the basement. It was quite a day, and poor Foxy had to get used to this new place and new people. He felt responsible.

Foxy wagged her tail at the bottom of the steps. She "arfed" a couple of times when Paul opened the door, but she didn't seem to be loud or excitable. Paul was glad. "Come on," he said softly. He picked her up and buried his nose in her fur, getting familiar with her smell. "Let's get away from all of these people and have a look around town," he told her.

Paul and Foxy took the shoveled paths out to the roads, from which the new snow was plowed. Foxy was happy to get outdoors. She wallowed in the snow on her short legs, but then she followed Paul around the block. A light was on at the Sherwoods and Paul couldn't resist knocking on the door.

When John answered the door Paul said, "This is Foxy. She's an early Christmas present. If you see her around, she's my new dog."

"Oh ho!" said John. "She's a beauty! Did you know she was coming?"

"No," said Paul. "Dad kept it a secret. We've been looking for a dog for a while, though. She's perfect! He couldn't have found a better dog!"

"You're right," said John. He called Alice to come to the door and have a look at Paul and Foxy standing under the porch light.

"I just wanted you to know, because she's an outdoor dog. She'll live in the basement during the winter, but I'm going to fix up a dog house for her. You might see her around," said Paul.

"Thank you for showing her to us," said Alice, bending down to put her hands in Foxy's ruff. "Oh, you're a good dog, aren't you. We'll keep an eye on her when you're at school."

On Christmas Eve, Marty and Line put the lace cloth on the dining room table, and set it with the best china and Mother's Fostoria wineglasses, which she would fill with Welch's grape juice. They put name cards at each place. The centerpiece was a lake made from a blue mirror, with a snowy hillside of fluffy cotton batting beside it. Little houses and trees surrounded it, a peaceful Christmas scene. Small candles shaped like carolers with wicks sprouting out of their heads stood around it. No one used the candles, which Mother brought out every Christmas, so as not to spoil them.

Before dinner, *Amahl and the Night Visitors* was broadcast on television. Paul knew it was coming. He looked up the time in *The TV Guide* because he wanted to do a little inner preparation.

Paul went down to the basement and explained to Foxy what he felt reluctant to tell anyone else, that he was always apprehensive about his feelings when the family watched *Amahl*. This year he was sure he wouldn't cry as he usually did. In spite of his feelings, he didn't want to miss it.

Paul felt he was himself Amahl, the lame shepherd boy who is a dreamy player of pipes and a storyteller, excited by the arrival of the three wise men at his humble cottage. Amahl and his Mother are so poor they have sold their sheep, and he expects they will have to go begging. "Won't it be fun!" he says to the kings.

Every one of the Mikkelsons, even Dad, watched the opera written by Menotti, introduced by Menotti himself. Mother made sure Grandma Bakken had the best chair and Aunt Rose sat on the sofa. Kristen stood squarely in front of the screen. Paul could see Marty's rapt face, listening to the melancholy oboe in the opening scene which imitated the shepherds' pipes.

Line teased Kristen, "You make a better door than window, Kristen! Can't you sit down?"

But Kristen stood in front of the screen, not hearing Line. She was beginning to understand everything this Christmas. It was fun to watch her.

"You can move, Line," said Mother. "Just let her be."

Line, Marty and Paul knew all of the songs by heart. They could sing the one in which the comical King Kaspar describes the box of delights he travels with, telling Amahl what is in each of the drawers and offering him the "black, sweet licorice" which is in the last one.

They knew the one the shepherds sing as they arrive, bringing whatever hospitality they can offer the kings: "Emily, Emily, Michael, Bartholomew, give me your hand, come along with me." And the one in which Amahl's mother tries to take some of the gold for her child, only to be caught by the kings' bodyguard.

While they watched, no one sang along, but Paul knew that when it was over, the songs would be running through their heads, renewed in power until they could hear them again next year. When Amahl decides to go with the kings and give his crutch as a present to the wonderful child they describe, he finds himself healed. He holds out his crutch and manages to walk toward the kings. All of Paul's efforts at hardening himself against the tears didn't work. He saw Line watching him, but she was crying too. Amahl sang, "Look, Mother, I can dance! I can jump! I can run!"

Paul felt himself a walking miracle that year. He was healed as well as current medicine could do it. He could do as he liked now. Paul offered himself and his life, and Foxy's for that matter, once again to Christ and his service. Amahl walked off stage, his crutch tied to his back, playing his reedy pipes as he followed the kings.

25

When Line saw Mother's old maternity clothes hanging on a clothesline in the basement, she rushed upstairs to ask what it meant.

"It means I'm having another baby," said Mother, calmly. She was making a list of groceries for someone to take to the store on an old envelope.

"Another baby! When?" asked Line.

"In September."

Line couldn't believe her nonchalance. "In September! Can I tell the other kids? That's so wonderful!" It would bring the number of Mikkelson kids to six and make a little brother or sister for Kristen to play with, since she was so much younger than the rest of them.

"You can tell them," said Mother. She smiled up at Line. "It's a little bit of a surprise to me too, but it will be a lot of fun. Now, could one of you, or two of you, go to the store?"

"Sure," said Line. "Is there a lot to get? I'll see if Marty wants to go." Paul and Kristen were playing with Foxy in the yard, so Marty must be upstairs reading. It was April and most of the snow and ice were gone, but there was a biting chill in the air.

Marty was clipping house plans from a *Better Homes and Gardens* magazine and filing them in a box. Her face shone when Line told her about the new baby. "Another baby! I can't believe it!" she said. Her face told Line she was thinking about the question they asked each other when Ellie got married, whether Ellie was pregnant. "This baby could be the same age as its nieces and nephews if Ellie has a baby soon."

But no one had heard anything about a baby from Ellie. She seemed to be happy, working as a secretary for a school district and fixing up the little apartment she shared with Bruce in Iowa City.

Marty hugged Mother when she saw her.

"I'm so pleased about the baby!" she said.

"Me too," said Mother, smiling.

Line and Marty put on their coats and scarves, but thankfully not their boots.

"Hang on to Foxy," said Line to Paul as they went out the door. "We're going to the store." Foxy rushed up to them and sniffed their heels, but Paul called her back.

There were groceries to get almost every day. Dad sometimes took the car downtown, but often enough the kids went down for a few things. It was only four blocks away.

"I can't wait until it gets warm," said Marty. "Another month or so, I guess." Unless there was a snowstorm in April, the ground and the air warmed up pretty fast as the days grew longer. It was almost the end of school. Since the girls didn't sleep in the same room any more, there was much less time to talk. Line welcomed the chance.

"I'll be happy when school's out," said Line. "But, on the other hand, I miss the other kids during the summer."

"You miss arguing about politics!" said Marty. "I know you love it. You love your old speech club, admit it."

"Okay, okay," said Line. "It's such an interesting time! Mr. Simons is so fired up against segregation, he wants to go sit in with Negroes at lunch counters in the South this summer. I think he will too." Mr. Simons was a substitute the school found to replace Mrs. Schneider who was ill. Just out of the University of Wisconsin, he taught history as if current events were as important as the ones in the distant past. He was excited about John F. Kennedy, the front runner for the Democratic nomination that year. Although the Mikkelsons were Republican like most Iowans, all of whom liked Ike, Mr. Simons fired up Line as well as her classmates.

"I wonder if he'll be around next year for my American history class," said Marty. When Line told Mother and Dad about Mr. Simons, Dad said, "Sounds like a hot head. But a rolling stone gathers very little moss remember."

The only Negro they had met was a pastor from Madagascar who spoke at their church. Line watched closely to see how he moved and talked. His smooth skin was very dark, but the palms of his hands were pink. He spoke English with an accent Line didn't recognize. He said he had learned French in school because Madagascar was a French colony.

"Mr. Simons wants me to give my speech on apartheid in South Africa. There was a massacre of people peacefully protesting the passbook requirement. He wants me to read *Cry the Beloved Country*," said Line. "He says it would give me some background, so I guess I will."

"I love the way Isak Dinesen describes Africa," said Marty wistfully. "It sounds so beautiful."

"There's a lot going on all over the world right now," said Line, sadly. "But not here."

"Well, keeping up with current events can't hurt," said Marty practically. "When is your speech? Do you have time to read the book before you write it?"

"It's in a week," said Line breezily.

Line took *Cry the Beloved Country* to her babysitting job that night. A young trucker's wife had asked Mother if one of her daughters could babysit for her two kids while she went out with her husband. They lived in a rented part of an old brick house near the river.

When Line arrived, the kids were just finishing up their supper. Line's heart constricted when she saw that white Minute rice was all they had to eat, and the kids left some of it on their plates. The thin young woman and her husband left Line with the pale little girl and boy, neither of whom said much.

Line was stung by how listless the kids were, and how sad the rented place was. She could not see that there was much to do. She took a pencil and paper from her school binder and amused the kids with the story pictures Ma showed Laura Ingalls Wilder when they were waiting for Pa to come home in a blizzard. One was a story of a pond which turned into a duck as you told the whole story, drawing with your pencil at the same time.

When it was time to go to bed, the quiet kids didn't put up any fuss. They showed Line to an upstairs room where there were a bunch of beds and cribs. The kids climbed into the cribs and lay down, quiet as mice. Line wondered at this too, as no other kids she knew would have been so docile. There was no tearing around, jumping on beds or yelling. Line wished them good night, turned out the light and crept downstairs, hoping that the kids would go to sleep on their empty little tummies.

There wasn't a peep from them, and Line sat uncomfortably in a rickety old-fashioned chair trying to read her book. The darkened living room was filled with ancient furniture. When the thin woman and her husband came home, they looked happy and loving, but there was a smell of beer or whiskey about them. The woman carefully paid Line her $1.50 for the three hours and wished her good night. The young trucker took Line home in his car. He was shy and polite, and so was Line.

At home, Mother was in the living room, watching a late night television show. She seemed happy to see Line. "How did it go?" she asked.

"All the kids had for supper was white rice," said Line. "And the parents were drinking."

"Yes, I know," said Mother. "But you're not to judge them. You can't know how things are for someone else unless you have put on their shoes and walked around in them."

"I'm glad I went," said Line.

"I was a little apprehensive," said Mother, "but I count on your good sense, Line. I didn't want to refuse Mrs. Arthur."

Line went out to the kitchen and got the can of salted peanuts off the shelf. She poured a few into her hand and went back to talk to Mother. "I'll never take a salted peanut for granted again," she said dramatically.

Mother smiled at her. "You shouldn't. And don't take your warm bed for granted either. You kids are very well off."

Line stood there, eating peanuts, as if there was nothing more to do in life.

But Mother thought otherwise. "Go to bed, Line. Tomorrow is another day."

Line leaned down and kissed Mother lightly on the cheek. "Thank you. Good night." She climbed the dark stairway to her own, familiar bed.

That week Line was invited to a baby shower for one of her classmates. Her name was Sharon Wagner, and Line loved her warm, farm-girl manner. Sharon sat beside Line in study hall and they were also in 4-H together. But all of a sudden Sharon didn't come to school and no one knew why. Line found out she had gotten married. Line felt hurt that Sharon never shared an inkling of this momentous fact. They were both 16 and Sharon was very bright. The Wagners didn't belong to the Mikkelsons' church. Would Line ever see her again?

But Diane's mother, who lived on a neighboring farm, decided the girls should give Sharon a baby shower. She invited all the girls in Line's class to a shower at her house. Line bought a baby gift of three tiny white cotton shirts and wrapped them in tissue paper with a card she made herself on yellow construction paper.

Line got a ride with Sylvia Hanson, whose sister brought them both. The atmosphere at the shower was deadly under dim electric light in a drab, linoleum-floored kitchen. Several mothers were there, and they encouraged the girls to get sandwiches and cake, and then sit around in a circle on chairs in the kitchen. But the girls were scared to talk. There was too much in the air that no one dared ask about.

All girls Line's age feared "having to get married." This had happened to Sharon in a secretive, sad way. Not the way you wanted to get married. None of the girls knew anything about the guy Sharon married, or where it happened. They wondered what it would feel like to get pulled out of school and married at 16. But Sharon never talked to anyone about it, and she certainly wasn't going to talk to a large group of classmates sitting around in a circle.

Diane's mother seated Sharon near the card table where the presents were piled. Line sat almost next to her, with Sylvia between them. Sharon didn't look any different than she always did, gentle and pretty, with soft brown hair turned up at the ends, thick bangs on her forehead. Like the rest of them, she wore a dress gathered at the waist, but her sweater was pulled down so you couldn't see if her stomach, where the baby must be growing, was getting any bigger.

Sharon just sat there silently and so did Sylvia, who also lived on a farm and was the best basketball player in Line's class. Line knew that most farm kids worked a lot harder than she did. They did chores, taking care of livestock both morning and evening, and helping with field work, haying and threshing. If there were enough men in the family, the girls might do women's work at home, but there was plenty of that! Heavy cleaning, cooking and baking for their families and the farm hands. Many of these families had lots of kids in them, so there were enough people to help out.

The reluctance of any of the girls to speak was oppressive and the mothers didn't know how to help. Diane's mother urged Sharon to open the presents. She passed them to Sharon one after the other, packages wrapped in dime store paper and tied up with bright paper ribbons curled into tight rings by drawing a scissor along them.

"Oh, that's so cute!" someone would say as a little sleeping suit emerged out of the crackling paper. Boys were supposed to wear blue and girls pink, and since no one knew whether the baby would be a boy or a girl, many of the clothes and blankets were white or yellow, or soft prints with several colors in them.

When Sharon got to Line's present, Line watched closely as she opened it. All babies needed these warm little undershirts, with tabs on them to pin their diapers to. Line reached over to touch the soft white cotton, remembering how tiny and red Kristen had been, and how it felt to fit her pliable little arms into an undershirt. Soon there would be another baby in the Mikkelson house!

Sharon smiled over at her shyly. "Thank you Line," she said in her gentle voice. It was the most intimacy Line was able to get.

Line wondered where Sharon lived. She thought of the tiny apartment where Ellie and Bruce lived, its kitchen bright with calico curtains Ellie made herself, a brave replica of their own big kitchen. Ellie could do what she liked in her own kitchen, but she also worked in an office every day of the week. Perhaps Sharon would now have her own kitchen, but it was unlikely. She was probably living with her parents, or her husband's parents, on a farm where there was lots of work.

One after another, the presents were opened and passed around for the girls to look at. Some of the girls drank the coffee Diane's mother prepared, trying on their grownup status. Line tried it, but the coffee tasted bitter and hot. After the presents there was nothing else to do, so the girls put on their coats and went home, Sylvia's sister dropping Line at the big parsonage at the edge of town.

Line felt relieved to find Mother up late again, reading a magazine. She sat down on the couch next to Mother. Perhaps Marty was right. Home, where you understood people, was best after all.

Mother was curious about the shower. "How is your friend Sharon?" she asked.

"She's fine," said Line. "She didn't even look pregnant. Not like you do!" she teased, patting Mother's swelling tummy.

"Well, maybe it's a little early for her to start showing yet," said Mother. "It was nice for Diane's mother to get you all together. I know you were worried about Sharon."

"Yup," said Line. "But it was really sad and awkward. I would have liked to talk to her, but there were too many other people around. I didn't want to embarrass her. She hardly talked at all, but I think she was touched by the presents."

"Did you find out anything about the boy she married?" asked Mother.

"No," said Line. "But I got the impression that he lived on a farm near them."

"My dear girl," said Mother. "I'm sure it is hard to see one of your friends have to give up her studies and plans to get married at such an early age."

"I don't know," said Line. "That's the sad part to me. She might be perfectly happy, but everyone is so flustered by the situation, that we'll never know. No one will even talk about it honestly."

"Perhaps you are right, Line," said Mother. "At any rate, I hope that by the time you girls want to get married you can do it with whole-hearted joy." She put her arm around Line. "And I must say, I hope it is a long time from now!"

Line could almost see Mother's eyes going back to Ellie's Christmas wedding, which was so hasty, and so quiet. She couldn't help but ask, "Mother, did Ellie and Bruce have to get married?"

"No," said Mother. "I don't think so. Ellie just got stubborn, said she was 18 and she didn't want to wait any longer to be with Bruce, and he supported her." Mother hesitated, but then she continued. "And of course, the same was true of me. Some people thought your Dad and I should have waited until he finished the seminary and got his first pastorate, so he could support us. And it was wartime too. But I got a job in the Lutheran orphanage. When we had Ellie, it was hard to have a tiny baby there. We missed your Dad every day. But, things worked out in the end."

Mother smiled at Line. "Ellie is happy, I think. But you kids will have the chance to go further. You are all good students, and you know the value of educating yourselves. You will be much more useful to others if you have an education."

"Yes, Mother," said Line, demurely, thinking of the grim atmosphere of the dimly lighted kitchen and the girls who couldn't speak. "I can't wait to go to college. The way Mr. Simons talks, it is the beginning of your life!" She knew Dad and Mother were a little leery of Mr. Simons. Line often made idols out of people, and later found their feet were made of clay!

That week, Marty and Line walked home from the bus on a wet, cold windy day. The rain held the promise of spring, however, and there were buds on every tree branch. It was growing lighter too, and the girls, carrying their books in their arms in front of them, felt that it wouldn't be long now until summer vacation.

In the house they smelled something sweet and strange. Paul and Mother were standing over the stove, peering at some shriveled brown things in a frying pan.

"They're morels," said Paul. "Mrs. Appelman showed Mother and Dad where to find them on the hillside."

"They're a great delicacy," said Mother. "We couldn't resist trying some, but we'll have the rest for supper."

Line looked dubious. She was surprised that Paul, who was the finicky eater in the family, was interested in them. But then Paul liked all growing things. Morels apparently had a crinkled top and a stem. Mother cut them down the center, so they each looked like half a mushroom and you could see that they were hollow.

Paul handed Line a fork and she cut off a tiny corner of one of the stems. The taste was rich and buttery, like nothing Line could imagine. She managed to swallow it, but she did not want more.

"They grow in the dead leaves under the trees," said Mother. "They're really hard to see, but Marjorie took us with her to look. The rain brings them out. Marjorie is an expert mushroom hunter and she said they eat them on toast for a treat."

Line didn't think they would be much of a treat. Mother used Campbell's cream of mushroom soup in the hot-dish recipes she found in magazines. But the taste wasn't nearly as intense as this. "I think I will leave this treat to the rest of you," said Line.

"Give it a try," said Mother. "We all will tonight."

"I want to go mushroom hunting," said Paul. His bright face was attentive as he put his nose toward the mushrooms in the frying pan. "They smell so good!"

"That's the butter!" said Dad, who came in from the study. "It's a little dangerous unless you know what you're doing. Many kinds of mushrooms are poisonous, and there's a false morel which looks a lot like the good one. Marjorie showed us. The stems of true morels are hollow."

At dinner Mother put a half slice of broiled toast with mushrooms on each of their plates. Line ate hers as quickly as she could, and chased it with corn and milk to get the taste out of her mouth. Marty and Paul looked as if they were trying to enjoy them, but the morels were rubbery, not like anything they usually ate.

"How is your speech coming?" Mother asked Line. There were no Lutheran missions in South Africa, so they didn't know much about apartheid. South Africa was settled by the British, and part of it by the Dutch, whose descendants, the Boers, now ran the country.

"It's hard to find facts when you are speaking about current events," said Line. "But more interesting. *Life* magazine printed articles on Sharpsville and even some on the history of South Africa!"

"Well, that's exactly what you need, isn't it?" said Mother. "How about the book?" She knew Line was reading *Cry the Beloved County*.

Line looked a little shamefaced. "I started it, but I haven't gotten very far. Marty read the whole thing when I wasn't looking!"

"You'll never get anywhere unless you learn to enjoy reading," said Mother. She looked pointedly at Dad.

"I learn more from people than I do from books," said Line. "I always have!"

"You know, Line," said Dad gently. "I was never much of a reader either, but I got through four years of college and four years of seminary, and let me tell you that was a lot of reading!" The books to prove it were lined up on the walls of Dad's study, but these days the kids knew that unless he was preparing a sermon, he mostly read ham radio magazines. "I love language, though," he said. "The turns of it, the phrases, the way it moves people."

"That's what I like about speech club!" said Line. "There have been some great speeches in America. History is all about them." She much preferred having someone in front of her speaking, to reading what they wrote. Looking at someone you knew so much more about them than if you just looked at words on a page. You could tell how they felt about what they were saying, whether they were being honest.

Kristen was squirming in her high chair. "Kristen, do you want to get down?" asked Mother. The littlest, she was the only one who was allowed to leave the table without finishing the food in front of her. The rest of them were old enough to know better.

"Well, Line," said Mother. "You better pull that speech together. I know it is due tomorrow. I don't think it will excuse you from doing the dishes though. You've had plenty of time to work on it."

"Yes, I know," said Line. "I will." The closer it got to an emergency, the easier it was for her to do things.

That night Line got Marty to tell her the story of *Cry the Beloved Country* and she settled down with the *Life* magazines from the past month, from which she was able to write her speech.

But when she showed it to Mr. Simons, he thought something was missing.

"You have a powerful speech here, Line, about something important. But I don't see its importance to you. I thought that if you read Alan Paton's book you would get a living sense of what it is like not to have the right to move freely in your own country. Or use public facilities. But your speech is just about external events. Have you ever read the *Declaration of Independence*? Or the *Bill of Rights*?" he asked. He looked impatient, intense, as if he could hardly sit still.

Line backed off a little, feeling blank. "Yes," she said hesitantly.

"What do you think people's rights are?" asked Mr. Simons, running his hands through his black hair, which wouldn't lie down.

"Life, liberty and the pursuit of happiness?" said Line.

"And what does that mean to you?" asked Mr. Simons. "Imagine that you didn't have these rights. Imagine that you are petitioning the government, or someone, to exercise your rights."

Line didn't know what to say to that. She just stood there.

"Well, try again," said Mr. Simons. "Try putting some of yourself into your speech. Make it so important to you that you are able to convince your listeners."

Line went home flustered. She never thought about rights or needed them. And *Cry the Beloved Country* wasn't about rights. It was about how love and respect for one's fellow man conquered their differences. It was about how a white man who loves Lincoln and writes that South African Christianity is hypocritical is killed by the son of a good Negro pastor. And how his white father manages to forgive and help the people of the valley.

Line told Marty about her conversation with Mr. Simons. "It's like we're almost not speaking the same language," she said.

"Put yourself in his shoes," said Marty. "He just came out of college, he's wishing that he is in the South, sitting in at lunch counters with Negro friends and being dragged off to jail. He might even get on television! That would be much more exciting than sitting here talking to us conformist kids. But I'm sure he likes you. I'm sure he is trying to convince you to think differently too."

"I do! I do think differently," said Line hotly. "But I don't know how to help! What can I do about a family of kids who just gets white rice for supper? Without shaming their family. The husband and wife were really nice. Or a nice girl who gets pregnant too soon?"

"Yeah," said Marty softly. "Problems right under our nose."

"I guess I just have to say what I think," said Line. "I can't do more than that."

Line sat down and wrote new paragraphs at the beginning of her speech. She wrote from her heart, from her own understanding:

"As Christians, and as Americans, we believe all people are created equal, 'that they are endowed by their Creator with certain unalienable Rights, that among these are Life, Liberty and the pursuit of Happiness,' as the Declaration of Independence states. But in regards to some races in the world, we do not act that way. Both in our own country, where we have segregated schools, washrooms and even drinking fountains in the South, and in South Africa, where apartheid is the law, people are not being treated with equality.

"Apartheid means 'apartness' in the Afrikaans language. The only reason laws are set up to separate people is when some people fear other people. There is no need for us to fear each other. I believe that if we were truly Christian and loved our neighbors as ourselves, people wouldn't have to struggle against each other to get the rights they deserve."

When Line gave her speech, Mr. Simons applauded her from the back of the room. "Excellent, Line!" he said. "Thank you for explaining how 'apartheid' came about in South Africa. It comes from fear, as anyone can see. Love conquers fear. Let us hope that it can do so here too."

But Dad was right, too. When school was out, Mr. Simons was gone. Line never found out where he went.

26

Early in the morning, Line stole out of her lower bunk. She could hear Paul's breathing across from her, and the sagging bunk above showed that Marty's body was still in it. She didn't want to wake them. Foxy, who lay on the floor beside Paul, raised her head, but Foxy wasn't going anywhere without Paul. Line slipped out of her pajamas and into shorts. The sprunnnng sound of the spring on the screen door couldn't be silenced, but she was careful not to bang the door.

The orange sun came through the birch and poplar trees at a low angle. Line wanted, just once, to wake before the sun lifted off the horizon on the lake. But being outdoors all day, she slept too heavily. She rubbed the sandy soil off her bare feet and stuck them into the rubber thongs she knew were hers because they were green.

In the worn Lande cabin, which was just as quiet as the bunkhouse, Line smelled coffee. Aunt Rose must already be up. Soon the sweet, rich smell of toasted wheat and melting butter joined it, as Line made herself a piece of toast and took it outdoors.

The air was soft, a little damp, and smelled like green things growing, new leaves and branches, though it was late July. At the bottom of the steps below the cabin, Aunt Rose sat in a lawn chair at the edge of the lake. She smiled at Line, and raised her cup in a quiet "good morning." The only sounds were of the ducks paddling by, looking for breakfast, and the call of a loon.

Not wanting to break the spell, Line walked quietly out onto the dock. The lake was as still as milk in a pan and mists lay along it near the shore. The sun was high, coming toward her like a shining path. A school of minnows swam under the dock, their silvery skins flashing in the light. Line sat down on the steps below Aunt Rose. From far across the lake came the thunk of someone putting oars in their boat. Across the still water, every sound carried.

"This is the life, isn't it Line?" said Aunt Rose.

"Yes," said Line. The quiet wouldn't last long. Soon the whole tribe of Mikkelsons and their Bakken cousins, whose family was building a new cabin a few lots over, would be up and hungry. Later, when the contractors came, bulldozers would crash through the woods, helping clear the space around the split-level cabin for vehicles in the front, and a patio and lawn at the back. The property was all forest, a woods of birch, poplars and pines which sloped steeply down to the lake. The men tried to save the birches and pines, but the poplars were fair game.

Line remembered a morning, years ago, when she and Marty and Paul came down the steps of this cabin early in the morning and visited the trolley car, scared to death that the angry owner would drive them off with a pitchfork. The trolley car was still up in the woods under the pines. She and Marty showed it to their cousins the first day they came. It was rumored that the ancient owner had died, however, and a pastor from the

Twin Cities bought the land. Lots were being sold for people to build cabins on.

Line and Aunt Rose heard the sound of sandals flapping along the woodsy lake path and two of the younger Bakkens, Esther and Naomi, emerged. They were about Paul's age, all long brown legs and arms, with tousled honey-colored hair.

"Good morning," said Aunt Rose, smiling at their sleepy faces. "Go up and get some breakfast, if you're hungry." The girls stood for a minute looking toward the lake and then at each other, like two deer peering out of the woods. Line could see they couldn't decide whether to go out on the dock or up the steps to the Lande cabin at the top of the hill. But hunger seemed to get the better of them and they climbed the steps.

There was no food at the Bakken cousins' new cabin. Mother, Aunt Rose and Aunt Helen Bakken spent all day cooking for the huge brood at the rented Lande cabin which had electricity, a stove and a refrigerator. The Lande's had no plumbing, however. Water was carried up from a pump below and heated for washing dishes. The kids used the outhouse, brushed their teeth at a tin washbasin by the door of the cabin and bathed themselves in the lake.

Aunt Rose sighed. Altogether there were ten kids and six grownups to cook for. "But you know, Line," she said. "It is so different from being a school principal, that it really is a vacation." If she was surprised at the size of her brother and sister's families, she never said so. She was the best aunt, thought Line. She was Line's mentor as far as drawing went. Aunt Rose sketched and painted herself, and brought drawing instruction books as well as new sketchbooks for Line and Paul.

"How's your chipmunk sketch coming," asked Aunt Rose.

"It's coming along," said Line. "I'll show you later. Yesterday I got them to eat some popcorn from my hand. I tried to get Kristen to feed them, but she couldn't sit still. And if Foxy's around, they won't come out at all." Foxy sent the chipmunks straight back to their homes with an anxious "chrrrrr."

"I doubt if drawing and painting are your life," said Aunt Rose, "but they are certainly a lovely pastime."

Line bridled a little. She disliked the idea of hobbies. She wanted to do one thing hugely, passionately and well. "You're probably right," she said mildly. "I don't see how painting helps the world really. I want to do something important."

Aunt Rose laughed. "Line, you are as bright and shiny as a new liberty dime. I am certain that you will do something important with your life."

"Yesterday, Fiona and I took the boat out," said Line. "The wind came up in the afternoon and we wanted to get away from everyone. So I sketched a tennis shoe out in the boat, like you suggested. Every detail! It was amazing!"

"That's the point," said Aunt Rose. "Drawing helps you to see."

"Yeah, I guess so," said Line, looking out toward the water.

As Line expected, the morning was noisy with the sound of chainsaws and trees falling. Also with the sounds of kids swimming and splashing in the lake. The grownups worked, though Mother was very pregnant and needed to rest often.

* * *

After lunch, Marty shadowed Kristen up the stairs to the loft above the crowded kitchen in the Lande cabin to put her down for a nap. She read to her softly. It was hot and stuffy up in the loft as there wasn't any ventilation, but Kristen's little body grew heavy and sleepy and Marty put her down on the daybed. Then she stealthily went over to the card table and looked at the game of solitaire which she and her cousin Rebecca had laid out.

She flipped the deck over in threes, putting down cards, black queen on a red king, black jack on a red queen. Marty was fascinated by the deck of cards, known to be instruments of the devil. Idle hands were the devil's playground in any case, and Marty had never touched cards before. Rebecca played with abandon, showing off her superior knowledge. Rebecca didn't seem to know that cards were wicked.

Silently, hoping people would forget she was above them, Marty played card after card. The queens looked angry and bitter and kings were resigned. It was thrilling to play ancient games that people had played from time immemorial. Like chess. Aware that she was doing something illicit, wasting time that could be used more profitably, Marty couldn't stop.

In the kitchen below, Aunt Rose began making Toll House cookies for a treat. It was almost the last day of vacation. The Bakkens were leaving tomorrow and the Mikkelsons the day after.

Mother, Aunt Helen and Grandma Bakken were talking about curtains. "I don't even feel we need them," said Aunt Helen. "We're surrounded by woods!"

"I think Ellie made her curtains even before she moved into her apartment," laughed Mother. "They were the most important thing!"

"What did she use?" asked Aunt Helen.

"They're a sort of light blue calico. You know, flowered," said Mother.

"I think I'd use gingham in the cabin, if I were you," said Aunt Rose. "Thin cloth, so it didn't shut out the light. A gold and white gingham."

"So you are getting to know Bruce?" asked Aunt Helen.

"A little," said Mother. As a pastor's wife she never allowed herself to gossip or make intimate friends of church members, but with her mother and sisters she could talk. "He seems to be a go-getter. But I don't think he and his family have much appreciation for culture." Mother's eyes filled with tears. "I still feel I have failed her."

Grandma Bakken, who was thin and had a bit of Norwegian lilt to her sentences, said, "My dear girl. Ellie is a grownup now. You have raised her with the very best intentions. You must let go. You have all of your other children to worry about."

"Yes," said Aunt Helen. "My goodness, it's a difficult time. Our Jean is already at Luther, and Heather goes next year. Jean is very practical, but I do worry about Heather. She reaches out and tries to save people. And it gets her into trouble!"

"What kind of trouble?" asked Aunt Rose, beating the sugar and butter with all of the vigor of her strong arms.

"Oh, you know," said Aunt Helen. "She's attracted to these artsy, beatnik kids who think they should smoke and drink and use bad language. Stay out all night talking. It's terrible!"

"You have to trust them," said Grandma Bakken, her tongue struggling in her mouth. "You've brought them up in the Lutheran faith, taught them what's important and that the soul shines like a light. You must trust that they will walk in the light instead of in darkness."

"It's frightening," said Mother. "It's like they are drawn to darkness. Line loved her speech teacher last year, and a darker, more fiery guy I never met! And, as you said Mother, if you put a drop of ink into clear water, it never goes away. It just muddies the water."

Upstairs in the loft, Marty surreptitiously listened to the revealing adult conversation, laying jacks on queens, queens on kings, red on black. Her hands were sweaty and the cards were damp and ragged at the edges.

"That doesn't sound like Ellie, though," said Aunt Rose.

"No," said Mother. "Ellie's interested in kitchen appliances and furniture, and all the things money can buy. I was hoping that she would want to know about the finer things in life, music, paintings, books. She's so young."

"You still have a lot of influence I'm sure," said Aunt Rose. "Well, so are we having a wiener roast tonight? I think that's what we decided."

Aunt Helen laughed. "With this crew, you hardly finish one meal and you have to start thinking about the next!"

"And the dishes!" Mother sighed. A wiener roast helped, as there weren't as many dishes.

"Reminds me of the old days in Spring Grove," Grandma Bakken said. "You girls may not have it easy with all of your children, but it is definitely easier than it used to be."

"I'm the general's aide-de-camp," said Aunt Helen. "Herb being the general. I just deploy my troops and they do the dishes!" Uncle Herb was in the army when the two older girls were born. There were now more than enough girls in that family to get the housekeeping done.

"I just want to tell you," said Grandma Bakken. "I'm so proud of all of you, and your children. Such gifts! And your new little one, Lois."

"Thank you, Mother," Marty heard Mother reply. "Who would have thought? At my age!"

The heat in the loft grew, but Marty dealt out hand after hand, trying to get all of the cards to lay out in sequence. She was about to win, but Kristen sat up on the day bed, her hair wet and plastered to her face. Marty gave up and carefully packed the tattered cards into their box. "Come on, Kristen," she said. "Let's go over to the new cabin and bring Rebecca back her cards." She took Kristen's hand and helped her down the stairs.

"Tell everyone there will be cookies over here soon," said Aunt Rose as Marty and Kristen went out the door. She spooned small clumps of batter onto cookie sheets. "And remind someone to bring a pail of water when they come!"

Kristen slowly climbed down the steps to the lake with Marty holding her hand. Everything was interesting to Kristen; she could be distracted by a bug, a leaf, or a stone. But Marty held her firmly by the hand, making progress step by step along the forest path at the edge of the lake.

At the Bakken cabin, switchback paths zigzagged up the hill, through the trees and underbrush. There was poison ivy in there, shiny, with three leaves. But the men cut it away from the path. At the top of the hill, the new wooden building rose against the sky, two floors. The bottom floor was still dirt, with a pump room for water. Marty and Kristen climbed the steps to the porch at the front door.

Marty stood looking in the screen door with Kristen. She loved the simplicity of the big room where the smell of the new golden wood was so fresh. Light showed through the amber knotholes. It didn't look like one of the house plans she collected from magazines, because there were no rooms.

Along one wall windows looked down onto the lake, and on the other, smaller windows. Under the smaller windows was a row of sleeping bags neatly laid out, one for each of the Bakkens, including Aunt Helen and Uncle Herb, with their box or suitcase of clothing beside them. Later there might be walls to make rooms, but Marty loved it just the way it was. A big tent, secure against mosquitoes and small animals, but not much else.

Marty was shy about visiting, because Aunt Helen didn't want kids messing up the cabin. Rebecca and Fiona sat on their sleeping bags reading, keeping an eye on Little Hans, their brother, who was building a bridge with wooden blocks under the tall windows. Rebecca came to the screen door when she saw Marty.

"Aunt Rose is making cookies," said Marty, handing her the cards. "She told me to tell you. Thanks for the cards!" It was really just an excuse to visit the Bakken cabin. She could have left them in the loft. Kids were supposed to play outdoors. And the woods and the lake edge were full of places to go. No one cared where they went as long as they watched Kristen and little Hans. They couldn't get into much trouble.

"Great," said Rebecca. "Let's go tell the men."

The three of them went to the front of the cabin, where a sandy two-lane track came in from the gravel county road. The space was growing larger as the men cut trees and dragged them off to be cut into chunks and stacked in woodpiles. Dad, Uncle Herb and Bob Kautz, the contractor, wore boots and ragged old clothes as they worked in the woods. Dad took off his torn work gloves and wiped his sweaty forehead when he saw them. He picked up Kristen and stood her high on a cut log, his arms around her.

"Sure, we'll come over and have some coffee. We're ready for it!"

The men headed through the woods to the Lande cabin, taking Kristen with them, Rebecca following. Marty saw Esther and Naomi up in the treehouse. They were attaching ferns to ropes tied above the treehouse platform. Down below, Paul sawed a thin sapling with a short, dangerous-looking saw, Foxy at his side watching patiently.

"Aunt Rose is baking Toll House cookies," Marty said. The little girls instantly climbed down the rope ladder, their long tan legs bounding off toward the Lande cabin, following the men.

Paul looked after the retreating girls. "I was hoping it would be like the big tree," he said. "Remember? In North Dakota, where you could see things from high up."

"Yeah, I remember," answered Marty. "I'm sure it will be. But we have to leave in a couple of days! It will be covered with snow this winter."

"Yup," said Paul forlornly. The treehouse was bound to four living poplar trees with heavy twine, as Dad didn't want them to use nails. Dad helped bind the foundation logs, and then Paul and the girls cut saplings to make a rough floor. It was hard to believe it would survive a winter. "I hope we get to come next summer and see what happened."

"Yeah," said Marty. "I bet we will. Uncle Herb will probably rent out his cabin to us when their family isn't using it." Marty and Paul followed the others to the Lande cabin, where the men stood around outdoors with their coffee cups.

"He's planning on building next year," said Uncle Herb to Bob Kautz, the contractor. They were talking about Uncle David, brother to Herb, Aunt Rose and Mother. David was on the faculty of the Lutheran seminary in St. Paul. He had bought the lot next to Herb's. "Going with a Bach cabin," said Herb. The Bachs had perfected a technique of milling logs into even sizes and notching them together to make beautiful cabins at their lumber mill across the lake.

Marty passed the cookie plate, listening to the men talk. Pastors didn't own their own homes as the parsonages their families lived in was part of church property. But some pastors could afford to buy vacations homes. Lake Michigami was three miles long and a mile and a half across. Plenty of room. The spit of land that went into the lake on the eastern side was called Preacher's Point.

"He'll probably need your help," said Dad to Bob. Bob lived nearby and did handywork for people on the lake. He took in the Landes' dock in the fall. If it was left out in the winter, it would be crushed when the ice broke up in the spring.

"Yep," said Uncle Herb, "we appreciate it! You too, Carl. You're putting some sweat into this place!"

"Lots of building going on this year," said Bob Kautz. "This lake shore is being bought up." Between the Lande cabin and the Bakkens' new cabin, three pastors had bought land and one of the families was camping in a tent. They had kids too, so there were flocks of kids around, enjoying the ease of the lake and the primitive conditions.

"They've started an association for lake folks," said Dad. "I heard about it over at the Benedict store. Sort of get to know each other and watch out for our interests. You'll probably want to join, Herb." The lake was in Minnesota's Paul Bunyan State Forest and lake front lots were let out for sale by the state.

After "coffee," as the 3 p.m. break was usually called, the kids went in swimming. The older girls were reluctant, but they cajoled each other. If more kids went in it was more fun. The lake water was sun-warmed. In the winter it froze solid, many feet deep full of ice. In June the water was known to be very cold, but by the end of July, it was warm enough to stay in if you were energetic.

Mother sat in a lawn chair on the Lande dock, holding Kristen against her large pregnant tummy, until someone was ready to take Kristen into the water. Foxy hovered near her, watching them all and running up and down the dock with excitement. Swimming towels draped the dock and hung off the poles which anchored it. If they jumped off the end of the dock, the kids didn't cut their feet on stones and got used to the cold water all at once, but Marty couldn't.

Line stood at the end of the dock, screwing up her courage to jump in. The Bakken kids, whose father coached at a college and insisted they learn to swim, dove off the end of the dock into the shallow water. Finally Line jumped in, but Marty waded in, inch by freezing inch over the sharp stones, until the water was chest high and she could push off into a dog paddle. Flailing in the water, her body warmed up.

Under water, the stones gave way to smooth sand. It was shallow for a long way out from the dock, gradually growing deeper. The water came up to Marty's chest at the end of the dock. A few hundred yards out from shore, where the color of the water changed, was the drop off. Fishermen sometimes trolled there in the evening for deep-water fish, Northern pike and Muskellunge.

Despite lessons, none of the Mikkelsons knew how to swim properly. Marty and Line used black rubber inner tubes to float around the lake. The older girls took turns with Kristen and Little Hans in the water, holding them around their middles until they were comfortable and helping them use the inner tubes. They waded on the stones at the edge of the water and picked up mussel shells and pretty stones. But Kristen's fingers and toes turned blue and her teeth started to chatter. Marty got out and wrapped her thin little body in a towel.

"You better take her up and put dry clothes on her," said Mother. "She's shivering."

Marty quaked with chill too, a damp towel around her shoulders. She still needed to shampoo her hair, so when Kristen was dressed she brought her to Mother and got back in the water with the shampoo bottle. Line and Rebecca took some shampoo too, scrubbing their hair with their fingers at the end of the dock, then swimming off under water like mermaids to rinse it.

Aunt Rose didn't go swimming and neither did Mother. But Uncle Herb and Aunt Helen appeared in their bathing suits and so did Dad. Herb and Helen swam laps a few yards out from shore and Dad swam out farther and farther, exploring.

* * *

After the hot and sweaty work sawing logs in the woods, the lake felt cool and delicious to Paul. He dog paddled around happily, examining the crayfish, little clam shells, algae and the thick, hideous black spotted leeches which undulated through the water like snakes. In the water, it didn't matter at all if one of Paul's legs was stronger than the other. He could float and kick and dive, opening his eyes under water so he could see. Foxy sat on the dock watching. She wasn't much of a swimmer.

That evening Paul encircled a flat rocky place near the lake shore with big stones and helped Dad light a teepee of sticks and logs. They let the big logs become coals for cooking, watching for sparks flying up into the trees.

When they heard Aunt Rose calling from above, requesting a pail of water, Paul jumped up and went half way up the steps to the pump. "I'll get it," he called up. Taking an empty pail off its hook, he put it below the red pump, working the handle hard so the fresh water flowed. He remembered the long ago trip to this cabin when he was exempted from carrying water because his leg was braced and he couldn't get up and down steps well. Now he proudly carried water pails along with everyone else, struggling to lift his legs and strengthen them on the wooden steps. It wasn't easy, but he was determined.

"Good work, Paul," Dad called from below.

The Bakken kids came streaming down the lake path when they smelled the wood fire. Paul sat at its edge, watching the leaping flames as he cooked his hotdog. Line came and sat by him on a log, her hotdog threaded on a stick as she tried to find a spot in the red coals. Activity surrounded them.

Twilight took a long time in the summer in the Northern woods. Cooking marshmallows for their s'mores the kids got smoky on purpose to fend off mosquitoes.

After supper Dad dived into the lake again for a swim. The two families were so busy this year, no one even thought of fishing. Paul jumped in the lake with Dad. At night the water was smooth and glassy. Loons called to each other a few hundred yards off shore. After a whole day of sunshine, the water felt warmer than it had all day. The sky was huge above them and the sun sank into the horizon on the western side of the lake, the color of the water darkening as the sky did.

Paul did not want to leave the water. His body was protected from the few mosquitoes that came out in the evening and he was as weightless as he might have been in space. He turned over on his back and practiced floating, moving his arms and legs a little to keep his body from sinking.

"It feels more like it's our lake, doesn't it," said Dad.

"I hope so," said Paul. They lived a long way from northern Minnesota now, but the more often they came, the more it would be theirs. What was possession anyway? Perhaps you owned what happened to you and nothing else. That seemed right. Paul felt he owned the evening.

Under the trees at the platform above, a chipmunk poked his head out and "churrrred," but it sounded different, as if he were about to go to bed. The birds were making night chirps too, so different from what you heard during the day. The call of the loons was lonelier. A dark hump on the dock was Marty, her arms clasped around her knees, with Foxy beside her.

"How are the mosquitoes?" asked Paul.

"Not too bad. There must be a breeze," said Marty. Her quiet voice carried across the water. "Look! The evening star!"

Paul looked up and so did Dad. Only a few lights burned around the lake. There was no moon yet and the sky looked alive, a Prussian blue. A chill stole across the surface of the water.

"I think that's Venus," said Dad. "The brightest thing in the sky right now."

"Could we take the boat out one night, Dad?" asked Paul. The promise of more stars coming out was compelling. "I'd like to get to the middle of the sky."

"Maybe not that far," said Dad. "And we don't have many days left. We better do it tonight! Want to come, Marty?"

Marty didn't answer, but Paul looked around, excited. "Can we take Foxy?" The lake was calm. Above on the hill, screen doors banged and lights were on. A fisherman with a motorboat trolled quietly out near the dropoff. Nature, God's bountiful hand, enfolded them in its beauty. No one could ask for more, thought Paul.

* * *

ACKNOWLEDGEMENTS

The author would like to thank her siblings, friends and cousins who have shared in the experiences of which this is a fictionalized account. In particular she would like to thank Ruth Frost for the generous sharing of her own childhood experiences. She also thanks Don Starnes for his wonderful work designing the cover and for his support throughout the project.

Connie Kronlokken

ABOUT THE AUTHOR

Connie Kronlokken grew up in a large Norwegian/Danish Lutheran family. She spent her childhood in small towns across Minnesota, North Dakota and Iowa. In 1969 she moved to the San Francisco Bay Area and now lives in Los Angeles with her husband Don Starnes. Connie studied filmmaking in Denmark and has been a student of yang style tai chi for more than 25 years. She loves being with her family, the march of the seasons, cooking and gardening. She's been parsing romance from reality for most of her life.

www.ingramcontent.com/pod-product-compliance
Lightning Source LLC
Chambersburg PA
CBHW020738250626
47155CB00003B/812